The FORTUNE HUNTER

By Daisy Goodwin

Fiction:
My Last Duchess

Non-Fiction:
Silver River

The FORTUNE HUNTER

Daisy Goodwin

headline
review

First published in 2014 by
HEADLINE REVIEW
An imprint of HEADLINE PUBLISHING GROUP

1

Cataloguing in Publication Data is available from the British Library

ISBN 978 0 7553 4809 1 (Hardback)
ISBN 978 0 7553 4810 7 (Trade Paperback)

Typeset in Adobe Caslon by Palimpsest Book Production Limited,
Falkirk, Stirlingshire

Printed and bound in Great Britain by
Clays Ltd, St Ives plc.

Headline's policy is to use papers that are natural, renewable
and recyclable products and made from wood grown in sustainable forests.
The logging and manufacturing processes are expected to conform
to the environmental regulations of the country of origin.

HEADLINE PUBLISHING GROUP
An Hachette UK Company
338 Euston Road
London NW1 3BH

www.headline.co.uk
www.hachette.co.uk

In memory of my mother
Jocasta Innes
1934–2013

Part One

The Royal Menagerie

July 1875

WAS QUEEN VICTORIA A KITTEN OR A CODFISH? Charlotte hesitated. The monarch's chinless face did look remarkably similar to the glassy stare of the fish, but that would mean making the late Prince Consort a kitten, as that was the only animal she had left. It was hard to think of Prince Albert as feline, but now that she had superimposed the image of the fish onto his wife's face, it was undoubtable that the queen made the most magnificent kind of cod. She stepped back for a moment and looked at the overall composition, now that she had replaced each royal face with an animal head. The Prince of Wales was a satisfactory basset hound and Charlotte felt that she had done justice to Princess Alice's mournful demeanour by turning her into a calf. She dipped her brush into the pot of Indian ink at her side and began to shade around her work, blending the edges of the animal heads into the rest of the photograph. Later, depending on what time she could persuade Fred to bring her home from the ball, she would photograph her creation.

She sighed and stretched her folded fingers over her head. The sun had sunk beneath the rows of white stucco townhouses, throwing a warm glow into the room.

Charlotte would have her Royal Menagerie. She thought she would put it on the back wall of the drawing room at Kevill. Properly framed, it would look to the casual observer like any other family portrait; only the people who really looked would see that she had turned the Royal Family into a frock-coated and crinolined 300. It was possible that some of the starchier guests might be a little shocked, but as close observation of anything besides the lace on a visitor's gown seldom took place in the drawing room at Kevill, Charlotte did not feel she had much to worry about. The faint possibility of discovery might be enough to get her through those interminable afternoons spent at home entertaining lady callers. Charlotte hoped that the Bishop's wife, in particular, would look over her long, perpetually dripping nose and be so offended that she never called again.

The thought of the Bishop's wife and the way that she always referred to her as a 'poor motherless girl' was enough to make Charlotte's hand slip, and a drop of Indian ink fell onto one of the ivory silk flounces of her skirt. It was a very small drop of ink, but the silk was so absorbent that it quickly flowered into an unmistakeable stain. Charlotte was annoyed at her carelessness. The ink spot was barely visible, but she knew that her aunt would spot it immediately and would make it into a tragedy of epic proportions. 'What a calamity!' she would exclaim, the lace ribbons on her widow's cap fluttering. 'Your beautiful dress ruined and on the night of the Spencer ball too!' Charlotte's aunt Adelaide liked nothing better than a minor domestic mishap that she could turn into a drama worthy of Sophocles. She would feel it her duty to point out the blemish to everyone they met, and invite them to comment on the tragic twist of fate that had ruined her niece's exquisite dress. Charlotte was dreading the evening's entertainments quite enough without the added humiliation of her aunt's histrionics.

She thought for a moment, and then picked up her watercolour box. Perhaps there was some China White left. She took a clean brush, licked it thoroughly and started to paint over the stain. It wasn't perfect, but it covered the worst of it, and with any luck she might get through the evening without her aunt noticing. She was just giving it another coat when there was a perfunctory knock on the door and her brother Fred walked in wearing his dress uniform.

'Are you ready yet, Mitten? Aunt Adelaide is fretting about the horses and I want to be at the Opera early.'

He saw what she was doing and stopped. 'Why are you painting your dress?' He smirked. 'Is that the latest fashion, hand-decorating your ball gown?'

'Well, if it was the latest fashion, as you never stop pointing out to me, I would be the last one to know. I have spilt some ink on my dress and I am concealing it with paint.' Charlotte pointed at the blemish with her finger. 'There! Good as new.'

'But what on earth were you doing messing about with ink in a white ball gown? I thought girls had better things to do before a ball, like getting their hair arranged or choosing which jewels to wear.'

'If you look carefully, Fred, you will see that my hair has been arranged, and as for jewels, Aunt Adelaide thinks that diamonds are unsuitable for debutantes and so she is wearing Mamma's necklace. I thought I would occupy my time usefully while I waited for you all to get ready.'

Fred glanced over at the work table where the Royal Menagerie lay. He went over to have a closer look, and shook his head.

'You really are a rum one, Mitten.'

'Do you like it?'

'Like it! Of course I don't like it. It's peculiar, that's what it is. Why don't you have any normal accomplishments? Singin', piano playing, needlework, that sort of thing. It's deuced odd for a girl of twenty to be squirrellin' around with cameras and chemicals all the time. You need to be careful that you don't get a reputation. Augusta is quite concerned about you. She says that after we are married, her first task will be to launch you properly. She thinks that with the right approach, you could be quite a success.'

Charlotte smiled. 'How very kind of her.'

Fred looked at her suspiciously, his blue eyes bulging as they always did when he was cross. 'Augusta will be a real advantage to you. She says that making the right sort of marriage is like pilotin' a ship into harbour. It needs a steady hand at the tiller.'

Charlotte thought, but did not say, that despite Lady Augusta Crewe's navigational skills, it had taken her four London seasons to land a proposal of marriage. She decided to change the subject.

'You look very handsome tonight, Fred. Augusta will be proud of you.'

Diverted, Fred pushed his chest out and brushed his hand down the gold braid on his jacket.

'Went to Bay Middleton's tailor. He swears by him, won't go anywhere else.'

'Bay Middleton is clearly very discerning.'

'Best dressed officer in the Guards. It's all about the cut. Had to have three fittings for this.'

'Only three fittings! I must have had ten at least for this frock, and I think your uniform fits you rather better and is altogether more flattering.'

'Nothing wrong with your dress, or at least there wasn't before you started coverin' it with ink.' He put his hand on her shoulder. 'When Augusta and I are married she will advise you. Daresay you could learn something from her. Always very nicely turned out, Augusta.'

Charlotte thought that she had heard enough about the superiority of Augusta Crewe to last a lifetime. Even if her future
sister-in-law had been charming and generous, she might have
tired of Fred constantly invoking her name, but as Charlotte found
her affected and calculating, her presence in every conversation
between brother and sister was a scalding irritation.

There was a cough from the doorway. Penge, Aunt Adelaide's
butler, looked at them reproachfully.

'Her ladyship has asked to me to remind you that the carriage
was ordered fifteen minutes ago.'

Fred became officious. 'Come along, Mitten, nothing you can do
about the dress now. Captain Hartopp's not goin' to notice.' He was
halfway down the curving staircase before he turned back to look
at her. 'And you needn't worry about partners tonight. I know
Hartopp will claim the first two, and Augusta has promised to find
you some suitable young men.'

Charlotte was silent but thought that she would like nothing
more than to dance with an *unsuitable* young man. Despite Fred's
solicitude, she was not at all worried about finding partners: although
she had only been to a handful of balls, her dance card was always
full. Suitable young men and the odd unsuitable one had quickly
learnt that although Charlotte was not perhaps the most striking
looking girl in the room, she was undoubtedly one of the richest,
as the sole heiress to the Lennox fortune, which would be hers
when she was twenty-five. The money had not meant much to her
growing up in the Borders, but since she had come to London,
Charlotte had often heard the phrase 'the Lennox heiress' muttered
in conversation or seen it mouthed silently by one new acquaintance to another. She had noticed too that the mutterings and the
mouthings made Fred anxious. The money was hers alone – her
mother, the original Lennox heiress, had been their late father's

second wife – but Fred was as proprietorial about her fortune as if it were his to bestow. Under the terms of her father's will, she could not marry without his consent until she reached her majority, and Fred was enjoying the privileges of this role immensely. There had been some young men in the Guards who had made Fred feel uncomfortable about his tailor or his taste in claret, but those feelings of unease had subsided now that he was the guardian of the Lennox fortune, and, of course, the fiancé of Lady Augusta Crewe.

It was not therefore the fear of being a wallflower that made Charlotte inch down the curving staircase after her brother, one reluctant step at a time. She was probably the only girl in London who dreaded a full dance card. Sitting out a dance was better than being whirled around the room by some pink-cheeked younger son doing his best to secure the Lennox Fortune. Did she hunt? No. Silence. Had she been presented? Not yet. Pause. Did she like croquet? Sometimes she would volunteer that she enjoyed photography. This would generally make Percy or Clarence look anxious, as if being asked a question in an exam that they hadn't prepped for. Then Algernon or Ralph would tell her the story of how he had his photograph taken, 'for Mamma, y'know', and complain about how long it had taken: 'The photographer chap wanted me to stand with my head in a vice, otherwise he said it would come out blurry.' Did they like the results? she would ask, and the young men would pause; sometimes a blush would stain their bewhiskered faces. Despite their confusion, she would persevere: did the photograph look the way they had imagined themselves? At that point her partner would mumble that he never really gave much thought to his appearance, but he supposed that the photographs were accurate enough. Generally after these exchanges the young man would not insist on another dance. Once when a more imaginative young man had asked Charlotte if she would take his photograph, she had demurred, saying that he might not like the result. He did not ask a second time.

At the bottom step Charlotte tried to arrange herself so that her fan and reticule covered the ink stain on her gown. But it was clear that her concern was unnecessary, for Aunt Adelaide was much too preoccupied with her own appearance to give much thought to her niece. She was standing in front of the pier glass in the hallway, turning her head this way and that as the light caught the Lennox diamonds around her throat. Married late to an impecunious baronet who had died six months later, Aunt Adelaide had not had many diamonds in her life and she was enjoying her borrowed finery to the full. Charlotte could see that her aunt, who must be at least forty, was a good deal more excited about the evening ahead than she was.

'How well those pearl earrings go with your dress, dear. Just the right note of ornament without ostentation. I can't bear it when young girls cover themselves with jewels – do you remember Selina Fortescue at the Londonderry ball? She looked positively gaudy, such a shame with a fresh young complexion like that.' Aunt Adelaide looked at Charlotte as she said this but couldn't resist her twinkling reflection for long and turned back to the mirror.

Fred coughed. 'I notice, Aunt, that, unlike Charlotte, you have covered yourself in jewels. Is it quite the thing for you to be wearin' the Lennox necklace? The diamonds are Charlotte's property after all, and I think that as her guardian I should have been consulted.'

Underneath the diamonds, Charlotte saw the skin of her aunt's décolletage redden. She spoke quickly.

'Oh Fred, don't be so pompous. I would feel ridiculous wearing the necklace. It's much too grown up for me, and besides, it looks very becoming on Aunt Adelaide. I would much rather she wore it than for it to be locked up in a vault.'

Aunt Adelaide looked at her gratefully. Fred picked up his gloves and started to pull them down over his fingers, cracking each knuckle as he did so.

'I don't think it is pompous to express some concern about a valuable piece of property that belongs to my only sister. Perhaps you have forgotten the promise I made to Father to look after you, but I haven't. Everything that you do reflects on me. I don't want your future husband to accuse me of mismanagin' your affairs.'

'Well, I have no intention of marrying someone who would complain about me lending a necklace to a member of my family. I was going to offer it to Augusta to wear at your wedding, but if you feel so strongly about it, perhaps that would be a mistake.'

As Charlotte had intended, Fred's indignation subsided.

'Augusta did mention the necklace to me. I will, of course, make sure that she takes very good care of it, as I am sure that you will, Aunt. Now I suggest that we leave, or we will miss the first act.'

Charlotte smiled to herself. Fred's real anxiety was not that Aunt Adelaide was wearing the Lennox diamonds, but that Augusta would see her wearing them at the Spencer ball. Augusta was already planning to wear them to her wedding, and she would be unhappy if their magnificence was diluted by too many public outings on other necks than hers.

As her brother handed her into the carriage, she wondered how she would compose their wedding portrait. There would be the official one, of course, with the bride in white and orange blossom with the diamond collar round her not-quite-long enough neck with Fred standing stiffly behind her – Augusta would be seated as she was practically the same height as Fred. But in the unofficial one Charlotte thought that Augusta, with her flattish nose and wide apart eyes, would make a rather satisfactory Pekinese, and Fred, with his red face and his burgeoning chins, might pass for a turkey. It would not be a picture that she could hang anywhere, of course, not even in the darkest corners of Kevill, but it would give her private satisfaction to look at it when she was being 'launched' by Augusta after the wedding. Unless she could find a husband in the run-up to their nuptials, she faced the prospect of living with the newlyweds. The current arrangement with Lady Lisle suited Fred while he was a bachelor, but when he was a married man he would naturally want his sister to live with him and his wife. Fred's £1,000 a year would not stretch to a house in town, but as Charlotte's guardian, he and Augusta would be able to take Lady Lisle's place as Charlotte's chaperone in Charles Street.

There was a tap at the carriage window. She looked out and saw the large, whiskered face of Captain 'Chicken' Hartopp, Fred's great friend and a devoted follower of the Lennox fortune. Fred was not actively encouraging Hartopp's suit, as he was hoping for a title for his sister, or at least an alliance with one of the older landed families, but as Hartopp's fortune was almost as great as Charlotte's he could not rule him out entirely.

'Miss Baird, I am so glad I caught you before you left. I wanted to give you these; I thought perhaps you might like to wear them tonight.'

He handed her a corsage of white rosebuds through the window and Charlotte gave him what she hoped was a delighted smile.

'Thank you so much, Captain Hartopp. How kind of you to think of me.'

'My pleasure, Miss Baird.' He tipped his hat to Fred and bowed to Aunt Adelaide. 'Good evening, Lady Lisle. What a magnificent necklace. Are those the famous Lennox diamonds, by any chance?'

Adelaide Lisle simpered. 'They are indeed. Dear Charlotte has been kind enough to let me wear them tonight. I hope I can do them justice.'

Hartopp paused just a second too long before saying, 'You can have no doubts on that score, Lady Lisle.'

Charlotte saw the way Hartopp's eyes glittered when he saw the necklace, and thought that even living with Fred and Augusta would be preferable to looking at his face every morning over the breakfast table. She had not yet acquired any photographs of aquatic mammals, but when she did, she was sure that Captain Hartopp, despite his feathery nickname, would make a perfectly splendid walrus.

A Night at the Opera

THE OPERA HOUSE WAS FULL. IT WAS ADELINA PATTI'S last performance of *La Sonnambula* before she returned to New York. Every box was full, every seat from the stalls to the gods was taken. Bay Middleton sat in the second row, so close to the stage that he could see the lattice of blue veins that snaked across La Patti's décolletage, the rivulets of sweat that ran down her painted cheeks.

But though he had his eyes on the stage, Bay Middleton's senses were concentrated on a box in the Grand Tier. He felt Blanche's presence as vividly as if she were sitting next to him; he knew without looking round that her shoulders were bare and that two blond wisps of hair would tremble on the back of her neck. He could almost smell the cologne she used to bathe her temples. Still, he would not look up. He had been aware that he was making a mistake in coming tonight even as he fastened the dress studs in his shirt and adjusted the points of his white tie. But tomorrow Blanche would be gone and he wanted to be near her even if he could not bear to look at her.

The music fed his melancholy. He was not, like most of the audience, here merely to be seen. Bay felt the music; sometimes he would find the hairs on his arm standing on end, just as they did when he knew he was about to win a race, or when a woman looked at him in a certain way. It had happened the first time he had seen Blanche. She had pressed her foot against his at dinner and he had known, at once, that it was no accident. She had looked at him with her heavy-lidded eyes and had smiled, showing small white teeth and a glimpse of pink tongue. It had been the first of many such moments. She had been looking at him across dinner tables and ballrooms for the last year. There had been other women before her, of course, but Blanche Hozier was the first woman he had ever missed a day's hunting for.

She had not been smiling earlier that afternoon as she stood in front of the mirror, tucking away the curls that had come loose a few minutes before. He had been marvelling, as usual, at how quickly Blanche could change back from the woman who had led him by the hand to the chaise longue to the one who stood there now checking that every hair was in place. She was still flushed, but she was once again the mistress of the house and the Colonel's wife. She had caught his eyes in the mirror and had said without expression, 'I am going to Combe tomorrow.'

He had said nothing, sensing that this was a declaration.

'The Colonel is there all the time working on his drainage schemes, and as there is no chance of him coming to London, I must go to him.' She turned to face Bay, tilting her head a little to one side as she looked at him, one of her diamond ear drops catching the light and dazzling him.

He considered this for a moment. There could be only one reason why Blanche would leave London before the end of the Season. His eyes dropped to her waist.

He blinked. 'Are you sure?'

Blanche lifted her chin. 'Sure enough.'

He stood up and walked towards her. She crossed her hands in front of her like a gate. He stood still. 'A child? Oh Blanche, I am so . . .' But she cut him off, as if she couldn't bear the emotion in his voice.

'Combe is lovely at this time of year. Isobel has a cough and I believe the country air will do her good.'

The slight huskiness that he found so beguiling had gone and she had resumed the commanding tones of Lady Blanche Hozier, the daughter of an earl and the mistress of Combe. He looked in vain for some trace of her former softness, but she was as hard as the looking glass behind her. He felt both desolation at the thought of losing her and irritation that he should be so summarily dismissed.

'You will write to me.' It was not a question, but Blanche had shaken her head.

'No letters, not until afterwards. I have to be careful. If the child is a boy . . .' He had seen her twist the wedding ring around her finger.

'I will miss you, Blanche,' he had said, putting his hand out to take hers. But she had shrunk away from him, as if he had become red hot. He had punched his fist into his other hand in frustration.

'I wonder that you didn't tell me, earlier?' His eyes flickered over to the chaise longue.

Blanche looked at him, her drooping eyelids belying the fierceness of her tone.

'I think you should leave now before the servants come back. They have seen too much already.'

He had wanted, very much, to tear her hair down and to shake her porcelain composure, but he had let his arms drop and said, 'Are you sure the child is mine?'

This time she had turned her whole body away from him and had just pointed to the door. He had picked up his hat and gloves from the chair and left without another word.

Now, as he listened to Adelina Patti as Amina singing of her love for Elvino, he felt the blood creeping to his ears as he thought of that last remark. He wanted to look up and show Blanche that he had not meant to wound her, but he could not turn his head. He knew that her retreat to the country was the only prudent course, but he had been hurt by the manner of his sending off. If only there had been some expression of regret, some tenderness. But their liaison had ended as abruptly as it had started. He suspected that he was not Blanche's first lover, but she had always been discreet. Bay knew that her marriage with Hozier was not a happy one. Indeed, there had been a moment when he thought that Blanche had wanted more than their afternoons in the blue drawing room and he had been terrified and excited in equal measure. But that moment had passed and he had felt nothing but relief. To elope with Blanche would have meant leaving the regiment, the country, probably. So he knew he had no right to feel aggrieved, but still – a child. He remembered the way that Blanche had refused to look at him as he left that afternoon, as if she had already erased him from her life.

La Patti hung her head at the end of her aria to receive her applause. The stage was soon covered with flowers thrown by her admirers. Bay looked up at the other side of the theatre from Blanche's box and saw his friends Fred Baird and Chicken Hartopp in a box with two ladies. One he recognised as Fred's aunt and the young girl he thought must be Fred's sister. He supposed that Lady Lisle must be bringing the girl out as the mother had died years ago. He picked up his opera glasses to get a better look at the girl, conscious as he did so that Blanche might be watching him. It would do her no harm, he thought, to see that he had other interests.

But the Baird girl had drawn back, her face was in shadow, and all Bay could see of her was a kid-gloved hand tapping a fan on the side of the box. He held his glasses up for a minute longer, waiting for a glimpse of her face, but she did not reappear. It was almost as if she were hiding from his gaze.

At the interval he decided to leave; he thought he would go to his club and have a brandy. He thought of Blanche looking down at his empty seat. But as he reached the corridor he felt a hand on his shoulder.

'Middleton, what are you doing down here?' Chicken Hartopp looked down at him, beaming. His dundreary whiskers covered almost his entire face, but what skin there was visible was flushed with the heat. 'Thought you would be in a box, old man, not down here with the plebs. Couldn't help noticing a certain lady sitting opposite.' Chicken squeezed one eye in a clumsy wink.

Bay said quickly, 'I thought I'd listen to the music for a change. This is La Patti's last performance before she goes back to America.'

'An opera lover too, eh?' Chicken started to laugh at his own joke. Bay was about to leave him to his mirth when he saw Fred Baird coming towards them.

'Middleton, my dear chap, I thought I saw you down in the stalls. Will you come up to the box and meet my sister?'

Bay was about to refuse, but then he remembered the Baird box was in full view of where Blanche and her companions were sitting. He followed Bay and Hartopp through the crimson corridors to the box.

'Aunt Adelaide, you know Captain Middleton, of course, and may I present my sister Charlotte.'

Bay bowed to Lady Lisle and turned to Charlotte Baird, who was small and dun-coloured, quite unlike her brother, who was large and vivid. She stretched out her hand to him and as he brushed his lips against the knuckles of her glove, he felt her hand tremble slightly.

'How are you enjoying the Opera, Miss Baird? La Patti will be a sad loss to the company here, when she returns to New York.' Bay was standing with his back to the auditorium. He turned slightly to the left so that an observer might notice that he was talking to a young lady. Charlotte Baird looked up at him. Bay was not as tall as Hartopp or Baird, but Charlotte still had to tilt her head up to address him.

'I haven't had much chance to form an opinion about the music, Captain Middleton. I don't think my brother or Captain Hartopp have drawn breath since we arrived.' She gave a crooked little smile. 'Perhaps you can persuade them to be quiet. I should so like to hear the opera as well as see it.' Bay noticed that she had a trace of freckles across the bridge of her nose.

'I will do my best, Miss Baird, but I doubt that even the Archbishop of Canterbury himself could silence Chicken Hartopp.'

She looked at him and he saw that her eyes were the most definite thing about her face: large, with very long black lashes. He could not quite make out the colour in the gloom of the box. She held his gaze.

'But you, Captain Middleton, you like to listen. Is that why you sit down there in the stalls?'

The crooked smile reappeared. He realised she had noticed him earlier. He thought again, how different she was from her brother. Fred was an amiable bully who was happy as long as he was in front. But this girl came up on the inside, in the blind spot.

'I like to look up at the singers, Miss Baird; I want to feel in the middle of things.'

'But that's what I want, and yet here I am, surrounded by distractions.' She waved her hands at the young men who were standing with her aunt and shrugged. The bell rang to signal the end of the interval.

'Delighted to have met you, Miss Baird.' Bay looked over at Fred Baird and Chicken Hartopp and said, 'I hope you are allowed to enjoy the rest of the opera in peace.'

'I hope so too. But Captain Middleton, you aren't thinking of returning to your seat already? There is a lady in blue who has been staring at you these last few minutes while we have been talking; she looks as though she wants to tell you something. Won't you look round and see what it is she has to say?' Charlotte Baird's voice was soft but there was something sharp in there as well. Bay did not look round, but made his way to the door at the back of the box.

'I don't believe anything can be more important than the Second Act, Miss Baird.' He nodded to the others and left. Rather to his own surprise, he found himself making his way back to his seat in the stalls, aware now that he was being observed from two sides. He thought with some satisfaction of Blanche watching his conversation with Charlotte Baird from the other side of the House.

The Second Act was not as good as the first; the music could not push away his swirling thoughts. As he fidgeted in his seat he caught a faint whiff of the gardenia in his buttonhole. The flower had come from a corsage he had ordered for Blanche to wear this evening. He had been going to take it with him that afternoon, but it had arrived too late. It had been lying on the hall table when he had returned to his rooms, a mute reminder, as if he needed one, of how much had changed in the last few hours. His first impulse had been to throw it away, actually to crush the waxy white petals and the dark green glossy leaves under his heel, but as he picked up the flowers to destroy them he had been overwhelmed by their scent. The heavy sweetness was the smell of all their afternoons together in Blanche's blue drawing room. He remembered the dust-laden motes of light that had fallen like sequins on her bare throat. The smell of the gardenias was as abundant as Blanche herself, the waxy smoothness of the petals as dense as the white skin of her shoulders. He could not resist pulling out one spray and fastening it in his buttonhole. But now, as he touched the fleshy white petals, he thought that he had never seen Blanche completely naked and now he knew that he never would. The thought made him shudder, and crush the flower between his fingers.

He was still intending to go to his club, but as he was leaving he saw Fred Baird handing his sister and aunt into their carriage. They must be going to the Spencer ball. He had been sent a card, of course, having been one of Spencer's aide-de-camps in Ireland, but he had decided not to go. He didn't really care for balls; there was so much clamour he could never hear what the girls were saying in their light little voices. Not that it mattered. Those debutante conversations were all the same – did he care for waltzing or polkas? Wasn't the steeplechase most awfully dangerous? Had he ever been to Switzerland in the summer? He was standing on the corner of the Strand, when the Baird carriage passed him and he saw Charlotte's small face looking at him through the glass. He touched his hat and she raised her hand in reply but did not, rather to his surprise, smile.

He hesitated for a moment, before turning north towards Spencer House. Blanche would be there, but then so would little Charlotte Baird. She would be grateful for a dancing partner who was not Chicken Hartopp. He knew that Hartopp was seriously pursuing the girl – she was an heiress, of course, and like all rich men, Hartopp wanted to be richer. But now he had met Charlotte, Bay found that he did not like the idea of Hartopp marrying her. Any girl who went to the Opera to listen to the music was not the right match for the cloth-eared Hartopp. He looked around for a hansom but then decided he would walk. It was a fine evening and it would not hurt to arrive a little late. Perhaps Blanche would be looking towards the door, wondering if he would arrive.

The Spencer Ball

THE BALL WAS AT ITS HEIGHT. IT WAS AT THE POINT where the women were rosy from the dancing, but before the moment when coiffures began to slip – carefully curled fringes flattening in the heat. The guests, who had been delaying their arrival so that it would appear that they had been dining at one of the more fashionable houses before the ball, had finally dared to make their appearance. The parliamentary lobbies on the Suez bill had closed and the ballroom was spotted with MPs and ministers. It was the last event of the season before people disappeared to the country for the summer, so there was an energy to the occasion as the guests tried to make the most of this last opportunity to squeeze what they wanted from the world: a promotion, a liaison, a husband, a mistress, a loan, or simply a piece of delicious gossip. No one wanted to miss this party; it was the final opportunity to acquire the baubles of hope and intrigue that would make the arid summer months bearable before the fashionable world reassembled in the autumn.

As Bay Middleton made his way up the double staircase, he saw that Earl Spencer, the Red Earl as he was known, was still standing by the door to welcome his guests. The last time Bay had seen Earl Spencer in evening dress had been in Dublin at the Vice Regal lodge. There he had been the Queen's representative, and with his great height and golden red beard he had looked the part. But now the political wind had changed, the Whigs had been ousted by the Tories under Disraeli, and Spencer looked a little less burnished. His kingdom was on the hunting field, not here under the chandeliers. But he had daughters to bring out and a Party anxious to manoeuvre itself back into power, so there was no help for it. Still, he hovered on the edge of the festivities as if ready to follow more promising sport at any moment.

Spencer caught sight of Bay at the bottom of the stairs and called to him before the footman could announce him.

'Middleton, my dear fellow. I am uncommon glad to see you here.' He squeezed Bay's hand in his great freckled paw.

'It's not the same as Dublin, eh?' Spencer's pale blue eyes clouded. 'Still, we have royalty tonight. The Queen of Naples, no less, or should I say the former Queen. Very grand, like all these deposed monarchs, but lively enough.' He pointed a stubby finger at Bay. 'I shall rely on you to entertain her. She speaks perfect English but she has a way of sighing that is altogether foreign. I believe the King is not altogether to her taste. No doubt you could bring a smile to those handsome lips.'

Bay smiled. 'I don't think a queen would have much time for a mere cavalry captain, My Lord. But I am at your service as always.'

Spencer laughed and put his arm around his shoulders.

'They were high times in Ireland, eh Middleton? Best hunting in the world. Still, who knows? Disraeli can't last for ever and then we will be back with a vengeance.'

He propelled Bay into the ballroom where the orchestra was playing a polka.

'There she is, Queen Maria, the heroine of Gaeta. They say she took command of the garrison and fought against Garibaldi and the Risorgimento while her husband the little king locked himself in his bedroom.' Spencer pointed to a tall dark woman dressed in white who stood surrounded by a group of men in uniform.

'It appears that she is still in command of her troops.' Bay thought that the Queen looked as if she was posing for a portrait, her arms positioned in a perfect oval and her head turned slightly so that everyone could admire her clear profile and the long curve of her neck. She wore a small tiara that sparkled against her dark hair.

'At least she looks the part,' said Spencer. 'Not like the Widow of Windsor. And a horsewoman too. She came out with the Pytchley last year, led the pack all the way. I suppose a day out with the Pytchley is compensation for losing a kingdom, eh?' But Bay was no longer looking at the Queen in her frame of courtiers. He had seen Blanche's blond head and he could not help following it as it tacked across the dance floor. Spencer followed his gaze and made a small tutting noise.

'I believe you are not listening to me, Middleton. Still, I shall leave you to your own pursuits, even if no good can come of them. It's high time you got married. The right sort of wife would make all the difference.' The Earl moved off towards the supper room, leaving Bay watching Blanche as she danced around the room. He was dismayed to see how very gracefully she was dancing tonight. She was coming around again and he knew that if she were to turn her head she would see him. He stood there, unable to move, and then just as they were about to come face to face, he saw a flash of white to his left and turned his head. It was Charlotte Baird – still small and dun-coloured but just then a most welcome sight.

He pulled himself around to face her. She was standing beside her aunt and another lady, whom Bay recognised as Augusta Crewe, Fred's fiancée. Charlotte looked very small standing beside the other women. Middleton bowed to the group and moved next to her.

'I hope you can hear the music now, Miss Baird.'

She nodded. He thought she looked less sure of herself here in the glittering expanse of the ballroom than she had in the enclosed space of the box at Covent Garden.

'Yes, but this music is not intended to be listened to.' She smiled her crooked smile and Bay could see that her fingers were tapping her fan.

He bowed and asked her to dance. But before Charlotte could answer, Augusta said, 'Oh, but you are too late, Captain Middleton, Miss Baird's dance card is quite full. Isn't that right, Charlotte?' Augusta blinked her sandy eyelashes at Bay.

Charlotte laughed. 'Oh, but Augusta, I *must* make room for Captain Middleton. Haven't you noticed how magnificent Fred is looking tonight? It is all the work of Captain Middleton here who sent him to his tailor. I think I should express our gratitude, don't you?'

Augusta sniffed. 'I can't say that I have noticed anything in particular. Fred is always well turned out.'

'Oh, you are just being loyal. You may have the next dance, Captain Middleton, and Augusta, perhaps you would make my excuses to Captain Hartopp.'

The band struck up a waltz. Bay held out his hand to Charlotte. He was surprised at how small and how light she was. She barely came up to his shoulder, unlike Blanche, who had always been on a level with him. She was concentrating too hard on the steps to look at him at first. He could see her biting her lip with effort. He tightened his grip on her waist and finally she raised her eyes to his and said, 'You are a very good dancer.'

'I have had lots of practice. In Ireland there was nothing to do except hunt and go to parties.'

'But Captain Hartopp was in Ireland with you, was he not? He doesn't dance as well as you.'

Bay smiled. 'It's true, no one could call Chicken a dancer. He can ride, though.'

'Why do you call him Chicken, Captain Middleton? I've asked Fred but he won't tell me.'

'If your brother won't tell you, then you can hardly expect me to, Miss Baird.' He saw her frown and continued, 'Don't be cross. It is rather a sad little story and I am too fond of Chicken to repeat it.'

'But you don't mind taking his dancing partner away?'

Bay looked down at her, surprised. He hadn't expected Fred's sister to be so lively.

'Oh, but that was your decision, not mine. Once you had accepted my invitation I could hardly turn you down.'

'How chivalrous you are, Captain Middleton.' She looked up at him through her lashes and Bay decided that her eyes were grey, almost the colour of the blue roan he had ridden in Ireland last summer. She was not beautiful but he found he liked looking at her face.

'Well, I guessed that you didn't want to dance with Chicken all night.'

'Are you a mind reader then, Captain Middleton, as well as being the best dressed officer in the Guards?'

Bay laughed. 'And on what basis do you call me that? Are you an expert in Guards uniforms, Miss Baird?'

'Not at all, but my brother is. Fred doesn't praise people very often, so I am inclined to believe him. I am only sorry you are not wearing your uniform tonight so I can see what perfection looks like.'

'Oh, I think there are quite enough uniforms here tonight.' Bay's voice was dismissive. He felt there was something ostentatious about wearing uniform to every social occasion.

'Well, I am sure your tails are the epitome of understated good taste, Captain Middleton.'

Bay could not help but glance at his impeccable tail coat with its four jet buttons on the cuff. Charlotte smiled and he checked himself. 'You are mocking me, but I am not ashamed of taking the trouble to ensure my clothes fit properly.'

'I envy your attention to detail. Fred is always berating me for my lack of interest in clothes. He would like me to be a fashion plate like Augusta. But I find the rigmarole of dressmaking so tedious. Standing perfectly still while people stick pins into you is not my idea of an occupation.'

'So what would you rather be doing, Miss Baird?'

She didn't answer immediately and they did a turn around the dance floor before she said rather hesitantly, 'I like to take photographs.'

Bay did not conceal his surprise. How could this curious girl be related to stuffy old Fred? 'Really? What sort of things do you photograph?'

'Oh, a variety of things, landscapes, portraits, animals, whatever I think will make a good composition.'

'Have you ever taken a picture of a horse?'

'Not yet. Did you have one in mind?'

'I would like very much to have a likeness of Tipsy, my hunter. She is a thing of beauty.'

'Horse and rider would be interesting. Have you have ever had your photograph taken, Captain Middleton?'

'Never.'

'Has no one ever asked you for a picture? I am surprised.'

Bay was about to answer when he saw Blanche's golden head and white face inches away from him. He lost his balance for a second and stepped out wildly, then heard a gasp and a faint tearing noise.

'Miss Baird, I am so sorry, what have I done?' Bay looked down and saw that he had put his foot through the flounce of her skirt, leaving a grubby rent in the white silk.

He thought for a moment that Charlotte was going to cry but she shook her head and said, 'It doesn't matter, but I think I should get it sewn up.'

They retreated to some seats in the corner and Middleton told a footman to fetch a maid with needle and thread.

'Unless of course you would rather go somewhere more private like the cloakroom.'

She gave him a sideways look. 'Oh no, I would much rather stay here and try to figure out why such an excellent dancer should lose his balance.'

He made a little flourish with his hands. 'You could make anyone unsteady, Miss Baird.'

She did not reply for a moment, considering his remark, and then said, 'I don't think that was the reason, Captain Middleton.'

Bay was about to protest when the maid arrived and started to sew up the gash in her dress. Bay stood in front of Charlotte, shielding her from the room. When the girl had finished and the dress was whole again he said, 'I daresay you won't dance with me again, but can I take you into supper?'

Charlotte shook her head. 'I am promised to Captain Hartopp. I can't abandon him again.'

'How very irritating. Let me, at least, take you back to Lady Lisle.'

He put out his arm, but she hesitated and then took a flower from the corsage at her wrist. It was a small white rosebud whose tightly furled petals were tinged with pink.

'You've lost your buttonhole, Captain Middleton. Won't you take this instead?'

He picked up the flower from her outstretched palm and put it into his lapel. It was smaller than the gardenia and there was no scent that he could detect.

'You are very kind, Miss Baird.'

'Hardly that. It's just that I notice things.'

'Even without a camera?'

She smiled. 'Once you learn to look at things properly, you never stop.'

'Now I feel thoroughly nervous of having my likeness taken.'

'But I only see what is there, Captain Middleton.'

He was about to ask what she saw, but noticed Chicken Hartopp making towards them across the dance floor.

'There you are, Miss Baird. I have come to rescue you from Middleton. I hope you haven't forgotten that you promised to let me take you into supper.'

'Of course not, Captain Hartopp. I was just on my way.'

'My fault entirely, Chicken. Miss Baird here was furnishing me with a new buttonhole.'

Hartopp looked at the white rosebud on Bay's lapel and flushed. Bay realised that somehow he had offended him. Charlotte looked embarrassed and put her hand on Hartopp's arm.

'I hope you don't mind. Captain Middleton needed a new buttonhole and there are so many flowers in the beautiful corsage you gave me that I could spare one . . .'

'Of course I don't mind,' said Hartopp, who clearly did. 'We should get to the supper room before the ices are all gone.'

Bay knew that it was ignoble of him to enjoy Hartopp's annoyance, but he could not help himself. Hartopp and Fred Baird had never concealed their amazement that despite Middleton's inferior social position and fortune, he was not only a better rider than either of them but was also much more popular with women.

But satisfying though Chicken's chagrin had been, Bay took even more pleasure in the fact that little Charlotte Baird had had no qualms about giving him the flower. She liked him, and though Bay was used to being liked by women, he was pleased that this particular girl had decided to favour him. She was not a girl, he guessed, who was easily pleased.

The band started playing a tune that Bay recognised as one that he had danced to with Blanche. They had not danced together very often, as Blanche was careful of her public reputation, so Bay was able to remember each dance quite distinctly. This particular polka had been playing the night of the Londonderry Ball. They had just become lovers and there had been something intoxicating about being able to hold her in his arms in public. She had hardly looked at him, but he had seen the pulse beating in her neck. He found himself looking across the ballroom for her, wondering if she too remembered that other night, but there was no blond head among the swirling dancers. She must be at supper or perhaps she had gone home. Bay was surprised that she could have left without his noticing. He looked at his pocket watch; it was almost midnight. It was much later than he thought. He had been distracted.

There was a cough behind him. He turned to see a man wearing a dress uniform he didn't recognise.

'Captain Middleton?' The man spoke with an accent, French or Italian.

Bay nodded.

'My name is Count Cagliari. I am equerry to her Majesty, the Queen of Naples.' Cagliari looked over to where the Queen was sitting.

Bay bowed. Cagliari was tall and blond, his chest extensively be-medalled.

'At your service.'

'I believe you may know that Her Majesty will be hunting with the Pytchley this winter.'

Bay nodded. 'I hear that she is an excellent horsewoman.'

'Yes, that is the case. Her Majesty is quite without fear. But she is a queen and there is a feeling that she should have some assistance. She is after all riding with the public.'

Bay smiled. 'I don't think the members of the Pytchley would call themselves the public.'

Cagliari made an apologetic wave of his arm.

'Forgive me, sir, I am aware that the Pytchley is a very superior gathering. But that is perhaps, as you say here, the point moot. The Queen, as you know, is cruelly parted from the land whose name she bears. She has not the opportunity to lead, to shine, that should be hers by birth and upbringing. So it has become very important to her that she should be distinguished, to make her mark.' Cagliari paused, looking for the right words, then he continued.

'The Queen wishes to make her mark on the Pytchley, Captain Middleton. And to that end she needs a guide, someone to help her to take her rightful place.'

'The hunting field is not a court, Count.'

'No indeed, how clumsy of me to have given that impression. It is a place of excellence, of course, but as we know, Her Majesty already is a Diana. All she needs is some direction, from someone like yourself, so that she can be the Queen of the hunting field.'

'Direction? Are you asking me to be her pilot? To open gates and that sort of thing, tell her which way the wind is blowing, help her on her horse if she falls off?'

Cagliari beamed, not picking up on the irony in Bay's voice.

'Yes, precisely, Captain Middleton. A pilot. That is the mot juste.'

Bay paused. The Count did not understand the absurdity of his request.

'Please tell Her Majesty that, while I am aware of the honour she does me, I am sorry to say that I cannot oblige her.'

'Oh, but Captain Middleton, you do not appreciate the situation. The Queen would be extremely grateful . . .' He rolled his eyes as if to convey the extent of her gratitude.

'Really, your mistress would be better off with someone who enjoys making royalty grateful. Why don't you ask Captain Hartopp? You see him over there by the orchestra, tall chap with the whiskers? He is an excellent rider, quite as accomplished as I am and he would like nothing better than to ride out with the Queen of Naples.'

Cagliari looked over to where Hartopp was standing with Charlotte and shook his head. 'I am sure he is an excellent fellow, but Her Majesty has asked for you in particular, Captain Middleton. She has heard so many things about your *particular* talents.'

'I am flattered, of course, but I must still refuse. Even if my own Queen were to command my services as a pilot, I would decline. I love to hunt and I have no intention of spoiling one of the great pleasures in life by acting as a glorified royal nursemaid.'

Count Cagliari looked shocked, and Bay felt that perhaps he had gone too far.

'I have offended you, Count, with my frankness. Forgive me, but you see, I am not one of life's courtiers.'

The Count bowed. 'Her Majesty will be disappointed. Poor lady, she has so many crosses to bear.'

Bay patted the Count on the shoulder. 'Tell her I am rude and uncouth and quite unfit for royal company. I am sure that a man like you can make it seem like a lucky escape.'

The Count smiled wanly. 'Well, I shall do my best, Captain Middleton.'

Bay watched him thread his way back through the dancers towards the ex-Queen. It was time to leave. As he began to walk down the great staircase he looked up and saw Charlotte Baird, closely followed by Hartopp, coming down from the supper room on the mezzanine. He wondered if she would look down and see him. He stood there for a moment until he saw her spot him. She gave him a tiny smile, and Bay touched the rose in his buttonhole. And then Hartopp took her arm and hurried her back into the ballroom.

The Group Photograph

Melton Hall, Leicestershire January, 1876

THE GROUP ON THE STEPS AT MELTON SHIFTED about, trying to keep warm, their breath cloudy against the cold winter air. Lady Lisle looked particularly unhappy; her nose went red in the cold and she had so been looking forward to a delightful morning in front of the library fire, writing letters. But no house party these days was complete without a group photograph, and when Lady Crewe had written to invite Adelaide and her niece and nephew to stay at Melton, the Crewe seat in Leicestershire, over Christmas and the New Year, she had specifically requested that Charlotte should bring her 'equipment'. 'It would be so lovely to have a record of our entertainments,' Lady Crewe had written. 'When Archie went to Balmoral last summer, he said that the drawing room was full of photographs.'

Adelaide Lisle had passed on this message with reluctance. She did not approve of Charlotte's photographic exploits. Her niece had turned her dressing room in Charles Street into some kind of lair, which no one was allowed to enter without ringing a bell. She had remonstrated with Charlotte about the amount of time she spent in her 'dark room' but her niece had simply changed the subject. There was not much else Lady Lisle could do. As both parties were fully aware, it was Charlotte's money that paid for the house in Mayfair, the carriage and the handsome pair of liveried footmen who stood at the back of Lady Lisle's carriage when she paid her afternoon calls, and for the champagne that she liked to serve her guests at her Thursday afternoons. Charlotte would never be so vulgar as to point this out, but then she didn't need to. Adelaide Lisle's husband had died leaving her a title but not the means to support it, so she had lived a meagre existence in a small house in the Close at Salisbury, until she had been summoned by Fred to supervise his sister's debut. It had not been difficult to leave the privations of her Salisbury life for the comforts of Charles Street and the attentions of the liveried footmen; so while Adelaide Lisle did not enjoy standing about on a cold December morning while her niece fiddled about behind the green baize cloth that covered her camera, she was in no position to complain

The photographic session had been fixed for that morning. When the hunting season got underway the house would be half empty during the daylight hours. All the guests had now arrived. Bay Middleton and Chicken Hartopp had been the last to come, turning up the night before with their strings of hunters. Lady Lisle had been quite surprised that Middleton had been invited to Melton; at the Spencer ball a month before Augusta had been so very definite that he was not a 'suitable' young man. But his unsuitability was not, it seemed, an issue in the hunting season when all the great houses in 'the golden triangle' of the Quorn, Pytchley and Melton meets, competed to attract the best riders. Fred had told Lady Lisle that Bay had turned down five invitations, including one from the Spencers to stay at Althorp, in order to come to Melton.

In her tent of green baize Charlotte peered through the lens and counted the heads again: four, five, six, where was the seventh? She unmuffled herself from the drape and looked from behind the camera at the group. Her hostess Lady Crewe and her aunt dominated the middle of the frame; Augusta sat to the left of her mother, her body turned towards Fred, who stood behind her. Charlotte thought that if she were to tinker with this photograph, Augusta with her pale eyelashes and pinched mouth would be more rabbit than Pekinese, Fred with his high colour and receding chins would as always be an excellent turkey.

The men stood on the step behind, which made the difference in heights all the more evident: Chicken Hartopp's enormous frame towered over the others. Charlotte wondered if she could ask all the other men to go up a step so that the difference in height would not be so great; Lord Crewe was not excessively tall, and Captain Middleton had looked rather slight beside Hartopp. But now Captain Middleton was not there.

'What has happened to Captain Middleton?'

'Don't worry, Mitten, he's just gone to get something. He'll be back directly,' Fred answered.

'But I have the plate all set up. Couldn't he have waited?' Charlotte hated it when her brother called her 'Mitten' in public. He told her it was because she had looked like a mitten without a hand when she was a baby. She had often asked him to call her something else, but of course, the more she protested the more he clung to the nickname.

'Well, can't you just take the picture without him, Charlotte dear?' Lady Lisle said. 'It is is getting rather chilly.'

'But that would ruin my composition,' Charlotte said. This was true – she wanted the four men in the background to frame the women in the centre – but it was Bay's picture she wanted to take. She wanted to see how he would look through her lens.

Just then Middleton came running down the steps and took his position next to Hartopp.

'Forgive me, Miss Baird, I had to adjust my necktie. I thought you would want me to look my best.'

Charlotte put her head back under the heavy drape. She could see Bay's outline upside down on the plate, his head six inches below Chicken Hartopp's. She had told them all to stand perfectly still for as long as it took them to recite the Lord's Prayer in their heads from the moment she raised her hand and squeezed the bulb. Not only was the prayer just the right length, but the act of remembering the words stopped her sitters from fidgeting. Her godmother Lady Dunwoody had told her that taking a photograph of someone captured a piece of their soul, 'So you want to take them in a state of grace, Charlotte, if you can.' *For ever and ever, amen.* Charlotte came out from under the cloth and smiled at the group in front of her.

'Thank you for your patience. I hope you will be pleased with the results.'

The group began to stir, moving stiffly after the enforced stillness. Bay was the first to break ranks. He jumped down the steps to where she stood.

'May I help you carry your things inside?'

'That's very kind of you. I hope you don't mind waiting while I dismantle the camera.'

He watched attentively as Charlotte slid the exposed plate out of the camera and put it into its leather box.

'You have a great deal of equipment, Miss Baird. When you told me that you were interested in photography, I had no idea that you were such an expert.'

Charlotte smiled. 'Oh, I am hardly that, but I enjoy it very much. I am flattered that you remembered our conversation.'

'Of course I remembered. I don't often meet young ladies who tell me they would rather stand behind a camera than have a dress made.'

'No. I suspect that I am in the minority. Augusta, for example, finds it quite incomprehensible. She was very disapproving yesterday when I excused myself from a conversation about her trousseau because I had a print to make.'

Bay laughed, revealing white teeth. Charlotte was glad that he was as sympathetic as she remembered him from the Spencer ball. Even through the lens, he had looked so much more vigorous and alive than her brother or Hartopp. There was a springiness to him that made him a much easier presence than most of the young men she knew with their ponderous movements and their mutton-chop whiskers. He was wearing a suit made out of very dark green material. The jacket had an unusual diagonal facing and elaborate horn buttons. Charlotte recognised the style as the 'university' coat. Fred had told her about it: 'Latest thing, everyone's wearing them at the clubs.' It was not a style that suited Fred, as it accentuated his barrel-shaped torso, but on Bay's lean frame the cut looked stylish rather than absurd. She was relieved too that Bay had not grown the dundreary sideburns that were so fashionable at the moment. Charlotte had spent many evenings trying not to stare at a breadcrumb or tobacco strand adhering to the luxuriant facial hair of her dancing partners. She had once stopped Fred in the middle of one of his homilies about 'feminine behaviour' by finding a sizeable crumb of Stilton in his whiskers. Bay, she was pleased to see, had restricted himself to a neat moustache.

'Here, let me do that. I don't think I can do much damage to this.' He took the tripod out of her hands and began deftly to collapse the extendable wooden legs. 'I hope you haven't forgotten your promise, Miss Baird.'

'My promise?'

'To take a picture of Tipsy, my horse.'

'I don't think I am skilled enough to take a portrait of a horse alone, but I could probably manage horse and rider. Remember that you have to stay very still.'

'That won't be a problem for Tipsy, Miss Baird, she's a very serious horse. I, on the other hand, am a terrible fidget.'

Charlotte smiled. She picked up the camera and the slide case and started towards the house. As they made for the disused nursery that Lady Crewe had allowed Charlotte to use as her photographic studio, they had to pass through the crenellated gloom of the Great Hall. Although Melton was of Jacobean origin, it had just been extensively remodelled in the fashionable Gothic style, and all the windows of the hall had been replaced with stained-glass depictions of the Arthurian legends, so Bay's face was washed with yellow then blue then red as he walked across the hall under the windows depicting the Lady of the Lake, Sir Galahad and Lancelot and Guinevere.

'Will you be hunting on Monday, Miss Baird?' he asked as he followed her up the narrow staircase. He was carrying the tripod, a footman followed with the camera and Charlotte herself held the case with the photographic plate.

'I don't hunt, Captain Middleton, but I shall come to the meet. I am going to take some pictures.'

Bay laughed. 'Not sure you will get anyone to stay still enough to say the Lord's Prayer at a meet.'

He put the tripod down.

'But why don't you hunt, Miss Baird? I suspect that you are an excellent rider, and Fred has a quality stable.'

She laid the plate carefully in the developing tray. She tried to speak as lightly she could, not wanting the circumstances of her life to shadow the conversation.

'My mother was my father's second wife. He married her when

Fred was seven. My mother was very young, very rich and, I believe, very reckless. She died in a hunting accident when I was four years old. My father decided that he didn't want his daughter to run the same risk.' The silence was broken by the noise of the footman putting down the heavy camera.

Bay spoke. 'I think if I was your father I would feel the same.' He looked at her and then gestured around the room which was full of Charlotte's photographic paraphernalia.

'But you have something else to fill your time. I had no idea that photography needed so much stuff.'

'Oh, but this is only some of it. At home I have even more.'

Bay picked up one of the brown holland folders that Charlotte kept her work in.

'May I?'

'Of course. But I should warn you that I am more enthusiastic than expert.'

Bay started to look through the photos. 'They look very accomplished to me. I admire this one of Fred and Augusta, you have managed to make her look quite benign.'

Charlotte laughed. 'Yes, that was quite a test. I had to promise her that I would make her look just like the Princess of Wales.'

Bay chuckled and continued leafing through the photographs, then he stopped and made an exclamation.

'But this is capital.' He held up the Royal Menagerie print. Charlotte had photographed her original collage and set it in a black oval border. 'The Queen as a codfish, there is the most uncommon resemblance. And Bertie makes an excellent basset hound. I see that you have a sense of mischief, Miss Baird.'

'Perhaps. Fred thinks that I am peculiar.'

Bay studied the menagerie photograph closely. 'Well, I think on the evidence of this that he is quite right.'

He looked round and laughed when he saw Charlotte's look of disappointment.

'But much better to be peculiar than to be "fashionable" like Augusta. I, for example, collect porcelain and, as you know, I like to listen to opera rather than talk over or sleep through it. My fellow officers find that peculiar but I am rather proud of my eccentricities. Fond as I am of Chicken Hartopp, I don't want to resemble him more than I have to, and I am quite sure that you feel the same about Augusta.'

'You can't expect me to be rude about my future sister-in-law,' Charlotte protested. 'I am an orphan. Augusta will be my family.'

'You have my condolences.' Bay smiled. 'Tell me, Miss Baird, if you were to make one of these creations with the group you took this morning, which animal would you choose to replace me?'

Charlotte put her head on one side. 'Oh, but that is unfair. If I am truthful I may offend you, and if I flatter you, you will think I am a simpering young lady currying favour.'

'I promise that nothing you could say could offend me, and we have already established that you could never be mistaken for a simpering miss.'

'Well, in that case, let me see . . .' Charlotte half closed her eyes in mock deliberation. She had known from the moment she had first set eyes upon Bay exactly what sort of animal he was.

'I would say that you are something wild but not exotic. A predator who makes his own way. You are not to be trusted around chickens or ducks, but you are capable of giving a day's capital entertainment. I would make you a fox, Captain Middleton. I trust I haven't offended you.'

'On the contrary. I have a great deal of affection for foxes. They have given me some of the best days of my life.'

The gong sounded for lunch.

'We must go, Captain Middleton. Lady Crewe does not tolerate tardiness. And Augusta will be wondering why we have been up here so long without a chaperone.'

'Shall I tell her we have been flirting, Miss Baird?'

'Is that what we are doing, Captain Middleton? Thank you for enlightening me.'

Easton Neston

I T WAS RAINING THE MORNING THAT THE EMPRESS was due to arrive, so the servants were waiting inside. The first thing they heard was the sound of the wheels on the gravel; the second was a weird, high-pitched, pulsating yell. The head housemaid got to the window first.

'She's getting out of the carriage and there's something on her shoulder. It's a monkey. She's only got a pet monkey.'

'Nasty smelly things,' said Mrs Cross the housekeeper. 'My last lady was given one and luckily it died a couple of weeks later. No one missed it, I can tell you.'

Wilmot, the butler, shouted for them all to get into line. The housemaid took her place beside Mrs Cross. She could hear the housekeeper humming under her breath. It sounded like a hymn. Mrs Cross was Chapel and she was not happy about working for a Catholic, even if she was an Empress. She had almost resigned when the letter came from Vienna asking for a room to be set aside for the saying of mass. In the event, she had not given her notice, aware that a letter of royal approval would be valuable whether the monarch was protestant or catholic. But she had assigned the coldest, draughtiest room on the North Front for the popish ritual.

The doors were opened and the housemaid saw the silhouette of a woman walking up the steps against the grey morning light. She was tall, an inch or so taller than the man who was holding an umbrella above her head. As she stood in the doorway, the fur mantle slipped away from her body and the housemaid was astonished to see how slender she was – Mrs Cross had said she was a grandmother already – but she had the waist of a girl. The maid instinctively drew in her own stomach.

The Empress was walking towards them now, the man with the umbrella who, although he wasn't wearing a uniform, looked like some kind of servant following just behind. When she reached Mrs Cross, the housekeeper made a surprisingly graceful curtsey. The maid tried to imitate her, keeping her eyes lowered as instructed. 'Never get in their eyeline, Patience,' Mrs Cross had said, 'foreign royalty can be tricky.' But the Empress was stopping in front of her. Surely it would be rude not to acknowledge her in any way. She glanced up at the veiled face and heard the Empress say in a soft, lightly accented voice, 'What is your name?'

The housemaid tried to speak but found she could not make her mouth work. She heard Mrs Cross say, 'This is Patience, the head housemaid, Your Majesty.'

'Such a charming English face. I feel sure I will like it here.' As the Empress walked away the maid caught a trace of violets and something else that smelt rather like brandy.

There was another eldritch scream as the monkey, who had been lurking in the doorway, scuttled across the hall towards the Empress. She seemed not to notice the racket that the animal was making and continued down the line of servants. The housemaid saw the monkey stop in front of Mrs Cross and watched, horrified, as it squatted down and proceeded to urinate on the housekeeper's skirt. Mrs Cross made a sound like a badly oiled door creaking in the wind, and the Empress looked round just as the housekeeper was kicking the animal across the floor.

There was a moment of quiet and then the monkey started screaming again, this time with a high-pitched chatter that ricocheted around the pillars of the entrance hall. The housemaid saw that the Empress's shoulders were shaking, and she realised that she was laughing. The monkey was rocking back and forth on its haunches; Mrs Cross was muttering under her breath. The maid saw the Empress extend one shaking hand towards the monkey and heard her say something in German, then the little man, who had carried her umbrella, picked up the animal and carried it out of the house. As he turned his back on his mistress, the maid could see that his face was as sour as Mrs Cross's had been.

The Empress sat by the fire in the Great Hall. The monkey had been been sent to the stables, but her favourite wolfhound was lying at her feet. The room was enormous, the double height ceiling as high as a cathedral. Elizabeth felt faintly irritated – everyone imagined that because she lived in palaces that she could not be happy in anything else. Yet really she longed for a room where she could speak without hearing her voice echo. Still it was a beautiful house, and more importantly it was in the heart of the English hunting country.

Baron Nopsca, her chamberlain, came into the room, looking worried.

'Earl Spencer is here, Majesty. I told him that you were indisposed after your journey, but he was very anxious to pay his respects.'

Elizabeth smiled. 'But I am not in the least bit tired, Nopsca. Send him in.'

The Earl, Elizabeth noticed, did not kiss her hand. He bowed rather stiffly when he was presented, but there were none of the sycophantic contortions of a Viennese courtier. He was very tall and Elizabeth had never seen a man with quite such red hair before. She tried not to stare at him.

'I hope Your Majesty is happy with the house?'

'It is hardly a house. In Austria we would call it a palace; even the stables are magnificent.' She smiled and was rewarded by seeing the Earl blush.

'Stables are the most important part of the place in my view, Ma'am. When I was rebuilding Althorp, I had them do the stables first, so at least the horses would be comfortable. The Countess was not happy about it at all. She wanted the kitchen block done, said the food was always cold by the time it got to the dining room, but I said what was the point of eating if you couldn't hunt.'

'I can see that we are destined to be great friends, Lord Spencer. Like you, I would much rather hunt than eat.' Elizabeth laid one hand very briefly on the Earl's arm and watched as his skin darkened to a rich magenta. She enjoyed the Earl's confusion, such a delicious contrast from the perfectly controlled manners of the Viennese.

'I am so looking forward to my first "meet", I think you call it. I am relying on you to teach me all the right hunting argot. I don't want to disgrace myself.'

The Earl interrupted her gallantly, 'Oh I am quite sure there is no danger of that, Ma'am. I have heard what a fine horsewoman you are.'

'And I have heard how fierce the English are in the field.' She looked at him through her lashes. The Earl pulled a handkerchief out of his pocket and wiped his brow, which was beaded with sweat, even though the temperature in the room was chilly.

'What time is the hunt tomorrow? I should so hate to be late on my first day.'

The Earl froze, his massive hand at his temple. 'Tomorrow, Ma'am? But tomorrow is Sunday.' He was now such a regal shade of purple that Elizabeth wondered if he was about to have some kind of seizure.

'Sunday?' she asked. 'I suppose people will attend church first.' But Spencer shook his great head.

'No hunting on the Sabbath, Ma'am. Even though every parson round here is a hunting man, the Church won't have it.'

Elizabeth raised an eyebrow. 'I had no idea that the English were so religious. In my country we hunt every day, in fact the Sunday hunts are usually the best. Everyone rides with a clear conscience.' She laid her hand again on the Earl's arm.

'I am sure, Lord Spencer, that if you were to talk to these, how did you call them, parsons, you could persuade them to bend their rules a little? I have come such a long way, and I would so like to hunt tomorrow.'

Baron Nopsca, who was standing in attendance behind the Empress's chair, began to listen carefully. His English was not perfect but he could hear that note in his mistress's voice which indicated that she had set her heart on something, and he knew all about the repercussions if she did not get what she wanted.

The Earl opened his bulbous light blue eyes wide. 'Can't be done, I'm afraid, Ma'am. Not even Queen Victoria herself could ride out on the Sabbath.'

Nopsca noted with alarm the perfect stillness of the Empress's head. How foolish he had been to stand behind her instead of in the Empress's eyeline. His mistress was not used to having her wishes denied, and he feared for the consequences. Silently he prayed that the Empress would remember that she was a guest in this country and that she could not expect everything to be arranged exactly to her satisfaction as it would be at home. His job was, above all, to save the Empress and the Crown from any embarrassment, and he knew that he would no longer be in employment if he failed to prevent the Empress from breaking the law. Why did the English lord have to be so blunt? Nopsca knew that the way to handle his mistress at these moments was to distract her; an outright refusal would only provoke her.

He held his breath as the Empress replied, 'But I thought Victoria was head of the Church in this country!' She paused. 'But it is not my place to break your funny English laws. I shall have to contain myself till Monday . . .' and she laughed. It wasn't a very warm laugh but the relief of it made Nopsca exhale sharply. To his horror the Empress turned round and looked at him. She saw the relief in his face and this time she laughed properly.

'You worry too much, Nopsca.'

Earl Spencer cleared his throat. 'Your Majesty will need a pilot on Monday. Someone to guide you through the field. Twenty years ago I would have taken on the job myself but I am not the man I was. May I suggest a former equerry of mine, a Captain Middleton. One of the best riders in England and knows the country round here like the back of his hand. Better, if anything.'

Elizabeth tilted her head, her dark eyes narrowed. 'Someone to lead me through the field? But I will not be riding out alone; Prince Liechtenstein and Count Esterhazy have come with me from Vienna. They are both excellent horsemen. I believe they will provide me with all the "guidance" I need.'

The Earl looked down at his boots as if looking for his reflection in the polished leather. He seemed to take comfort from what he saw there because he came back strongly, 'With respect, Ma'am, they may be capital riders but they have not hunted with the

Pytchley. They don't know how things are done here. My purpose in suggesting Captain Middleton was to spare you any of the minor embarrassments that might arise from unfamiliarity with the terrain, or with some of our customs in the field. Middleton knows every ditch and fence between here and Towcester. I suggested him because I feel sure that Your Majesty will want to be at the head of the pack.'

Elizabeth considered this. 'And is he discreet, this captain? Would you send him out riding with your queen?'

'Indeed, Ma'am. He is not absolutely from the first rank of society, but he is a superb rider. And it would put my mind at rest to know that he was at your side. Your presence here is a great honour, Ma'am. But as Master of the Pytchley, your safety is my responsibility.'

Elizabeth smiled. She suspected that this Captain Middleton's real duty would be to report on her activities. But if he could ride as well as Earl Spencer said, he could at least be useful while he spied on her.

'Well, I should hate you to worry, Lord Spencer, so I will accept your pilot. But he should know that I am not some porcelain doll to be protected. I am here because I want to ride out with the famous Pytchley hunt. I hope I won't be disappointed.'

The Earl picked up his hat and gloves from the chair beside him. 'No danger of that, Ma'am.'

Elizabeth held out her hand, and this time the Earl bent over to kiss it, his bushy moustache prickling against her skin. She was surprised to see him turn and walk out of the room. Surely he must know that it was disrespectful to turn your back on a monarch? She heard Nopsca behind her make a noise. She guessed he was thinking the same thing. In Vienna such an act would be inconceivable; a courtier would sooner cut his throat than commit such a grievous act of *lèse-majesté*. But, Elizabeth thought, with a sudden rush of exhilaration, she was not in Vienna now. She had escaped for a moment, from all the layers of custom and faux servility, from the courtiers who were obsequious in public and vicious the moment she turned her back.

'I think we shall have to get used to English manners, Nopsca,' she said.

Clementine

THAT EVENING, LADY CREWE HESITATED FOR A MOMENT before announcing who would take Charlotte into dinner.

The Baird girl was a funny little creature – always fiddling with that camera – but she would be family when Augusta married Fred. Lady Crewe had once hoped for a more glittering marriage for her only daughter, but now she was simply relieved that she was to have a son-in-law at all. The Bairds were a respectable family, not perhaps the smartest, but Augusta at twenty-four could no longer afford to be choosy. Edith Crewe looked at Charlotte, who was standing next to Augusta. She really was no beauty but the fortune, of course, made her attractive enough. It seemed unfair that all poor Dora Lennox's money should have gone to the daughter; Fred was comfortably off, but the Lennox fortune would have made all the difference to Augusta's future position. Fred would gain some benefit from the money now, but when Charlotte married, that would all change. She could see that both of Fred's friends were interested. Hartopp was the more suitable – there was no gossip linking him to married women – but feeling the injustice of Augusta's four fruitless seasons in search of a husband with a shrug almost of irritation, she beckoned to Captain Middleton.

As Lady Crewe announced her decision, Bay heard something

like a sigh somewhere over his left ear. Chicken Hartopp was not happy. But Bay could see from the smile on Charlotte's face that he had been her choice.

He offered her his arm.

'My print has come out well, Captain Middleton,' she said.

'I would expect nothing less, Miss Baird. You strike me as a most competent person.'

She looked up at him, surprised. 'Competent is not a word often applied to young ladies; we are usually called accomplished.'

'But accomplished suggests something rather fanciful and ornamental. You seemed so practical with your cameras and your chemicals, your hobby is hardly that of a young lady,' Bay said.

'Actually, Captain Middleton, some of the finest photographers are ladies. My godmother Lady Dunwoody has had her work exhibited at the Royal Photographic Society.'

'Don't be cross. I was trying to pay you a compliment. I would much rather be competent than accomplished.'

Charlotte paused, uncertain as to the extent of her crossness. A footman pulled out her chair and she sat down. She was about to reply to Captain Middleton when she heard Fred call across to her.

'I say, Mitten, do you remember who the painting of the pheasants in the library at Kevill is by? It's the spitting image of that one in the corner.'

Charlotte tried not to flinch at his use of her nickname. 'Greuze, I believe. Father bought it in Italy.'

Bay leant towards her and said, 'Mitten? Why does Fred call you that?'

'I have no idea,' Charlotte said, 'I hate it.' She glared at her brother, who was trying to impress his future father-in-law with the quality of his picture collection.

'Pity. I rather like my nickname. Much more interesting than

John. I was called Bay after the Grand National winner. We have the same colouring, apparently. Sadly the resemblance ends there.'

'Sadly?'

'I haven't won the Grand National, Miss Baird.' Bay bowed his head.

'Oh, is that what you want?' Charlotte was surprised that he had such a definite ambition. He hadn't struck her as a man who made efforts.

'Of course.' He turned to look at her.

'And will you?'

'I hope so. I might have a shot this year. It's all about the horse, and Tipsy is a contender.'

'Ah yes, the famous Tipsy.'

'I hope you are not mocking me, Miss Baird.' He looked at her with uncharacteristic seriousness. 'You don't ride, of course, so I can't blame you for your ignorance, but believe me when I tell you that horses are remarkable creatures. If you find the right one, as I have in Tipsy, it is like finding the other half of your soul. She understands me better than any woman has ever done. And she will never desert me.' He picked up his wine glass and drained it.

Charlotte said, 'Perhaps you haven't found the right woman, Captain Middleton,' and then, realising how forward that sounded, she blushed and added, 'I believe there are some examples of my sex who may be as sympathetic to your feelings as a horse, even if they aren't much use in the hunting field.'

Bay smiled. 'I shall take your word for it. Perhaps I am better at choosing horses than women. You know what you are getting with a horse, whereas with a woman all you can see is what's on the outside. You can feel a horse's soul the moment you ride out together, but with a woman – well, I don't think I have ever met a woman who says what she means.'

'But Captain Middleton,' Charlotte said, 'let's not forget that horses, even remarkable ones like your Tipsy, cannot actually speak. Who knows what white lies or polite half truths your favourite mare might utter if she could. Or perhaps you would prefer a woman who did not speak at all, but gazed at you in mute adoration, ready to obey your orders instantly. I think you are in the wrong country. I think if you were to go to Constantinople you might find the kind of woman you want in the sultan's harem.'

'I would go like a shot if I thought you were right, but I suspect that even the sultan has difficulty in finding a woman who means what she says.'

'I'm afraid that you are a misogynist, Captain, and that nothing I say will make any difference.'

'Possibly, Miss Baird, but please don't stop trying. I am enjoying your efforts.'

The footman took away the soup plates and Charlotte turned to talk to Augusta's younger brother on her other side. He was round-eyed and earnest and he was soon telling her about his studies at Keble College, where he was an ardent supporter of the Oxford movement. As the soufflé was replaced by the turbot, Charlotte turned again to her right but she saw that Bay was listening to the conversation across the table. He was sitting very still, and Charlotte thought this was the first time she had ever seen him motionless.

Lady Crewe was talking to Fred.

'I am always amazed at the names that perfectly sensible people choose to give their children. Do you remember when everyone was calling their daughters Aurora, on account of Mrs Browning's *Aurora Leigh*? And now I had a letter this morning from Stella Airlie to say that Blanche Hozier has called her new baby Clementine. I mean, what kind of name is that? It sounds like a medicine. You must promise me, Fred, that you and Augusta will choose decent English names that people can pronounce. Nothing worse than a foreign sounding name.'

Fred was nodding enthusiastically, his face flushed. Charlotte could see that he was nervous. Fred's mother's name had been Leonie.

She was about to tell Captain Middleton this – she sensed that he would be more than happy to help her tease her brother – but he was holding himself so rigidly that she felt if she touched him he might shatter. The only thing moving was a muscle that twitched in his eyelid.

For a moment she sat silently, but then, feeling her aunt's eye upon her, she knew she must say something. Her aunt was always scolding her for her lack of conversation, saying, 'A man wants to be soothed by feminine conversation, you don't want to make him work too hard. Your job is to make it easy for him to talk to you.' Charlotte had been surprised at this advice, as in her experience most men were more than happy with the sound of their own voice. But she leant towards Captain Middleton and said, 'What do you think, Captain Middleton? I think Clementine is rather a pretty name.'

Rather to her surprise, Chicken Hartopp, who was sitting opposite them, picked up her remark.

'Yes, what do *you* think, Middleton?' he said, so loudly that the table went quiet.

Bay paused for a moment and then he smiled.

'It's not a name I would have chosen, but then the only thing I am competent to judge is horseflesh.' He turned to Charlotte.

'What do you say, Miss Baird?' She sensed that Chicken Hartopp, her aunt and Lady Crewe were all listening, and she saw that Middleton was labouring to keep his mouth stretched into a smile.

She took a breath and then she said, 'I suppose the question is whether one's name is a self-fulfilling prophecy? My real name is ordinary enough, but I feel quite belittled if Fred calls me Mitten. Perhaps you feel the same, Captain Hartopp, when people call you Chicken?' She saw that Bay's smile had lost its tight rigidity and, encouraged by this, although a little ashamed to have teased Captain Hartopp, she continued.

'When you are at the races, do you bet as confidently on a horse called Treacle as one called Pegasus? How confident would you feel about the diagnosis of a Dr Pain?'

Captain Hartopp was about to answer when Lady Crewe said, 'We have an undertaker here in the village whose name is Coffin. I wonder if he ever contemplated another profession. I must ask him.' The conversation drifted off into maids called Polish, judges called Gallows and a surgeon called Saw. Charlotte felt that the moment, whatever it had been, had passed.

She turned to Middleton, who had slumped back against his chair.

'I hear that there is royalty hunting with the Pytchley this year.'

Middleton laughed. 'If you mean the Queen of Naples, she is ex-royalty. The Italians chucked her out.'

'Still, I should like a picture. My album has nothing grander than an earl. A queen, even a deposed one, would be a coup. Will you help me, Captain Middleton?'

He looked across the table as he replied, his eyes resting for a moment on Chicken Hartopp's red face. 'For you, Miss Baird, I would do anything, even make myself agreeable to one of the vainest woman in Europe.'

'Is she really so bad? I thought she was generally considered rather handsome.'

Chicken Hartopp leant over. 'The Queen of Naples has rather a weakness for Middleton. Wanted him to be her pilot. Not a job I would have turned down, but I suppose you are spoilt for choice, eh Middleton?'

Charlotte felt a tiny brush of saliva on her cheek as Hartopp leant towards her. She sat back involuntarily.

'I didn't fancy being at the beck and call of a woman, even if she is a queen. There are other things I want to do.' Middleton laughed. 'I realise that makes me sound very ungallant.'

'A little, Captain Middleton.' Charlotte was about to say that at least he was honest when Hartopp leant forward again. 'Time was, Middleton, when you liked nothing better than to be at the beck and call of a woman.' This remark hit a pause in the table's hum of conversation.

Lady Crewe clucked audibly, 'I couldn't help overhearing you mention the Queen of Naples, Captain Middleton. Did you know that her sister the Empress of Austria has taken Easton Neston from Lord Hesketh for the season? She is to hunt with the Pytchley. I hear she is coming over with ten horses.'

Lady Lisle spoke. 'Not only horses. Lady Spencer told me that she travels everywhere with a pet monkey, a dairy cow and a pack of wolfhounds. They have had to make all sorts of alterations to Easton Neston. Apparently one of the bedrooms is to be turned into a gymnasium.'

'A gymnasium? What on earth can she want with such a thing?' Lady Crewe was astonished.

'The Empress is so proud of her figure that she does calisthenics every single day,' Augusta said. 'I read in the *Illustrated London News* that she has taken lessons from a circus performer and can make her horses jump through hoops of fire.'

'Honestly, Augusta, how can you be so credulous?' said her mother. 'Empresses don't do circus tricks, even foreign ones. People will say anything to sell a newspaper. But I must say I am looking forward to seeing her. They say she is the most beautiful woman in Europe. '

Lady Crewe rose to her feet and beckoned to the other ladies to follow her.

As Middleton got up to pull out Charlotte's chair, his hand brushed across her bare shoulder. She felt its heat and looked up at him, startled.

'Oh how clumsy of me, Miss Baird, I am sorry,' but Charlotte thought that he didn't look sorry at all. He was staring at her and she stared back, feeling that to look away would be cowardly somehow. At last he laughed. 'Look at me. I have the manners of a stable hand. Will you allow me to escort you to the door, Miss Baird?' He extended his arm with exaggerated deference. Charlotte laid the tips of her fingers on it and they walked in silence to the door. As she walked up the stairs to the drawing room she still felt the touch of his hand on her shoulder, her collarbone to be exact.

Hair Brushing

THE BRUSH STOPPED, ARRESTED BY A KNOT. SO MUCH hair, it came down to below the Empress's knees; the imperial hairdresser had to bend almost double to brush its entire length. To wash it took a dozen eggs and a bottle of brandy. And it was so heavy the hairdresser could see the relief on her mistress's face when she took out the pins at the end of the day. It was like carrying a baby on the back of your head. Sometimes it felt so heavy that the Empress would lie in bed with her hair tied to the ceiling with ribbons to relieve the weight.

The hairdresser stood back, the hair in front of her pacified and smooth at last.

'Shall I tie it up, Majesty?'

Elizabeth put her head on one side and smiled at her in the mirror, 'No, I need it tonight to keep me warm.'

She stood up and shook the hair around her like a cloak. The hairdresser made her deepest curtsey, saying as she always did, 'I lay myself at Your Majesty's feet.'

'Thank you. You may leave us.' The imperial hairdresser walked, as custom dictated, out of the room backwards, hesitating a little as the route was as yet unfamiliar to her.

Elizabeth sat down in front of the mirror. She thought there was a new line underneath her left eye. It was what her mother would call a laughter line: 'Never forget that every smile leaves a crease on your face, girls.' Every time she said that, Elizabeth and her sisters would wipe their faces smooth as china for a minute and then one of them inevitably would start giggling and their mother would sigh and say, 'But your faces are your future, you know.' Her mother had been right, of course. It was Elizabeth's fifteen-year-old face that had changed everything that day in Bad Ischl. She had gone as an afterthought: to be a companion to Helena, her eldest sister and the one who had been chosen by their aunt to marry her son the Emperor. But Franz had seen Sisi, as Elizabeth was known to the family, and after that he was blind to anyone else. For the first and last time in his life, he had acted on impulse. He chose her, Sisi the shy one, not the suitable Helena who was so good at saying the right thing. Helena, who always looked regal, even when she was asleep.

But it was unfair that she should be getting laughter lines. There had not been so very much to smile about. There was a scratching at the door and Elizabeth smelt the monkey as it bounded into the room.

Elizabeth thought of the expression on the English housekeeper's face when she saw the dark stain spreading on her skirt. She knew that it was cruel of her to laugh, but it was such a relief to see something real in the middle of all that stiffness. It had felt like a good omen. Maybe, she thought, she could be happy here. She smoothed the skin round her eyes with her fingertips. The lines would come anyway; perhaps it was more important to find something to laugh about.

There was a knock at the door. Countess Festetics, the thin Hungarian lady-in-waiting, came in, her sleek head down and slightly forward as if she were an otter parting the waves. She was carrying a letter.

'Majesty.' She curtsied and handed the envelope to Elizabeth.

'Dearest Sisi, I hope you have arrived safely and that the house is to your satisfaction . . .'

It was a letter from Maria. Elizabeth felt her face tighten. Of her four sisters, Maria was the nearest to her in age, and they had been very close when they were little, but like so many things the relationship had changed with her marriage. Helena had been dignified about losing the chance to be Empress, but Maria was too young to conceal her envy. Things had improved when Maria had married the King of Naples, but she had barely had a chance to enjoy her status before the Revolution. And now she was a queen in exile, married to a man she could barely tolerate, with no children to comfort her.

The letter went on, 'I have been sorely tried these last few months; when I think of the riches I took for granted in Naples . . . and there are so many minor indignities. Only the other day the Duchess of Savoy was given precedence over me at a Drawing Room.' The letter continued with a catalogue of misfortunes and slights that Maria had been forced to endure. At the end there was a postscript, 'But now that you are here, dearest Sisi, I feel sure that my fortunes must improve. I hope that a little of your imperial glory will reflect on me.'

Elizabeth put the letter down; reading Maria's letter had made her feel weary. She knew that her sister wanted sympathy, but Elizabeth felt something close to irritation. Why should she be made to feel guilty for still wearing a crown?

Festetics was saying something in Hungarian about the dinner tomorrow. Elizabeth felt her spirits lift as she replied in the same language, 'Tell Count Esterhazy and Prince Liechtenstein that my sister is coming for dinner tomorrow.' Her cavaliers could be relied upon to pay court to Maria. Max and Felix were always charming, and so handsome. Of course, she would always be the object of their most intense adoration, but she would not object to a little flirtation with Maria. She was probably starved of that kind of distraction. Judging by the lumbering manners of Earl Spencer, English men had no idea how to flatter a woman. Her life had become considerably more pleasant now that Max and Felix had become her *cavalieri serventi*. The fact that they were inseparable meant that there could be no flicker of scandal in their slavish devotion to their Empress. Her husband, Franz Joseph, had made one of his rare jokes about them, 'I shall call them the dual monarchy – an Austrian and a Hungarian yoked together in the service of a greater cause.'

She looked at the clock; it was a little after ten. At this hour her husband would be sitting in his apartments in the Hofburg going through the state papers with his magnifying glass.

In the early days of their marriage she had been so jealous of those piles of paper. They were always there, waiting for him at five in the morning and still there at midnight when he went to bed. When she had dared to complain, he had looked at her as if he didn't understand what language she was speaking. 'I am the Emperor, this is my work.' She had retreated then in the face of his seriousness, but as time went on she realised that even if the country didn't need him to approve every appointment in the civil service or to sign every document relating to the management of his vast empire, Franz could not wake up in the morning or go to sleep at night without his paper mountain of responsibilities. Once she had resented the time he spent scratching through forestry reports from Carpathia; now she thought of those bundles of paper tied up in red tape with relief. While he had his head down over the paper trail of his empire, he could not look up and reproach her for leaving him alone.

She pictured his study. So spartan for a Hapsburg emperor. Franz slept every night on his iron campaign bed. The only colourful thing was the Winterhalter portrait hanging over his desk, the one of her holding up her hair in a great knot. Not her favourite portrait, but Franz was so fond of it. Probably by now he preferred it to the real woman. In the picture, at least, she was smiling at him.

Sisi picked up her pen and started to write. She certainly found it easier to write affectionately to her husband now that they were safely in different countries. At this distance Franz's inflexible routine seemed comforting rather than irritating. She liked the idea that she always knew where he would be and what he would be doing at any hour of the day. But it was better to know of it than to see it in its daily monotony.

By the end of her letter Sisi felt quite warm towards her husband. She thought that if he were here she would like to put her head on his chest for a moment and feel his warm hand on her shoulder. A moment, though, would be enough.

Franz had not protested when she had proposed this trip to England. In fact he had been almost eager, doubling her allowance and giving her the imperial train to transport her horses. For a moment Sisi wondered whether he actually wanted her to go and felt a little hurt; but then she dismissed the thought as incredible, Franzl would never ever admit even to himself that there was anything untoward about their marriage.

She signed her name Sisi with her usual flourish and sealed the letter. Her duty done, she allowed Festetics to settle her into the vast bed. The day after tomorrow she would be hunting.

The Orchid House

THE NEXT DAY WAS A SUNDAY. THERE HAD BEEN A private chapel at Melton since it was built in the early 1600s. The original had been an austere building, almost Lutheran in its simplicity. But Lord Crewe's enthusiasm for the Gothic had extended to every part of the house, and the architect, who was a disciple – there was no other word – of Pugin, had transformed the chapel into a polychrome tribute to High Anglican devotion. The simple clerestory windows had been replaced with a riot of stained glass depicting Noah's Ark (Lord Crewe had always wanted a menagerie). The flagged stone floor had been taken up and a tessellated pavement of the latest encaustic tiles had been laid down in a design taken from the floor of the Cathedral at Chartres. Every pew had a gilded finial; the ceiling was covered in lavishly painted beams with wooden gargoyles sprouting at every groyne. Lord Crewe had done very well out of the railway boom, so no expense or trouble had been spared. Many visitors had, in his Lordship's hearing at any rate, compared Melton favourably with Keble College in Oxford or even to the Houses of Parliament.

But the Gothic splendours of Melton were not popular with everybody. Every time Augusta knelt to say her prayers on a tapestry kneeler depicting the Miracle at Cana, she would reflect rather bitterly that the lavishness of the chapel was the reason for the modesty of her dowry. As the daughter of an earl, Augusta had expected from childhood to make a Great Match. She had gone into her first season fully prepared to flirt with younger sons, but to save her affections for the heir. To her surprise and chagrin, however, she had found that none of the names she had perused in the nursery copy of Burke's Peerage was finding its way on to her dance card. At the end of her first summer, she had danced with a couple of baronets and had supper with the younger son of a viscount and had taken one heady turn round the conservatory of Syon Park with the nephew of a duke, but none of these young men had come back for more. In her second season she had had high hopes of an Irish peer, who was most attentive until a tenants' revolt had summoned him back to his estates. She had waited for him to return the following year, only to find that he had become engaged to one of the Drummond sisters, who happened to have a dowry of £50,000. When Augusta looked at the gold and lapis mosaic of the Virgin Mary above the altar, she could not help thinking that if the chapel had been left in its original unadorned state, she would now be Lady Clonraghty.

Fred had proposed in her fourth season, just at a point when she was beginning to wonder whether she, like poor Princess Beatrice, was doomed to be the unmarried daughter living at home for ever. She had refused him the first time, of course; it was vital that he realised that she was not an easy conquest and she had not altogether given up hope of a title. But Fred was so excited by the thought of winning an aristocratic bride that he pursued her from ball to ball, claiming every dance that decorum allowed and making sure that he always procured her the peach ices that she coveted from the supper rooms. Although Fred was not aristocratic, or particularly handsome, he was more than respectably connected, and the shortcomings in his face and figure were disguised by the splendour of his Guards Uniform. Kevill, the Baird estate in the Borders, was not as grand as Melton, but thanks to the novels of Sir Walter Scott its location and its ancient pele tower had become quite fashionable. Border society was not so illustrious that it would be indifferent to the importance of a Lady Augusta Crewe. It was not the match she had hoped for, but it was a great deal better to be Mistress of Kevill than to be the domestic angel of some rural deanery. Fred had an estate of 20,000 acres and an income of £10,000 a year. She hoped it would be enough to take a house in town during the season, for while Augusta was an admirer of Walter Scott, she did not want to moulder in the Scottish foothills for ever, like the Bride of Lochinvar.

It was unfortunate that the Lennox fortune would leave the family when Charlotte married. Fred had confessed to Augusta that he had managed to save a substantial amount in the past few years since his father's death by living off the interest on his sister's inheritance. The house in Charles Street and the refurbishment of Kevill had all been paid for with Lennox money, so that the heiress might live in suitable style. Of course, that style would continue if the heiress remained unmarried, but Augusta could not believe that Charlotte, even with all her peculiarities, would be single for long. Hartopp was clearly making a play for her, however Augusta had seen the look on Charlotte's face when Bay had taken her into dinner. Middleton was handsome, of course, and she had observed that he was an excellent dancer, although Bay had never actually asked her to dance. But he was quite unsuitable and only a girl as naive and inexperienced as Charlotte would fail to recognise that.

Augusta thought, not for the first time, how fortunate Charlotte was in having her as a mentor. How easy it would be for Charlotte, without Augusta's guidance, to be swayed by the smooth tongue and nimble feet of a Bay Middleton and diverted from the excellent match that surely lay ahead for her. Not that there was any hurry. Charlotte's prospects would be much improved by spending a season or two under Augusta's tutelage.

Augusta was not the only member of the congregation whose attention was diverted from the young curate, who was preaching a heartfelt sermon on the subject of brotherly love. The Hon. Percy, Augusta's younger brother, was a fervent Tractarian, and he could tell from the priest's elaborate robes and choice of quotations that he too was of the same mind. Lord Crewe was admiring, as he always did, the procession of lions, elephants and zebras making their way up the ramp to the shelter of the Ark. Next to him, his wife was wondering if Lady Spencer would hold a reception for the Austrian Empress; she couldn't help but be curious.

In the pew behind, Lady Lisle was thinking about lunch.

Fred was contemplating whether he should have a coat made up with the new American shoulders as his tailor had suggested. Next to him, Charlotte was trying to decide whether the pricking feeling on the back of her neck meant that Bay was sitting in the pew behind her.

It did. Bay had not woken up with the intention of attending the service, but when he saw Hartopp wearing his frock coat and clutching his prayer book, he realised that he too might benefit from communing with the Almighty. He made a point of sitting directly behind Charlotte Baird and singing as loudly as he could. He wondered if she would turn round. But she didn't.

At the back, the indoor servants enjoyed the respite. If you had been up since dawn laying fires, then half an hour sitting down listening to the importance of Christian charity was divine intervention indeed.

After the service the household dispersed. Lord Crewe went to the gun room; Lady Crewe and Lady Lisle took the carriage to visit a sick villager; the Honourable Percy stayed behind to have a word with the vicar about a recently acquired translation of Josephus; and Augusta and Fred went to see if the lake had frozen. The housemaids stood up, their knees clicking as they got to their feet, and waited for Charlotte, Bay and Chicken Hartopp to leave the chapel.

Charlotte walked quickly. She had no intention of lingering, but if anyone chose to intercept her, well, she could not be held responsible for that. She walked up the flight of steps that connected the chapel to the rest of the house. There were fourteen steps, and on the thirteenth she heard his voice.

'Miss Baird, I think this is the moment.'

She stopped and turned her head.

'The moment for what?' She knew, of course.

Middleton was bounding up the steps towards her, two at a time, as if trying to escape from Hartopp. When he reached her, Bay said, 'You haven't forgotten poor Tipsy? She has been beautifying herself all morning.'

Charlotte laughed. 'I very much doubt that I can do such a paragon justice, but I will attempt to take a picture of you both if you can promise to keep her still.'

'Splendid.' He turned to Hartopp, who stood on the steps below, visibly dismayed by their banter.

'Chicken, old fellow, why don't you help Miss Baird with her equipment while I bring Tipsy round to the front of the house?'

Hartopp hesitated, but when Charlotte said, 'Oh that would be very kind, Captain Hartopp,' he followed her obediently.

As they climbed the stairs to the old nursery, Hartopp said, 'Middleton has some cheek expecting you to take a picture of his horse. He thinks altogether too much of that creature.'

'Oh I don't mind, and besides, I want to take a picture of Captain Middleton, and I suspect that he will be a much better behaved subject if his horse is present.'

They entered the nursery, and Hartopp saw the print of the group photograph that Charlotte had taken yesterday on the table. He looked at it carefully and saw that Bay was the only person in the photograph who was smiling. Hartopp bristled.

'Middleton looks very pleased with himself in this picture.'

Charlotte turned around from the shelf of photographic plates. 'Not many people can smile in a photograph like that. Holding your expression can make even the most genuine expression seem forced.' She took one of the plates over to the window to examine it.

Hartopp did not reply immediately. He stood staring down at the picture, his face filling with colour, one massive hand pulling at his whiskers. His chest heaved and the buttons of his jacket strained at the buttonholes. Finally he spoke, his voice emerging in a rapid mutter.

'Miss Baird, Charlotte if I may call you that, you must be aware that in the last few months I have come to admire you greatly. My admiration is so great that it compels me to take a step which might appear to be premature, but which I, after much deliberation, have decided that I can no longer put off. You see, I am at that stage in a man's life where he feels the need to settle down, and there is no one in the world that I would rather—'

He broke off as Charlotte, who had clearly not heard a word of his speech, gave a squeal of excitement. 'Oh, look at that! Captain

Middleton is making his horse stand on its hind legs, surely he will fall off.' She pressed her face against the window.

Hartopp sighed and cleared his throat, preparing to start again. 'Miss Baird, Charlotte if I may call you that—'

Charlotte, who was picking up her camera and plates, interrupted, 'Come along, Captain Hartopp, we must hurry. I am afraid that if we don't go down there and restrain him, Captain Middleton will break his neck.'

'Oh, there's no chance of that,' said Hartopp with regret.

But Charlotte did not hear him, and put the tripod into his hands.

Outside, Bay was preening and curvetting on Tipsy as if he was in a circus ring. He could see the white faces of the housemaids pressed against the glass, and he couldn't resist jumping up so that he was standing on the saddle as Tipsy cantered around the turning circle. Then he bent down, held onto the edge of the saddle and pushed himself up into a handstand. He managed two circuits before bringing himself upright. He could hear the faint sound of clapping from inside the house, and he gave his audience a little bow.

'Oh, I was hoping that you were going to stay like that a little longer. It would have made a delightful picture.' Charlotte was standing on the front steps setting up her equipment, a thunderous looking Hartopp at her side.

'I'm afraid I was showing off. I don't want to blacken Tipsy's good name with my antics.' Bay jumped to the ground and patted his horse's neck.

Charlotte gestured to Captain Hartopp where she wanted him to set down the tripod. 'If you could just pull out that leg, perfect. Thank you so much, now I am quite ready to do justice to this remarkable horse.'

'Then if you have no further use for me, perhaps you will excuse me, I have letters to write.' Hartopp did not wait for Charlotte to answer before setting off towards the house.

Bay gestured towards the retreating figure with his crop.

'What have you done to Hartopp, Miss Baird? He looks quite fierce. Did he offer to make you Mrs Hartopp and you spurned him with a girlish laugh? I had no idea that you were so heartless. You must temper your refusals with paltry compliments to assuage a man's pride, y'know. Poor Chicken, he looks quite crestfallen.'

'Don't be absurd. Captain Hartopp has, no doubt, decided that he has more important things to do than to watch you cavorting around on your horse.'

'Well, if you say so, but he looked like a disappointed lover to me.'

Charlotte hesitated. Bay was joking, of course, yet Hartopp's pique was clearly genuine. But having given him no encouragement, she really could not be responsible for his feelings.

'So, Captain Middleton, do you think you can persuade Tipsy to stand still?'

'Absolutely. How would you like us?'

Charlotte looked at them. She had imagined Bay sitting on the horse, but now that she saw him with the animal and observed the way he looked at Tipsy, she knew that was the image she wanted.

'Why don't you stand just there with your hand on the bridle like that?' She pulled the cloth over her head and looked at the upside-down image. She moved the camera a little so that the horse and rider were in the centre of the frame. Coming out from under her shroud she said, 'Remember, when I raise my hand I want to you to keep still for as long as it takes to recite the Lord's Prayer. If you or Tipsy move, the image will be blurred.'

'We will be as still as statues. Won't we, Tipsy?'

Charlotte looked up at the sky and saw a procession of dark clouds heading towards the weak winter sun. She needed to take the picture now, before the light went. She disappeared underneath the baize, steadied herself and raised her hand.

She was at 'Forgive us our trespasses' when Fred's voice broke across her thoughts.

'Oh, what a charming scene, dear Mitten taking a picture of Middleton and the love of his life.'

Charlotte willed Bay not to move; another ten seconds and the photograph would be done. 'The power and the glory . . .'

'A horse is the love of Captain Middleton's life? I am surprised,' Augusta's voice came from behind her.

Charlotte was determined not to lose her concentration. 'World without end, Amen.' She thought she saw Bay flinch. She came out from under her shroud, to see the engaged couple standing behind her. She turned on Fred.

'Really, Fred, how many times have I told you not to disturb me when I am taking a picture? You wouldn't like it if I started talking to you just when you raised your gun.'

'Completely different, Mitten. Shooting is a serious business.'

'And photography isn't? Well, why don't you try and take a photograph, Fred? You might find that it's slightly more complicated than pointing a gun at a bird and pulling the trigger.'

Fred took a step towards her

'Really? It looks to me that all you are doing is pointing a camera at your subject and releasing the shutter. Where's the skill in that?'

Bay's voice broke in with mock plaintiveness. 'May we move now, Miss Baird? Tipsy is getting rather restless. It's feeding time at the stables and she doesn't want to miss her oats.'

'She has been an excellent sitter, I didn't see her move a muscle,' Charlotte said.

'She's terribly vain, didn't want to produce a bad likeness.' Bay jumped on Tipsy's back and, with a touch of his heels, galloped off towards the stables.

Charlotte was left at the top of the steps with Fred and Augusta. There was a little pause and then Fred said, 'You and Middleton seem very pally.'

'I find him amusing.'

'Well, of course he's amusing – he's famous for being amusing and agreeable and an excellent dancer – but I must warn you, Mitten, that he is what is called a ladies' man.' Fred whispered the phrase 'ladies' man' as if somehow to make it less shocking.

'I think you forgot to say, Fred, in your list of Captain Middleton's accomplishments, that he is the best dressed officer in the Guards. Didn't he give you the name of his tailor?' Charlotte asked.

'I don't see what that has to do with anything,' blustered Fred. 'I am simply trying to point out that he is to be treated with caution. I like the man, he's a fellow officer and one of the best riders in the country, but he just isn't suitable.'

Charlotte collapsed her tripod with a sharp snap.

'Suitable for what?' she said.

'For you, of course!' cried Fred.

'So what you are saying is that he is good enough for you, and for Earl Spencer and the Queen of Naples, but he isn't suitable for me. I fail to follow you, Fred.' Charlotte felt herself flushing.

Fred was about to reply, but Augusta put her hand on his arm. 'Dearest Fred, why don't you carry all this equipment upstairs for your sister? I should so much like to show her the new orchid house before luncheon.'

Brother and sister obeyed her with equal reluctance. Fred had a great deal more to say to Charlotte about the unsuitability of Bay Middleton and Charlotte had no desire to look at orchids with Augusta, but neither could think of a way out. Charlotte handed the tripod and the camera to Fred, keeping only the plate she had just taken – she didn't trust Fred not to drop it. Augusta took her arm and propelled her towards the walled garden where the orchid house had been built.

'I daresay you have never seen an orchid house before in a private residence. Papa got the idea after a visit to the botanical gardens at Kew. He is so very fond of exotic plants that he simply couldn't rest until he had created his own orchidarium.'

They walked through the frosty kitchen garden with its blackened cabbages and tall asparagus cloches to the round glass pavilion on the south wall.

Augusta pushed open the door and they both exclaimed at the warm, humid air. A spike of orchids brushed Charlotte's cheek; as she pushed it away she noticed the cold waxiness of the petals and the complete lack of scent.

'Do you like the orchids, Charlotte? My father's collection is famous, of course. There are specimens here that come from as far as the Kingdom of Sarawak.'

'Goodness! I have only a vague notion of where Sarawak is, almost unimaginably distant.'

'Yes, distant to us, but not to my father, who has spared no expense to get the choicest items.' Augusta's tone was unmistakably bitter.

There was a pause. Charlotte decided on closer inspection that Lord Crewe might have better spent his money elsewhere. She did not care for the floral contortions around her; the orchids felt to her like monarchs in exile, their magnificence incongruous with their new surroundings.

Augusta picked up a hot pink flower and began to stroke one of its pendulous lower petals with one kid-gloved thumb.

'As we are going to be sisters, Charlotte, and because you have no mother, I feel that it is my duty to give you some guidance.'

'That is very kind of you, Augusta, but you are forgetting Aunt Adelaide. She is very conscientious.'

'Perhaps. But Lady Lisle has been away from London society for a number of years, and while she is no doubt a delightful companion, her judgement on certain matters is a little rusty. She is out of the swim, and is not quite aware of all the potential hazards that lie in your path.'

'Hazards?' said Charlotte.

'It will be much easier, of course, when you are living with us I will be on hand to guide you. I have had so much more experience in these matters.'

'But Augusta, you are only four years older than me.'

'Only three years, I think you'll find, but those three years have given me a sense of the pitfalls that lie ahead of you. I know how easy it is to be led astray.'

Charlotte smiled. 'Led astray? Augusta! Are you about to confess to an indiscretion? How very exciting. Does Fred know?'

There was a pop, as Augusta crushed the pink cushion of the orchid's lower lip.

'I am talking about you, Charlotte, as I am sure you are aware. You and Captain Middleton.'

'You really ought to be more careful with your father's orchids. That was a very fine specimen until you started playing with it,' Charlotte said.

Augusta sighed. She spoke slowly and with an air of great patience.

'Fred was perhaps a bit clumsy earlier, but you must understand that he was only trying to protect you.'

'Protect me from what, though? I have danced with Middleton once, sat next to him at dinner once, and taken his photograph twice. He has not made love to me, indeed the bulk of our conversation has been about his horse. Frankly, if he is an example of a dangerous ladies' man, then I am disappointed.'

'Captain Middleton has a reputation. He has been friendly, too friendly, with a married woman. She was mentioned at dinner last night – Blanche Hozier. You must have noticed how Middleton reacted when my mother mentioned her name. I believe the liaison is at an end, but that is hardly the point.'

'But I am not a married woman, and Captain Middleton is not a married man. Our meetings are in public, and as yet, there has been no talk of Gretna Green. I know nothing of Blanche Hozier, but if Captain Middleton's behaviour has been so very shocking then I am surprised to find that he is a guest here at Melton.' Charlotte lifted her chin defiantly.

Augusta gave Charlotte a look intended to convey sisterly compassion.

'Oh dear, this is exactly what I was afraid of. You are taking his side, and that is because he has preyed upon your emotions. You have had so little experience of men, and when an accomplished young man like Captain Middleton makes himself agreeable, you are quite defenceless. You imagine, of course, that he is interested in you. But dear, sweet, innocent Mitten, here is a man who has displayed a fondness for a married woman. Why then would he be attracted by a young girl with no experience or sophistication, if it were not for the fact that you are a considerable heiress? I am afraid that Captain Middleton, who comes, I understand, from a very modest background, is a fortune hunter.'

Charlotte would have liked very much to pick up one of the orchids from Sarawak and poke it into her future sister-in-law's bulging blue eye, but she retained her composure by imagining her instead as an overbred Pekinese holding a parasol.

'A fortune hunter? I fail to see, Augusta, how that distinguishes Captain Middleton in any way. Are you telling me that Captain Hartopp isn't interested in my money, or that you and Fred would be quite so eager to have me share your newly wedded bliss if I were a poor relation? Perhaps Captain Middleton is only interested in my fortune, but if that is the case he does a much better job of concealing it than anyone else.'

Augusta, no doubt thinking of the Lennox diamonds and how distinguished they would make her look on her wedding day, laid a conciliatory hand on Charlotte's arm.

'We mustn't quarrel, Charlotte. I mean no harm. Every girl is entitled to a flirtation. All I ask you to remember is that Bay Middleton may be a wonderful dancing partner and a charming photographic subject, but he is not a serious prospect. I don't want you to be compromised. With your advantages you could marry someone of real standing – a man whose position will give you a role in life. I have such great plans for you next season. If you don't end the year as a future countess or even a marchioness, I will be very disappointed.'

Charlotte felt suddenly weary. She could not hope to explain to Augusta that her disappointment was inevitable. For if the conversation had convinced her of one thing, it was that she would never marry a man who had been procured for by her future sister-in-law.

'You have been very generous with your advice, Augusta, and there could be no better counsel, I daresay, to a girl who wants to make a dazzling marriage. But now you will have to excuse me. I must take this plate back to the house – or I am afraid the humidity in here will affect the result.'

Augusta smiled, revealing her prominent overbite. 'Of course, I know how important your hobby is to you. I just wanted to make sure we had a little tête-à-tête before you took any more "photographs" of Captain Middleton.'

But Charlotte was already at the door, desperate to breathe in the cold winter air.

She didn't consciously intend to go back to the house via the stable block, but somehow she found herself walking through the yard. The stable was the only part of Melton that had not been given the Gothic treatment. Although Lord Crewe had talked about replacing the stable clock with a campanile with revolving figures, his architect had never quite got around to completing the design.

As it was the start of the hunting season all the stalls were full. Charlotte looked for Tipsy's grey coat, but there were so many horses there that she found it very hard to tell them apart. She was almost at the other side of the yard when she saw Bay. He was crouching down on the ground, tying a hunting bandage around his horse's leg. He had taken his coat off and had rolled up his shirtsleeves, revealing sinewy white arms covered in freckles. Charlotte watched him for a minute as he pulled the bandage tight and then soothed the horse, who was stamping and snorting from the indignity. But as Bay whispered in the animal's ear and let it lick the flat of his hand, the horse subsided.

Charlotte willed him to look round. At last he turned his head and saw her and the plate case in her hand. He ran over to where she was standing, just under the stable arch.

'Don't tell me you have done it already? Have you come to show Tipsy the results?'

Charlotte shook her head. 'Even though the printing process is much faster than it used to be, it is not that speedy. You will have your print tonight, if I am not waylaid by something else. No, I came through here to escape from Augusta. She has been giving me sisterly advice, and I find that it is best taken in small doses.'

Bay ran a hand through his hair and Charlotte noticed the swell of his forearm.

'What was the advice about?' he asked, and when Charlotte did not immediately reply, he said, 'I can tell from the way you are blushing that she was advising you about me. Am I right?'

Charlotte looked down at the floor and kicked a piece of straw with her foot.

'She is very concerned about my future.'

'And let me guess, she doesn't think that your future should include reprobates like Bay Middleton?'

'I don't believe she used the word reprobate. I think she might have said that you were "unsuitable".'

Bay laughed and stretched his arms out wide. 'And what do you say, Miss Baird? Do you agree with the Lady Augusta? Am I to be cast into the outer darkness?'

Charlotte raised her eyes to his. 'I find that I agree with Augusta very rarely.'

'Thank goodness for that. But she is right in some respects. I am unsuitable. I am not rich, and while I am a gentleman, you won't find me in Debrett's. I am not the sort of man that makes mamas happy.'

Charlotte interrupted him, 'The one advantage of being mother-less is that you learn how to make up your own mind about people.'

'And have you?'

'I think so.'

They were both silent for a moment and then both began to speak at once. Charlotte was saying that she must go back to the house to change, as Bay said, 'I am really very glad that you are at Melton. I have wanted to see you again since the Spencer ball. If only to make amends for my clumsiness in ruining your dress. I am hoping you have forgiven me for that.'

'I have forgiven you, although my dressmaker hasn't,' Charlotte said lightly, but then, seeing the expression on Bay's face, she lowered her voice. 'I think you were distracted that night, Captain Middleton; something had thrown you off balance.'

Bay put his fingers through his hair again and Charlotte realised to her surprise that he was nervous.

'You are right. I was distracted, but I must tell you, Miss Baird, that I am not distracted any more.' His gaze was steady. Charlotte gripped the plate in her hands tightly. Attempting a smile, she said, 'Oh, my dressmaker will be so relieved.'

But Bay did not smile back. 'I was lucky to meet you that night, I can't tell you how lucky. You were right, I had lost my balance but now I have found it.'

Charlotte felt the blush spread across her face. 'I don't know how I helped you, but I am glad that I did.'

'Are you? I think you may be the only one that can help me. I so wish that I had something to offer you in return.'

Charlotte wanted to tell him that he had already given her so much – a sense of possibility, that her future might be more than she had hoped, but she did not have the words. She looked at his arms and saw that the reddish hairs were standing on end. She wanted to stroke them. She realised that she had never wanted to touch a man before. Almost involuntarily she took a step towards him. He began to raise his arms as if perhaps to embrace her, but at that moment there was a clatter of hooves behind them and they both drew back. A groom in blue livery came to a halt when he saw Bay and dismounted.

'Captain Middleton? I have a letter for you from the Earl. He says I am to wait for a reply.'

The groom pulled a letter out of the pocket of his saddlebag and gave it to Middleton.

Bay broke open the seal and scanned the contents. Frowning slightly, he reached into his breeches pocket and found a coin.

'You must have ridden like the wind to get here so quickly. The Earl says he is writing at twelve o'clock and it is now only quarter past one. Tell his lordship that I will come over to Althorp this afternoon, but I shall go at my own pace. I am not going to ruin my horse on his account.' He threw the coin to the groom.

'Yes, sir, and thank you, sir.'

Bay turned to Charlotte and shook his head. 'We have been monstrously interrupted, Miss Baird. Earl Spencer, who was responsible for bringing us together, is now forcing us apart. He says that he has a matter to discuss with me of the utmost urgency. I don't believe that it is urgent at all, but as the Earl is both my patron and my commanding officer, I have no choice but to go.'

Charlotte was disappointed, but also a little relieved. She knew that Middleton had been on the point of saying something significant, which would tip them from a flirtation into something more serious. She wanted to have that conversation, but she also found the prospect terrifying. Things were happening so quickly. She had no patience with Augusta's view of Bay, but she wanted more time to observe him. She shook her head saying, 'But we are in no hurry, are we, Captain Middleton? Surely we can wait a few hours?'

'Of course we can wait – for you I can be the most patient of men – but it goes against my every instinct.'

Charlotte laughed.

'You are not in a race now, Captain. I will still be here when you return. And who knows? If I can evade the ladies of the house I might even be able to print up your photograph.'

The stable clock began to chime the half-hour, startling them both. Charlotte reacted first.

'Heavens, I must go and change at once and so must you. If we are both late for lunch, I think Augusta will have you arrested for abduction.' She turned and began to walk through the arch.

Bay followed and put a hand on her arm. 'But Miss Baird, Charlotte, am I right to feel lucky that I have met you?'

Charlotte smiled. 'I think we both might be lucky, don't you?'

All the Trimmings

MIDDLETON FOUND THE EARL IN THE ALTHORP stables, looking over a handsome chestnut mare. As Bay had found the horse for him, he was happy to agree with Spencer that she was a beauty, but he couldn't believe that he had been summoned to look at a horse he knew better than its owner. Spencer broke a carrot into pieces and offered it to the horse on the palm of his hand. The horse snorted and filled the stable with its steaming breath. The Earl turned to Middleton and clapped him on the shoulder.

'Apologies for summoning you over here on a Sunday, Middleton. Matter of some urgency.'

'So I gathered from your note. But you didn't give me much to go on,' Bay said.

'Too sensitive to put in a letter, Middleton, and besides, some things need to be explained man to man.'

'That sounds a little worrying,' Bay smiled.

'Nothing to worry about. This is what I would call pleasure masquerading as duty.' The Earl took Bay's arm and started to walk around the yard, stopping briefly in front of each horse. 'I don't know if you have heard, but Easton Neston has been let to the Empress of Austria.'

'Lady Crewe mentioned something about it last night at dinner.'

'I called on the Empress yesterday. Remarkable woman, really looks the part if you know what I mean. I am no stranger to royalty but she is quite something. The face that launched a thousand ships and all that . . .'

'But I thought the Empress was a grandmother already.'

'You would never know it, Middleton. She is as slender as a young girl and her complexion is quite perfect. I can't say this in front of the Countess, of course, but I think she is the most beautiful woman I have ever seen.'

Bay laughed. 'You appear quite smitten, sir. Have you summoned me here to act as your Cupid?'

'If only . . .' The Earl shook his massive head. 'She is the sort of woman to turn a man's head. You should see her hair, Middleton, all piled up on her head like a crown – and what a profile!' The Earl fell silent for a moment, lost in admiration.

Bay, who was feeling impatient by now, took out his pocket watch. It was a quarter to four. If the Earl did not get to the point soon, he would have to ride back to Melton in the dark.

'My curiosity is aroused. I hope I shall get the chance to see the Empress in the flesh.'

'You will, Middleton. That's why I asked you over here. The Empress has come here to hunt. She is going to ride out with the Pytchley tomorrow.'

'I shall look forward to seeing whether she is as beautiful as you say,' Bay said with a touch of irritation, 'but I still don't understand why you summoned me over here.'

'Stop interrupting and I will tell you,' the Earl said. 'The Empress needs a pilot, and while I would do it myself like a shot, I am too old to keep up with her. There is only one man for the job.' He pointed his meaty forefinger at Bay.

Bay was silent for a moment and then he shook his head. 'I am flattered, of course, that you would entrust me with such a responsibility, but I am afraid I must refuse. You know very well that when the Queen of Naples asked me to be her pilot I said no. What makes you think that it should it be any different for the Empress? Surely there must be somebody who wants to open gates for royalty? Hartopp, for instance, would jump at the chance to be a royal nursemaid.' He tried to keep his tone light, but he could not prevent his annoyance from poking through.

Spencer simply ignored his outburst, smiling patiently as if talking to a child.

'There is quite a difference between an ex-queen of an Italian principality and the wife of the ruler of the largest country in Europe, Middleton. Refusing the Queen's request, while a touch ungallant, was your own business, but when I ask you to look after the Empress of Austria' – the Earl stopped in front of a pretty grey mare and pulled back her gums to look at the teeth – 'you are not really in a position to decline.' Satisfied with the animal's mouth, the Earl moved on to the next stall.

Bay was silent. Although he no longer worked for Spencer since they had returned from Ireland, the Earl was his patron and supporter. If Disraeli lost the confidence of the House in the next few months, as everyone expected, then Spencer would be back in the Government. Bay had no great desire for an official appointment, but he knew that a position of some kind would make it much easier for him to pursue his interest in Charlotte Baird. As an impecunious cavalry captain on half-pay he was not much of a catch, but if Spencer was to give him some post, he would have a salary and some claim to be a coming man. And while he had no desire to pilot the Empress, there was some consolation in being offered a position that both Chicken Hartopp and Fred Baird would covet.

'But what is an empress to me? How will I look after her?' Middleton looked at his patron's red face, which still held its patient smile, and realised that there was nothing he could say that would change the desire on one side and the obligation on the other. He bowed his head and said quietly, 'I will do it, of course, since you ask me, but I wish you hadn't.' He hit the side of the stall with the flat of his hand and the grey mare snorted in sympathy.

'Oh, don't worry, Middleton, there won't be any gates to open. The Empress is an excellent rider. And as for looking after her, I am sure a man of your experience will have no difficulty in keeping her happy.' The Earl winked at Bay.

'And it is important that she is happy, Middleton. Relations with Austria are delicate at the moment, and we need to keep them as an ally against the Prussians. So anything you can do to further the cause of Anglo-Austrian friendship will be appreciated by the Foreign Office. The word from Berlin is that Bismark is furious that the Empress is here, and anything that riles old Otto is good news for us.'

'I will do my best, of course, but you of all people know that I am no diplomat,' Bay said.

'I think even you will manage to make yourself agreeable to a beautiful woman. What is more, although the Empress has brought her own string of horses, my guess is that she is going to need some new ones, and who better to help her find them than you, Middleton?' Spencer started to shake with impending mirth.

'So . . . don't look . . . a gift horse . . . in the mouth, old man.' When he had finished laughing at his own joke, he said in his normal voice, 'Will you come in for a quick tot of something to keep out the cold? If we go in by the kitchen, we can get to the library without being disturbed by the womenfolk.'

Bay hesitated. He did want a drink, but it was getting dark and he didn't want his horse to lose its footing on the way home, the day before the hunting season started.

'I should like to get back to Melton before the light goes completely.'

'Pity. Still, I am sure you have your reasons, eh Middleton?'

The Earl gave Bay another of his enormous winks.

'My wife tells me that the little Baird girl is staying at Melton.'

Bay looked at him in surprise.

'Nice little thing. I knew her mother, wonderful horsewoman. But absolutely reckless. Would jump anything. The husband tried to stop her but she wouldn't be told. Can't say I was surprised when she broke her neck. She left all the Lennox money to the daughter, so Miss Baird comes with all the trimmings. You could do a lot worse for yourself, eh Middleton? Just the sort of wife a man needs if he wants to win the Grand National.'

Middleton said nothing. He was embarrassed by the Earl's directness. Men and women of Spencer's generation saw nothing wrong in talking about marriages as if they were market transactions, but he found it distasteful. The last thing he wanted was to be thought of as a fortune hunter. He liked Charlotte Baird a great deal. There was the way that she remembered everything he said to her, the way she listened with her head slightly tilted. It was true that he might not have married her a year ago, but he was a different man now. He wanted a quiet place that he could call home. He could imagine Charlotte waiting for him in the drawing room, puzzling over one of her albums but listening all the time for his step on the stair. But then there was the money. He told himself that when he had first met Charlotte at the ball, he had not known that she was an heiress, or rather he had not remembered until a day or two afterwards, when Hartopp had taken him aside at the club and told him about the fortune and his own prior claim to it. 'I was winnin' her over, Middleton, winnin' her over, and then you come along and turn her head. Leave her alone, Bay, she's a nice gel and I want to marry her.' Bay had felt sorry for Hartopp. He knew after one dance with Charlotte that she would never become Mrs Hartopp. But as Chicken was rich, no one would accuse him of being on the make, although Bay knew that Hartopp found the money quite as appealing as Charlotte's other charms.

'It's time you settled down, Middleton. Found yourself a wife of your own.' Spencer emphasised the last word. Bay wanted to punch the Earl's beefy, smiling face, but instead he adopted what he thought of as his courtier demeanour.

'Miss Baird is certainly a charming girl.'

'Charming and rich. Capital combination.' The Earl raised his arm, and Bay evaded the inevitable slap between the shoulder blades by stepping aside and gesturing to the groom to bring his horse up to the mounting block. 'I'll write to the Empress, then, and tell her that she will be in your capable hands.' The Earl winked at him. 'No better hands with a horse, and quite good at handling women too from what I hear.'

Middleton looked up at the sky. A low ray of winter sun was pushing through the swollen grey sky.

'It looks like snow. I hope the Empress is prepared for the going to be heavy.'

Royal Sisters

ARL SPENCER'S NOTE WAS DELIVERED TO THE EMPRESS after dinner. Baron Nopsca brought it into the drawing room himself, knowing that his mistress would want to read this right away. The Chamberlain hoped very much that the letter did not contain bad news about the arrangements for tomorrow. Her Majesty was looking forward to taking part in a real English hunt so much, and she did not like to be disappointed. As he walked into the double cube of the drawing room, he realised to his horror that he had forgotten to put on his gloves. He wondered if he should go back and fetch them, but it was too late – the Empress had seen him. She was sitting next to her sister, Queen Maria, on the sofa in front of the fire; her brother-in-law the King, Prince Liechtenstein and Count Esterhazy were standing by the mantelpiece; Countess Festetics was sitting in the corner, sewing.

He put the note in the Empress's outstretched hand as quickly as he could before she noticed his naked hands. But the Empress merely thanked him in German before opening the envelope and then saying in English, 'It is from your friend Earl Spencer, Maria. He says that he has found me a pilot for the hunt tomorrow. His name is Captain Middleton. Do you know him?'

Her sister flushed, 'Yes. I have heard of him.'

'I don't understand why I have to have a pilot, but the Earl insists. He claims that this Middleton is the best rider in England.'

'Only the best rider in England would be able to keep up with you, Majesty,' said Count Esterhazy.

'Oh, don't be such a courtier, Max.' The Empress laughed. 'I am sure that the English ladies ride like the wind.' She turned to her sister. 'What do you think, Maria, will I be able to stand the pace?'

'I don't know why you ask me, Sisi. You know very well that you always come first.'

If Sisi caught the bitterness in her sister's voice, she didn't show it. She carried on, 'And did you see the famous Captain Middleton when you were hunting last year?'

'I did. He can ride, certainly, but I doubt that you will find his manners to your taste,' Maria replied.

Sisi put her hand on her sister's arm. 'Oh dear, was he rude to you? I shall have to scold him. But I have had enough of good manners. Dear Felix and Max are so relentlessly charming that a little roughness will make an interesting change.'

The Empress stood up and moved towards the windows. The curtains were drawn against the dark, but she drew one back and looked out into the night.

'It is snowing.' She turned and asked her sister, 'Will the hunt still go ahead?'

'I guarantee it. The English cannot bear to be deprived of their sport. And everyone will turn out tomorrow to see *you*,' said Maria.

'But I am here incognito. I am travelling as Countess Hohenembs, so it won't be the Empress hunting tomorrow.' Elizabeth stood very straight, her face flushed. 'This is meant to be a private visit. I don't want to be a circus attraction.'

Count Esterhazy and Prince Liechtenstein glanced at each other, hearing a familiar note in the Empress's voice. Countess Festetics looked up from her sewing. Count Eszterhazy was the one to speak first.

'But Majesty, the people tomorrow will be your favourite company – riding folk whose only desire is for a good day's hunting. Perhaps there may be a frisson at having royalty among them, but my guess is that it will be your horse attracting all the attention.'

Elizabeth stared at the Count for a moment and then her face relaxed, her lips almost curving into a smile.

'But which horse? I am worried that none of them are used to jumping these English hedges.'

The men pounced on this conversational opening and began to discuss the merits of the Empress's horses at length. Countess Festetics resumed her sewing.

Elizabeth went back to sit next to her sister.

Maria said, 'You mustn't blame the English for wanting to look at you, Sisi. Their queen has shut herself away since her husband died. And the papers are full of you, even though you are travelling incognito. Everybody wants to see "the most beautiful woman in Europe".' Maria smiled thinly at her sister.

'But I am so tired of being stared at. Can you imagine what it feels like to know that everybody is looking at you, all the time?' Elizabeth spoke in a rush of emotion but kept her voice low. She looked to her sister for sympathy but saw that Maria's face had closed up.

There was a little pause and then the ex-queen of Naples said, 'There are worse things in life, Sisi, than being stared at.'

Silver Nitrate

THE SNOW BEGAN TO FALL JUST AS BAY REACHED Melton. While he waited for someone to come out and open the gates he watched the flakes fall and settle on the gravel underneath the lighted windows of the lodge. Inside he could see a woman feeding a baby in a wooden high chair while her husband looked on. The baby was laughing and trying to pat her cheek as she held up the spoon. The child had managed to smear a good dollop of his porridge on his mother's face and Bay watched as her husband, the gatekeeper, tenderly brushed it away.

Tipsy neighed with impatience and the man looked up and saw Bay. Seconds later he came out.

'Sorry to keep you waiting, sir. Would you like me to light you up to the house?' He held up a lantern.

Bay felt unaccountably guilty for having disturbed the peaceful domestic scene. He found a coin in his pocket and handed it over. 'No need for you to come out on a night like this. I'll take the lamp myself.'

The gatekeeper was delighted. 'If you're sure, sir. Thank you very much indeed.'

At his usual gallop, Bay would have covered the drive from the lodge to the house in minutes, but now the snow and the lantern slowed him down. He felt the flakes settle on his eyelashes and moustache. Charlotte would laugh if she could see him now. He thought that he wouldn't mind being laughed at by Charlotte. When Blanche Hozier had made fun of him for some slip of the tongue or social awkwardness, he had felt the scorn beneath her smiles. Charlotte, though, was different. She might tease him, but there would be no derision in her laughter.

The baby in the lodge had made him think of Clementine, the daughter he had never seen. He could not see Blanche – blonde, immaculate Blanche – feeding a baby with a spoon and having her face smeared with porridge. Instead he imagined Charlotte holding a baby out to him.

Tipsy stumbled, jolting Bay out of his domestic daydream. The snow was laying a blanket of hush over the landscape and there was no light apart from the flickering gleam of the lantern. Then he heard the chimes of the stable clock sounding seven times – if he hurried he might be able to find Charlotte before dinner. Forgetting his concerns about the hazardous snow, he nudged Tipsy into a canter.

The dressing gong was sounding when Bay came into the house. He knew that he should change out of his wet clothes, but he thought there was a chance that Charlotte might still be in her studio. He didn't think that she was the kind of girl who spent more time than she had to changing for dinner. He ran up the stairs two at a time, praying that he would not run into anyone.

He had reached the first landing when he heard a voice.

'Captain Middleton, where have you been in this weather? You must be frozen.' Lady Crewe was standing on the other side of the landing.

Bay chewed his lip. The last thing he wanted was to be waylaid in conversation by his hostess. He said, as curtly as possible, 'I had to ride over to Althorp. The Earl wanted to speak to me.'

'It must have been very important business for you to go all that way, and on a Sunday too.' Lady Crewe sniffed; she was a keen observer of the Sabbath.

Bay knew that if he told Lady Crewe what the Earl had wanted he would never get away. Instead he shook his head and said, 'I am sorry to say that the Earl is not observant. Why, in Ireland, we would sometimes hold amateur theatricals on a Sunday.'

Lady Crewe gasped and Bay shook his head.

'You can imagine my feelings, Lady Crewe. Now, if you will excuse me.'

He did not wait for a reply but dashed off in the direction of the nursery, hoping that she would not remember that his bedroom lay the other way.

Bay sighed with relief when he saw the light under the nursery door. He walked in and saw Charlotte standing with her back to him. She was wearing what looked like an evening dress – white silk trimmed with green velvet – but she had swathed herself in a brown holland apron.

She was examining a print. Bay noticed that her hands were covered with brown stains. As he reached her, Charlotte gave a little shriek of surprise and then smiled broadly.

'Captain Middleton! You are just in time.'

'I am so glad.'

He tried to look at the print, but she held it away out of his view, saying, 'Promise me that you will be honest. I won't be offended if you don't like it.'

'Really?'

'Well, I might be a little piqued, but only a little.' Slowly she held up the print.

Bay had never seen a photograph of himself before. He was disappointed to find that he was not as tall or as broad as he had imagined himself. In the picture his head was level with Tipsy's, the horse nestling into his shoulder. The unspoken bond between horse and rider was quite evident in the photograph. They were undoubtedly a team.

'My dear Miss Baird, Charlotte – can I call you Charlotte? I can't tell you how happy this makes me.' Bay found himself blinking. 'Tipsy is magnificent.'

'And what do you think of yourself?' asked Charlotte.

Bay shrugged. 'Does anyone really like their own portrait?'

'You would be surprised. Fred liked the *carte de visite* he had done at Gaillevant so much that he ordered three dozen and sent them to all his friends.'

'I only want one copy, but I promise you that I will treasure it for ever.' Bay took one of Charlotte's hands in his and touched a brown stain on her forefinger.

Charlotte blushed. 'It's the silver nitrate I use on the plates. I can't get it off. I must put on some gloves before dinner.'

'Not on my account, dear Charlotte. These stains on your hands are like the calluses I get from riding; they are the price we pay for doing what we love.' He stroked her palm with his finger. Her hand trembled a little.

'I don't think Augusta would agree.'

'I don't care in the slightest what Augusta thinks, or her mother, or anyone else for that matter. Do you?'

He held her hand tight. She did not pull it away.

'No, I don't think I do.' There were two spots of red on Charlotte's cheeks.

Bay leant towards her and kissed one of the red cheeks.

'I have made you blush, Will you forgive me?' he said and kissed the other cheek.

'I think so,' Charlotte said softly.

Bay leant forward and kissed her, this time on the mouth. He felt her body soften and lean into his, her mouth opening and the touch of her hand on his arm. He could smell rose water and the tang of chemicals. He wanted to pull her to him, to gather her up completely.

There was a loud creak from the nursery staircase, followed by the sounds of stertorous breathing.

Bay and Charlotte were examining the print when Fred reached the doorway.

'Mitten, I just wanted to . . .' He saw Bay. 'Oh, hello, Middleton.' And then, registering Bay's riding clothes, he said, 'Shouldn't you be changing for dinner?'

'I was just on my way. But I couldn't resist a glimpse of Tipsy.' Bay gestured towards the photograph on the table.

'May I suggest that you hurry up? Lady Crewe does not like to be kept waiting.' Fred fingered the facings of his tail coat, scraping his fingernails against the satin.

'Keeping a lady waiting, that would never do.' Bay made Charlotte a little bow. 'Thank you, Miss Baird, for the photo. For everything, in fact.'

As he left the room, Fred turned on Charlotte.

'I am surprised to find you in here alone with Middleton. You know his reputation.'

'Oh yes. Augusta was punctilious in letting me know about that,' Charlotte replied.

'Then you are either foolish or wilful. A young girl cannot be too careful of her good name. What seems like a harmless flirtation now, could have a major impact on your future.'

Charlotte smiled. 'I hope so. I like Captain Middleton extremely. If he proposes, I shall accept him.'

'Of course he will propose. You are an extremely wealthy woman, but there is no question of you accepting him. You cannot marry without my consent and I have absolutely no intention of giving it.' Fred rose on the balls of his feet to give his point more emphasis.

'That is only true for the next nine months, three weeks and four days, until I am twenty-one. Then I can marry whomsoever I choose.'

Fred rocked back on his heels. 'You forget that I am still your trustee for another four years.'

'Oh, I haven't forgotten, but I don't care about the money. I can wait.'

Fred showed his teeth in a facsimile of a smile. 'You can wait. But what about Middleton?' He pointed to the picture of Bay and Tipsy. 'He is a man with expensive tastes.'

Charlotte said nothing. She was staring at the photograph.

Her brother continued, 'Let's not quarrel, Mitten. I have no desire to play the tyrant.'

Charlotte looked up at him. 'I am not your Mitten. My name is Charlotte.' She unfastened the tapes of her holland apron and folded it neatly, then picked up her reticule and took out a pair of white lace mittens, smoothing them over her hands until all the stains were hidden.

'Come on, Fred. You don't want to keep Lady Crewe waiting.'

'But you do understand me, Charlotte?' Fred put his hand on his sister's arm.

'Of course I understand you. I even promise to think about what you have said.'

'Good girl.'

'But I am not promising to obey you. That will be Augusta's job when she marries you.'

Charlotte was the only one smiling as they both contemplated the likelihood of Augusta being an obedient wife.

Greensleeves

IT WAS CLEAR FROM THE PLACEMENT AT DINNER THAT Augusta had spoken to her mother. Charlotte was taken into dinner by the Hon. Percy and seated at the other end of the table to Bay.

It was not a lively meal. Lady Crewe generally liked to restrict the conversation to topics suitable to the Sabbath. But after an almost silent fish course, she could not contain her curiosity any longer.

'Did you see Laetitia Spencer at Althorp this afternoon, Captain Middleton? She had a chill before Christmas and I am hoping that she is quite recovered. I was thinking that I might call on her this week.'

'I didn't see the Countess, Lady Crewe. But then the Earl and I were in the stables.'

'In the stables? What on earth were you doing there on a Sunday?' asked Lady Crewe.

'I fear that the Earl visits the stables every day. We had some business to discuss,' Bay said, as neutrally as he could.

But Lady Crewe was not to be put off.

'But what business could be so urgent that you had to go over there at once?'

By now the whole table had given up the pretence of conversation and twelve heads were looking at Bay.

'The Earl had an assignment for me.' He paused and, seeing Lady Crewe's expectant eyebrow, he added, 'Of a confidential nature.'

Lord Crewe snorted. 'I hear that Austrian woman is hunting with the Pytchley tomorrow. Daresay Spencer wants you to pilot her.' Lord Crewe had little time for Catholics, even royal ones. 'Am I right, Middleton?'

Bay bowed his head. 'I can't lie to you, Lord Crewe.'

There was a moment of silence as the assembled company digested this revelation along with their turbot à la crème.

Hartopp was the first to speak, attempting but not altogether succeeding in keeping the jealousy out of his voice, 'Quite a last-minute request if she is hunting tomorrow. Do you think someone else dropped out?'

'Very likely,' said Bay.

'Nonsense,' interrupted Lord Crewe. 'Middleton is the best rider in England. Spencer will have been told to get the top man and he has. Congratulations are in order. Quite an honour to pilot an empress, even if she is a foreigner.'

'It is certainly a responsibility,' said Bay.

'I think it is tremendously exciting,' said Lady Lisle. 'But I hope she speaks some English, unless of course you speak German, Captain Middleton.'

Fred snorted. 'Of course he doesn't speak German! But I am sure you will have a way of making yourself understood, eh Middleton?'

Bay said quietly, 'I believe the Empress speaks excellent English, but I don't anticipate much conversation. My job is to guide her during the hunt. There won't be much time for talking.'

'But we ladies expect a full account of the Empress, Captain Middleton, whether you talk to her not,' said Augusta. 'In the *Illustrated*

London News it says that she has taken riding lessons from a circus artist, and that she has been seen to jump through a ring of fire.'

'Well, if I see her jump through a ring of fire when we are out with the Pytchley tomorrow, I will be sure to remember every detail, Lady Augusta,' said Bay.

It was fortunate that the footmen were coming round with the salmis of pheasant, so that the sound of Charlotte's laughter was drowned in the clatter of serving spoons on silver salvers.

Lady Crewe was still thinking about the Empress. 'I wonder if she will be attending dinners while she is here. I am sure Laetitia Spencer won't miss the opportunity to show her off. But it would be a pity if the Empress did not have the opportunity of visiting some of the other important families in the county. Althorp is all very well, but so old-fashioned; it would be such a shame if she went back to Austria without seeing the best examples of the modern style.' She looked up at the hammer-beamed roof of the dining room with its roundels picked out in scarlet and gold, and the frieze of Sir Galahad in search of the Holy Grail, with great satisfaction.

'You must be sure to tell her, Captain Middleton, that Easton Neston and Althorp are quite old-fashioned. If she wants to see an English country house that is really up to the minute, she should come to Melton.'

'If she's hunting with the Pytchley she will be here on Tuesday,' said Lord Crewe, 'as the meet is here.'

'Of course! Well, Captain Middleton, you must tell the Empress that I would be only too pleased to show her around Melton. She won't find a house like this in Austria, I daresay.' Lady Crewe leant forward as she said this and looked directly at Bay, so that he had no choice but to answer.

'If she asks me, I will certainly pass on your invitation, Lady

Crewe. But I suspect that we won't have many opportunities to talk about architecture. And who knows, I may not be to the Empress's taste and I will have lost my post by Tuesday.' Bay smiled.

'Nonsense, Middleton. We all know how good you are with the fair sex.' Fred Baird rolled his eyes at Augusta.

Lord Crewe looked up from his pheasant and let his fork drop with a clang.

'Middleton, you are not to encourage the woman to come inside the house. If she insists, we can't stop her, but I don't want some foreign royal traipsing about Melton. Nothing but trouble. She won't come alone, I am quite sure, and before we know it the house will be full of Austrians.'

'But George, it would be an honour to receive the Empress,' protested Lady Crewe.

'No, it would be an honour to receive *our* queen at Melton. There is no comparison,' said Lord Crewe, his face reddening.

Adelaide Lisle, who hated unpleasantness, turned to her host with her most winning smile. 'Now, you must tell me about the wonderful frieze you have here in the dining room. I am awfully stupid about legends and so forth, and I can't for the life of me figure out who is the handsome young knight with curly blond hair – the only knight whose name I can remember is Lancelot, and that's because I have a cousin called Lancelot, but this young man looks rather different.'

As Lady Lisle chattered away and Lord Crewe began to unravel the Arthurian legends, the other diners began to talk among themselves, tacitly agreeing to avoid all further mention of the Empress.

The men did not linger over their port. Fred and Hartopp felt that they could not talk about the Empress in front of their host and yet it was the only thing they wanted to discuss. Although both men would, if asked, claim to be a friend of Bay Middleton, both of them took the news of Bay's advancement into imperial circles as a profound injustice. When all three of them had been ADCs to Earl Spencer in Ireland, they had jostled for position on a daily basis. Both men could understand why Bay as the better horseman should have been picked to pilot the Empress, but it seemed quite unfair that mere talent should take precedence over superior birth and breeding. How could a man like Bay, be expected to understand the niceties of imperial protocol? True, the father had been an officer who had died fighting in the Crimea, but the mother had remarried some kind of coal merchant in Co. Durham. There was also a lurking suspicion that Bay had been preferred because he was as good with women as he was with horses. Fred felt this a little less keenly than Hartopp; he still reckoned that his successful wooing of Lady Augusta had been the result of his own charms rather than her increasing desperation. So when Bay rose after one glass of port, nobody protested.

But in the drawing room, the conversation among the women was unfettered. Augusta, who had seen the look of surprise on Charlotte's face when Bay had announced his new role, lost no time in asking her what she thought of Bay's elevation into imperial circles, or as she put it, 'to be the Empress's groom'.

'Oh, is a pilot the same thing as a groom? I understood the roles to be quite different. I don't ride myself, of course, but surely the groom looks after the animal and a pilot guides the rider?' Charlotte said.

'It's quite an honour for Captain Middleton,' said Augusta, 'and, of course, he is an excellent rider, but I am surprised that Earl Spencer thought he was a suitable escort for royalty, even foreign royalty.'

'What do you mean, Augusta?' asked Lady Lisle in surprise. 'Captain Middleton seems to be a very personable young man. What objection could there be?'

'I think some people might say that he was altogether too personable,' said Augusta, and, lowering her voice, 'I believe that there are some husbands who would rather he wasn't quite so charming.'

'Augusta!' warned her mother. 'You shouldn't be talking about such things, and on a Sunday too! May I remind you that Captain Middleton is our guest. And I am quite sure that Earl Spencer knows what he is doing. Now perhaps you would like to play for us, instead of spreading slander.'

Augusta, realising that her mother was going to support Middleton so long as there was a chance of being introduced to the Empress, took up her place at the piano and gave her own trenchant version of a Chopin nocturne.

She had moved on to Beethoven when the men came in. Fred went straight to the piano. Bay walked over to the sofa where Charlotte was sitting and stood behind her. Bending down, he said softly in her ear, 'I am just trying to remember where we were before we were interrupted.'

Charlotte looked straight ahead of her and kept her face as bland as if they were talking about the weather. 'I think you were admiring the photograph of you and Tipsy.'

'Tipsy, as you well know, is the apple of my eye, but she wasn't the object of my admiration. Now where exactly had we got to in our conversation?'

Charlotte turned to look at him. 'I think you were about to tell me about your new role as the Empress of Austria's pilot.'

'Why would I waste a moment of our precious tête-à-tête, talking about something so uninteresting? I am being asked to be a nurse-maid on horseback, running after my royal charge and making sure she doesn't get her habit too muddy, or get trampled by the pack,' Bay said, his hand on the back of the sofa, his fingers so close to her bare shoulders that she had goosebumps.

'You can be as dismissive as you like, but it's an honour to be chosen. Fred certainly thinks so.' Charlotte looked at her brother, who was standing next to his fiancée at the piano. 'He was pea green when you made your announcement. Fred would like nothing better than to be at the beck and call of an empress.'

'If you want me to resign my nursemaid duties in favour of your brother, you only have to say the word. I would be more than happy to oblige.'

Charlotte shivered, acutely conscious of the fingers that were now stealthily grazing her shoulders. 'I think even Fred would admit that he is not the rider that you are. And besides, at this moment I am very much in favour of anything that makes him cross.'

'Did he give you a lecture on unreliable cavalry captains, by any chance?' Bay said.

'He was anxious to remind me that I can do nothing without his consent. Which means Augusta's consent, of course. I am not sure Fred is still capable of independent thought.'

'Poor Fred. He is entering into a life of servitude.'

'Oh, he doesn't mind. To be married to a peer's daughter is enough.'

Bay touched one of the vertebrae above her neckline, and Charlotte gasped.

'Are you sure you don't remember what we were talking about before? Perhaps this will remind you.' Bay bent down again and blew lightly into her ear. 'It was such a delightful conversation.'

Charlotte dug her nails into the sofa. 'Perhaps I do remember, just a little. It's not the sort of conversation I am used to, after all.'

'Every conversation is different, but none more charming than with you.' He ran his nail down the groove in the nape of her neck and was gratified to see Charlotte arch forward like a cat. But the sudden movement was noticed by Augusta, who was not so lost in her music that she was unable to monitor the situation of the sofa. It was time to intervene.

She stopped playing and called out, 'I have been playing long enough, it is someone else's turn. Charlotte, won't you give us something?'

Charlotte shook her head. 'Oh, but I am a wretched player compared to you. You are being very unkind to everybody here if you make me perform.'

'Nonsense, Charlotte, there is nothing wrong with your playing that a little practice wouldn't remedy. And I think we would all like to hear you. Isn't that right, Captain Middleton?' Augusta said pointedly.

'Perhaps I might offer to entertain the company too? I can't play but I like to sing.' Bay turned to Charlotte. 'Can you play "Maud"?'

'Yes, if you don't mind a few wrong notes.'

'Perfection is boring. Shall we?' He put out his hand to Charlotte. 'That is, if you don't mind, Lady Crewe.'

Lady Crewe nodded and smiled, while Augusta, realising that she had been outmanoeuvred, left her post at the piano to stand next to her fiancé. As Bay passed she said, 'I had no idea you could sing, Captain Middleton.'

'I am an only child, and as my mother was very fond of music, I had no choice. But as to my ability, you had better reserve judgement.'

Charlotte sat at the keyboard, Bay standing just behind her. As she began to play the introduction, he put his hand on the piano, brushing her shoulder as he did so. She immediately played a wrong note and he looked at her her and smiled.

> *Come into the garden, Maud,*
> *the black bat, night, has flown,*
> *Come into the garden, Maud,*
> *I am here at the gate alone.*

His voice was powerful and true, a warm baritone that wrung every shade of meaning out of Tennyson's lush lyric. When she hesitated over the accompaniment he slowed down so that they were always in step. When he reached the line 'And the planet of Love is on high', he looked at Charlotte with meaning. He was singing, it was clear, to her. On the last line, when the melody went up an octave and he had to sing, 'Come, my own, my sweet', he looked straight into Charlotte's eyes and held her gaze while the final chord died away. There was a moment's silence, which was broken by Lady Lisle, who was dabbing at her eyes with a handkerchief.

'That was one of my dear late husband's favourite songs. But I don't think I have ever heard it sung so well before. Thank you, Captain Middleton, for bringing back so many happy memories.'

Bay made her a little bow. 'My pleasure.'

'Will you sing something else?'

Bay looked at Charlotte, who nodded.

'Play me a G minor chord.'

Charlotte played the chord and Bay sang,

> *Alas, my love, you do me wrong,*
> *To cast me off discourteously.*
> *For I have loved you well and long,*
> *Delighting in your company.*

Charlotte recognised the tune and began to accompany him in earnest, *'Greensleeves was my delight'*.

As he sang the chorus, he gestured at the green velvet ribbons that punctuated the puffed white sleeves of Charlotte's frock. When the song was finished, Bay took Charlotte's hand and kissed it.

'Thank you for playing so beautifully.'

'I think you encouraged me to be better than I am.'

'I don't think that is possible, Miss Baird.'

Augusta broke in, 'You must be sure to serenade the Empress tomorrow, Captain Middleton. She is from Vienna, and we know how the Austrians love their music.'

Bay did not miss a beat. 'I think you may have an exaggerated idea of a pilot's role, Lady Augusta. I doubt if I will be talking to the Empress, let alone singing to her. I am merely a guide, a flag for her to follow, not a troubadour.'

Augusta folded her arms, but made no reply.

Lady Lisle got to her feet, her widow's streamers fluttering.

'What a perfectly splendid evening, but I am ready for my bed. Charlotte, dear, will you hold the candle for me on the stairs? You know how shaky I get in the evenings.'

'Of course, Aunt,' Charlotte said.

They made their way to the door, Charlotte following in her aunt's wake. All the men rose and made a movement to open the door, but Bay was there first. As Charlotte passed him, he touched her elbow. 'Unfinished business,' he whispered.

In her bedroom, Charlotte held up her candle close to the cheval glass so that she could examine her face. It was not, she knew, a beautiful face, and yet Bay had kissed her nonetheless. For a moment she wondered whether he had been kissing her or the Lennox fortune, but she pushed that thought away. If Bay was a fortune hunter, he was very good at disguising his cupidity.

The door opened and Grace the housemaid came in. Charlotte did not have her own maid, since the superior French personage who had attended to her in London had given in her notice after an accident involving silver nitrate and lace. Charlotte did not miss her; she had hated the way Mam'selle Solange had made a sharp intake of breath every time she did her hair.

'I meant to be up here sooner, miss.' Charlotte sighed with relief as the maid loosened the strings of her corset. 'But we were outside in the hall listening to the music and I lost all track of the time. Was that Captain Middleton singing? What a fine young gentleman! He was doing tricks earlier on his horse – standing on his head and all sorts of stuff. Had us all laughing our heads off. He makes it all look so easy.'

'Yes,' Charlotte agreed. 'He does.'

She caught sight of her reflection again in the glass. She looked better now in her chemise, with her hair down.

'Grace?'

'Yes, miss?'

'Do you think you could do my hair differently tomorrow? Perhaps with some ringlets hanging down. Do you think that would look nice?'

'You leave it to me, miss. I will make sure that Captain Middleton has eyes for nobody else.'

A Flawless Complexion

TEN MILES AWAY IN A MUCH LARGER BEDROOM, Countess Festetics was laying strips of raw veal on her mistress's face.

Sisi had been looking at her face in the mirror before she went to bed and decided that her complexion was dull. This was unacceptable, as she wanted to look radiant at her first English hunt. Everyone would be looking at her, she knew, trying to decide whether she lived up to her reputation. Her silhouette was still good; her waist was as small as it had been when she married. She knew that on a horse from a distance, she looked like the dashing Empress that people wanted to see.

She would wear a veil, of course, with the riding habit, but then there was the moment when she lifted the veil. Sisi could not bear that look of disappointment when her audience was forced to replace their mental image of fairy-tale beauty with the worn reality before them. She had hoped that her visit to England might be anonymous, her real identity known only to a few; but that had been a fantasy. Stories about the beautiful Empress with her ankle-length hair sold too many newspapers, even here, for her identity to remain a secret. On the way down to Easton Neston she had spent the night at Claridge's. During the night word had got out that she was staying at the hotel, and when she left in the morning there had been a small crowd outside the door who had come to see the Austrian Empress. She had looked out over the sea of faces, most of them female, and seen that combination of expectation and disillusion that was so difficult to bear. A young woman at the front had held out a bunch of violets to her and Sisi, seeing how desperately she wanted to be chosen, had taken them with a smile. As Sisi got into her carriage, she heard a voice say, 'I thought she was lovely too, but did you see her teeth?'

Sisi knew that it was hopeless to live up to the fairy-tale princess with stars in her hair of the Winterhalter portrait, an image that sold everything from chocolates to liver salts in Vienna, but she found it impossible not to try. Beauty was her gift, her weapon and her power, and she dreaded its passing.

There were some things she could do, like remaining slender. She liked the rigour of her morning exercises, the ache in her arms as she pulled herself up on the rings. But maintaining her nineteen-inch waist had meant that her face had lost its youthful plumpness. There were days when, confronted by an unexpected mirror, she saw a gaunt, middle-aged woman looking back at her. Festetics had found her crying after one of these glimpses of mortality and had told her about the beauty regime of the Princess Karolyi, her grandmother, who at the age of eighty had skin 'as soft and smooth as a baby's'. The veal had to be fresh and pounded very thin, but if used once a week it would keep the complexion radiant for ever.

After she had covered the Empress's face entirely with the raw meat, save for the eyes, nose and mouth, the Countess Festetics took a leather mask out of its case and put it gently in place. She fastened the tapes that tied it at the back so that her mistress could move her head in the night without the meat falling off. The mask was also a necessary protection against the Empress's wolfhounds, who had once mistaken the beauty treatment for an evening meal.

There were times when the Countess had regretted telling her mistress about the secret of the flawless complexion. It had been a family story, much embroidered in the telling, that she had pulled from her memories in a desperate attempt to comfort the weeping Sisi. She knew from ten years' experience that the only thing to do when her mistress was consumed by one of her spells of self-loathing, was to distract her as quickly as possible. Therefore she had turned her vague memories of her grandmother's soft and scented cheek into the elixir of eternal youth. Sisi had insisted on sending for some veal immediately; the next morning she had declared that the treatment was indeed a miracle. Countess Festetics was not as sure as her mistress as to the veal's efficacy, but she had long ago realised that Sisi had only to believe in something for it to be true. If she had convinced herself that veal would restore the lustre to her complexion, then there was no reason to disabuse her.

'I will wear my green habit tomorrow, I think.' The Empress's voice was muffled by the layer of meat and the leather mask.

'An excellent choice, Majesty. You always look so fresh in it and the colour perfectly sets off your hair.'

'And be sure to tell the servants that I will need a very hot bath when I come back tomorrow. I haven't hunted for weeks and I don't want to get stiff.'

'I have already told them, Majesty.'

'Thank you, Festy. I would be lost without you.' The Empress pointed to her face and tried to laugh.

'I am sure that the English milords will be astonished when they see you tomorrow. I have seen pictures of their Queen and she is small and completely round like a *Zwetschkenknödel*.'

Sisi shook her head. 'Oh, I am sure she was young and slender once. How many children did she have? Her husband must have found her attractive.'

'Or maybe he was a Coburger with a taste for *Zwetschkenknödel*,' said the Countess drily.

'I suppose if you are Queen in your own right, it doesn't matter what you look like.'

'Perhaps the English don't know that a queen can be beautiful, which is why you will dazzle them tomorrow. But I think you must sleep now, Majesty. You know that the veal will only work if you rest properly.'

'What you mean is that you are longing for your own bed. Run along then, Festy, but make sure you call me in good time tomorrow. I want my hair to be perfect.'

'Of course, Majesty.'

As she looked at the Empress one last time before closing the bedroom door, Festetics wondered what the world would make of the modern Helen of Troy if they could see her now – wearing a leather mask with veal juices running down her neck, and her hair tied to the ceiling in two long ropes. But no one save the Countess would ever see her like this; it was their secret.

The Lennox Diamonds

THE THREE HOUSEMAIDS SAT AWKWARDLY ON THE nursery sofa. They were trying to hide their work-roughened hands under their skirts, or by twisting them together on their laps. Charlotte wanted to tell them not to worry, she wanted to see the hands in their reddened, chapped reality, but she knew better than to say so.

She waited for them to settle and then she said, 'When I raise my hand, I want you all to take a deep breath and say "bosom" as you exhale.'

The housemaid on the left, the prettiest one, began to giggle.

Charlotte sighed. 'I know it sounds peculiar, but saying the word will put your mouth into the right shape for the photograph. Look what happens when I say it.' She stepped away from the camera and said the word, exaggerating the dignified pout that the final syllable gave her mouth.

'Bosom', 'bosom', 'bosom'; the maids tried the word out, but the giggles were spreading and soon all three were shaking with laughter.

Charlotte walked over to the window to hide her impatience. She wondered when the hunting party would return. She had hoped to go out with her camera that morning and take pictures at the meet, but there had been too much snow. She turned back to the maids and clapped her hands.

'Are you ready? I only have you for half an hour, so if we don't take the picture now it won't get done.'

The maids heard the sharpness in her voice. Sitting up, they tried to compose their faces. Charlotte looked at them through the viewfinder. She asked the pretty one, Grace, to sit in the middle and then posed the other two in profile. Every so often one of them would shudder with suppressed laughter. She waited for a moment and then she raised her hand.

'Bosom,' the maids whispered. Charlotte held her breath Would they keep still for the whole minute? Twenty-five, twenty-six – she could see that the maid on the right was going red with the effort involved in not laughing. Fifty one, fifty-two – she saw a tear sliding out of Grace's eye. Fifty-nine, sixty. She dropped her hand and the girls collapsed together in a quivering heap.

'Thank you, girls, you can go back to work now.' She had wanted to do several poses, but she could see that they were never going to stay still for long enough.

'But ain't you going to show us the picture, miss?'

'I have to print it first. Come back tomorrow and I'll show you.'

The maids clattered out, their voices echoing down the back stairs.

Charlotte looked at the clock on the mantelpiece. Ten minutes to five. She should be downstairs having tea, but she couldn't face all the talk about the wedding. Augusta and Fred had settled on a date in March and Lady Crewe was telling everyone who would listen that the trousseau would never be ready in time. Charlotte knew that she ought to be taking an interest in the arrangements, but she found it hard to concentrate on the endless chatter about the best place to buy Valenciennes lace.

Grace returned and put her head round the door.

'Lady Crewe was asking if you wanted some tea sent up, miss.'

Charlotte sighed; the message meant that her absence had been noted and disapproved of. She would have to go down now. Another day she might have pleaded a headache, but that would mean missing Bay at dinner.

'Thank you, Grace. Please tell Her Ladyship I will be down directly.'

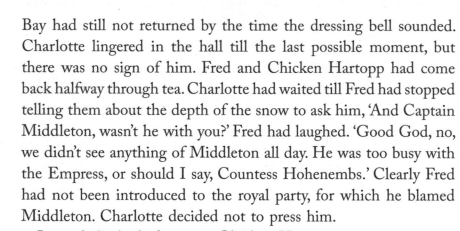

Bay had still not returned by the time the dressing bell sounded. Charlotte lingered in the hall till the last possible moment, but there was no sign of him. Fred and Chicken Hartopp had come back halfway through tea. Charlotte had waited till Fred had stopped telling them about the depth of the snow to ask him, 'And Captain Middleton, wasn't he with you?' Fred had laughed. 'Good God, no, we didn't see anything of Middleton all day. He was too busy with the Empress, or should I say, Countess Hohenembs.' Clearly Fred had not been introduced to the royal party, for which he blamed Middleton. Charlotte decided not to press him.

Instead she looked over to Chicken Hartopp.

'What did she look like? Is she as beautiful as they say?'

Chicken shook his great head. 'Really couldn't tell you, she was surrounded the whole time by flunkeys. She must have had at least six men with her. Austrians and such. She could have had her own hunt.'

'It makes you wonder why she needed Middleton,' said Fred.

'Surely the Austrians know how to take an English fence. They ride well enough.'

'Perhaps Middleton's fame has reached Vienna,' said Augusta, 'or should I say his reputation?' She looked hard at Charlotte as she said this, but Lady Crewe lumbered to her feet at this point and the group broke up.

Charlotte thought, not for the first time, that her wardrobe was not adequate for her stay at Melton. She had imagined that three evening dresses would be enough, but she realised her mistake when she saw that Augusta appeared to be wearing a new dress every single night. Her choice was between the blue moire, the pink figured silk or the white with the green trim. She decided on the pink; in truth she would have liked to have worn the white dress that had inspired Captain Middleton to sing 'Greensleeves' the night before, but she knew that Augusta would remember and would make some remark. The pink was pretty enough, and at least the bustle had this season's narrow silhouette.

'There, miss, what do you think of that?' Grace put down the curling tongs and invited Charlotte to look at her handiwork in the mirror. Charlotte usually wore her hair pulled back from a centre parting into a simple chignon, and so she gasped when she saw her reflection. The maid had piled Charlotte's hair on top of her head with loose ringlets hanging down at the back, and curly tendrils framing her forehead.

'Do you like it, miss?' Grace said anxiously.

'I hardly recognise myself,' said Charlotte. It was true, she did look different. She knew that she would never be beautiful, but for once she felt pleased with her reflection. The hairstyle had softened the angles of her face. The curled fringe called attention to her eyes, which tonight looked almost green. Her hair, which was a nondescript shade of brown, seemed to have an unaccustomed lustre. Her mouth, which was too wide to be fashionable, for once did not look too big for her small face. There had been a time when it would have taken all her courage to go downstairs and face the scrutiny of all the other women with their perfect ringlets, but since she had met Bay she no longer felt their stares so keenly.

'I expect Captain Middleton will like it,' said Grace. 'He looks like a gentleman who notices feminine things.'

'Yes, I believe he is.'

Charlotte thought that Bay must propose tonight. He would not have kissed her like that yesterday if he was not serious in his intentions. He could hardly think that she was the sort of girl who could be kissed with impunity. And yet, there was a part of her that was rather taken with the notion that he might think she was 'fast' and worldly enough to take his embraces in her stride. It had been her first kiss, but she hoped that Bay had not known that at once. And if he did propose, what would she say? She thought of the lectures she had received from Fred and Augusta on Bay's unsuitability as a husband. Bay Middleton was not the match they had in mind for the Lennox fortune, but Charlotte suspected that they would only really be happy if she died an old maid leaving the fortune intact to the little Freds and Augustas. No matter what they said, she thought that Bay liked her for herself, and while she had nothing to compare it with, she thought that his impulse to kiss her yesterday had been genuine enough. And for her part, she knew there had been nothing that she wanted more than to kiss him back.

She fastened her pearl drops into her ear lobes and surveyed the effect. They were pretty but not striking. In honour of her new hairstyle, her new look, she needed something more.

'Grace, could you ask my aunt for my jewellery case?'

She would wear the Lennox diamonds tonight. She had never felt equal to their magnificence before, but tonight she felt that she could carry them off. Perhaps not the whole parure, the earrings alone would be dazzling. She had brought the jewels to Melton with her so that Augusta could try them on with her wedding dress, but it would do no harm to remind the world to whom the diamonds actually belonged.

Grace returned carrying the jewellery case, accompanied by Lady Lisle, who started to speak the moment she walked into the room.

'Charlotte dear, when the maid told me that you wanted the diamonds I had to make sure she hadn't made a mistake. Are you going to wear them yourself? Are you sure that's wise? They are quite serious jewels for a young girl to carry off.'

Charlotte smiled. 'Don't worry, I am not going to deck myself out like a Christmas tree. I thought I would just wear the earrings and perhaps the brooch. And if I look ridiculous, well, I hope that no one here will judge me too harshly.'

She opened the box and was gratified by the sparkle within. Charlotte had almost no memories of her mother, but she fancied that she had once kissed her before she went to a ball and had been entranced by the glittering stones hanging around her mother's neck and arms.

The earrings were in the shape of teardrops – the large central stones surrounded by smaller faceted ones. When Charlotte held them up to her ears they flickered and flashed in the candlelight.

Grace smiled at Charlotte in the mirror.

'They look splendid, miss.'

But Lady Lisle looked worried.

'I wonder if it is wise to wear them tonight, Charlotte. I am worried that Augusta might think you are being tactless. After all, dear Fred won't be able to give her jewels like these.'

'I have already offered to lend her the diamonds for the wedding. I think she can't grudge me a night with my earrings,' Charlotte said with some force. Lady Lisle retreated, as always, at any sign of resistance.

'You are probably right, dear. After all, they are your jewels, so why shouldn't you wear them?'

She looked at her niece properly, taking in the new hairstyle, the diamonds and the glint in the grey-green eyes.

'I have to say that you are looking remarkably well tonight.'

'Thank you, Aunt. Grace has worked miracles with my hair.'

'It's very becoming, certainly. But it's not just that, you look different somehow. Perhaps it is the earrings. I always remember your poor mother wearing them. Tonight I can really see the likeness.'

'But she was so lovely. I am not nearly as pretty as her,' Charlotte said.

'Nonsense, child. I don't know where you have got that idea from. You are very like your mother. Not just in your features, but in the way you hold your head, your way of speaking. She would be very proud if she could see you now.' Lady Lisle was a kind woman. Charlotte was so self-possessed that it was easy to forget that she was, after all, an orphan.

'I wish I had a photograph of her. Father had one done of her in her coffin, you know, but I have never been able to look at it. There is the portrait at Kevill, of course, but it's not the same.'

'I have a pen and ink drawing of your mother that I made just after she got married. I shall find it for you. It's not a photograph, of course, but I remember your mother was very pleased with it at the time,' Lady Lisle said.

Charlotte went over to her aunt and kissed her on the cheek. 'That would be very kind.'

Charlotte and Adelaide Lisle were the last of the guests to join the group gathered under the Arthurian murals in the Great Hall. The chairs in the room had been designed by Pugin himself, but they were so ornately carved and exquisitely uncomfortable that people preferred to stand. Augusta and Fred were huddled by the fire, looking at the *Illustrated London News*. Augusta's brother, the Hon. Percy, was talking to the local curate; Lord Crewe was explaining the significance of the Lady of Shalott mural to an indifferent Hartopp; and Lady Crewe was sitting on the only upholstered chair in the room. There was no sign of Bay. As they approached the group, Charlotte saw Augusta's eyes flicker as she took in the hairstyle and the earrings. Fred gave her a puzzled look, as if he couldn't quite decide what was different about her, but then his fiancée whispered something in his ear. His face clouded, and for once, Charlotte found herself grateful for Captain Hartopp's attempts to flirt with her. He seemed to have regained his good humour and bounded up to her as if nothing had happened the day before. He was full of a cartoon he had seen in *Punch*, the humour of which, Charlotte felt, was rather being lost in his telling. But she smiled and nodded as if it was the most amusing story in the world.

Augusta, though, was not to be deflected.

'My goodness, Charlotte, you look very splendid tonight. Is there a special occasion? I feel quite dowdy beside you,' she said, her thin lips stretched into a tight smile.

'Your maid, Grace, has been so clever with my hair. I am so

grateful to you for lending her to me.' Charlotte's smile matched Augusta's exactly.

'She has a real way with hairpieces, it's remarkable what a little artifice can do.' Augusta carried on, 'But those earrings are all your own, of course. They are quite dazzling.'

'They belonged to my mother.'

Hartopp, who had been listening to this exchange with incomprehension, broke in, delighted to have a point of reference,

'The famous Lennox diamonds, eh? Shame to leave them in a strong box.'

'Exactly my thoughts, Captain Hartopp. What's the point in having lovely things if you don't use them?' Charlotte said.

Augusta was about to reply when the dinner gong sounded. As there was still no sign of Bay, Charlotte put her hand on Chicken's meaty arm.

But just as they were filing into dinner she felt a touch, his touch, on her shoulder.

'Glad to see that Chicken is looking after you in my absence,' Bay said. He looked flushed, as if he had just ridden in from the outside, although he was wearing evening dress.

'I must go and apologise to Lady C. I am damnably late.' He moved ahead into the dining room and Charlotte felt a little sparkle of excitement. Bay was back and he had claimed her.

She looked up at Captain Hartopp and smiled. 'Do you know, Captain Hartopp, I think you must tell me that story again. You do it so killingly well.'

Bay was sitting next to Augusta. Charlotte realised that his status had risen at Melton since he had become the Empress of Austria's pilot.

Augusta might disapprove of him, but she clearly could not resist the glamour of his imperial association. Charlotte listened to her trying to prompt Bay into telling her about his royal charge, but he was clearly enjoying having the upper hand and would only talk about the glories of the Pytchley. Finally Augusta could bear it no longer.

'Captain Middleton, I want no more details of the hounds and the kill. All I want to know is whether she is as beautiful as they say.'

Bay said in mock puzzlement, 'But who do you mean, Lady Augusta?'

Augusta rocked backwards on her chair in annoyance. 'The Empress, of course, who else would I mean? Is she really the loveliest woman in Europe?'

Bay paused for a moment and Charlotte tried not to smile. She was enjoying Augusta's torment.

'Do you know,' he said, 'I really couldn't say.'

Augusta's fork clattered on her plate. 'But Captain Middleton, I thought that you were at her side all day, surely you have some idea of what she looks like. Or is a pilot so far in front that he never sees the person he is guiding?'

Hartopp, who like Charlotte was following this exchange, boomed across the table, 'Come on, Middleton, you are quite the connoisseur of the female form. Surely you have formed an opinion?'

Bay smoothed the end of his moustache with his fingers, making them wait. 'The Empress certainly knows how to ride. I don't think I have ever seen a woman with such good hands. It was hard going today in the snow but she was right behind me the whole way. Took every fence, even cleared the gates. She would have made an excellent cavalry officer.' He smiled across the table at Charlotte.

But Augusta would not give up; information was currency in her world and she was determined to exact her price. She saw Bay smile at Charlotte and so she said, 'Charlotte, please can you help me persuade Captain Middleton to vouchsafe some opinion as to the Empress's looks?'

Charlotte hesitated. She wanted to know just as much as Augusta but she didn't want to side with her against Bay.

'I was hoping to see the Empress for myself tomorrow. I want to take some photographs at the meet, I would so like to have an image of her.'

Bay emptied his glass. 'I am afraid you may be disappointed. The reason I can't give you my opinion of the Empress's looks is that she wore a veil. She only took it off right at the end of the day when it was too dark to see her face.'

Hartopp laughed and said, 'Sorry, Middleton, that's just not good enough. A man like you can take the measure of a woman whether she is wearing a veil or not. You and I both know that beauty has its own smell.'

'Do we indeed?' said Bay. 'I detected no smell from the Empress beyond the usual aromas of the field. All I can tell you is that she is tall for a woman and very slender. Oh yes, and she appears to have a vast quantity of hair of a brownish hue. She holds herself well and she speaks quietly. There were times when I could barely make her out.'

'Tall and slender with good bearing,' said Augusta. 'Sounds as if you were quite smitten, Captain Middleton.'

Bay said, 'You must draw your own conclusions, Lady Augusta. I have merely tried to answer your questions.'

Charlotte said quickly, 'And how is the Empress's English, does she have a strong accent?'

'No, hardly at all. I was surprised at how good it was, much better than that of her entourage. But to be honest, there wasn't much conversation. She is very serious about her sport.'

'Then you are two of a kind,' said Hartopp. Bay smiled in reply but Charlotte could see his hand curling around the handle of his knife. Lady Crewe called out querulously from the foot of the table.

'I want to hear all about the Empress, Captain Middleton.'

'She is tall and slender and has lots of hair, Mama,' said Augusta. 'She speaks English without an accent and she is an excellent horsewoman.'

'Yes, yes, but is she exotic looking? I always think foreign women look so mysterious,' Lady Crewe said.

'There is certainly something mysterious about her, Lady Crewe,' said Middleton, 'but as to whether she is exotic, I really have no other Empresses to compare her with.'

Lady Crewe lost interest and the conversation turned to other things.

When the ladies withdrew, Charlotte lingered in the Great Hall for as long as she dared before joining the others in the drawing room. Luckily for her, Lady Crewe had insisted on playing bridge, so she was able to retreat to a far corner of the drawing room behind an enormous potted palm. She spent an anxious twenty minutes shifting her gaze from the door to her distorted reflection in the brass pot that contained the potted palm. When she turned her head from side to side she could see the earrings sparkle.

The rubber was coming to an end. Any moment now Augusta would be released from her card-playing duties and Charlotte would be forced to talk to her. At last the men sauntered in, and Bay spotted Charlotte at once behind her palm.

'What are you doing hiding over here?' he asked, amused.

'I wanted some shade,' she said.

Bay laughed. There was a pause until Charlotte could bear the silence no longer.

'What do you think of my hair? I hope it is worth the effort. Normally I can get dressed in minutes but this took what seemed like an hour.' She turned her head from side to side.

Bay tilted his head and half closed his eyes as if admiring a painting.

'I think you look charming, but then you always look charming, whether you are wearing ringlets and bedecked with diamonds or wearing an apron with your hands covered in stains. It makes no difference to me.'

Charlotte was both flattered by this speech and faintly annoyed. She had, after all, gone to some trouble on his behalf.

Bay seemed to catch her thought and said, 'But having said that, I think your ringlets and your diamonds are delightful.' He hesitated. 'Charlotte,' she felt a little thrill as he used her Christian name, 'I wish we could go somewhere and talk privately. I can feel Augusta watching me through the back of my head.'

Charlotte looked up at him. 'Is there something particular you wanted to talk about, Bay?' Her voice shook a little as she said his name.

'I think you must – or rather I hope you do – understand that there is. But before that, there are some things I must tell you about my circumstances. I am not a rich man. My stepfather makes me an allowance because he is a generous man and he adored my mother, but when he dies the money will go to his children. I have my army pay and the profits I make from selling horses. I have no debts at least, and I live well as a bachelor, but I am not a man of means. And yet you are an heiress. Tonight I see you in your diamonds and it makes me wonder if the gap between us is too great.' He stopped and looked at the floor.

Charlotte rushed in, 'It's true, I have diamonds. But you have Tipsy, the future winner of the Grand National. It would be hard to say which is the greater treasure.'

Bay looked up and smiled. 'I agree with you, of course, but I wonder if the world will feel the same.'

Charlotte began to pull off one of her evening gloves. 'Look at this hand, at these stains. Do you really think that I care what the world feels?'

Bay took the naked hand and was raising it to his lips when Augusta's patrician drawl shattered the moment.

'Oh dear, am I interrupting something?'

Bay squeezed Charlotte's hand, before releasing it.

'As a matter of fact, Miss Baird and I were discussing a matter of great importance to us both. But as it is a private conversation we should have known better than to start where we would inevitably be interrupted.'

He winked at Charlotte and turning to Augusta he said, 'And as you are so interested in the Empress, I should tell you that the thing that struck me most about her was her lack of pretension. It is a rare quality in a lady of such high rank.'

Augusta's eyes gleamed at this morsel. She was distracted just as Bay had intended, and did not appear to notice the implied insult.

'Really, Captain Middleton, and yet I have heard from Fred that her sister the ex-Queen is very particular about protocol. When Fred was presented to her, he made a quite a faux pas by forgetting to walk backwards out of her presence – even though they were in a ballroom! The Chamberlain came to reprimand him afterwards.'

'Poor Fred,' said Charlotte, 'he must have been mortified.'

'Mortified about what?' said her brother, who had come to join them.

'Your contretemps with the horrid Queen of Naples,' said Augusta.

Fred looked embarrassed. 'I had not intended to cause offence. Didn't think the walking backwards thing applied in the middle of a ballroom – dangerous business.'

'Well, I am sure that the Empress will expect no such niceties tomorrow, Baird,' said Bay.

'Do you think you will be able to present me?' said Fred, unable to conceal his eagerness.

'If the opportunity presents itself. But, of course, I am only the pilot.'

'Perhaps tomorrow, when the hunt is here at Melton, there might be a moment?' Augusta came as close to pleading as her pride allowed.

'I shall certainly do what I can,' said Bay.

There was a general clatter and scraping of chairs from the other side of the drawing room as Lady Crewe announced her intention of going to bed. Augusta made to follow her and beckoned to Charlotte, saying, 'That is our cue to retire. My mother does not hold with late nights.'

Bay bowed to Augusta. Turning to Charlotte, he said, 'We must finish our conversation tomorrow, it seems.'

'I look forward to it.' Charlotte shook her head a little so that her diamonds sparkled.

'So do I, Miss Baird, so do I.'

The Left Foreleg

WHEN THE LADIES HAD BEEN ESCORTED TO THE door, Fred turned to Chicken and Bay.

'What do you say to a game of billiards?'

Bay shook his head. 'Not tonight. I want to check on Tipsy.' And he left them before they could protest.

The temperature had dropped and Bay shivered as he stepped outside. But he was grateful for the cold, as he needed to clear his head. He was furious that Augusta had interrupted his conversation with Charlotte just at that moment. They had been almost there. But now his proposal would have to wait until tomorrow. It did not matter really – he was confident that Charlotte's feelings would not change overnight – and yet he would have felt much easier in his mind if the matter had been settled.

For he had not been entirely accurate when he had told Augusta that he had been unable to form an opinion of the Empress's looks. It was true that he could not say whether or not she was beautiful; his impression of her had little to do with her face. Yet he could draw a precise silhouette of the Empress on her horse – the straight back, the tilt of her head – as accurately as if she was standing in front of him.

The day had started badly. When Spencer had presented him to the Empress, she had given him the very briefest of nods and had resumed her conversation with two men, who from the colour and cut of their hunting clothes must have come with her from Austria. These courtiers made no move to acknowledge Middleton at all, evidently taking him for some kind of servant, and Bay found himself hovering awkwardly at the edge of the group, waiting for the hunt to start. When at last the huntsman blew his horn and the pack moved off, Middleton kept himself a few yards ahead of the Empress and her courtiers, who were riding abreast. At no point did she look at him or acknowledge his presence, and as Bay looked out across the sparkling fields crosshatched with black thorn, he cursed Spencer for spoiling a glorious day's hunting. He had no desire to act as some glorified groom.

The hounds had picked up the scent and were travelling at speed towards a small copse. Between the pack and its quarry was a hedge at least twelve foot tall. The hounds had found a hole at the base of the hedge and were squirming through, one at a time, yelping with excitement. The huntsman had stopped, evidently deciding that the obstacle was too high for him to clear, and was making his way further down the hedge, looking for an opening. Bay could see that the rest of the field were following him down to the other end of the field where there was a gate. The hounds were all through now and Bay could hear them squealing from the other side. They would be well into the copse before any of the riders could get into the second field. They were all lining up behind the gate, politely waiting in turn to jump over it.

He hesitated for a second, thinking of Earl Spencer's expectations and the web of obligation he was under, and then he felt Tipsy tremble under him and he felt his spirits lift as he pressed his heels hard into her sides and rode straight towards the hedge. He thought for a moment that Tipsy might refuse, but then she sprang and they were clear of the hedge and, by a whisker, the snowdrift on the other side. His heart was thudding in his chest as he slowed to a canter across the unbroken snow. This was what he loved, to be ahead of the pack with nothing to worry him but the going ahead. He could hear the yips of the hounds in the wood, and as he stood up in the saddle to see which way they had gone, he caught a flash of movement in the corner of his eye. He turned his head, a little piqued that someone else had dared to jump the hedge, and to his amazement saw the solitary figure of the Empress riding a few feet behind. She was sitting quite upright on her horse, looking as spruce as she had done at the beginning of the day, her elegant silhouette precise against the snow. That hedge had been a gamble, even for Bay, but she had taken it with ease and independently, it seemed, of her retinue.

Bay had not believed Earl Spencer when he told him the Empress could ride – he had assumed that this was the kind of hyperbole that hung around anyone of rank. But if anything, Spencer had underplayed it: the Empress could not only ride but she could ride almost as well as Bay himself. He couldn't think of many men who could have taken that hedge, let alone women. He raised his crop to her in congratulation – realising as he did so that he was probably breaching some royal protocol, but he felt the need to acknowledge that, for the moment at least, they were equals.

Bay did not wait to see how she responded, since he could see the rest of the hunt beginning to gallop up the field towards them. He could just make out the green jackets of the Austrian contingent and he urged Tipsy forward into the copse. But as he plunged on into the wood, he did not have to look round to know that she was behind him.

She had been there at the kill. Bay had been surprised to see that the Empress had watched the fox being torn to pieces by the hounds without a tremor. Only when the huntsman offered her the brush did she appear to falter, waving him away.

On the way back, he noticed that she followed him rather than rejoining her own clique. The light was beginning to go, so he let Tipsy subside into a slow trot. He was thinking that Tipsy might be ready for the National in the spring when he heard her say, 'Captain Middleton.' He turned round, surprised and pleased somehow that she should remember his name.

'I think your horse is going lame in the left foreleg.' He had been riding just ahead of her so that he had not heard her to begin with, and she had had to attract his attention by tapping his arm with the leather fan that hung from the pommel of her saddle. Her voice was low and quiet, with almost no accent. It was the precision of her speech that betrayed her as foreign; she didn't have the drawl or lisp of an English society woman. He looked down at Tipsy's leg, but he could see nothing wrong with it.

'I will take a look when we get back to the others, Your Majesty.' She tapped the fan on her saddle. 'I don't think it can wait, Captain.'

He heard the note of command in her voice and he pulled Tipsy in and dismounted to have a better look at the foreleg. The Empress had been right, there was a small rock lodged in the hoof which was making Tipsy limp. He had not even noticed. He dislodged the stone with his pocket knife. The frog of the horse's hoof was red and inflamed; if it had gone on any longer Tipsy could have been lame for weeks, and her National chances would be dashed. He was astonished that he hadn't spotted it earlier. He put the horse's leg down, and when he looked up he saw that the Empress had lifted her veil and was looking down at him.

'Was it something in the hoof?' Her face was pale in the fading light; he could only just make out her features – dark eyebrows against white skin, a straight nose, high cheekbones, a few lines around the eyes.

He held out his hand flat and showed her the rock. She reached over with her fan and poked it. 'It was a good thing you caught it, Captain Middleton. It would be a pity if such a fine horse was to go lame so early in the season.'

'I am in Your Majesty's debt then, for I admit I had noticed nothing.'

'I was brought up with horses, Captain Middleton. My father had not much interest in education but he did teach us all to ride.'

'He was a good teacher, then, Your Majesty, if I am allowed to say that.'

She looked down at him and smiled faintly without showing her teeth.

'If we were in Austria it would not be considered proper for you to talk to me so directly, but then we are not in Austria. I take it that you cannot show sixteen quarterings in your family tree?' Middleton shook his head. He wondered what she would say if she knew exactly how humble his origins were.

'Then you could not be part of the imperial household, Captain Middleton.' The Empress's face was serious.

Middleton got up on his horse. Now their faces were level, and the Empress smiled again, and a dimple appeared in one cheek. 'But that is one of the reasons that I prefer the sport here,' she said as she rode on.

The Leather Fan

CHARLOTTE WAS WOKEN BY A NOISE THAT SOUNDED like a thousand plates cascading onto a stone floor. It took a few moments for her to realise that it was the barking of the fox hounds. As they poured into the stable yard their yelping reverberated around the stone walls, creating a cacophony of sound that made sleep impossible.

She lay in bed listening to the sounds of the house coming to life. There was the clanking of the housemaids with their coal buckets, the hall boy leaving the polished riding boots outside bedrooms, the footmen and valets brushing and starching the hunting coats. The maids when they came in to light the fire were talking excitedly in low voices about the hunt, and the possibility of seeing the Empress. 'Cook says that her hair comes right down to her ankles.'

At home, when the local hunt met at Kevill, Charlotte would bury herself in the innards of the house – developing prints in her dark room or retreating to the linen cupboard, where she liked to check the sheets that her mother had brought as part of her trousseau. Each one was embroidered with her monogram, DAB – Dora Alice Baird – and the little owl that had been her symbol. The second Mrs Baird had not had time in her brief life to make much of a dent on the surface of Kevill – she had been too busy with her horses and her parties – so Charlotte had few reminders of her existence apart from the jewels in the strongbox and an ever-dwindling number of Irish linen sheets. She would look for those small tears that, if snagged by an unsuspecting toenail, could cause a serious rent. It was satisfying work: catching the loose threads before they unravelled. It was her own way of preserving her mother's memory.

Safe in the starchy cool of the linen cupboard, she could allow herself to remember the last time she had seen her mother. Charlotte had been waiting on the landing with her new doll, which she had christened by painting a red cross on its porcelain forehead. At last her mother had come down the stairs, her riding habit looped over one arm. Charlotte remembered the lacy borders of her mother's pantaloons and the shining buttons on her boots. Every detail of her mother's outfit lay crisp in her memory, but not the face. Her mother had laughed when she saw the baptised doll. 'What a solemn little girl you are, Lottie.' Charlotte could still feel the rough grain of the serge riding habit against her cheek and hands when she had pushed her face into her mother's skirts. She could hear the click click click of the riding crop as her mother had trailed it against the banisters as she went downstairs away from her. Her mother had been so young, married at eighteen, dead at twenty-three. Her horse had stumbled over a fence, and Dora Baird née Lennox had been thrown head first into a ditch and broken her neck. They had brought her body back on a hurdle, covered with one of the huntsmen's coats. Charlotte had watched from the nursery window, wondering what the pink speck was that the men were carrying so slowly across the fields, until her nurse had found her and taken her away.

Charlotte's father had said after the accident that he would never hunt again, but the winters in the Borders were very long and the amusements were sparse, so his self-imposed exile from the Orrington did not last beyond the following Christmas. But he had been adamant that his only daughter would not follow the same route as her mother. The Shetland pony was sent away and Charlotte was sent to play in the nursery when the hunt came to Kevill. It was only when her godmother Lady Dunwoody had given her the camera and taught her how to use it, that Charlotte found an occupation that filled the long winter days with meaning.

But there was no escaping the hunt today. Of course, she could have pleaded a headache and kept to her room until the riders set off, but she wanted to see Bay. If she and Bay were to marry, she could not hide in the linen cupboard from November till April. Besides, she wanted to see the Empress.

Charlotte was curious to know if she was as beautiful as everybody said. She had seen an engraving in the *Illustrated London News* after one of the Winterhalter portraits, where she looked romantic and soulful, her long hair studded with diamond stars. But that image must be at least ten years old now, judging by the crinoline. Would Elizabeth still be as appealing a decade later? When questioned at dinner last night, Bay had not been very forthcoming. Charlotte had rather admired him for that. He had so clearly not wanted to descend to Augusta's level by answering her questions. Of course, in matters of feminine beauty, men were not always reliable witnesses. There was, in Charlotte's experience, a great gulf between the charms that men found appealing and the kind of beauty that could withstand female scrutiny. The camera lens was equally ruthless. The kind of women that were all 'wriggle and chiffon', in her aunt's phrase, did not translate well to the photographic plate. All the conventional accoutrements of feminine charm – the pouting, the lowered lashes, the trembling bosom – were deadened by the long exposure time demanded by the photograph. To look unflinchingly into a lens for a whole minute was not easy, and in Charlotte's experience women found it harder than men. Even though the new cameras meant that the exposure time now was shorter, the women who required sleight of hand to dazzle the eye were always disappointing in photographs.

After breakfast Charlotte went up to the old nursery to fetch her equipment. She looked at the photograph she had taken of Bay with Tipsy. His very pale blue eyes shone out of the print. Later, she thought, she would retouch the surroundings so that there was nothing to distract the viewer from the man and his horse.

Carrying her equipment across the Great Hall, she almost collided with a footman carrying stirrup cups on a silver tray. As he opened the door and she could see the red, black and brown mass punctuated by points of silver, hear the shouts and the snorts of the horses and smell the excited animals, she found she could not move. There had been exactly this combination of light, colour and sound the day her mother had set off on her favourite grey. She wanted very much to retreat into the cool gloom of the house and pretend that none of this was happening.

'Stirrup cup, miss?' The footman waved the tray in front of her. Charlotte picked up one of the silver goblets and took a gulp of the steaming liquid. She had imagined it was some kind of mulled wine, but it was stronger than anything she had tasted before, coursing like liquid fire down her throat and melting the butterflies in her stomach. A horse whinnied in the distance and she took another gulp.

By the time she saw Bay cantering across the park with Chicken

Hartopp, the goblet was empty. As they jumped the ha-ha that separated the garden from the park, although she could not really see Bay's face, Charlotte knew that he was smiling.

She took a deep breath and stepped out onto the terrace.

Bay pulled up his horse in front of her. From where she was standing on the terrace, she could look him in the eye. He tipped his hat to her.

'No jewels this morning, Charlotte?'

'I believe diamonds in the daytime are considered vulgar.' Charlotte pursed her lips in her best imitation of Augusta. Bay laughed and leant towards her.

'How I wish you were riding out with me this morning. It is such a glorious day to be hunting. There is really nothing like it.'

'Unless you're a fox, of course,' Charlotte said.

Bay looked surprised at her tone.

'I would love to have your company in my dark room today.' The stirrup cup made it possible for Charlotte to say exactly what was in her head.

'And I would happily attend you in your dark room. But I'm afraid Tipsy wouldn't like it. Look at her, she is dying to be off.'

'And you have an empress to look after as well.'

'Her too.' Bay waved his hand as if to brush the Empress away.

'Is she here yet? I want to see her very much. I am hoping to take a photograph of her. I am becoming quite practised at riders and horses.'

'The Empress isn't here, though I believe she is riding over from Easton Neston. We can't start without her, of course.'

'Of course. But I thought punctuality was the politeness of princes,' Charlotte said.

'But not of empresses, it seems. The hounds have caught the scent twice already this morning. They are working themselves up into a frenzy. They're desperate to be off – they know it's a perfect hunting day.' As Bay looked out over the horses and hounds he shouted a greeting to an elderly gentleman with a face red from years of hard riding and strong drink, mounted on a shiny chestnut horse.

'Good day to you, Colonel. How is Salamander proving?'

The Colonel stopped, his head craning round as he heard Bay's voice. As he turned to face them, Charlotte could see that his eyes were covered by a milky film.

'Is that you, Middleton? Didn't see you there for a moment. Salamander is doing very well. Worth almost every penny I gave you for her.'

Bay laughed. 'I'll take her back any time, Colonel, on the same terms.'

The Colonel patted Salamander on the flank. 'Couldn't part with you now, could I, old girl?' He looked up and Charlotte could see that he was looking for Bay, who was a few feet away. She realised that the man was almost blind.

'Over here, Colonel,' Bay said. 'May I present Miss Baird?' The Colonel looked in the opposite direction.

'Miss Baird, Colonel Postlethwaite – longest serving member of the Pytchley, and the hardest rider in the Shires.'

Charlotte nodded and, realising that was useless, she said as loudly as she could, 'How do you do, Colonel Postlethwaite.'

The Colonel turned his great, blind head towards her.

'Honoured, Miss Baird.'

Bay spoke quickly. 'The scent's well and truly up. I think it is going to be a capital day for it. You can give Salamander her head.'

'Oh, I intend to, Middleton.' The Colonel dug his heels into his horse's flanks and disappeared into the throng.

Charlotte looked at Bay. 'Can he see anything at all?'

'Precious little. But Salamander's a good horse. She'll see him through.'

'But isn't it fearfully dangerous?' Charlotte said.

Bay looked as if he was about to laugh but then clearly thought better of it. Instead he said gently, 'Postlethwaite doesn't think it's dangerous, Charlotte. He's been hunting round here all his life. It's not the danger he's scared of, it's the day when he can't ride out anymore.'

Charlotte felt her eyes fill with unbidden tears. The stupid, blind old fool. She looked down at her camera, and started to fiddle with the shutter so that Bay would not see the emotion in her face. But just then there was a shout and a great murmur ran through the crowd. Charlotte looked up and saw that the royal party were making an entrance. She knew it was the royal party because everyone at the meet, with the exception of Colonel Postlethwaite, had turned to watch the Empress and her attendants cantering down the hill that led to the house.

As a composition it could not be bettered, Charlotte thought. If only they were not moving so fast, it would make a magnificent photograph. The Empress in a dark green habit, slender and erect on her strawberry roan, was flanked by two male riders in coats of a lighter green and silver spurs, with a groom bringing up the rear. Charlotte saw that the Empress rode as if she was glued to the saddle; her slender figure did not waver or wobble as the horse came down the slope. She heard a gasp as the royal party sailed over the ha-ha that Bay had jumped earlier. The male riders flanking the Empress leant forward as they took the ditch, but she stayed quite motionless in the side-saddle, seeming to float with her horse.

'At last,' Bay said. He dug his heels into Tipsy's flanks and with a brief wave to Charlotte, he trotted off towards the royal party.

The Empress had stopped in the middle of the forecourt, still flanked by her escorts. She was talking to Earl Spencer, her face tilted up on account of his immense height, and as she had lifted her veil, Charlotte could see the Empress's profile, a small, sharp counterpoint to the immense weight of hair at the back of her head. The other riders were keeping a respectful distance from the royal party and Charlotte thought she had her picture. She had brought down a plate with a new emulsion that required a shorter exposure time. Lady Dunwoody had said it was quite effective in daylight. She put her head under the cloth and angled the camera so that her subject was at the centre of the frame. It felt strange to be taking a picture without the subject's knowledge, but Charlotte knew that she would probably not get as clear a view again. She moved the viewfinder so that the Empress was in the upper third of the plate; a little asymmetry, she found, always made for a more pleasing effect. She found the bulb and squeezed it. She heard the muffled bang and started to intone the Lord's prayer. At 'Hallowed be thy name', she felt that she had exposed the photo long enough and she unclenched the bulb and came out from her shroud. The Empress was still talking to Spencer, but she had turned her horse a little so that the whole face was visible. She was about fifteen feet away and Charlotte could see that she had regular features, a straight nose, and dark eyes under thick, arched brows. Was she beautiful? Charlotte found it impossible to tell, but there was something intense about the older woman's gaze that surprised her. Charlotte sensed that the other woman was full of emotion, she could almost see her quivering. Charlotte wondered what the Red Earl could be saying to the Empress to create such an effect. But she must capture this moment. As quickly as she could, she put in a new plate and had a look at the composition in her lens. She moved the camera a fraction to the right and squeezed the bulb again. This time she took it as far as, 'On earth as it is in heaven', just to be sure.

Charlotte straightened up. As she looked over to the scene she had just photographed, she noticed two things: the first was that the Empress was holding something that looked like a fan in front of her face. The second was that standing directly beside Earl Spencer was Bay Middleton. The fan was large and unlovely. It was not there for decorative or ventilation purposes. It was being used as a shield.

Although it was a cold day, Charlotte felt the humiliation rise over her like a scorching tide, stinging her face and neck, as if she had just been slapped. She looked over at Bay, trying to catch his eye. Surely he could explain to the Empress that she was just an amateur photographer who meant no disrespect? But Bay did not seem to see her; he was completely held by the face behind the fan.

Major Postlethwaite

BAY SET OFF TOWARDS THE EMPRESS, WHO WAS talking to Earl Spencer. As he approached he could see her profile clearly, her veil was up. Yesterday he had only seen her face in the silvery gloom of the twilight; now there was a bright winter sun and he gazed at her. She was full of contrasts, the dark eyebrows against the pale skin, the mahogany-coloured hair against the green habit, the red lips and the white throat. She must have felt the heat of his glance because she turned her head towards him, but as she did so she saw something that made her frown and her mouth compressed into a tight line. She started to tug at the reticule attached to her saddle with sharp, angry movements and pulled out what looked like a baton. The Empress gave the object a flick with her wrist and Bay saw that it was a fan made from smooth brown leather. She held it up so that her face was hidden from the front. Bay looked over to see what she was shielding herself from, and saw Charlotte's small figure standing beside her camera, the bulb in her hand. Behind Spencer, he could see the Empress's two companions stiffen and look at each other in alarm.

The Empress now noticed his presence.

'Captain Middleton,' she made an angry gesture with the fan, 'it's too much. Nowhere is safe.'

Earl Spencer, immediately on his guard, said, 'Your Majesty, I can assure you there are no threats to your person at the Pytchley.'

'I am afraid you are wrong. There is a . . . person over there taking photographs of me, Earl Spencer.' She did not raise her voice but Bay thought that the low intensity of her tone was somehow more terrible.

'I came here as a private individual to hunt, not to be hunted. I thought I should be safe here. But once again, I find that I am a fairground attraction to be captured as a souvenir, a prize to sell newspapers.'

The Earl look round, bewildered, and then he saw Charlotte on the terrace, fumbling as she tried to dismantle her equipment.

'Oh, but Ma'am, that is just the Baird girl; she's a guest at the house. I am sure she meant no harm by it. A lot of these young girls play around with cameras now. In my day it was sketchbooks and easels, but I suppose we must all move with the times. Isn't that right, Bay?'

The Earl turned his huge head towards Middleton, the look in his bulbous blue eyes unmistakeable – Charlotte Baird was Bay's responsibility, and as she had caused this faux pas, he must make amends.

Bay saw the hard tilt of the Empress's chin and found it unaccountably attractive. He couldn't understand why she was so angry but he liked the way her temper highlighted her features. He couldn't help himself taking stock of her as a woman, the narrow waist, the mass of hair, the dark, unreadable eyes. He noticed a small mole on the Empress's upper lip. It was the only blemish on the white skin. He found himself wanting to touch it. But then a flick of the fan reminded him that this woman was also a monarch. He hesitated – he knew he should defend Charlotte, but he sensed that the Empress would not like him taking another woman's part.

'If only we *could* move with the times. Literally, I mean. I would so much like to have a record of Tipsy here in full flight.' Bay smiled, willing the woman in front of him to respond in kind. She looked at him directly, clearly surprised by his deflection of her anger, and for a moment Bay thought that she would snub him, but then he saw her face soften and the set of her shoulders relax. 'I have a charming photograph of me and Tipsy, but can you imagine what it would be to actually see her gallop?'

'If it is possible in the imagination, Captain Middleton, then I am sure that one day it will become a reality.' Slowly, the Empress lowered the fan and the corners of her mouth moved upwards into the beginning of a smile. Spencer let out a great sigh and the two Austrians relaxed back into their saddles. Bay saw the courtiers taking him in, registering his existence for the first time.

He was about to reply to the Empress when a great yelping went up from the hounds, who had found the scent. He looked at the Empress and she lifted her crop, gesturing for him to ride on. He pulled Tipsy round and started to follow the others down the drive. At the gate, as the Empress passed in front of him, he turned back to look for Charlotte, but she had already gone.

The day was fine and clear, the thin layer of snow on the ground crisp under the horses' hooves. The hounds had picked up the scent halfway up a hill topped by a small Greek temple, so positioned that it could be seen from the drawing room of the house. As Bay cantered past, he saw that the statue was of Diana the huntress, holding her bow. Bay's classical education had been scant but he recognised Diana – he had taken an interest in the hunting deities. He knew the story of Diana and Actaeon, the hunter who had been been turned into prey for trespassing on the goddess bathing. Spencer had a painting at Althorp of Actaeon surprising upon the deity and her attendants in their nakedness. When Bay had seen it he had thought that the fleshy figure of Diana would have needed quite a substantial mount. This statue, though, was slender, the body taut as it twisted round to take aim. She looked like a woman who didn't miss. There was something in the clarity of its profile that was familiar. He turned his head to take another look and just then the Empress came up on his right flank; the resemblance between the sylph-like statue and the lissom, intent figure beside him was unmistakeable. He raised his crop to show the Empress but she had already passed by, following the hounds ahead.

The going was good. Bay liked a long run at the beginning of the day. He preferred it when the pack thinned out a bit and the riders were strung out in order of ability and courage. He had nothing to prove, but still it pleased him to find himself at the front. There were so many places where he had to curb his instincts, but here in the field there was no deference, no order apart from the natural one. Even the Empress, his social superior in every way, was here to follow his lead.

The hounds had stopped at a stream. They had lost the scent. The huntsman was urging them across, but the animals were confused, reluctant to go through the icy water. Bay looked around for a crossing place. The stream was just too wide to jump and he didn't want to get soaked this early in the day if he could help it. There was a bend in the stream a hundred yards away and Bay urged Tipsy down towards it to see if it offered a better vantage point. He looked back and saw that the Empress was behind him, as was, to Bay's surprise, Colonel Postlethwaite. How the Colonel had followed the Empress, Bay could not imagine. The man might not be able to see a thing, but he could still find the best-looking woman in the field. The Colonel had been one of the many admirers of Skittles, the famous courtesan who had hunted with the Quorn in the Sixties. She had been famous for the tightness of her habits, into which she was rumoured to have been sewn naked, and the ferocity of her riding. The gossip went that she had been quite taken with the Colonel, so much so that she had forgiven him his lack of fortune.

The clamour of the hounds suggested that a few had crossed the stream and had found the scent on the other side. Bay looked at the stream. It was slightly narrower here and there was a sandy slope. He could either try and jump to the other side or take the safer but wetter route and wade through the water. He didn't hesitate, but urged Tipsy into a run and, to his enormous relief, cleared the brook. The Empress landed a moment after and then, with a great bellow, Colonel Postlethwaite, a beaming smile on his scarlet face.

One of the Austrians riding with the Empress was trying to catch up with her and was now readying himself to jump over the stream. Bay watched as the horse stumbled and tried not to smile as the man fell head first into the water. The stream was not deep and the man managed to scramble onto the bank, but he was a comic sight: soaking wet, the gold braid on his coat sodden and his breeches transparent.

Bay heard what sounded like a snort of laughter and turned round to see that the Empress was convulsed. He caught her eye and she shrugged.

'Esterhazy pulled the horse up short. He should have had the courage of his convictions. If you are going to jump, then you must be decisive. There is no room for second thoughts,' she said and cantered after Colonel Postlethwaite, who seemed drawn after the hounds by an invisible thread.

Bay lingered for a moment to watch the unfortunate Esterhazy attempt to recapture his mount and then he turned his own horse in the direction of the pack.

The hounds were swinging around in a great arc – Bay was always impressed by the refusal of foxes to run in a straight line. The endless circling and doubling back was the element that made hunting so endlessly fascinating. There was no logic to it, no order. The railways that now crossed the English countryside might proceed in inexorable parallel lines for ever, but Reynard would never be ruled by Bradshaw. Bay relished the random syncopation of the hunting day; the recklessness of a good run followed by the idle moments as the hounds looked for the scent. All his other days were ordered in a procession of meals, costume changes and ritualised pleasure, but in the field nothing could be predicted. No two days were ever the same. In London, in the season, Bay knew almost to the minute where he would be at any time of the day on any day of the week. The battlefield, Bay supposed, was equally unpredictable, but he was a soldier who had never seen action. The Pax Britannica had made the Shires his battleground.

The rest of the field was beginning to catch up. It had thinned out since the morning; the royal sightseers had given up and gone home when they realised what was required of them to keep up with the Empress. Bay saw Spencer grinding down the middle of the line, the flanks of his horse crusted with a white tidemark of sweat. Spencer was a superb rider but his great bulk meant that he would never be at the front of the pack. Bay turned his head and saw that the Empress was ahead of him, once again. She was riding at full tilt towards a nasty-looking fence, Colonel Postlethwaite at her heels. Bay felt a sick lurch in his stomach as he realised that she was about to take a fence that even he would baulk at. He shouted, 'Look out!' and dug his spurs into Tipsy, hoping to head her off. But the Empress could or would not hear him. He watched as she let her horse's reins go slack and allowed the animal to take off. She cleared it all right, but had she landed safely? Bay could not see over to the other side. He urged his own horse on and over the fence, feeling Tipsy shudder as they cleared the highest bar. And they were down. He looked up and saw the Empress's horse standing in front of him, riderless. He felt his mouth go dry.

Then he heard the awful, unmistakeable shriek of an animal in pain, and turning his head, he saw Salamander, the chestnut mare he had sold Postlethwaite, lying on the ground, the body of her master pinned beneath her legs. The Empress was attempting to soothe the animal, but the horse's leg was bent and broken and it was thrashing about in agony. Bay sat frozen for a moment. He saw Postlethwaite's head bent back at an unnaturale angle. The horse's dreadful screaming grew louder. Bay made himself dismount and walk towards the Empress. She was standing very still. Bay watched as she raised her hand.

At first he thought that the object she was holding was the leather fan, but then he saw that it was a revolver. Slowly and deliberately, her hand quite still, she aimed the weapon at the centre of the horse's forehead and fired. The screaming stopped as the mare's body collapsed. Bay gasped, and the Empress turned her head – the dark eyes burning in her white face.

'The Angel of Death is always with us,' she said and crossed herself, the revolver still in her hand.

Bay walked around the dead horse to Postlethwaite's head. The milky eyes were staring at the sky and the mouth was open in a grotesque smile. Bay knelt down and pushed the old boy's eyelids shut. He tried to pull the body out from beneath Salamander, but the carcass was too heavy. He saw that Postlethwaite's stock was tied with a gold pin in the shape of a horseshoe. He thought of the old man fumbling with the pin that morning and felt tears running down his cheeks. Postlethwaite had been a gallant creature and this was probably the end he would have hoped for, but still Bay felt desolate as he looked down at the bodies of horse and rider. He felt in the pockets of his coat for a handkerchief but could only find his hip flask. He brushed his face as best he could with the rough wool of his sleeve and took a swig from the flask. The brandy tore his throat and made him cough, but at last he could control his tears.

He felt a touch on his arm.

'I am sorry, Captain Middleton. He was a friend of yours?' The Empress held out a small scrap of fabric edged with lace. He realised she was offering him her handkerchief. The gun had disappeared.

'He used to be the Master of the Pytchley. I sold him . . .' Bay found he could not go on. He took the handkerchief from her and tried to wipe his eyes. It smelt of lavender.

'I think, though, that to die like this is a blessing, no? To jump into the next world.' The Empress looked at him directly and Bay saw that there were golden flecks in the dark irises.

Bay nodded. 'He was riding for a fall. Damn fool was almost blind. Shouldn't have been out today.'

'So maybe he chose the manner of his going, Captain Middleton?' She was still gazing at him and he couldn't look away.

'But the waste of it . . .' Bay gestured to the dead body of Salamander, but kept his eyes on the Empress's face.

'No, no. You must think of it as glorious. He died a free man.'

Bay could hear the noise of the field on the other side of the fence. In a moment they would be surrounded. She was still looking at him. He thought of the blind gallantry of Postlethwaite, charging down the field with no thought of the consequences. He took her hand and kissed it.

She did not pull her hand away immediately. It was Bay who pulled back, as if astonished at his own action.

He was about to apologise, when she spoke. 'It is only when I am hunting that I feel free. Perhaps it is the same for you, Captain Middleton?' Her voice was soft and warm but she was not smiling.

'I have taken a liberty, Your Majesty. Forgive me, I forgot myself.'

He waited for the reprimand, but she only tilted her head a little to one side.

'Don't apologise, Captain Middleton. You were paying a tribute to your friend, I believe.' She smiled then.

Bay tried to smile back. It struck him that she was exactly right; he had been inspired by Postlethwaite's recklessness.

'I think Postlethwaite might have kissed both hands,' Bay said.

Elizabeth laughed. Even though smiling made the skin round her eyes crease, she looked much younger. Bay realised that she had neither been shocked nor surprised by his action.

'I see I have had a lucky escape. Now, Captain Middleton, could you help me get on my horse?'

Bay linked his hands and bent down so that she could use them as a step. He saw as she drew up the material of her habit that there were no petticoats, and as she put her foot in its elastic-sided boot in his palm he realised that she was wearing suede breeches underneath the riding dress, and he knew that the glimpse had been quite deliberate. His hands shook as she swung herself into the saddle. As she looked down at him, he saw her face regain its regal composure.

'Thank you,' and she nodded to him as if he had been a servant.

A Proposal

THE HUNTSMEN HAD ARRIVED WITH SPENCER. THE
Earl took in the situation and bowed his head for a moment.
'Who's down?' he said to Bay.

'Postlethwaite. Broke his neck,' Bay replied.

'You shot the horse?' Spencer asked.

'The leg was broken.' Bay felt reluctant to admit that it had been
the Empress who had administered the *coup de grâce* to Salamander.

'Capital fellow, Postlethwaite,' said the Earl. 'Shame about the
horse.'

Bay helped the grooms lift the gate off its hinges. The unwitting
cause of Postlethwaite's death would serve as a stretcher for his
body. It took five men to lift him from under the dead horse. Bay
crossed the old man's hands over his chest and put his silver-handled
crop by his side. One of the huntsmen blew a long note on the
horn as the grooms picked up the makeshift bier and started to
carry it back over the fields.

What was left of the hunt started to make its way back towards
Melton. Bay caught up with the Empress but she had pulled her
veil down and they rode back to the house in silence. When they
reached the house, Count Esterhazy, who had changed into dry
clothes, came out to greet her and they rode off together towards

Easton Neston. The Empress did not say goodbye to Middleton, but as she set off down the drive she turned and raised her hand in farewell.

Bay watched the Empress ride away down the drive until she was out of sight. As he pulled Tipsy's head round towards the stable yard he felt the tension in his body. His jaw ached as if he had been clenching it for the last two hours. Dismounting, he felt his legs tremble beneath him. He stood still for a moment, leaning against the wall of the yard, pressing down on his heels, trying to find his balance. Closing his eyes, he waited for the shaking to pass. He had been so reckless earlier, inspired by poor doomed, gallant Postlethwaite.

Bay opened his eyes and saw that Charlotte was standing in front of him, her face screwed up with distress. She put her small white hand on his arm.

'Oh Bay, I am so sorry.'

He tried to make his face into the appropriate shape.

'Poor old Postlethwaite. Still, he had a good run of it. Not such a bad way to go.'

A shadow of surprise crossed Charlotte's face. 'Colonel Postlethwaite is dead?'

'Came off after a jump and his horse rolled on top of him. It was very quick.'

The party bringing Postlethwaite's body back to the house would be arriving soon. Bay took Charlotte's arm and led her out of the stable yard into the park. It would not do for her to see Postlethwaite's broken remains being carried back into the house. He could feel her arm trembling under his hand. They walked in silence towards the vista which ended in the Temple of Diana. When they reached the ha-ha, Bay made to open the wicket gate, but Charlotte stopped him.

'Were you there when Colonel Postlethwaite fell?' she asked.

'I didn't see it happen. I was the other side of the fence, but I was there directly afterwards. He died instantly.' Bay tried to sound reassuring, remembering that Charlotte's mother had died in a hunting accident. 'That kind of thing is over in a second.'

'And the Empress? Was she there too?' Charlotte said.

Bay paused. He thought of the Empress holding the pistol at Salamander's head and his own behaviour after.

He said, 'Postlethwaite was with us at the head of the field. The Empress was there before I was.'

Bay saw, to his surprise, that Charlotte's eyes were filled with tears.

'But what's the matter? Surely you are not crying for old Postlethwaite, a man you met but once, who died a death of his own choosing?' He took her small hand between his two palms. 'Don't cry for him, Charlotte. He was smiling at the end.'

Charlotte shook her head, as if to scatter the tears. She raised her head and looked directly at him.

'Will the Empress will be hunting with you again, tomorrow?'

Bay looked at her. He didn't understand the question, or rather, the urgency behind it. She couldn't possibly know about his foolish gesture towards the Empress.

'Well, yes. Spencer has asked me to be her pilot for the whole visit.'

But at that her face relaxed. Bay felt in his pockets for something to dry her eyes, and pulled out a handkerchief with which he dabbed her wet cheeks. It took him a moment to register that the handkerchief was the one that the Empress had given him beside the body of the Colonel. He wondered if Charlotte would notice, but she was too preoccupied to take in what he was wiping her face with.

Charlotte continued, 'You see, I thought I might have made her angry. When I took the photograph. She put up her fan. And then I saw you next to her, and I was so worried that she would be cross with you, because of me, I mean.'

Bay remembered the hard tilt of the Empress's jaw behind the fan, and the colour in her cheeks.

'And I thought you might be tarnished,' Charlotte burst out. 'With the connection.'

Bay hesitated. He could not admit to Charlotte that he had not acknowledged the relationship between them, that he had entirely failed to defend her, that he had simply changed the subject. She expected more of him, and he rather liked the version of himself that he saw reflected in her eyes. He would like to be that person, not the man who had kissed the hand of the Empress next to the body of a dead friend.

'Dear Charlotte, as if any association with you could do such a thing,' Bay said, and as if to prove it he bent down and kissed Charlotte on the mouth. Her lips were dry and slightly salty from the tears. She trembled so gratifyingly that he kissed her again, pulling her to him with one hand around her waist. It was too late to turn back now. He wanted to jump, without second thoughts.

'I long for the day when you are my wife,' he whispered into her ear. 'I want to marry you. As soon as possible.'

He felt her relax into his arms and she kissed him this time, making it quite clear what her answer was.

At last Charlotte pulled back from him to look at his face. She put one hand to his cheek.

'Bay, you should know that I can't marry without Fred's consent, at least not until I am twenty-one.'

'I shall ask him tonight.'

'And he will lecture you about the virtues of a long engagement. He and Augusta have waited for a year.'

Bay smelt lavender water and a tiny whiff of fear. 'I know there are good reasons to wait, but are they really so very important?' He wanted to kiss the inch of neck that was visible above the boned collar of her dress; he wanted to cover the red blotches that were forming there with his mouth.

'I am afraid that money is always important. Fred is my trustee and at the moment he enjoys the income from my inheritance. When I marry he will lose that money, and that is not something he is looking forward to.' Bay was not listening, he wanted so much to capture that flush. He bent towards her again, but this time he felt a hand against his chest stopping him.

'I can't marry you right away, even if I would like to, so we must be,' she tried to smile as he pressed against her, 'we must be prudent.'

'Prudent?' said Bay, taking the protesting hand in his and finding that inch of neck with his mouth. Charlotte shuddered and for a moment she seemed to surrender, but then she stiffened and this time she pulled away from him in earnest.

But he would not let go of her hand. He looked down into her small, worried face, saw the hectic flush on her cheeks, the filling eyes.

'Do I look like a prudent man? I think you have confused me with somebody else.'

She almost smiled, but his voice was urgent.

'Charlotte, I am . . . unsteady.' His grip on her hand was hard, almost painful.

The look on her face made him regret those words.

'Not in my affection for you, never that. But in myself. I would like to be settled.'

And as he spoke Bay felt that there was nothing he would rather do than settle down with Charlotte in the country.

'Let's elope, Charlotte. We could manage on my income to begin with. I could sell my hunters and we could live very quietly at first.'

Charlotte thought she understood his unsteadiness; she remembered the scene at dinner when Blanche Hozier's baby had been mentioned. But she did not understand Bay's urgency.

'Sell your hunters? Even Tipsy? You would give up your chance of the Grand National to elope with me? Well, I am flattered beyond measure, but are you sure that such a sacrifice is really necessary? I shall be twenty-one in the autumn, – surely we can wait nine or so months to be married. I don't see there is any reason for us to behave like fugitives. Fred may not welcome my marriage, but once I have achieved my majority there is nothing he can do to stop me. I see no compelling reason to run away like thieves in the night, when we could be married quite respectably within a year.'

Bay's handsome face turned away from her.

'You're right, of course, it is unreasonable of me to expect you to give up your trousseau and your wedding finery. I know these things mean a lot to a woman. But Charlotte, I so wish it could be done now.'

Charlotte moved so that she could look at him face on.

'But why? I care nothing for wedding finery, but I do care about what family I have left. Fred can be insufferably pompous sometimes, especially now he is engaged to Augusta, but I would still like him to walk me down the aisle.' She paused for a moment, trying to read his face.

'What makes you so desperate to run away? You must know that my feelings for you will be the same in September as they are now. I will not change.'

Bay sighed. He knew that he had done this all wrong. The only reason for haste was his own inconstancy. He could not tell Charlotte that he was afraid for his own heart.

'Forgive me, dearest Charlotte, I am not myself. Major Postlethwaite's death was a great shock. It made me think that we must take our happiness when we can.'

Charlotte kissed his cheek.

'I think we are young enough to risk waiting a few months. Meanwhile you must be nice to Augusta. If she thinks of you as a desirable husband for me, then Fred will hardly dare to object. Perhaps you could present her to the Empress? Have you noticed how much more civil she is to you now that you are riding out with royalty?' She put up her hand and traced his moustache with her fingertip.

Bay nodded.

'I promise to marry you as soon as it is practical.' She smiled. 'And you won't have to sell Tipsy or disappoint the Empress. I think she would be very sorry to lose you.'

A Summons

THE INVITATION ARRIVED AFTER DINNER. THE LADIES had gone to bed and only a few of the male guests were lingering in the billiard room. This, like the rest of Melton, had been fitted out in the Gothic style, with a vast wrought-iron lamp over the table which cast a cathedral-like gloom over the proceedings. Each cue had its own carved niche against the wall, set in a row like truncated choir stalls.

The game was coming to an end. Hartopp was winning and his face was crimson under his dundrearies. Bay and Fred were making half-hearted efforts to catch up with him, but they knew they were beaten. The men had almost finished the brandy that had been left out on the butler's tray, and Hartopp made for the bell to ring for some more, but Fred put his hand on his arm.

'Don't think we can ring for reinforcements, Chicken. Gives the wrong impression.' To make amends he emptied the decanter into Chicken's glass.

'To the victor, the spoils.'

The three men were toasting Hartopp's triumph when the door opened. All three men looked round a little guiltily – they had been quite loud in their toasting – but the figure at the door was not an irate butler but a small boy. In his hand he carried a letter.

'Please, sirs, I have an urgent message.' The boy, who was no more than eleven years old, was consumed by the importance of his mission. This was his first time beyond the green baize door. His normal post was cleaning boots behind the scullery – but when the groom had arrived from Easton Neston with the message, the butler had not thought it worth his while to get dressed again as it was only for one of the young gentlemen, so he had sent the boy. The message had arrived a good half an hour before, but the boy, who was not familiar with the company side of the house, had lost his way in the dark and had blundered into a good number of dark, echoing spaces before he had found the billiard room.

'And who is the message for, boy?' Fred Baird held out his hand.

The boy hung his head. In his panicked stumblings through the dark rooms he had forgotten the name that the butler had told him. He held up the letter in answer, but Fred, who had been largely responsible for emptying the brandy decanter, was feeling playful.

'Well, which one of us three graces is the lucky recipient of the enchanted apple, eh?' he said, laughing immoderately at his own joke.

The boy had no idea what Mr Baird was talking about, but he heard the drink in the man's voice and he knew better than to answer. He continued to stand there, mute, still holding out the letter.

'Surely you can make out the letters – is there an M for the magnificent Captain Middleton here, an H for the heroic Captain Hartopp, or a B for Baird of the Borders?'

The boy shook his head and Baird, on the other side of the billiard table, shook his head too in imitation. His face looked ghostly and mad under the shade of the green light and the boy began to shake with fear. He knew how men could be when they had too much drink in them. He longed to be back beside the kitchen fire, polishing the riding boots until he could see his reflection in the leather.

'Come on, boy, the suspense is too much. Who is the lucky fellow, eh?'

The boot boy said nothing. The writing on the envelope was nothing but a black scrawl to him, as he could not read.

Baird turned to Chicken. 'In my house, a boy like that would speak when addressed by his betters. He would not skulk like a mangy cur when asked a direct question.'

Bay, who until that point had not been paying much attention to Baird's drunken posturings, heard the thin note of cruelty in Fred's voice and he turned to look at the boy. He saw the shake in the outstretched arm still holding out the letter. He put down his brandy glass and began to move round the billiard table to the door where the boy stood.

'Stop, Middleton, damn you. I have asked the boy a question and I will have an answer.'

Fred had tipped over from jocular to bellicose. Bay had seen this before in Ireland, where Baird had been notorious in the mess as a mean drunk. He carried on round the table till he was next to the boy and touched him on the shoulder. The boy's arm was rigid. Bay took the letter and found a shilling in his pocket which he put in the boy's still shaking hand, folding his fingers around the coin like an envelope. The boy stood still for a second longer and then he ran out of the room as fast as he could.

'Insolent little devil. And you, Middleton, what do you mean by interfering? I had asked the boy a question, I was waiting for an answer.' Fred was nearly shouting.

Bay looked down at his name on the letter and turned it over, and when he saw the double-headed eagle outlined on the black sealing wax, he put the letter into his waistcoat pocket.

'Most likely the boy couldn't read and he was too scared to admit it. Didn't you see how he was shaking? But in answer to your question, the letter is for me.'

But Baird's rage was escalating now. Thwarted in his persecution of the hall boy, he turned his fury on Middleton.

'And who is sending you letters in the middle of the night, Middleton? One of your lady friends? Perhaps the Empress herself, eh Chicken?' Hartopp made a noise from beneath his whiskers that sounded like laughter.

Bay smiled. 'More likely a creditor.' He turned to the door. 'And now, gentlemen, I bid you goodnight.' But Baird was not to be deflected.

'Show me the letter, Middleton. I believe it could have been for any of us.'

'But it was, in fact, for me.' Bay put his hand on the doorknob.

'So why won't you show it here? Or do you have something to hide? Don't want us to know that you are getting billets-doux delivered in the middle of the night?'

Bay knew that he should turn the handle and walk out of the room. He knew that once Fred got into one of his drunken rages, there was nothing to be done until the alcohol had subsided. But he hesitated for a moment, and in that moment Fred, with tipsy alacrity, had come round the billiard table and seized him by the shoulder.

'I will see that letter.' And he pulled it triumphantly out of Bay's waistcoat pocket.

Bay stood perfectly still. Fred started pawing the letter – 'Look at this, Hartopp, a fancy black seal. I reckon it is from the Empress. Well, I have to say, Bay, you've lost no time in securing the filly. Fine-looking woman too.' Fred described the Empress's curves with his hands and turned to Hartopp, who drunkenly imitated the same gesture. 'Damn fine looking.'

'Give me the letter, Baird,' Bay said as lightly he could.

'Why? Are you worried that I might tell Charlotte about your royal correspondence? Think it might spoil your romance?'

Fred waved the letter in front of Bay's face, his eyes glittering with drunken malice.

'She might not think so highly of you, if she knew you were getting letters from empresses at midnight.' Bay could smell the brandy on Baird's breath.

'You flatter me, Baird. This letter is undoubtedly some message concerning the meet tomorrow. The Empress thinks no more of me than one of her horses, rather less, in fact, as she is uncommonly fond of animals.'

He spoke confidently, but there was a shade of doubt in his mind. Suppose the Empress made some reference to his presumption that afternoon, perhaps the letter was a note telling him that she no longer required his services as a pilot. He felt his heart lurch and he made to take the letter from Baird, but the other man was too quick for him and darted to the other side of the room.

'Well, I think as my sister's welfare is at stake here, Middleton, it is only right that I should find out whether you are speaking the truth or not.' Baird picked up a cue and started to use it as an improvised letter opener.

Bay said very clearly, 'Don't touch that letter, Fred.'

But Fred was not listening. With one twist of the cue the seal broke. Greedily, he pulled out the letter, while Bay stood frozen. He knew that there could be nothing incriminating in the letter and yet he felt paralysed with guilt. The Empress had moved him today, he hardly knew how much; but he had come back and had proposed to Charlotte. If this letter contained some secret then he would only have himself to blame. In that moment, he knew himself to be a man without character.

Baird threw the letter across the billiard table, where it fanned out across the green felt.

'It's from the Empress's chamberlain, requesting your presence at dinner tomorrow night.' Fred paused, as if he had to adjust to this information.

'Well, you are going up in the world. One minute she's treating you like her groom, and the next moment she's asking you for dinner,' Fred said.

Bay could hear the envy in Fred's voice. He realised, too late, that Fred had never thought for a moment that there could be anything between him and the Empress. It had simply been a drunken taunt. But now Fred was resentful, not for some slight to his sister's honour, but because he had not been singled out for distinction himself. True, he was about to have an earl for a father-in-law, but he was not asked to dine with empresses. What had Middleton done to deserve such marks of distinction? Bay could see these thoughts forming themselves on the other man's flushed face. He tried to keep his own expression neutral. He had felt an unreasonable jolt of pleasure at the invitation – she had not, after all, convicted him of *lèse-majesté*. But there was another part of him that knew that this dinner was the start of something. She had noticed him as a man, just as he had seen her that afternoon, with the gun in her hand, as a woman.

It was not an invitation but a summons, though Bay knew that he should not go. He remembered Charlotte's soft, dry lips and her distress at the thought that she might have angered his patron.

He said aloud, almost without meaning to, 'I can't very well refuse.' He realised his foolishness almost as the words left his mouth, but Fred's rage was deflected in astonishment.

'You can't very well refuse? Why on earth would you? The Empress of Austria, who is also the Queen of Hungary to boot, asks you for dinner and you wonder if you should accept?' Fred turned to Hartopp and said in a falsetto voice, holding out imaginary skirts with his hands, 'Dearest Captain Hartopp, I am the Empress of Austria. Would you do me the honour of favouring me with your presence at dinner?'

Hartopp, who was relieved that the quarrel between Baird and Middleton seemed to have subsided, picked up his cue.

'Well, that would be very nice, Your Majesty, but I promised the Queen of England I would see her tonight, and there's the Empress Eugenie tomorrow. She used to be the Empress of France, you know. I might be able to accede to your most gracious request sometime next week. Would that suit?'

Baird said in tones of mock outrage, 'But don't you know that *I* am the most beautiful woman in Europe?'

Hartopp looked him up and down with lecherous scrutiny and said, 'Well, that's as maybe, Your Majesty, but the others asked first and you will just have to wait your turn.'

Bay made himself smile. He was grateful for the turn in Baird's mood. Of course he had to accept the invitation. Nobody refused an invitation from royalty, even foreign royalty. Perhaps if the invitation had not been made public, he could have written back to say that the honour was too great for someone in his relatively lowly position, but to do so now would be impossible; Baird and Hartopp would consider it swank and would begin to ask themselves why.

He gathered up the letter and stuffed it back into his pocket.

'Do you know what we need, gentlemen? Another drink. I have a flask of brandy in my room. I suggest that we put it to good use.'

As they variously walked and staggered back to the bachelors' wing, Bay felt the awkwardness of his situation. If only Charlotte had agreed to marry him right away. But she had refused, and Bay could not blame her for that. He could not tell her the real reason for his urgency, and so they had agreed to wait until the end of the hunting season before announcing their engagement. Charlotte had been quite clear: 'If we go to Fred now, he will feel bound to refuse, as he has given me so many warnings about your unsuitability. If we wait until the end of the season, then, who knows, maybe the Empress will have given you an Austrian dukedom and then he will have no reason to object to the match except on the grounds of jealousy. And if he won't consent, then I will marry you in September when I am of age and no one can stop me. Of course, I won't be able to touch my inheritance without my trustees' consent till I am twenty-five, but I am sure we will manage. It will be much easier if there is no unpleasantness.'

Bay knew that Charlotte's plan was the sensible course of action. One of the things he found so appealing about her was that strength of character; she was someone who knew her own mind. And yet he wished that he had been able to sweep her off her feet and gallop through the night to Gretna Green. It would be foolish, of course, but it would be irrevocable. There would be a scandal and he would be branded a fortune hunter and a cad, but he thought that he would not mind that so very much if he were actually married to Charlotte. Instead he had received an invitation from the Empress which he could not refuse, even if he had wanted to.

As he climbed the stairs he caught sight of his face in a mirror, and as he turned towards the looking glass the candle he was carrying bathed his face in upward light, casting strange shadows so that his eyes and teeth gleamed and he looked almost devilish. Bay had never thought of himself as a bad person before, but now he wondered what sort of person he really was: the devil in the mirror or the noble-looking young man in Charlotte's photograph?

But before he could decide, Chicken Hartopp lurched up behind him and said, 'Admiring your handsome physog, Captain Bay Middleton, the famous ladies' man?'

'I hope, if I am famous for anything, it is my riding,' said Bay evenly.

Chicken shook his vast head. 'Any man can learn to ride, but not many can make all these women fall for you. How *do* you do it, Bay? Why can't they see what a shallow feller you are?'

'Maybe that's what they like about me,' said Bay.

An Invitation

THE ROOM WAS SO DARK WHEN CHARLOTTE WOKE up, that she thought it was still the middle of the night. But then her door opened and the maid came in with her fire lighting equipment. Charlotte put on her shawl and went over to the window. There were fingers of light just appearing over the hill, turning the temple of Diana a pearly pink. Charlotte put her hand to her lips and felt the dry skin there that yesterday Bay had kissed.

She had gone to bed directly after dinner the previous night, claiming a headache. Part of her, the ignoble half, would have liked very much to have sat in the drawing room with Bay at her side, bursting with the knowledge that this famous Lothario and breaker of female hearts had proposed to Charlotte Baird, the girl with stains on her fingers. But she knew that it would be a short-lived triumph, for if Augusta suspected the truth it would lead to exactly the sort of scene that Charlotte was hoping to avoid.

It was a shame, she thought, that Bay had never flirted with Augusta. If only her future sister-in-law had been able to dismiss Bay as a beau she had toyed with and discarded, then his interest in Charlotte would be much easier to bear. The only way Bay could redeem himself was through the Empress. If he could persuade Elizabeth of Austria to notice Augusta, then anything was possible.

So she had avoided Bay's eye at dinner, only glancing at him briefly as the ladies withdrew, and was rewarded with his most brilliant smile. She had been in her bedroom for a full ten minutes before the blush had subsided.

The maid had got the fire lit at last. The new wood was crackling and spitting. A spark flew out and landed on the hearthrug and smouldered there until the maid stamped it out with her boot. Another spark landed and the smell of burning wool filled the room. The acrid smoke shocked Charlotte out of her reverie.

She plunged her face into the icy water of the hand basin. The maid protested, 'Sorry, miss, I was just going to bring you up some hot water, but I wasn't expecting you to be up and about so early.'

Charlotte felt her skin tingle. 'Sometimes cold water can be just what is needed.'

There was a noise from the corridor, a voice raised, some laughter.

'That'll be the hunting party, miss. The meet's at Greystock today, which is twenty miles off.'

Charlotte looked out of the window; the pink-tinged dawn was now overcast with black rain clouds.

'It's a long way to go, to get wet.'

At breakfast there was a letter waiting for her. It was from her godmother Lady Dunwoody. She was, she wrote, preparing for an exhibition at the Royal Photographic Society in March.

It is both a great honour and an undertaking. The Queen herself is to open the gallery, which is quite an event because, as you know, she hardly goes out these days. But then the Prince Consort was such a keen photographer. I wondered, dear Charlotte, if you would help me in my preparations. You are without question my most talented pupil. Your eye is so good. I would love to include some examples of your work in the exhibition.

Of course, you may be reluctant to leave Melton if the rumours
I hear of an understanding between you and a certain gentleman
are true, but then this is an opportunity that you could hardly avail
yourself of as a married woman.

Celia Dunwoody was her mother's cousin. She had married a wealthy baronet, Sir Alured Dunwoody, who was rather older than herself, and had used his money and influence to set up an artistic salon in her house in Holland Park. Celia Dunwoody's Thursdays were famous as a place where up-and-coming artists could meet their society patrons. In the last few years Celia had taken up photography, and her soulful tableaux of young girls dressed as Circassian slaves, or characters from the Idylls of the King, were much admired in her circle, and as her circle included everyone of taste, her reputation was assured. It was true that some of her guests had preferred Lady Dunwoody's Thursdays before they included viewings of her latest photographic compositions, but given the lavishness of her hospitality and the high quality of the lions that she attracted, these thoughts were only uttered in the privacy of the carriage going home from Holland Park.

Lady Dunwoody had offered to bring Charlotte out in London, but Fred had not been happy with idea of his sister becoming part of 'the Holland Park set'; he had heard too many stories about the kind of 'artists' that frequented the famous Thursdays. So Charlotte's debut had been overseen by her paternal aunt, Lady Lisle – whose artistic ambitions did not extend beyond the odd watercolour of the Cathedral Close. Charlotte would have very much preferred to live with Lady Dunwoody in Holland Park, where she could have spent all day in the studio or the dark room, instead of being dragged to balls by Lady Lisle. But, of course, she had not been consulted.

Charlotte was aware that she was being watched across the table by Augusta, who was clearly waiting for her moment to pounce. Augusta had not received any letters that morning. She did not like the sensation, however brief, of being less popular than her mousy sister-in-law-to-be. They were alone in the breakfast room: the men had gone hunting and the older ladies had gone to visit the wife of one of the gamekeepers, who had just had her tenth confinement. The delivery had been complicated and the details had not been thought suitable for the ears of young ladies.

Charlotte kept her head down, studying the letter, hoping that Augusta would leave her alone. But only a minute or two passed before Augusta said in her affected drawl, 'Looks like a very satisfyin' letter. You must have read it through five times at least.'

Charlotte looked up. She saw that she could not escape.

'It's from Lady Dunwoody. She is to be part of an exhibition at the Royal Photographic Society and she has asked me to go to London to help her prepare her prints.'

'The Royal Photographic Society? I never knew such a thing existed. What next, the Royal Hot Air Ballooning Society?' Augusta smirked.

'The Queen and the late Prince were very keen photographers. The Queen is going to open the exhibition herself.'

'Well, I hope Lady Dunwoody won't be too disappointed that you can't go.' Augusta's smile did not reach her eyes.

Charlotte said nothing. Until that point, she had not thought seriously of accepting. But suddenly she saw the next six weeks stretching ahead of her – full of her brother's condescension and Augusta's malice. Bay was the only reason to stay, but he would not be at the house for much longer. He and Hartopp had rented a hunting lodge in Rutland for the rest of the season. And now she had made it clear that she would not elope with him, perhaps it would be better if they did not remain under the same roof. She did not feel very confident of her power to resist him; there had been something unsettling about his urgency yesterday. Furthermore, there was the very appealing prospect that if she were to leave Melton now, it would not only confound Augusta's suspicions about her relationship with Bay, but it would also annoy her very much. Charlotte knew that her main role at Melton was to be the unmarried foil to Augusta's triumphant young bride-to-be.

So with these thoughts running through her mind, Charlotte lifted her chin and said, 'But I have no intention of disappointing her. Lady Dunwoody is my mother's cousin and she has always been extremely kind to me. As she has asked for my help I don't very well see how I can refuse it. I shall go to London tomorrow. The exhibition is in March and I am sure there is a great deal to be done. I am sure your mother will understand how I am placed.'

'I think that Mama will think it very odd, as do I. Why would you go down to London to mess about with some smelly chemicals when there is so much to be done here? Never mind the exhibition, *I* am getting married to your brother in March. Forgive me if I consider that to be rather more important.'

'But Augusta, as you have often pointed out, I know very little about the fashionable way of doing things. Why do you need me in attendance when I am clearly not qualified? Forgive me, if I would rather go somewhere I can actually be of use.'

Augusta looked at her in surprise. She had never heard Charlotte speak with such vehemence.

'And what will Captain Middleton say, I wonder, to your sudden departure? I thought you were such great friends?'

'I am sure that he will understand.'

Augusta looked puzzled for a moment, and then her eyes narrowed as she took a new tack.

'I suppose Captain Middleton is very busy with his own obligations. My maid told me that a letter came for him last night, hand delivered.' She paused for effect, but Charlotte said nothing.

'It was from the Empress, summoning him to dinner tonight. He has clearly made quite an impression on Her Majesty.' Augusta emphasised the last two words.

'How fortunate,' said Charlotte, trying to hide her surprise, 'as he is her pilot. I hope that the association will be of some use to him. It must be a good sign that she has asked him to dine with her.'

Charlotte spoke with a shade more confidence than she felt, but now she had declared her intention of going to London she was not going to allow Augusta's insinuations to derail her.

'I am not sure I would be entirely happy if Fred was having dinner with the most beautiful woman in Europe,' Augusta said.

'How fortunate then, Augusta, that the Empress did not invite him. And now, if you will excuse me, I must see to my packing.'

Charlotte swept out of the room, her cheeks pink. She knew it was a mistake to engage with Augusta, whose reserves of spitefulness were far greater than her own, but she could not resist the feeling of satisfaction that for once she had had the last word. But now she would have to go to London and leave Bay behind, or Augusta would think that she had changed her mind because the Empress had invited him to dinner.

On the Chocolate Side

A S THE FOOTMAN OPENED THE DOUBLE DOORS OF the Great Hall, Bay felt a surge of relief that he had, after all, decided to wear his dress uniform. It had meant hiring a chaise to get here, an expense he could ill afford after his losses at billiards the evening before; but as he took in the scene before him, he knew that, sartorially at least, he would do. Esterhazy and Liechtenstein were standing by an enormous carved mantelpiece, both wearing the white and gold uniform of the Austrian cavalry, their chests emblazoned with campaign medals and jewel-encrusted orders. Bay wondered how much active service they had seen. Perhaps they had been part of the imperial army that had been so roundly beaten by the Prussians three years ago. All he had was an ADC's ribbon, but he would rather have that, than a chestful of campaign medals from an infamous defeat. He was glad that he belonged to a regiment with the most splendid uniform in the British army – the Hussars were called the Cherry Pickers on account of their red trousers, ornamented with a gold stripe down the outside leg. Bay hoisted his jacket to sit at exactly the right angle on his shoulder and practically marched into the room.

Liechtenstein and Esterhazy did not look round as Bay was announced. Only a slight bristling of the gold-braided shoulders betrayed their awareness of his presence. At the other end of the room there were two women sitting on a sofa talking. Bay could barely see them across the cavernous room, but he knew at once that neither of them was the Empress. He hesitated. The two men clearly meant to snub him, and while he felt confident of a warmer reception by the ladies, he did not know quite how to cross the room to them, imagining the echo of his spurs tapping against the hard floor. In desperation he looked up as if to admire the frescoes on the ceiling. He tried to appear absorbed by the goddesses and cherubs floating above him, but he found it hard to disguise his own awkwardness. He wished now that he had had the courage to refuse the invitation. He should have stayed at Melton and spent the evening being attentive to Charlotte, who had never seemed more attractive to Bay than she did at this moment. But just as his neck was beginning to ache from his scrutiny of the ceiling, he heard the doors open and the footman announcing the Spencers.

'Middleton, what a splendid surprise!' The Earl was clearly delighted to see him. 'Glad to see that you have made yourself indispensable to the Empress.'

Middleton stiffened at the Earl's tone, but a second glance reassured him that Spencer meant nothing particular by his remark. He bowed to the Countess, who gave him a look which suggested that Bay's presence had rather devalued the occasion. She had, Bay noticed, made an unusual effort with her appearance. Her dress was made from a bright magenta silk over which she wore a slightly dingy diamond stomacher. There was a tiara in her fading blond hair. Middleton had never seen her wearing so many jewels, even when presiding over the vice-regal balls in Dublin. The gems were at odds with her weatherbeaten English looks. In her large, beringed hands she carried a fan which she tapped on her skirt like a riding crop.

Her husband, though, betrayed no such nervousness. He surveyed the Great Hall, nodded briefly to the Austrians and clapped Middleton on the shoulder.

'You didn't tell me it was the Empress who shot poor old Postlethwaite's horse. Quite the Amazon. Remarkable horsewoman, too. I don't think anyone but you could keep up with her, Middleton.'

Bay was saved from having to answer by Countess Spencer. Ignoring her husband, she said to Bay, 'Edith Crewe must be so relieved that Augusta is finally to be married. I felt such a weight lifted from my shoulders, when my Harriet was settled, and she was only twenty-two. And Baird is really quite a good match. But then I don't need to tell you that, Captain Middleton – I hear that you have quite an affection for the Baird family.'

Bay spread his hands in a gesture of submission. He knew from experience that the Countess would not be deflected. She addressed her husbands's ADCs in the same tone as she used with her dogs, and she expected the same level of obedience.

'And if you are successful, you can tell Miss Baird that I shall be happy to call upon her.'

Bay bowed again. He sensed that Charlotte might not be over-whelmed with gratitude at this sign of the Countess's favour and that thought made him glad.

'But mind you make sure of her, Captain Middleton. You can't afford to . . .' But the Countess did not finish her thought as at that moment the doors were opened and the Empress entered the room.

Bay made his deepest bow, although he did not click his heels like the Austrians. As he straightened up, he saw the Empress glance at him and then immediately look away. She was wearing a dress of green velvet that exposed her shoulders and décolletage. In her hair she wore several diamond stars, arranged randomly as if they had been sprinkled there by some divine hand.

Her naked shoulders were startlingly white against the forest green of her gown. He found himself almost shaking as she offered him her hand. As he bent over to kiss it, touching her skin with his lips, he had to fight to compose himself. Looking up, he caught her eyes for an instant, but then she had immediately moved on to greet the Spencers.

Her hand had been dry, the skin a little rough, the hands of a horsewoman. But it was something to remember, the first touch of a woman's skin; it was the delicious forerunner of so many things . . . but there he checked himself. He forced himself to think of Charlotte's small, serious face, and the way she had trembled when he had kissed her. It had been her first kiss, he felt sure.

As he stood up he saw that there was another woman following the Empress. This, Middleton realised with an unpleasant lurch of his stomach, was her sister, the ex-Queen of Naples. And for the second time that night Middleton wished himself back at Melton Hall.

He felt a fool for not guessing that this ordeal lay ahead of him. The Queen would, of course, remember the man who had refused even to meet her at the Spencer ball. It had been unwarrantably rude, Bay could see that now, and for a moment he regretted his action. The woman before him was beautiful but everything about her was a little less splendid than her sister. Her face was longer, her lips were thinner, her eyebrows were straight while her sister's rose in graceful curves. She had the same heavy mass of hair, but as she was a couple of inches shorter it seemed to dwarf her. Tonight she wore it in the same diadem of plaits as the Empress, but on her the style looked more like an imposition than a crown.

Baron Nopsca made the introduction. 'Your Majesty, may I present Captain Middleton? He has been acting as the Empress's pilot.'

Once again Bay bent to kiss the hand that was offered to him. The Queen's hand was softer than her sister's but, he noticed, slightly moist. He hoped that the Queen would pass on at once, but she was frowning at him, making an elaborate pantomime of remembering something.

'Captain Middleton, I believe I remember the name.' She looked at him directly and Bay saw that she knew precisely who he was.

'My sister tells me that you are invaluable to her. She says she can't imagine how she could have managed without you.' The Queen smiled with her mouth only. 'I told her that she was very lucky to have secured your services. The famous Captain Middleton is not to be hired as easily as a hackney carriage. He is a man who follows his own inclinations. Sisi has no idea how lucky she is.'

The Queen glanced over at her sister, who was standing now between Liechtenstein and Esterhazy, listening to some story of Spencer's.

Bay wondered if he should make some apology to the woman in front of him, but he sensed that nothing he said could make a difference. Maria would always be the runner-up, in looks, in position, in everything. Instead he said, 'I hope I will have the honour of riding out with the Empress *and* her sister.'

'That will be for my sister to decide. We may be in England, but we are all her subject to her will.'

At this, Baron Nopsca, who had been hovering at the ex-Queen's elbow, looking for a moment to interrupt this worrying conversation, stepped forward and murmured in her ear, 'May I present you to Countess Spencer, Your Majesty,' and to Bay's relief they moved on. The rest of the royal party included the ex-King, a small man with a waxed imperial, who spoke no English and who looked surprised when Nopsca described Bay to him as *'le chef d'équipe de l'impératrice'*. The King looked at Bay and shook his head, as if pondering what the world was coming to when monarchs sat down to eat with their grooms.

Bay was assigned one of the Empress's ladies-in-waiting to take in to dinner. The Baron introduced her as Countess something, but the name sounded thick and foreign to Bay and he stumbled as he repeated it.

'I apologise for my German pronunciation. The only languages I learnt at school were dead ones.'

The Countess, who was a thin woman some years older than the Empress, gave an unexpectedly charming smile.

'I will forgive you, Captain Middleton. My name is Festetics. It is not German but Hungarian, which is famously the most difficult language on earth.' She had a deep voice and spoke with a strong accent, her words coming out fitfully in little staccato gusts.

'Thank goodness then, that you speak such good English,' Bay replied.

'We Hungarians have no choice but to become linguists. We never expect people to speak Magyar. The only person I know who has learnt to speak it fluently is the Empress.' She nodded. 'Yes, the Empress is like a parrot. Sometimes when we are talking, if I am to close my eyes, I am thinking that I talk to one of my own people.'

Bay, whose knowledge of Hungary did not extend much beyond some notion of gypsy violins and Tokay wine, wondered why the Empress had bothered to learn such an esoteric tongue.

'But Captain Middleton, she is Queen of Hungary as well as Empress of Austria. And such a Queen! We Hungarians are for ever thankful that she has married the Kaiser. He is not learning Hungarian, beyond saying "My loyal subjects", but my mistress she wants to understand us. The people say that she has a Hungarian soul.'

The Countess's eyes were shining and she looked over to the Empress, who was seated in the middle of the table between Earl Spencer and her brother-in-law, the little King. As she turned her head to the Earl, the candlelight caught one of the diamond stars in her hair and the refracted sparkles danced across the table, stippling the faces of the other diners.

Bay and the Countess were seated at the end of the table, firmly below the salt as protocol dictated. Bay had not expected anything else and yet he felt uncomfortably aware of his lowly status. In the field, the difference in rank seemed irrelevant; what counted was horsemanship, and in that department he felt the equal of anyone. But here in this vast, coffered dining room, where he had nothing to recommend him but his looks and his cherry picker uniform, he felt awkward. At least he could make himself agreeable to the woman beside him.

'Are you enjoying your stay in England, Countess?'

'It seems to me that it is, how you say, a splendid country,' Bay nodded his approval of her linguistic foray, and the Countess continued, 'if you are a horse or perhaps a dog. The Empress she does not care about food, but I am not so fortunate. Even when we have visited your Queen at her palace, the food was grey like stones, and tasting very much the same way.'

Bay had to laugh at her vehemence. He gestured at his plate, at the perfectly cooked Sole Veronique.

'Not all English food is bad, Countess.'

Countess Festetics leant over to him. 'My point exactly, Captain Middleton. The chef is Hungarian. He comes here with the Empress. Of course, I have to give him the menus. The Empress, she would live on bouillon and pumpernickel if I was to permit it. You are very fortunate that I am here. Because of me you do not have to eat grey food.'

Bay smiled. 'Your presence would be a boon, Countess, whatever the menu.'

The Countess laughed. 'You are very gallant, Captain. The Empress has mentioned to me how fine a rider you are, but she did not tell me that you could also talk so . . .' she searched for the word, 'delicately.' She turned to look at Bay directly as she said this and he felt a prickle of sweat on the back of his neck.

'There hasn't been much time for conversation on our rides together. The Empress likes to ride at the front of the pack. I spend most of my time trying to keep up with her.'

'We are all trying to do that, Captain. But she likes you . . . I am glad, because when she is happy, I am happy.'

'I am not sure all the Empress's party feel the same way,' Bay said.

The Countess saw Bay glance over at Liechtenstein and Esterhazy.

'Max and Felix? No, they are not happy at all to be eating with the stable boy.' The Countess pointed at him and smiled. 'But you must remember that they are Viennese and nobody is good enough for the Viennese. And, of course, they do not like to have a rival. For three years they have been everywhere with the Empress, to Bad Ischl, to Gödöllő, and in Vienna, of course. They are a fine pair of *cavalieri serventi*. The Emperor calls them Castor and Pollux. But now the Empress is talking about you, and asking you to dinner. You have made their noses . . . crooked.'

The footmen came round with the entrée. There was no one sitting on Bay's other side, so when the Countess turned to the man on her left, he was left alone. He tried to make conversation with the woman opposite him, but as she spoke no English they could do little more than smile at each other. He took a surreptitious look at the Empress. She was, as the Countess predicted, not eating, but her wine glass was half empty and there were two spots of colour in her pale face. She turned her head and caught Bay's eye. To his surprise she called out to him.

'Captain Middleton, I should like to hear your opinion of my horses.' She gestured to Spencer. 'The Earl says you are the arbiter of these things. Are they as good as your English hunters?'

The table went silent. To be addressed like this directly was a definite sign of royal favour. Bay felt the shift in atmosphere as the other diners reassessed his status. He hesitated before saying, 'Your horses are magnificent, Ma'am. I would be proud to be seen riding any of them.'

He paused, and wondered if he should continue, but then he saw the expression on Esterhazy's face and decided he would say what he really thought.

'But a great hunter needs more than good looks. To ride out with the Quorn and be in at the kill, you need more than breeding, you need heart. I mean the kind of animal who will ride twenty miles at a gallop over open country and still be ready for more. Your horses, Ma'am, will do anything you tell them, but a great horse doesn't need telling, it will give you everything it has without you asking, and when you think there is nothing left, it will find the legs for that last jump.'

There was a moment before Liechtenstein said, 'Are you really suggesting that Her Majesty's thoroughbreds, the product of five hundred years of breeding, are inferior to the grey mare you were riding yesterday?'

'You may not like her looks, sir, but you have to admit that she covered the distance as well as any in the field,' Bay said, aware that Liechtenstein's horse had refused a gate the day before.

'And these horses, the ones with heart that you speak of, I suppose they are English.' As Liechtenstein turned his head, Bay saw the faint gleam of a duelling scar on his cheek.

'I am sure that there are horses with spirit and courage everywhere, but so far I have only found them in England.'

Liechtenstein was about to answer but the Empress broke in, 'Earl Spencer, I must have one of these English horses. Will you help me find one?'

'Middleton's the man for that, Ma'am. No better judge of horseflesh in the country.'

The Empress turned her head towards Bay. He bowed and murmured that it would be an honour. The Empress clapped her hands and turned to her brother in law, the King of Naples, and translated the exchange for him into rapid Italian. As he listened the ex-King turned to stare at Bay and shook his head again, still baffled by his presence.

The conversation around the table picked up again, and as the footmen brought round the pudding, the Countess leant over to him and said in a low voice, 'Well, Captain, you are, as they say in German, on the Empress's chocolate side — the one where everything is sweeter. It is where every courtier wants to be.'

'But I am not a courtier,' said Bay, a little too loudly.

The Countess smiled and Bay saw the glint of a gold tooth.

'Perhaps. But you are a man, I think.'

Having made her point, she carried on, 'This is a Hungarian cherry torte, Captain. Even the Empress likes this.'

Bay, who did not really care for sweet things, felt himself obliged to finish every crumb.

After dinner the Empress led the ladies out of the room, but to Bay's relief the men did not stay behind to drink port. The King of Naples left first, followed by the other men, in strict order of precedence, which meant that Bay was the last to leave the room. His face was aching from the effort of appearing agreeable. Alone for a moment in the dining room, he let out a silent scream, stretching his mouth as wide as it would go.

There was a noise behind him, a discreet clearing of the throat. Bay composed his face and turned around. Baron Nopsca was standing in the doorway, his hands clasped together in front of him.

'Captain Middleton, I have a message from the Empress.' He paused and looked down at the floor for a moment. 'Her Majesty would like you to meet her in the stables.' He delivered his message in the expressionless tone of a man who had trained himself not to react to his mistress's caprices.

Bay, though, could not hide his surprise.

'Now? She wants to meet me there now?'

'I am not precisely sure when the Empress will be joining you, but I think her intention is that you should wait for her there.'

The Chamberlain bowed from the waist in the continental manner, signifying that there would be no further conversation, and left the room as quickly as he could. Bay followed him into a corridor that appeared to lead to the servants' wing.

'Baron Nopsca!'

The Chamberlain turned round to face him. Although the corridor was dimly lit, Bay could see that the other man's face was white and sweating.

'The stables? How do I get there?'

Nopsca's face sagged with relief. 'My apologies.' He gave Bay directions, and then said, 'But it is a cold night. And it is possible you will have to wait. Her Majesty can sometimes be unpredictable. One moment, please.'

Nopsca disappeared through a door and came back a few moments later with a footman, who was carrying a decanter filled with a colourless liquid on a silver salver. He poured out a generous glass for Middleton and one for himself.

'Schnapps. In Vienna we call it the sentry's friend. It is very good at keeping out the cold.'

He raised the glass to his lips and emptied it. Bay followed suit, enjoying the hot rush of alcohol as it caught the back of his throat.

The Baron blinked and smiled faintly. 'One more, I think.'

Bay did not refuse. There was a kind of desperation about the Baron. They held their glasses aloft for a moment and the Baron said with a broader smile, 'To the Empress!' Bay repeated his words and felt the schnapps working its way down to his knees.

'Goodnight, Herr Captain, I hope that your wait will not be too long.'

On his way to the stables, Bay caught sight of his reflection in a speckled pier glass hanging in one of the Great Hall's many alcoves. He stepped towards it, unable to resist admiring the splendours of his uniform. Just as he was adjusting his cape to the requisite angle, he caught a flash of white in the corner of the mirror and heard the sound of voices. It was Liechtenstein and Esterhazy. They were speaking German in a low tone but Bay heard his own name spat out by one of them, followed by a harsh laugh. Bay did not dare turn round; he did not want the Austrians to think he had been eavesdropping. It was hard to see them in the foxed and wavy glass; the white shapes kept shifting and buckling. At one point the two white shapes merged into one as if the two men were locked in a fierce embrace. Bay squinted at the glass but it was impossible to make out exactly what was going on behind him. At last the white mass separated into two distinct shapes and he heard the sound of boots and spurs clanking up the great stone staircase. Bay felt a little unsteady, the schnapps was catching up with him. Had he really seen Castor and Pollux in a distinctly unfraternal embrace? He dismissed the idea as an alcohol-induced hallucination. He had been in the army long enough to know that such things took place in the barracks among the men, but between two officers? He brushed the thought away.

He found the stable easily. Like the house, it was a baroque confection – the bas reliefs on the ceiling were equal to the ones in the Great Hall. There were twenty or so animals in the stalls, and Bay felt calmer as he breathed in the familiar smell of horse and hay. He walked down the aisle between the stalls, wondering why the Austrians shaved their horses. He thought the barbering looked unnatural; it offended his notions of the respect due to such noble animals. But then the Austrians, he was beginning to see, cared a great deal about the surface of things – the gold braid on their uniforms, the precise order in which people of different ranks should go into dinner; even the halters around the horses' heads were made of silk rope. He thought of the impossible narrowness of the Empress's waist in her riding habit, her unrelenting carriage. She always looked immaculate, even after a long and muddy day in the field. She was a woman who cared about the way things looked, and yet she had asked to meet him here. What would Lichtenstein and Esterhazy, the ex-King of Naples and even the Emperor himself make of that?

The chestnut horse in front of him switched its tail irritably, kicking out against some unseen demon. The stable clock started to chime, it was ten o'clock already. Bay thought of the hired chaise and wondered how long he would have to wait. The excitement he had felt on receiving her summons, boosted by Nopsca's schnapps, had now began to subside into a feeling of giddy unease.

When, at last, he heard her voice behind him, Bay hesitated a moment before turning round. He wanted to see her face and yet he wondered what he would see there.

The Empress was smiling. She was wearing a velvet cloak with an ermine-trimmed hood over her evening dress. As he turned to look at her, she pushed back the hood and he saw the diamond stars, shining in the chestnut mass of her hair. Behind her was the Countess, sniffing audibly, her nose red from the cold.

'I have kept you waiting.' This was not an apology, but a statement of fact.

Bay bowed, he could think of nothing to say. The Empress turned to Countess Festetics. 'Captain Middleton must be cold. Can you ask Nopsca to bring us something warm to drink?' The Countess looked at her for a second and then left the stables.

The Empress looked around her for a moment and then waved a white hand towards the horses in their stalls.

'Do you really think I need new horses, Captain Middleton?'

Bay swallowed. 'I think, Ma'am, that you need ones that are worthy of you.'

'Worthy? But these are the best horses in Austria.'

'Perhaps, but they are still not good enough for you.' Bay moved a step towards her. 'You are the finest horsewoman I have ever seen. You should have the best.'

She moved a little to her left to stroke a horse's muzzle, and the light from one of the stable's sconces fell across her face and made the diamonds in her hair sparkle. She put her hand under the horse's mouth and let the animal nuzzle at her fingers.

'Does it matter so much? These are good horses. Perhaps I should be content with what I have.'

'Perhaps, Ma'am. We should all be content with what we have. But you deserve perfection.'

She shook her head faintly. 'You sound like a courtier, Captain Middleton.'

Bay felt the sting of this.

'But I am not flattering you for the sake of some advancement.

I speak the truth as I perceive it. If you dismiss what I say as flattery, then I am sorry for your sake, not mine.'

She looked up at this, pleased.

'Well, no one from Vienna would speak to me like that. But if you are not a courtier, then why are you here?'

Bay said very quietly, 'I think you know why.'

'Because I am the finest horsewoman you have ever seen?' she said.

'I came because you asked me to.'

She smiled. 'How very obedient. My sister would be surprised.'

Bay looked down at the straw at his feet. The two things he fancied he knew in life were horses and women. If any other woman in the world had asked to meet him in the stables, alone, at night, he would have been in no doubt as to what was expected of him. At some point he would put his hand on the woman's waist and it would begin. Here, though, any such action seemed impossible. The Empress was not like any other woman. There was her position, of course, her husband the Emperor, as well as the *cavalieri serventi*, but it was not just her rank and status that made him uncertain. He had not seen that slackening, the wide-eyed stare that told him when a woman wanted to be touched.

'Tell me something,' the Empress said. 'Why do they call you Bay?'

He looked up. 'It was was the name of a Derby winner that came in at odds of a hundred to one. After the race my friends started calling me Bay. I suppose they think I am a lucky man.'

'And are you?'

'Sometimes. With a good horse and a clear field I feel as lucky as any man in the kingdom.'

'And now? Are you lucky now, Bay Middleton?'

She was looking straight at him and Bay stared at her, searching for permission in her face for what he wanted to do. She was standing just out of arm's length. To kiss her he would need to step forward. But to move towards her now would make his intentions quite clear – if she recoiled he would not be able to pretend that he had meant nothing by his actions. He wanted to act, to end the uncertainty, to bring that cool, pale face next to his, and yet he knew that if he did, he was lost.

'Lucky and unlucky,' he said slowly.

She shook her head. 'That is a courtier's answer. I want to know, what does Bay Middleton make of his current situation?'

As she spoke, the horse behind her gave an enormous snort and flicked its tail out of the box, swiping the Empress's sleeve. She started forward in surprise and Bay put out his hand to steady her. His hand touched the smooth white skin of her shoulder and before he could think about what he was doing, he was putting his hands behind her head and pressing his mouth to hers. For a moment she was rigid and then he felt her hand on the back of his neck. Her kiss was like a sigh. Bay could smell violets, brandy and the faint musk of her hair. Her head felt heavy in his hands. Behind them the horse whinnied.

At last she pulled away and turned her head to the side. Bay could not see the expression on her face. He took one of her hands in his and said in a low, urgent voice, 'I have taken a liberty. You must forgive me. It was a moment's madness. You are so beautiful and so near. I could not resist.'

She smiled and put a finger against his lips.

'There is nothing to say . . .'

Bay saw the creases at the corner of her eyes and leant forward to kiss her again, but as he did so he heard a cough, a masculine clearing of the throat, and looking up, he saw Baron Nopsca, accompanied by the Countess, with two tankards on a salver. The

Empress saw the look on Bay's face and turned around. She did not falter.

'At last,' she said lightly. 'Poor Captain Middleton, you have been freezing to death. What have you brought, Nopsca? It smells wonderful.'

'It is called negus, Ma'am.'

Bay took the tankard that Nopsca offered him and had a sip of the spicy liquid. It was little more than tepid and Bay wondered how long the Baron had been standing there watching them. The man's face was impassive; if he had seen anything, he was too well trained to show it.

The Empress liked her negus. 'The coffee here is terrible but this is quite good. I think I shall have this every night, Nopsca.'

She turned to Bay and extended her hand. 'Thank you so much, Captain Middleton, for all your help. I am looking forward very much to riding one of your horses. I feel sure that we will get on very well together.'

'Undoubtedly, Ma'am.' Bay pressed his lips to her fingers just a little longer than he should.

'Goodnight then. Where are we hunting tomorrow?

'With the Quorn, Ma'am. The finest hunt in the three counties.'

'Then I have much look to forward to, Captain Bay Middleton.'

Bay found the way she said his full name as intimate as the kiss that preceded it. He looked to see if the others had noticed. Nopsca had already turned away but Festetics was looking straight at him. As he caught her eye, she smiled and gave him an unmistakeable wink before following her mistress out of the stable.

The Empress's Correspondence

BAY SLEPT IN THE CHAISE ON THE WAY BACK TO Melton Hall, as soundly as he did after a successful day's hunting. The chase was over for the day. There would be time for doubts tomorrow, but for now he closed his eyes, revelling in the memory of the Empress's head in his hands, his mouth upon hers.

But while he slept, the woman who was occupying his dreams was wide awake. She was standing by the window of her bedroom looking out over the snowy fields bathed in moonlight. In the corner of the room Countess Festetics was also awake. She was thinking not of love but of her bed. The Countess was exhausted but she could not retire until she was dismissed, and she knew from long experience that when her mistress was excited, she simply forgot to sleep. Festetics yawned as loudly as she dared and the Empress turned around.

'How you startled me, I had forgotten you were there.'

'Forgive me, Majesty, it has been a long day.'

'But a good one. I thought the dinner went off very well.'

Festetics smiled. 'I had a very pleasant companion, certainly. Captain Middleton is so gallant, he could almost be Hungarian.'

'You must see him ride and then you will be convinced that he was born a Magyar.'

The Empress was wearing a lace nightgown and her hair was loose over her shoulders. Her face softened with pleasure when she talked about Middleton. Festetics thought that she had not seen her mistress look so happy for years.

'He is certainly as devoted to you as any of your subjects. At dinner he praised you at every course. I think you have quite dazzled him.'

The Empress wound a great lock of hair around her hand.

'I did not expect this,' she said quietly. Festetics moved closer to her and put her hand on the other woman's.

'No one desires your happiness more than I do, Majesty. But I beg you to be careful. You know that Nopsca and I serve only you, but there are other people here who do not love you as we do.'

The Empress tossed her head and her hair shifted heavily. 'You know, Festy, I have spent all my life being careful. I have been watched and measured and judged since the age of fifteen. Observed as closely as a wild beast in a menagerie. From the moment I married I have been . . . scrutinised.' She leant forward and the hair fell around her face.

'Do you know that on the day of my wedding, my mother-in-law told me that my teeth were so crooked that when I smiled in public I should always keep my mouth closed? I didn't open my mouth for months.' She smiled then, revealing teeth that were a little crowded, the two incisors pushing out a little. They jarred with the symmetry of her features, giving the mournful perfection of her face a wolfish quality.

'But I am not scared now.' She bared her teeth at Festetics and then, seeing the alarm on her lady-in-waiting's face, she said, 'Oh, don't worry, I am not going to bite anyone. But,' her voice became serious, 'if I see a chance of happiness, even a small one, I will take it.'

The Countess bowed her head.

'My only desire is to protect you, Majesty.'

The Empress squeezed her hand. 'Yes, I know. Now go to bed. I don't need you any more tonight.'

The Countess curtsied. 'As Your Majesty wishes.' She was just at the door, thinking of the bed that awaited her at the other end of the corridor, when the Empress called after her, 'I need some writing paper, I only have a couple of sheets left and I want to write to the Emperor tonight.'

Dearest Franzl,

I have just read your letter of the 15th. You complain that I am a wretched correspondent. But you see, liebchen, I have been so busy that I really haven't had the time to write you the long letter that you so richly deserve. There has been so much to attend to here, and, of course, I have been hunting almost every day. Long hard days where we ride for hours without stopping, when I get home I am so tired that Festetics and Nopsca have to carry me to bed. I sleep so well here, I close my eyes and then, oblivion.

Tonight Maria and Ferdinand were here for dinner, with the Spencers — an English milord with a red beard and many acres and his wife, who has a red nose. Maria is happier here than she was in France but she thinks always of what she has lost. I think Ferdinand is more resigned to his lot. Of course they are still short of money; I believe that Maria relies very much on the generosity of Baron Rothschild. She is pressing me to visit the Rothschilds with her. The stables at Waddeson are, apparently, quite magnificent. Sadly my horses are quite inadequate to the hunting here. But I have a very able advisor in Captain Middleton, who has promised to find me some animals better suited to the conditions. You are always urging me to make friends among the English — I think I shall become very popular among the horse-breeding fraternity!

It was so easy to write to Franzl tonight, she felt buoyant with happiness. Sisi could not suppress a frisson of pleasure as she wrote Middleton's name for the first time. There was no need to mention him really, but she could not resist the urge to bring him into her letter, under her husband's nose. Of course Franzl would not notice; it would take a great deal more to make him look up from those stacks of boxes and feel a flicker of jealousy. But she felt that by writing down Middleton's name she had given warning.

You would be so happy to see your Sisi now. Festetics says that she has never seen me looking so well. The nervous exhaustion that kept me to my bed last summer has gone. What a fine idea this hunting has been. Of course, I miss you very much, but it is doing me so much good to be here. I think of you now poring over your boxes, and it pains me to think of you being alone, but I know you with your great generous soul would much rather that I was here and happy than in the spirits that I was in last summer. So please, dear Franzl, do not press me to give you a date for my return. I am happy here, and as you know, I have not had much happiness since the day we met all those years ago in Bad Ischl. Of course it would be the pinnacle of my happiness if you were to join me here, I think that you would enjoy the hunting enormously. Alas, I know that your devotion to duty means that you are chained to your desk, the father to your people but never perhaps the husband to your wife.

Please kiss my darling little Valerie for me. I would so much like to have her here with me, but I don't want to deprive you of your little dumpling. I know how much comfort she brings you, so I will put aside a mother's needs so that you can have her by your side.

I kiss your hands and your forehead.

your very own Sisi

She folded the letter and sealed it. When Festetics came back with the paper, she laughed and said, 'I didn't need the extra paper after all, I managed to get it all onto one sheet. But you can take the letter to be posted. And then I insist that you go to bed. You look quite fatigued. Get your rest, Festy, you mustn't get ill, as I would be simply lost without you.'

The Countess curtsied again and left the room. This time she managed to get all the way to her bedroom, and despite the tensions that the day had brought, she was asleep in minutes.

Holland Park

IT WAS ALMOST DARK WHEN THE CARRIAGE DREW UP outside the house in Holland Park. Charlotte could see the round turret of the house silhouetted against the dark blue sky, the lights from the narrow windows shining out. At this time of day, the house really did look like an enchanted castle, rising out of the dark forest of the Kensington streets. The whimsical shape was comforting to Charlotte; she felt as though she had reached not just her destination, but a place of refuge.

It had been a long journey. The night before she had stayed up as late as she could in order to catch a moment with Bay on his return from Easton Neston. Sitting in the drawing room after dinner while the gentlemen were at their port had been excruciating. Augusta was barely speaking to her and she had evidently complained about Charlotte to her mother, who had not, as she normally did, asked Charlotte to come and sit next to her by the fire. Even her aunt had been distant; Adelaide Lisle did not approve of Lady Dunwoody, and when Charlotte had told her that she was going to Holland Park the next day, the widow had dabbed her eyes and said plaintively that she had always tried to do her best by Charlotte, even if her best was clearly not good enough. Charlotte had been upset by this, until she reflected that one reason for her aunt's distress was that, as Charlotte's companion and chaperone, all her expenses were covered by the trustees of Charlotte's estate. When Charlotte assured her that she would join her in London after the exhibition, Lady Lisle became noticeably more cordial, since Charlotte's fortune would be paying for the establishment in Charles Street. Adelaide Lisle lived in fear of the day when Charlotte no longer had need of her services as a chaperone and she would be forced to return to her drafty little house in the Cathedral Close.

Charlotte had sat in the corner of the great Gothic drawing room, pretending to be engrossed in a copy of *Punch*. She looked up eagerly every time someone came in to the room, hoping against all rational expectation that Bay would come sauntering in and rescue her from social purdah. But by eleven o'clock there was still no sign of him, and when Lady Crewe announced that she was going to bed, Charlotte had no choice but to follow her.

She did not go upstairs at once, though, but lingered as long as she could in the Great Hall, peering closely at one of the pair of Canaletto scenes of the Grand Canal that an earlier Lord Crewe had brought back from the Grand Tour. She stood in front of the the dimly lit scene of boats and churches for a good five minutes until the butler appeared behind her and asked her if she required a candelabra brought up – was there something in particular she wanted to see? Charlotte realised that this was his discreet way of suggesting that the household was winding down for the night and that it was not altogether seemly for a young female guest to be scrutinising pictures in the darkness. She went up the stairs to her bedroom as slowly as she could, pausing almost at each step as if short of breath, but when she got to the gallery at the top and heard the single chime of fifteen minutes past the hour, she knew that she could not linger any more. Much as she wanted to see Bay on his return, the danger of being discovered lying in wait by Augusta or her mother was too great.

But it was vital to see Bay before she left. She had to explain to him why she was going. He could not be left to think that she was running away from him. He must be told that her feelings for him were undiminished.

As an unmarried woman of limited importance Charlotte had been given one of the lesser bedrooms, on the opposite side to the south-facing facade of the house, so she could not even watch at her window for Bay's return. She would have to send him a message asking him to meet her in the morning. Her train was an early one, but there would still be time for them to see each other before breakfast. She kept the message brief.

I am going to London tomorrow by the morning train. I will be staying with my godmother, Lady Dunwoody. I hope we can meet before I leave. Yours, CB.

She wanted to write something warmer at the end – your very own Charlotte, perhaps – but in a house as big as Melton a letter could so easily be intercepted. Although her 'understanding' with Bay was known, they were not formally engaged, and respectable young women did not arrange meetings with young men without a chaperone. Charlotte wondered how she could get the note to Bay. She was reluctant to trust a servant with it, but as his room was in the bachelor wing on the other side of the house, she could not deliver it to his door herself.

She tugged the bell pull and waited for what seemed like an age, until Grace, the pretty maid who had done her hair the night before, arrived, yawning and rubbing her eyes. She had clearly been in bed because her dress was half-unbuttoned and her hair was hanging down her back.

'I am sorry to disturb you at this hour, but I wonder if you could deliver this note to Captain Middleton.'

The maid stared at her.

'You see, I am going to London tomorrow by the early train, and I am most anxious to speak to him before I go.'

Grace shook her head. 'I am sorry, miss, but I am not allowed to go over to the bachelors' wing at night. If I was found out I would lose my position.'

Charlotte said, 'Can you give it to someone else? One of the footmen? It's very important.'

Grace seemed to consider this, and Charlotte realised that she was waiting for something.

'I am happy to give you something for your trouble.' She looked around for her reticule and took out a guinea; it was too much, she knew – she was giving herself away.

The girl's eyes widened when she saw the coin Charlotte was holding out to her.

'I'll see if I can find the hall boy, miss. He will be doing the gentlemen's boots now. It will be no trouble for him to give it to the Captain.'

'Is he reliable, the boy?'

'I would say so, miss.' But her glance flicked over to the reticule.

Charlotte took out another coin, a sixpence, and said, 'Give this to him, it's very important that Captain Middleton receives the letter.' The maid put the note and the coins in her pocket.

'You see, I don't want to leave Melton without saying goodbye to him.'

Charlotte said this as much to herself as to Grace, but the maid smiled and said, 'I understand, miss. He's a fine gentleman. I wouldn't want to leave him either without saying goodbye.'

Still smiling, she left the room, and Charlotte threw herself on the bed, her face burning. She had always been proud of the fact she was the one who observed other people's behaviour, but now she was turning into one of those people that the servants gossiped about. She was glad that she had made the decision to leave.

In the morning Charlotte was up and dressed by seven. The Great Hall was grey in the morning light and smelt of woodsmoke. It was empty apart from a maid in a brown holland apron who was cleaning out the vast fireplace. Charlotte went into the breakfast room, where the footmen were setting out chafing dishes of eggs and bacon, devilled kidneys, and kedgeree. Lord Crewe was sitting at one end of the table reading *The Times*. The rule at Melton was no conversation at breakfast; everyone ate and drank as if wrapped in individual membranes like eggs. Charlotte drank tea and ate a piece of toast while Lord Crewe dismembered a kipper with lip-smacking thoroughness. One by one the other members of the house party drifted in: only married ladies were allowed the luxury of breakfasting in their rooms. Charlotte had sat with her back to the window so she could see who came in, and she could not help but raise her head every time the door opened. But there was no sign of Bay. She heard the stable clock strike eight o'clock. It was time for her to get ready for the train.

She was standing in the hall in her bonnet waiting for the carriage to be brought round when she felt a light touch on her shoulder. She wheeled around in expectation, only to see the florid face and ginger whiskers of Chicken Hartopp.

'I am so glad I caught you, Miss Baird. Fred told me last night that you were leaving this morning. I didn't want you to leave without saying goodbye.' Hartopp took one of Charlotte's small gloved hands in his huge paw and squeezed it. 'Melton won't be the same without you, y'know. Very much hope I may call upon you in town.'

Hartopp gave her a look that she knew was intended to convey just how much he would miss her.

'Well, I am sorry to be leaving Melton, but my godmother says she really cannot manage without me. The Queen is to open the exhibition, you see, and apparently my presence is essential.' She retrieved her hand. 'Perhaps you would do me a favour, Captain Hartopp. Can you say goodbye to Captain Middleton for me? I was hoping to see him this morning, but I am running out of time.'

Hartopp nodded his great head. 'He must have had a very late night with the Empress. My room is next to his and he wasn't back when I retired for the night. Found the poor wretch of a hall boy asleep outside in the passage on account of having to deliver a message to Middleton. Sent him to bed and told him I would give it to him myself.'

Charlotte felt herself blushing. 'I am afraid the message was from me. You see, I didn't have a chance to tell him I was going away.'

'Haven't seen Middleton myself to talk to in days. Now that he is the confidant of royalty he's got no time for us less exalted beings.' Hartopp was smiling but Charlotte noticed the edge in his voice.

'Being the Empress's pilot is a great honour. I dare say it is very demanding.' Charlotte held out the challenge.

Hartopp tugged at his whiskers. Charlotte thought that rarely had she seen someone thinking so visibly. She fancied she could see his brain bulging with the effort. But his ruminations were interrupted by Fred, who came strolling down the stairs.

'So you are really off then, Mitten? Augusta is not happy with you, you know. Thinks you are deserting her in her hour of need.

Wants me to forbid you to go, but I told her it was no use. I know how much you enjoy hobnobbing with Lady Dunwoody and her aesthetic cronies. Almost as much Middleton enjoys rubbing shoulders with royalty, eh Hartopp?'

'He's quite the courtier. He'll be wearing silk stockings and knee breeches next,' said Hartopp. Both men laughed.

Charlotte did not join in. She saw that the carriage had drawn up outside the door and that the maid who was to chaperone her on the journey back to London was already sitting inside.

'I am sure you will find a way of mollifying Augusta, Fred. Goodbye, Captain Hartopp.'

She walked down the steps to the carriage, where a footman was holding the door open for her. As she climbed into the back beside the maid, she looked back at the house to where Fred and Hartopp were standing. As the carriage set off down the drive, she saw Bay come out of the house and stand between them. Hartopp said something to him and all three men laughed.

Charlotte had tried not to think about that laugh on the train to London. She did not want to see the three men standing loose and complicit on the steps. She did not want to calculate exactly when Bay had learnt that she was leaving, nor to speculate what Fred and Hartopp had said to him to stop him running down the steps to say goodbye. Had Hartopp told him about the note? Or had they been laughing about something quite different, some morsel from the night before? Whatever it had been, Charlotte felt the injustice of that laughter, and it burned at the back of her throat all day. As the carriage had drawn up outside Melton Halt, she had found herself reluctant to take the hand of the coachman waiting to hand her down; she had almost said, 'I do believe that I have changed my mind, please take me back to the house,' but somehow the words would not come. She had walked out onto the platform, half expecting another tap on the shoulder, and to turn round and see not the whiskery Hartopp but Bay. But no one had come. She had boarded the train, choosing a window seat, just in case Bay should make a last-minute appearance, but as the guard blew his whistle and the engine started, there was no sign of him. When the train pulled into St Albans thirty minutes later, Charlotte realised that she had a crick in her neck from looking backwards.

Just as the hansom cab stopped and Charlotte got out, the door to Lady Dunwoody's house flew open and a man came out walking backwards down the front steps as he called out his goodbyes to his hostess. In his haste he missed the bottom step and he fell backwards into Charlotte's unsuspecting arms. He was very tall and smelt of limes and tobacco. He was also heavy and Charlotte was almost winded by the weight of him.

'Oh my. What a situation.' The man, who was young and had an accent that Charlotte thought might be American, righted himself and turned to face her. He was wearing a cloak made out of a dark red velvet and a kind of soft hat that Charlotte had before now only seen in cartoons in *Punch*.

'Now that we have embraced, perhaps we don't need a more formal introduction. But if we are to start as we mean to go on, perhaps I should tell you my Christian name, which is Caspar, although you can call me Dearest if that's too formal.'

Charlotte found herself smiling. Caspar had a wide, freckled face and he beamed at her as if meeting her was the most delightful thing that had ever happened to him in his whole life.

'My name is Charlotte Baird, I am Lady Dunwoody's god-daughter.' She held out her hand and Caspar took it.

'It's an honour to meet you, Charlotte Baird,' Caspar said. 'Lady D talks about you all the time. You are the photographic paragon, her proudest creation. She showed me some of your plates. If we weren't practically engaged I would be quite jealous. But now that we are almost as one flesh, I am prepared to make allowance for your talents; in fact I think we will be quite a formidable team. We will take New York by storm, Charlotte Baird.'

'But would I ever get a chance to speak, Mr . . .?'

'Hewes!' Lady Dunwoody, who was standing in the doorway, broke in. 'Leave Charlotte alone, she will be exhausted after her journey and in no mood to deal with your nonsense.' She came down the steps and kissed Charlotte on the cheek. 'I am so happy to see you, my dear. Mr Hewes is very skilful in the dark room but he is so talkative!'

Caspar Hewes was not abashed. 'Oh Lady D, you may want to work in silence, but I fancy that Charlotte Baird is a conversationalist. For the dark room is not a tomb but a confessional. I think that as we labour side by side pulling out plates hither and thither, there will be chatter, there may even be confidences. Am I right?' He finished his speech by making Charlotte an extravagant bow.

'I think, Mr Hewes, that you will talk and I will listen, but I think that we will both be content.' Charlotte put her hand to her cheek, suddenly aware that there might be a smut from the train on her cheek.

'Only content? Oh Charlotte, Charlotte, what a decorous English word. You may be content but as a vulgar American I will be irradiated with happiness.'

'That's quite enough, Caspar,' Lady Dunwoody interrupted. 'Go back to wherever it is you live and we will see you in the morning. Miss Baird is not used to Americans.'

'I am not Americans, Lady D. You must not prejudice your divine goddaughter against my race. I am Caspar Hewes, late of San Francisco, California and now resident at twenty-one, Tite Street. You could travel the breadth of my fair country and never come across someone quite like me.'

'Well, that is a relief. Now do go home, won't you, or I shall be forced to shut the door in your face.' Lady Dunwoody led Charlotte up the stairs, leaving the maid to navigate the trunks and boxes.

'Very well, I will accept my banishment. Goodnight, Charlotte Baird, I look forward to entering the darkness with you tomorrow.' Caspar drew the claret folds of his cape around him and walked off down the dark street, his voluminous silhouette fading in and out of the yellow gaslights. Charlotte turned to go into the house.

'Such a particular young man,' said Lady Dunwoody. 'Talented, but so unpredictable. I never know what he is going to say or do from one moment to the next. Perhaps that is an American thing.'

'How did you meet him?'

'He came to one of my Thursdays. I noticed him at once, of course – he looks like a heron in my drawing room – and of course, his ridiculous clothes.' Celia Dunwoody was wearing a red kimono. Charlotte had seen pictures of Japanese geishas wearing this garment, but it looked rather different on Lady Dunwoody, who was tall and barrel-shaped. The kimono, which had clearly been made for a shorter person, ended mid-calf, revealing a rather un-Oriental expanse of buttoned boot. But Lady Dunwoody was not someone who was defeated by detail. She continued talking at rather than to Charlotte in her loud voice, which swooped up and down the octaves like a parrot.

'I assumed that he was one of Violet's aesthetes – you know how she likes to go about with a brace of poets – but then he announces that he is Caspar Hewes of San Francisco and that he has travelled five thousand miles because he wants to see a great photographer at work. Since then he has practically lived here, holding things, making suggestions. He is always saying, "Have you thought about doing it this way?" I don't think I have ever met anyone who asked so many questions.'

Lady Dunwoody swept Charlotte through the hall into her drawing room. 'But enough of Mr Hewes. You must take off your bonnet and I shall ring for some tea. I can't tell you how pleased I am to see you. There is so much to be done.'

That night as Charlotte went upstairs to her room in the turret, she wondered why her godmother had not mentioned Caspar Hewes in her letter. From the work she had seen in Lady Dunwoody's studio, he seemed more than capable of assisting her with the exhibition; if anything he was more skilful than she was. And yet Lady Dunwoody had been so very urgent that she should come.

Charlotte looked around the room which was furnished in the very latest aesthetic fashion. The wallpaper was festooned with peacocks and pomegranates and there was a collection of blue and white china arranged on a shelf that ran all the way around the room just above eye level. It was not a large room, but everything in it was pleasing to Charlotte. She liked the intricacy of the wallpaper and the contrast to the simple bamboo furniture. In most houses, Melton for example, Charlotte imagined herself rather like the drawings in *Alice in Wonderland*, always monstrously out of scale with her surroundings. But she was just the right size for this room.

Her trunk and cases with all her photographic equipment and plates stood in the corner of the room. Usually Charlotte unpacked her plates the moment she arrived at a new place – it was her way of asserting her own order in unfamiliar surroundings – but tonight she felt reluctant to open the leather plate case.

There was a tap on the door and Lady Dunwoody came in. She was ready for bed – the kimono had been exchanged for a paisley wrapper, and her hair was hanging down her back in a long grey plait.

'Are you comfortable, Charlotte, dear? Have you got everything you need?'

'Oh yes, Aunt Celia. It's so lovely to be here.' Lady Dunwoody's eyes swivelled round the room and came to rest on the plate case lying on the bed.

'May I have a look?'

Charlotte was minded to refuse but knew it would be useless. Lady Dunwoody always got her way.

The first plate the older woman pulled from its red velvet casing, was the tableau of the maids. She held it up to the light and examined it critically.

'Good composition.'

The next plate was the group portrait of the house party that Charlotte had taken on the steps of Melton. Lady Dunwoody peered at it. 'Goodness me, Edith Crewe has grown stout. This young lady must be your future sister-in-law – with that chin she has to be Crewe's daughter. Fred looks wonderfully smug, but he has no reason to be: the Crewes have terrible tempers. How old is the girl, twenty-four? Edith must be relieved to have got her off her hands.'

Celia Dunwoody leant forward over the plate and peered at it more closely. 'And I wonder which of these fine young gentlemen is the object of your affections, hmm? Is it this young buck with the splendid whiskers? No, I can tell from your face that he is not the one. Which leaves this elegant creature in the back row.

Can this be the famous Captain Middleton?' Aunt Celia's tone was light but she looked closely at Charlotte.

'I don't know about famous, but yes, that is Captain Middleton,' Charlotte said.

'I can hardly make him out here, do you have another picture? I feel sure that you do.'

Charlotte hesitated, there was something in her godmother's tone that made her reluctant to continue, but Lady Dunwoody was waiting. She reached over and pulled out the plate she had taken of Bay and Tipsy in the Melton stables. He was looking straight ahead, his profile aligned perfectly with that of his horse. ·

'What a handsome animal. And Captain Middleton too is clearly a fine specimen.' She laughed when she saw the expression on Charlotte's face. 'I don't get many cavalry officers at my Thursdays. I had forgotten how splendid they are. Such good subjects for a photograph.'

'Not all cavalry officers are like Captain Middleton, Aunt,' Charlotte said, taking the plate from her and putting it back smartly into its case.

'Oh, I can believe that. I saw him once at the Airlie ball, in the days when I used to go to balls. I believe he was making himself most agreeable to the younger ladies. He danced with Blanche Hozier three times; so fortunate that her husband wasn't there. Hozier is exactly the sort of man who enjoys a scene.' She paused and looked at Charlotte to see how she was reacting.

Charlotte said slowly, 'I understand that Captain Middleton has a past, Aunt Celia. But I have also met gentlemen without pasts, and I prefer Captain Middleton. And he prefers me.'

'Well, of course he does. You would make any man happy, not to mention your delightful fortune.' Lady Dunwoody laid her hand on Charlotte's and leant over so that Charlotte could feel her warm, clove-scented breath.

'I have nothing against Captain Middleton. I can see that he is exactly the sort of man that a girl would fancy herself in love with.' She saw the expression on Charlotte's face. 'He may be your first love, my dear, but that doesn't mean he will be your last.' She patted Charlotte's hand and stood up.

'Now I must leave you to get some rest. You will need all your reserves of strength to handle Mr Hewes in the morning. I guarantee that he will be here before you have finished your breakfast.'

Charlotte lay down in the narrow brass bed. She had unpacked everything, and now there was nothing to be done except sleep. As she closed her eyes she saw Bay standing on the steps at Melton, laughing. She turned over and pressed her face into the mattress, pulling the pillow over her head, trying to stifle her fears. She breathed in the downy sweetness of the feather bed and forced her thoughts elsewhere until at last they rested on the ungainly figure of Caspar Hewes loping along the pavement in a puddle of red velvet. The contrast with Bay's precise silhouette was so absurd that she almost smiled before falling asleep.

Forest Green

BAY WAS HAVING TROUBLE WITH HIS BOOTS. HE LIKED them polished to a high shine, so at the beginning of the day, at least, he could see the red gleam of his coat reflected in the surface. Normally he left them outside his room at night, matt with grime and dust, and in the morning they were miraculously restored to shine and sparkle. But this morning his boots were dull. The boot boy had cleaned off the mud but had not spent the twenty minutes or so that was needed to bring the boots up to their full lustre. Bay was irritated. This was the boy he had protected from Fred's drunken malice that night in the smoking room – it piqued him that this chivalrous act had not been repaid by devoted service. He attempted to polish them himself with the wrong side of his chamois leather waistcoat, but he could not coax a gleam from the cracked leather. He could ring the bell and summon the wretched boy, but then he would miss breakfast, and he was anxious to see Charlotte before setting off for the hunt.

He had come back to Melton the night before in a state of elation – the only time in his life he had come close to feeling like this before was when he had won the Viceroy's Steeplechase in Dublin. He had ridden then with skill and daring that he had not known he possessed. He had taken the outside track, gambling that his horse could outpace the others and that he would not be caught in the melee of riders and men that followed every jump. The risk had paid off; he had jumped free and clear and had finished first. Last night he had been boxed in by those Austrian flunkeys and that sour sister, but he had outmanoeuvred them; he had sailed over all the obstacles and had reached his prize. He had risked everything and he had won again.

Bay did not reflect for a moment that his victory might have been engineered. It did not occur to him that the impediments to his progress had been deftly swept away, that he had been positioned so carefully before the last fence that he could only leap in one direction. Nor did he remember in his triumph last night, what had happened after the victory in Dublin. Agnes, the chestnut mare that had carried him so gallantly, had collapsed afterwards. Her heart had failed her. Bay had cried then. Even now his eyes would fill with tears when he remembered the way that Agnes's legs had simply crumpled beneath her. She had been his finest horse and the race had killed her.

Bay was thinking of Agnes this morning. He could not escape the image of the chestnut mare's crumpled body as he rubbed at the parched leather of his boots. He threw away the chamois leather. The boots would have to do. He must find Charlotte before he set out. He needed to see her small, anxious face.

He pulled the boots on; they were three years old at least and the leather had learnt the contours of his feet precisely. He could ride all day in them and never feel their grip. Most men had several pairs, but Bay had never found any that were as perfect as these, so he wore them every day.

He set off down the long narrow corridor of the bachelors' wing with its narrow oilcloth covering. As he reached the main part of the house, the floor covering grew progressively softer and more luxurious. By the time he reached the main staircase he was walking on fine red broadloom Wilton woven with motifs of gryphons and fleur-de-lis in the best Gothic style.

Bay put his head around the breakfast-room door, looking for Charlotte, but he could only see Augusta and her father eating in the kipper-scented silence. Walking back across the Great Hall he saw that the huge, studded oak door was open onto the porte cochère. He looked out of the window and saw Fred and Chicken standing on the steps. As he joined them outside, he saw a carriage setting off smartly down the drive.

Fred saw him first, and greeted him with a mock obeisance. 'It is Sir Lancelot himself. Surprised to see you here, Middleton. Don't you have royal duties to attend to?'

'If you mean eating cold soup at the end of the table with only an old Hungarian governess with a beard to talk to and those Austrian popinjays sneering across their moustaches at me, then I am quite prepared to join the Republic.' Bay felt a moment's disloyalty to the charming Countess Festetics, but he had to diffuse the envy that he could see on Fred's face.

'What a disappointment. We thought that you would come back with the Order of the Golden Fleece at the very least.'

Bay shrugged. 'The only royal decoration I have is this catch on my sleeve where the Empress's spur caught me when I was helping her onto her horse. Not the highest order of chivalry exactly.' He laughed and Fred and Chicken joined in. This was the laugh that Charlotte had seen as she looked back out of the carriage window and saw the three men together on the steps.

Encouraged by the laughter, Bay went further. 'Do you remember the Queen of Naples, Chicken? The one who asked me to be her pilot at the Spencer ball? And I turned her down. Well, she was there last night and not at all happy to see Bay Middleton. Of course, she is the Empress's sister. So I suspect my days as the imperial pilot are numbered.'

Fred looked rather pleased by this admission and Chicken clapped Bay on the back. 'Never mind, old man, we plebs will stand by you. Never thought you were cut out be a courtier.'

'No indeed. Don't have the knees for it, or the stomach.' Bay turned to Fred. 'I was hoping to speak to your sister. Have you seen her this morning?'

Fred and Chicken looked at each other, and Bay saw something pass between them that he did not understand.

'You've just missed her,' Hartopp said. 'We were seeing her off. Shame you didn't wake up a bit earlier. But I suppose you must be exhausted after your royal visit.'

Bay saw the look of pleasure on their faces. They were enjoying his ignorance. Fred would welcome any setback to Bay becoming his brother-in-law and Chicken Hartopp resented Bay's success with Charlotte. He was torn between his desire to know where Charlotte had gone and why, and his reluctance to admit that she had left without letting him know. He felt his hands grow clammy despite the chill of the morning. Could Charlotte have somehow found out about the scene in the stable? But that was impossible. Besides, in this bright morning air he himself was having difficulty in believing in the events of last night.

He tried to keep the smile on his face, but without success.

'Oh dear, Bay, it looks like you have fallen out with all your lady friends,' said Chicken, grinning broadly. 'You must be losing your touch. Stick to horses, that's my advice. You know where you are with a horse.'

'Well, you should know, Chicken old boy.'

Bay could not resist the retort, but regretted it when he saw the flush creep up behind Hartopp's dundrearies.

The three men stood in silence for a moment until Fred spoke. 'Well, I am going down to the stables. Morning prayers are just about to start and I don't want to be caught by Lady Crewe. Yesterday she made me read the collect for the day, and then told me off for going too fast.' He set off down the steps, followed by Hartopp. Bay could see that the back of Hartopp's neck was dark red.

Bay hesitated for a moment. He needed to go to the stables too, but he did not want to encounter Fred and Hartopp again so soon. He went back into the house, thinking he might find a cigar in the smoking room, but he was intercepted by Augusta so neatly that she might have been waiting for him.

'Did you have a pleasant evening, Captain Middleton? We missed you here, of course, but I am quite sure you didn't miss us.'

Bay bowed stiffly. 'It was a big party, certainly.'

'Oh come, you can do better than that. I think if you desert your friends for the charms of royalty, the least you can do is to come back prepared to recount every last detail.'

'Then I am bound to disappoint you, Lady Augusta. If you wanted me to describe the Empress's horses I could do a creditable job, but when it comes to dresses and jewels you are going to find me sadly deficient.'

'But I thought you had such an eye for the ladies, Captain Middleton. What did the Empress look like in her evening clothes? Was she very splendid? She is a grandmother, after all, so she probably looks better by candlelight.'

'I think all women look better by candlelight, don't you?' Bay said.

But Augusta was not to be deflected. 'Did you see her pet monkey? My maid told me that all the servants at Easton Neston are giving in their notice because the animal is allowed to go round biting people.'

'I saw royalty, but no monkeys, I'm afraid.'

'Well, I think you are very dull. You must have seen something worth repeating.'

'Could you possibly entertain the notion that I might well have seen something worth repeating, as you put it, but that I might prefer to be dull than to be indiscreet?'

Augusta narrowed her pale blue eyes in disbelief. 'Goodness me, how very pompous you are, Captain Middleton. I had no idea you were so attached to the Empress.'

'Perhaps I have a weakness for grandmothers,' Bay said. He took out his pocket watch. 'Is that the time already? Will you excuse me? I don't want to keep the Empress waiting.'

'No, that would never do. How lucky she is to have such a devoted and loyal servant.'

Bay paused. He should, of course, have asked Augusta where Charlotte had gone, but he knew that she would enjoy the fact that Charlotte had left without telling him even more than Fred and Hartopp had done. But it would be foolish to antagonise her completely.

'Perhaps it wouldn't be betraying a confidence to say that the Empress was wearing a green dress and she had some diamond ornaments in her hair. Her sister, the Queen of Naples, was in red.'

'What kind of green?' Augusta said.

'Oh, very dark, the colour of a Scotch pine. The combination of the diamond stars against the dark brown hair and the green put me in mind of a forest at night.'

'A forest at night? Captain Middleton, you are quite the poet. I now have a very vivid picture of your dinner. You must be sure to tell Charlotte. It is the sort of detail we young ladies relish.'

Middleton realised that he had said too much. But he could at least find out where Charlotte had gone.

'I was hoping to see Miss Baird this morning, but I was too late. Her carriage was leaving, just as I arrived.'

'She didn't wait to say goodbye? I am surprised.' Augusta opened her eyes wide. 'I thought you were such good friends. Do you mean she went off without a word?'

Bay said nothing and Augusta continued, her eyes shining, 'I can understand her not wanting to say goodbye to me. She knows I am excessively annoyed with her for deserting me on the eve of my wedding. But you? You must have blotted your copybook, Captain Middleton.' She put a finger to her forehead. 'I wonder what you could have done to upset her? Surely she can't resent your having dinner with the Empress in her forest green dress? What a shame you were back so late last night, as I remember that Charlotte was quite the last lady to retire. The butler found her wandering the Great Hall at midnight pretending to look at the Canalettos.'

Bay said, as evenly as he could, 'Do you know where she has gone? I should like to write to her.'

'I wonder if I should tell you though, Captain Middleton?' Augusta put her head on one side. 'As the lady has left without saying goodbye, it may be that she doesn't want any further communication from you.'

Bay found himself clenching his fists and put them behind his back.

'I find that hard to believe but I won't ask you to betray a confidence. Good morning, Lady Augusta.'

He turned away from her and made his way towards the stables, kicking the paving stones as he walked. He was so full of rage that he took no account of the damage he was inflicting on his favourite boots. He knew that Augusta had been toying with him and that with some cajoling he would have found out where Charlotte had gone, but he could not bear to give her the satisfaction. He was angry with Fred and Hartopp, angry with Augusta and even with Charlotte. Why had she gone away without letting him know? There was probably an innocent enough explanation but still he was angry. He had been quite ready to run away with her, and she had persuaded him that they must wait, and that he should cultivate the Empress to boot. He had merely been doing what she had asked him. It would almost be fair to say that the scene in the stables had been Charlotte's doing.

He would not have been there alone with the Empress if Charlotte had agreed to elope with him. And now, just when he needed to see her, she had disappeared.

Bay had worked himself up quite successfully by the time he reached the stables. Tipsy was waiting for him all tacked up. But as he patted his horse's nose and rubbed her flank in greeting, he remembered the photograph that Charlotte had taken of the two of them in this very spot, and his indignation faltered. He swung up himself up into the saddle and urged Tipsy into a gallop. It made no sense to tire the horse so early in the day, but he needed to shake himself out of his mood.

It had not been a successful morning. Now he had to meet the Empress and his boots were dull.

Part Two

The Quorn

IT WAS THE FIRST FINE DAY OF THE HUNTING SEASON. The snow had melted at last. The sky was blue and clear and there was no wind. The members of the Quorn expected no less. They would hunt in any conditions, of course, but it was only fitting that for the biggest meet of the year the weather should be perfect. The God they worshipped in their parish churches on Sunday was undoubtedly a Quorn man, who understood the importance of a good clear run. The railway companies, too, understood the importance of the day ahead and had laid on special trains from London, packed with men and the odd woman who looked forward to a day out with the Quorn all year. The thought of riding to hounds across the trim fields of Leicestershire, their hearts pounding, their muscles straining to be in at the kill, was the talisman they touched in dreary barristers' chambers, or the innermost confines of the Foreign Office, or the committee organising the refreshments for the Lady Mackinnon's *tableaux vivants* in aid of Bulgarian orphans. This already splendid sporting occasion was made all the more piquant by the presence of royalty. The Prince of Wales was hunting with the Quorn this season, and now the papers were full of the equestrian exploits of the Austrian Empress. The idea of a galloping queen was peculiar and splendid to the minds of the passengers on the special trains, so far removed from the image of their own queen, a tiny figure shrouded in black who had kept to the same mournful pace since her husband's death fifteen years earlier. If some of the travellers felt the peculiarity of the wife of one of the most powerful men in Europe laying aside her duties as a wife and sovereign to chase foxes in a foreign country, they did not give the thought much room – this was the Quorn, after all.

Perhaps the only person on the hunting train that morning who did not understand that the claims of the Quorn were paramount, was the Austrian Ambassador, who received regular press reports from Vienna where journalists were less than sympathetic to an absent empress who preferred riding to hounds in a Protestant country than doing her imperial duty. But while he read these reports and in his heart agreed with them, he knew better than to mention his misgivings to the Empress. Her sense of the obligations of her position was, he had discovered, idiosyncratic. She had been in the country for some weeks now and had not yet paid a call on Queen Victoria. When he had suggested, on her arrival in London, that this visit might be politic, she had thrown nuts to that vile little monkey of hers and said that she thought that Queen Victoria did not like her and would be relieved not to have to entertain her. He had tried writing to the Emperor to impress upon him how important it was for the Empress to observe the niceties of royal etiquette, pointing out that there had been several hints dropped by Foreign Office ministers which made it clear that Victoria was 'surprised' that the Empress had not yet called on her. But the Emperor had reproached him for his insensitivity, writing that 'The Empress is travelling incognito to recover her health and strength; her well-being is as you know infinitely precious to me, and I am determined that she must be left in peace until such time that she is sufficiently restored to take up her duties again. I do not wish to sacrifice the well-being of my wife on the altar of diplomacy.' The Ambassador could not help reflecting that a woman who rode to hounds nearly every day was hardly the invalid, broken in mind and body, that the Emperor referred to in his letter.

The Ambassador was enjoying his posting to London – the sport was excellent and he was enjoying a special friendship with Lady Hertford. He did not at all want to be summoned back to Vienna in disgrace, and yet he feared that was exactly what would happen if reports appeared in the British press suggesting that the Austrian Empress was deliberately avoiding Queen Victoria. The Ambassador had been sufficiently perturbed by a conversation he had had with the editor of the *Morning Post* at one of Lady Hertford's drawing rooms to make this journey up to Leicestershire today. The editor had seemed remarkably well informed about the Empress's movements, which suggested that he had been briefed by someone either from the Foreign Office or, worse still, from the court itself. Either way it was a warning – the Queen was not happy and she was letting her displeasure be known. The Ambassador was on the train, not for the sport – although he appreciated the charms of the Quorn – but to persuade his empress to do her royal duty. He was not at all confident of success.

In the crowd gathered outside Quorndon Hall, the glorified kennel that gave its name to the hunt, the Empress was unmistakeable. She sat ramrod straight on her chestnut hunter, with the rest of the hunt arranged in a respectful semicircle around her. She was talking to another rider, who the Ambassador suspected from his girth and the relaxed set of the shoulders, could only be the Prince of Wales. The Ambassador sighed. His mission had just become considerably harder. If the Empress was to ride out with the Prince of Wales today then she would undoubtedly think that she had fulfilled her obligations to the British royal family. But as the Ambassador knew, an audience, or even a day's hunting, with the son was no substitute for a formal audience with the mother. Indeed, if, or rather when, the Queen heard of the day's events, she would fancy herself doubly wronged. Although Victoria was still a semi-recluse, she was not entirely grateful for her son's efforts to keep the monarchy before the public and was sensitive to the idea that his popularity might actually eclipse hers. If the Empress of Austria was seen to be hunting with the Prince of Wales before calling on the Sovereign, then what had been merely a worrying situation would turn into a full-blown diplomatic incident. He must try and talk to the Empress before the hunt set off. The Ambassador knew that as soon as the Empress was in the field he had no chance of catching her.

The Prince of Wales was in the middle of a story. The Ambassador took advantage of the laughter that always followed a royal anecdote, to put himself in the Empress's eyeline. She saw him, frowned and pulled on the reins of her horse as if to move off, but before she could get away the Prince of Wales called out to him, 'Good day to you, Karolyi, so you have come to try the delights of the Quorn as well? Her Majesty is quite the toast of the Shires.'

Karolyi bowed as graciously as he could on horseback. 'I am sorry to say that I cannot hope to represent my country in the field as nobly as the Empress.'

The Empress gave him a brief nod, acknowledging that this was no more than the truth. She turned to the Prince.

'It is such a pity that I cannot persuade the Emperor to join me. He is a magnificent horseman and I know he would enjoy the hunting here as much as I do, but he claims that the country cannot spare him.'

'We must be thankful that he can spare you, to show us how the

Austrians ride.' The Prince stroked his moustache with one gloved hand, as if to show his appreciation of the Emperor's gesture.

'Well, I hope one day you will come to Gödöllő, our estate outside Budapest. That is where I like to ride when I am at home. We don't have the ditches and fences you have here, but you can gallop for miles without stopping.'

'What a prospect. I should like nothing better. My country might be able to spare me for an unchecked gallop across the Hungarian plains, I think.' The Prince of Wales shrugged and then, gathering himself, he said, 'But now, my dear Empress, I must pay my respects to the Master or I suspect we will never set off today.'

Seeing his opportunity, Karolyi brought his horse as close to the Empress as he dared.

'I am so pleased to see Your Majesty looking so well. It seems that the English air agrees with you.'

Although Karolyi's words were automatic, the compliments of a professional courtier, they were for once completely truthful. The Empress did look well. There were pink tones in her pale cheeks and the whites of her eyes were clear. Karolyi was used to seeing her in Vienna where her usual expression was one of simmering boredom, but here she looked as if there was nowhere else she would rather be.

'Yes, I have to say that I am happy here.' As if to prove her point she smiled, and Karolyi, who had never seen her smile before, began to wish that he had not come on this self-appointed errand. But he could see that the hounds were being brought out of the kennels and the huntsmen were beginning to assemble. He would have to say his piece.

'Majesty, I wondered if you had given some thought as to when you might visit the Queen. I know that you are here unofficially, but I fear that she will take offence if you do not call on her soon. Especially now that you have met the Prince of Wales. It would be very unfortunate if the British press was to make some comment. The newspapers here can be quite outspoken.'

Karolyi braced himself for the reproof, but to his surprise the Empress's smile did not waver. She looked not at him but over his shoulder, as if she were looking for someone.

'Poor Karolyi, you worry too much. I promise I shall go and see the Queen. In fact I shall go on Sunday, as there is no hunting then. Please make the arrangements. You are quite right, I cannot put it off any longer.'

The Ambassador almost fell off his horse in surprise. The last thing he had expected to encounter was smiling acquiescence. Clearly the English air agreed with Her Majesty very much indeed.

'Of course, the Queen does not normally receive visitors on a Sunday but I am sure she will make an exception to see you, Majesty.'

But the Empress was not listening. She had seen someone over his shoulder who clearly interested her more. Karolyi turned to see a young man approaching whose hair and moustache were about the same shade as the Ambassador's bay gelding. The Empress raised a hand in greeting.

'Bay Middleton, I was beginning to think you were not coming.'

She turned to Karolyi. 'Count Karolyi, may I present Captain Middleton, my pilot. But for him I would probably be lying at the bottom of some Leicestershire ditch.'

Middleton bowed to the Ambassador. 'Is this your first time with the Quorn, Count? Best hunting in this part of the country, but don't try to keep up with the Empress. She rides like a woman possessed.'

Karolyi glanced at the Empress. Middleton's remark struck him as over-familiar. In Vienna he could not imagine anyone talking about the royal family in such a way in their presence. But in England, evidently, things were done differently. This man was clearly not a groom and yet he had no title. Karolyi noted the fact that the Empress had called the man by his curious first name. That too would never have happened in Vienna. He cast about in his memory for what he knew about Captain Middleton. It was a name that had certainly been gossiped about when he had first arrived in London.

'I have had the pleasure of seeing the Empress at the Spanish riding school in Vienna. No Austrian would ever dream of keeping up with her.'

'Well, it is lucky for me, then, that I have an English pilot,' said the Empress and again she smiled.

Karolyi saw that the smile was intended for Middleton and his courtier's sensibilities told him that his presence was no longer required. But he decided to linger. He was interested in the frisson he had detected between the Empress and this young man

'Very fortunate indeed. I am sure that we Austrians are all grateful to Captain Middleton for keeping our finest ornament safe from harm.'

Middleton smiled. 'I am doing my best, but the Empress is a true sportswoman. She puts the thrill of the chase before her own safety.'

There was a sudden clamour from the hounds, who had picked up the scent. The Empress pulled at her horse's reins.

'We must be off.' She nodded to Karolyi, a clear dismissal.

The Ambassador again attempted a bow. 'Your Majesty can leave all the arrangements with the Queen to me.' The Empress flinched; she had clearly forgotten already her promise, but the bugles were sounding now and she was anxious to be gone.

'Thank you, Karolyi, on Sunday, yes?' Then she and Middleton were off, picking up speed as they joined the gaudy pack of riders and hounds that swarmed across the hillside opposite. He watched as the two figures, the Empress in dark blue, Bay in red, began to cleave their way through the mass of riders. As the hunt approached a hedge, the hounds began to fight their way across it – finding a hole in it and pouring through in a quivering, excited mass. The riders started to move down the field, looking for an easier place to cross, but the Empress and Middleton did not go with them. Karolyi gasped as he saw the Empress, without even breaking her horse's stride, go straight at the hedge. For a moment he thought that she had misjudged it and he had a sudden vision of standing in the Emperor's study in the Hofburg trying to describe to him the precise moment at which his wife had fallen from her horse and broken her neck; but then Middleton was beside her, urging her horse on with his own, and miraculously both horses cleared the hedge at the same time. The Ambassador held his breath as they disappeared from view but then he looked up and he could see them again, the blue and red figures distant specks now, charging up the hill after the hounds.

Karolyi dug his heels into his horse's sides and prepared to join the gaggle of latecomers, mostly 'Cits' from London who had decided to take full advantage of the hunt breakfast. There were some ladies too, who were sitting in carriages ranged around the grounds following the progress of the hunt through their opera glasses. Karolyi was just about to join the riders when he saw that one of the ladies was Countess Festetics, who was his cousin on his mother's side and an old dancing partner. He trotted over to her, but she was so engrossed in following the hunt through her binoculars that she did not notice him. Finally he called out to her in Hungarian and she turned immediately.

'Ah Bela, how lovely to see you. Have you come for the hunting?'

Karolyi jumped down from his horse and went to kiss the Countess, twice on both cheeks as was the Hungarian custom.

'I came to talk to the Empress. It seemed to be the only way to see her. Your vague little notes never actually contained an invitation.'

Festy shook her head. 'I know, Bela, and I am sorry. But you know how she is when she doesn't want to do something. She just shakes her head and says, put him off. I have tried to make her listen but she only hears me when she wants to.'

'Poor Festy, Her Majesty is very lucky to have you at her side.'

'No, Bela, I feel privileged to serve her in whatever way I can.' The little countess gave him a fierce look. 'I know that sometimes to other people she can seem . . . difficult. But I know her kindness and her nobility of spirit.'

She tilted her chin at him as if daring him to defy her.

Karolyi laughed.

'As I said before, Cousin, she is very lucky to have you at her side. But today she has not been difficult at all. I came to ask when she would visit the English Queen, and she said very sweetly that she would go on Sunday and please could I arrange it. I was surprised to find her so amenable.'

Looking closely at the Countess's face to gauge her reaction he continued, 'Her visit to England seems to be agreeing with her. In fact I have not seen her look so well and in such fine spirits for a long time. Not since the coronation in Budapest, I think. I wonder what it is about England that suits her so well?'

The Countess shook her head. 'Bela, Bela, you know me better than that. I will not gossip about the Empress to you or anyone else. You should rejoice as I do that she is in such good spirits.'

Karolyi took her reproof with a smile. 'Indeed I do. But I have to say that I worry about the hunting. She is perhaps too fearless. I thought just now that she must break her neck at that first hedge.'

'Oh, I know. Every time she goes out I am sick with worry. Today

I had to come and see for myself; somehow that is better than imagining all kinds of accidents at home.' She sighed. 'Sometimes I think that she is really trying to kill herself.'

Karolyi shrugged. 'Yet she has everything to live for. Her husband adores her and lets her do anything she wants. She is still beautiful; in fact I would say she is as lovely now as she has ever been, lovelier even.'

The Countess sighed again. 'It's true. She is still beautiful, but she can't see it. All she sees when she looks in the mirror are the lines and the wrinkles.' She picked up her field glasses and scanned the horizon, but by now the Empress and her escort had vanished from view. She turned back to the Count.

'It is such a waste. She has all the gifts – she speaks six languages fluently, she writes poetry. I sometimes think her mind is like a museum full of great treasures, unseen and unused. If only she had some great cause, some purpose that would occupy her completely – she could do great things.'

'She is an empress, there is no greater position. And she has every opportunity to do good at home, but instead she chooses to come to England and hunt,' Karolyi said.

'I don't mean opening hospitals and giving alms to orphans, Bela, I mean a cause – something for her to believe in. Look how much she did for Hungary. Do you think that Franz Joseph would ever have been crowned King in Budapest without her? I will always be grateful to her for that. But now that time has passed and she has no cause to fight for.'

Karolyi smiled. 'She has the Quorn . . .'

'Exactly. But I wish there was something else.' There was a pause.

'And how are the Empress's *cavalieri serventi*, Castor and Pollux?' Karolyi asked. 'I don't think I have seen them this morning.'

'They are . . . they are indisposed. The Empress made it clear that she wanted to hunt alone.'

'Apart from the gallant Captain Middleton, of course.'

'Apart from him.' The Countess pressed her lips together.

'Her Majesty was kind enough to present him to me. I am glad that she has such an –' Karolyi paused for a moment, ostentatiously looking for the right word, 'such an *able* escort. Captain Middleton is famous for his horsemanship, I believe.'

'He was recommended to Her Majesty by the English Lord with the red hair, Spencer. The Queen of Naples was furious as she wanted him for herself and he refused her.'

'So he is ambitious, then? Why ride with a mere queen, when there is an empress on offer?'

'Ambitious? No, I don't think so. He is not a courtier and he is definitely not a spy. You don't need to worry on that score, Bela.'

'But you have another concern? Captain Middleton has a reputation for more than horsemanship, I hear. He is very popular among the ladies, but not so much with their husbands.' Karolyi had remembered where he had heard Middleton's name before. There had been some tendresse with a married woman, who had left in the middle of the season to join her husband in the country. The lady – what was her name? Blanche, or something like that – had not been seen in town for a while; there had been an addition to the family, which fortunately had been a daughter. The provenance of daughters could stand a little vagueness.

'He is a handsome young man in uniform, why would any husband like him?' said the Countess with a shrug.

Karolyi knew better than to press the Countess any further. She was not a woman who could be flattered into indiscretion. An Austrian lady-in-waiting would have told him everything about the Empress and Captain Middleton, and more, but Countess Festetics was

Hungarian and she felt that it was almost her patriotic duty to resist the swirling gossip and jockeying for position that characterised the Viennese court.

There was a clamour from behind them and the hounds began to pour over the brow of the hill on the other side of the Manor. The Countess picked up her glasses. Realising that the conversation was over, the Ambassador decided that he might as well have his day out with the Quorn and he took up his horse's reins.

'Goodbye, Cousin, I am glad to have seen you. It is so nice to speak Hungarian again. I feel quite rusty.'

'I am lucky, the Empress always talks to me in Magyar, she is very proud of her fluency.'

'And how fortunate that she speaks such good English as well. I assume Captain Middleton does not speak Hungarian, or even German?'

The Countess laughed. 'Enough, Bela, enough. Go away and chase your fox. The exercise will do you good.'

The Ambassador accepted his dismissal. Even though the Countess had told him nothing, as a true diplomat he had gleaned all he needed to know.

Falling

THERE IS A MOMENT TOWARDS THE END OF A DAY'S
hunting when the light begins to fail and even the most
sure-footed horse begins to stumble; it is a time when hedges loom
ominously in the winter light and muscles are cramped from long
hours spent in the saddle. After a couple of falls at the end of the
last season, Bay had learnt to recognise that sudden waning of his
strength, the point at which his mind no longer knew the limits
of his body. It was the first sign that, at thirty, he was no longer as
physically indomitable as he had been at twenty-one. He was a
more skilful rider than he had been then, so his form had been
unaffected but he knew the decline had begun. For a while Bay
had mourned the notion that life would only get better. But today
there were no regrets. The sun had shone and the fox had eluded
them for three hours, making it one of the best runs of Bay's
hunting career. He found himself hoping that this particular animal
might evade the hounds in the end; it deserved some reward for
having given them such glorious sport.

The hounds were careering across a ploughed field towards a
small copse. He looked across at the Empress, who was riding
alongside him; her habit was splashed with mud and a loop of hair
had come unpinned and was flapping against her back like a noose.

But her back was as straight as ever and she sat so lightly on her horse that she seemed, to Bay, to hover in the saddle. They had barely spoken that day, the pace had been so fast, but every time he caught her eye Bay felt the thrill of the connection between them. All the anxieties of the morning had been pummelled away by the relentless pursuit of the fox. Now he felt nothing but an intense joy in the moment, hurtling across the Leicestershire earth with the Empress at his side.

They reached the copse. The question was whether to wait to see if the hounds ran the fox to ground, or to skirt the edge of the wood to see if the animals came out the other side. Most of the riders, including the Prince of Wales, were pulling their horses up, grateful for a moment's respite. Bay made to do the same, but the Empress raised her riding crop and urged her horse to carry on. Bay touched Tipsy's flanks with his heels and followed her.

The ground began to rise and Bay's horse faltered at the steepness of the gradient. When he had brought her up to speed and looked up, the Empress had disappeared over the brow of the hill. Bay raised his crop and brought it down on Tipsy's flank. The horse crested the ridge but coming down the steep escarpment on the other side, she stumbled, and Bay, who was looking ahead for the Empress, suddenly saw the earth rising towards him.

In a stupor he heard German and felt a drop of rain falling on his face. A red wave of pain scalded him awake; he opened his eyes and saw the Empress's face very close to his own. He wanted to smile but the pain was too intense. He heard himself groaning.

'Bay? Bay Middleton, can you hear me?'

Bay tried to nod.

The Empress pulled off her glove and put her hand in his. 'If you can hear me, squeeze my hand.' Bay felt the cold, rough fingers, but as he tried to press her hand in return he felt an excruciating jolt of pain in his shoulder and a horrible looseness. The bile rose in his throat. He knew that he must have dislocated his shoulder; it had happened to him once before when he had fallen steeplechasing. Chicken Hartopp had been there and had known what to do. He had given him his crop to bite on while rotating the joint back into place. Afterwards he had teased Bay for the bite marks that had almost severed the pigskin.

Bay tried to speak. But no words came out.

'Are you injured? Can you move your limbs?' The Empress's voice was cracking with tension. She stared intently into his eyes. He tried again to speak, but all he could manage was a moan of pain. The Empress reached into the pocket of her habit and brought out a silver flask. She poured a little brandy between his lips. The alcohol hit the back of his throat and made him cough, but it cleared away the fog in his head and he was able to say, 'My shoulder, dislocated . . . Help me put it back.'

The Empress nodded, 'Tell me what to do.'

'More brandy . . .' She held the flask to his mouth and poured out a few drops, but seeing the expression on his face, she tilted it so the brandy cascaded down his throat. Bay waited for a moment while the alcohol numbed the acute edge of his pain and then he forced himself to speak again.

'Can you feel the joint?'

The Empress put her hand gingerly on his shoulder.

'Yes, I can feel something here that is not right.'

'Can you turn my arm and push it back in at the same time?'

The Empress bit her lip. 'I don't want to hurt you. Perhaps we should wait for help.'

Bay felt himself wobble with nausea. 'Please, just do it now. I can't bear this.'

He felt her grasp his hand and he said, 'Now turn it outwards and push down.'

He heard his own scream as the Empress rotated his arm and pressed the shoulder socket into place. Then suddenly it was all over. The agony had gone, his shoulder, though sore, was no longer the all-consuming centre of his existence. He was still holding the Empress's hand; he tried to raise it to his lips, but the effort was too much.

'Thank you,' he said. She turned her head away. He saw that she was rubbing the hand that he had been holding. He thought of what he had done to Chicken's riding crop.

'I'm sorry, did I hurt your hand? At least you didn't have to shoot me.' He attempted to smile.

She looked at him then, her face white and tear-stained, but she managed to smile back.

'It was I who hurt *you*. You see, I am not so ruthless. If you were a horse, I think I could not shoot you even if you broke your leg.'

'I am grateful for that. I would be even more grateful if I could have some more brandy.'

She gave him some more, and then, without wiping the flask, she took a swig herself.

'I am sorry, you need this more than I do, but you see, when I saw you fall, I thought you must be dead.'

Bay tried to laugh.

'Don't you know that it's very bad form to die at a Quorn meet? I would never hunt again. Have you seen the Master? I am much more scared of him than I am of dying.'

'I think that you are not enough scared of dying. I think perhaps I am the same way. But I was scared when I thought *you* were dead.'

'Then we must be reckless together, or not at all,' said Bay.

'I warn you that I am not so good at being careful.'

She looked at him directly then, and Bay saw that there were shiny trails on her cheeks where the tears had dried.

'Nor me.'

He wanted to touch her, but his arms would not move. They stayed immobile for a moment, Bay lying on the muddy ground, the Empress kneeling beside him, until a gust of noise from the hunt bellowed out over the hill.

The Empress cocked her head in the direction of the sound. 'Should I go and fetch help?'

'I think I will be all right, if you can help me. But I will need some kind of sling.'

'A sling? What is that?'

'Something to hold my arm up.'

Sisi stood up, and picking up the long tail end of her riding habit, she tore it along the seam. As she started to rip it against the grain to make a triangle, Bay saw that she was wearing the chamois leather britches he had glimpsed before. They fitted as tightly as a jockey's, revealing every contour of her slim thighs and long calves. It was both shocking and thrilling to see a woman's legs so accurately represented. Through his pain he felt a frisson of desire.

Now she was kneeling beside him again.

'Can you sit up?'

Bay tried to raise himself with his good arm but the effort was too much for him.

'Will you let me help you?' Her voice was hesitant.

Bay tried to smile. 'I would be very grateful for your help, Ma'am.'

She very carefully slid one hand underneath his bad shoulder, leant over and clasped her arms around him. Her upper body was pressed against his; he could feel her breath on his face.

'Are you ready?' she said. 'I hope I am strong enough .'

He heard her intake of breath, and then a jolt of pain as she pulled him upwards. Now they were looking directly into each other's eyes, their noses almost touching. He only had to lean forward a fraction to kiss her. He tried to read the expression in her dark eyes, but in that hesitation the moment was lost. She drew away from him and started to fiddle with the piece of material she had ripped from her habit.

'If I tie it like this, does it feel right?' She drew the ends of the material into a rough knot behind his neck.

'Perhaps a little tighter.' The sling was already supporting Bay's arm but he liked the cold touch of her fingers against the back of his neck.

'Like this?'

'Exactly.' Bay leant back slightly and felt the swell of her bosom behind his head. He thought how pleasant it would be to remain exactly as he was now. But the light was already beginning to fade and the occasional noises that were carried through the gloom were a reminder that the Quorn could not be far away.

Putting his good hand out to support himself, he scrambled to his feet. He swayed a little as he stood upright. Sisi put out her arm to support him. He gave a rueful laugh.

'As your pilot, Ma'am, I would have to conclude that I am a failure. I am meant to be protecting you from harm.'

'Oh, I have all the protection I want. It is not often that I get the chance to be useful.'

Their horses were grazing together a little further down the bank. Bay whistled through his teeth to Tipsy, who came over and nuzzled his hand. Bay realised his next challenge.

'Now my uselessness is complete. I think I can mount Tipsy with one arm, but I won't be able to help you.'

Sisi laughed.

'Do you think that I am the kind of rider who can't mount her own horse unaided?' She made a clucking noise through her teeth at her horse, which to Bay's amazement bent its forelegs and knelt in front of the Empress. She swung herself lightly onto the saddle and the horse rose to its feet.

'In another life, I could have had a career in the circus.'

Bay considered her. Since she had torn her habit in half to fashion his sling, her legs in their suede britches were quite visible.

'You certainly have the legs for it, Ma'am.'

Sisi looked down. 'It is a mercy it is getting dark. Otherwise we might cause quite a scandal.'

Bay shivered. The impossibility of their current situation struck him. To be seen riding about the countryside with a half-dressed empress was compromising to both of them. If he was to leave her, he would be equally at fault for abandoning a woman in a strange country. But perhaps that might be the wiser course.

'I should really leave you. Easton Neston is only half a mile away. I don't think I should come to the house. Baron Nopsca would have a seizure. If I set off now I can get to Melton Mowbray before dark and find a doctor. I hope you will forgive me if I desert you.' He smiled ruefully. 'I am not much good, am I? First I fall off my horse and then I propose to leave you to find your own way home.' He pulled Tipsy's head round in the direction of the road and started to move off, but Sisi held out her riding crop to bar his way.

'I forbid you to leave, Captain Middleton.' Her tone was light but it was a command nonetheless.

'But I am only thinking of you, Ma'am.'

'It is not your place to worry about my reputation,' she said. And then, softening, 'The thing about my position is that people will talk about me whatever I do. I learnt a long time ago that there was no point in being worried by it. At least this will give them a decent story.' She tilted her chin up. 'You must come back to Easton Neston now; you cannot possibly ride all the way to Melton Mowbray in your condition. I will send for the doctor and you will stay with me until you are quite recovered. We will have your things sent over.' She tapped the horse with her crop and set off smoothly up the hill.

Bay had no choice but to follow. His attempt at chivalry had been definitively countermanded. He was not entirely unhappy about this. There was no reason to go back to the web of rivalry and half-friendships at Melton Hall now that Charlotte had left. Indeed he rather relished the thought of Chicken, Fred and especially Augusta learning that he was now staying with the Empress. Then he wondered what Charlotte would make of the news, and whether he could get a letter to her before Augusta did. But he didn't have her address, and he felt uneasy about the fate of any letter that was sent to her via Melton. Augusta was quite capable of intercepting any missive that she thought was from Bay. That morning's feeling of irritation with Charlotte returned. Why on earth had she slipped away without a word? Was it some mysterious act of feminine caprice? If so, she was not the woman he had thought she was.

A pothole in the road made Tipsy stumble and the jolt sent a stab of pain through Bay's shoulder. He knew that the Empress was right; he was not strong enough to ride ten odd miles in the dark across open country. He would most likely fall off and die of exposure. He could already feel the initial shock of his fall wearing off, and an awful cold weariness numbing his body. He knew that if he was to slide off his horse now, he would be unable to get on it again. It was a relief that she had made the decision for him. His longing to lie down was so great that he did not dwell too much on the fact he was not accepting an invitation, but obeying an order.

The Ex-King's Bedroom

THE JOURNEY BACK WOULD NORMALLY TAKE TWENTY minutes, but though Bay could ride well enough one-handed, anything faster than a walk was too painful for his shoulder, and so the journey took them over an hour. He had urged the Empress to go on ahead, but she had refused.

'If you were to fall again, you would be quite helpless.'

'But I won't fall again.'

'Nobody ever thinks that they are going to fall, Captain Middleton.'

Just after they had had this conversation and were riding slowly along the broad river valley that led to Easton Neston Park, the Quorn came into view, spreading like a scarlet stain down the hill towards them on the other side of the river. The fox was clearly visible in front, running from side to side, trying to shake off the hounds who poured after it. The riders had thinned a little from the morning. As they grew nearer Bay saw the massive figure of the Red Earl and beside him the Prince of Wales. For a moment it looked as though the fox was going to cross the river and bring the whole hunt after it, but at the last moment the terrified animal swerved into a thicket of trees overhanging the water. It must have found some refuge there – possibly in a deserted badgers' sett – as it did not emerge. The hounds set up a terrific row, and the riders began to rein in their horses, waiting for the kill.

The Empress did not stop to watch the hounds at work, riding steadily on, with Bay following. But she was hailed by one of the riders on the other side of the stream who, recognising her, came right down to the water's edge.

'Your Majesty! I was afraid that you were lost.' There was relief in the Austrian Ambassador's voice, but also a note of warning.

The Empress turned her head and said, 'As you can see, Count, I am quite safe. It is poor Captain Middleton who has been injured.'

Bay nodded to the Count. 'Put my shoulder out. The Empress set it for me.'

Karolyi was too well trained to show any surprise at this, although his eyes did widen when the Empress checked her horse and he saw her chamois leather-covered legs gripping the side saddle.

'I am taking the Captain to Easton Neston. Perhaps you would be good enough to send for a doctor.' The Empress gave Karolyi no opportunity for further conversation.

'Of course, Majesty. I will attend to it directly.'

Without another word, the Empress turned her horse towards the road at the end of the valley. Bay nodded again to Karolyi and went after her.

As soon as they were out of earshot, the Empress laughed.

'Well, my new riding costume will be the talk of the Hofburg now,' she said. 'Karolyi would be far better off to keep it to himself, but he lives to gossip, and he won't be able to resist turning this into a story. It will all be about my heroic act in setting your shoulder, but he will find it impossible not to mention the state of my dress.'

Bay said nothing. He had seen the look on Karolyi's face at the sight of the Empress's legs. He hoped that the Ambassador was not a club man. The story of the man wearing a sling made out of an imperial riding habit would keep the gossips of Brooks and White's busy for weeks. It was not an entirely comfortable thought. But his worries about a possible scandal dissipated as he saw the gates of Easton Neston and he started to follow the Empress along the long drive to the house.

When he dismounted he could barely stand. Noticing this, the Empress clapped her hands and ordered the grooms to fetch Baron Nopsca immediately.

The Baron arrived a moment later, looking flushed. He almost managed to conceal his surprise at seeing the Empress's costume. The Empress spoke to him in German and the little man nodded, touching the ends of his moustaches as if to reassure himself that some things at least were unchanged.

Sisi put her hand on Bay's uninjured arm. 'Now you must get some rest. The Baron will take care of you.'

'You are very kind, but I feel that I am an imposition.'

She put up her hand to stop him.

'One of the prerogatives of royalty is that no one is allowed to contradict me. Isn't that right, Nopsca?'

The Baron bowed. 'Majesty.'

Inside the house, the Baron helped Bay up the broad marble staircase to a large bedroom on the first floor.

'This is the room formerly used by His Majesty the King of Naples. The Empress has directed me to accommodate you here.' The disapproval in the Baron's tone did not escape Bay. 'She has told me of your accident and has instructed me to send for the doctor. Please let me know if there is anything that you need.'

As the door closed Bay murmured some thanks, then, sitting down on the bed, he lay back and fell instantly asleep.

He woke with a start. The room was dark apart from the glowing fire. Moving gingerly, Bay felt the ache in his shoulder. It was so stiff that he could hardly move. Someone had taken his boots off and put a blanket over him, but he was still in his riding clothes apart from his jacket. Someone – the doctor, presumably – had strapped up his shoulder. Bay realised that he must have been unconscious.

It was impossible to know what time it was. He could have been asleep for minutes or hours. His head began to fill with worries. Had anyone sent word to Melton about his accident? He knew that he had to send a letter before the hunt gossips turned his accident into the story of the season: 'the pilot who had to be rescued by his royal charge'. He must write to Charlotte before she received some spiteful retelling of the day's events courtesy of Augusta. But even if he could get out of bed, he didn't think he could hold a pen with his injured right arm.

It was an unfamiliar feeling to be powerless – immobile in a strange house, surrounded by foreigners in his own country – yet there was something thrilling about this helplessness. Something was coming, he knew, but would it be pleasure or pain? It was like the moment before jumping an unfamiliar fence, the surge that went with taking off followed by the fear of landing.

Outside a high wind was sweeping across the Leicestershire plain, rattling the panes in the large baroque windows, sending drafts through every chink in the walls and gap in the glazing. Bay felt himself listening to every squeak and groan from the house around him. He tensed when he thought he heard the sound of whispering voices followed by a cry, but then relaxed when he realised that it was a combination of the wind and a squeaking door. Then there was another noise, a rhythmic creaking. Was it his imagination, or did he hear that quick, familiar step outside his door?

He tried to sit up when the door opened, but the pain in his shoulder made it impossible.

Sisi's face was lit from below by the Nightingale lamp she was carrying. The light cast a strange glow upwards on her face. There was something strange about her silhouette, he did not recognise the shape of her head, and then he realised that her hair was down.

'Are you awake?' Her voice was low and covert.

'Yes, over here.' He answered in the same whisper,

As the light came towards him, he saw that she was wearing some kind of white gown, and as she moved her head he saw the great sheet of her hair fall over her shoulders to the ground. When she approached the bed, he knew that he should not, indeed he could not move; to reach out his hand and touch her hair would be the moment of no return – the start of the race. But now she was so close to him that he could smell it – that mixture of violets, brandy and something more animal that he thought of as fox. His hand moved towards it. The hair felt warm and somehow springy, as if possessed with its own life force. He took a lock and wrapped it round his good hand. It was so long that he could wind it three times through his fingers without pulling at the scalp.

'Do you like my hair, Captain Middleton?' The same low whisper.

'Yes, Your Majesty, I do.' Bay tugged gently on the lock in his hand and pulled her face down to his. 'It is very useful to an injured man.' As he put his lips to hers he felt the hair fall around his face like a silken cocoon. He put up his good hand and felt the firm curve of her uncorseted waist under the silk of her gown.

'You may kiss me again, Captain Middleton.'

'Is that an order?'

'Not an order, I think, but a wish.'

'Then, Your Majesty, you will have to lie next to me, if I am to kiss you properly. Remember I am an injured man.'

'Oh, I am very worried about your injuries.' She put one finger lightly on his bandaged shoulder.

'Does that hurt?'

'No.'

'And this?' She leant over and, pushing back his shirt, put her lips to his skin. He felt her tongue touch his flesh, it felt rough like a cat's, and the caress sent a shock of pain and pleasure through his whole body.

'That was the best kind of hurting.'

She licked him again, this time bringing her tongue down to the hair on his chest.

'You taste of salt and something else also, the stable, perhaps.'

'You should have told Baron Nopsca to give me a bath,' Bay said.

She laughed. 'Oh, but I like your taste. I find it interesting.'

'So long as I can amuse you, Ma'am, I shall be content.'

Sisi began to undo the buttons on his shirt and when she had them all open she laid her head on his chest. He felt her breath against his skin and and her hair tickling his armpits.

'Your heart is beating most rapidly, Captain Middleton. Perhaps I should send for the doctor.'

'I don't think that will be necessary. If Your Majesty were to leave now I am sure that my heart rate would soon return to normal.'

'I see. Would you like me to leave? I don't want to endanger your health.' She was leaning over him directly and he could feel her breasts pressing against his chest.

'No, Ma'am, I would not.'

She lay there for a moment, her fingers tracing the outline of his lips.

'But you can't sleep like this, in your riding clothes, like a peasant.'

'It is very hard to undress with one arm.'

'Then you need help. Perhaps I should call Nopsca. No, it would be too cruel to wake him at this hour. I will just have to help you myself, Captain Middleton. I hope that I am equal to the task.' She sighed and her breath made the hairs on his chest tighten.

'So do I, Ma'am. But I feel sure that we will both rise to the occasion.'

She laughed and put her finger to his lips.

'Now be quiet, I need to concentrate.'

Later he listened to her breathing in the dark and thought that she had fallen asleep. Her head lay on his chest, her hair covering them like a blanket keeping them warm. He wondered what time it was. Somewhere in the darkness, he heard a clock strike four. There was still time then, before the household began to rumble into life. This was not a house, like some that Bay had stayed in, where they rang a bell in the small hours to summon the unfaithful to their rightful beds.

The Empress moved and Bay felt the blood return to his good arm, the one that she had been lying on. In the darkness he could just make out a glimpse of white as she stood up. He felt the cool brush of the linen sheet as she drew it over his bare skin and he sighed.

'Are you in pain? Did I hurt you?' Her voice was almost anxious in the dark.

'Not exactly,' he paused, 'Ma'am.'

He felt her hand against his cheek. 'When we are here you can call me Sisi. That is what my family call me, and my friends.'

Bay could not suppress the flicker of jealousy. 'Do you have many friends?'

'Not in England. No friends at all, apart from you. You are my

English friend, Bay. And now you must sleep. I need you to get better. I can't hunt without you.'

'What about your courtiers in the gold braid?'

'Max and Felix are not reliable. They can be distracted.'

Bay thought of what he might have seen in the mirror, in the gallery after the dinner at Easton Neston.

'I shall have to ride with one arm then. I hope I can manage.'

'Oh, I think you will manage. You have so far'. He heard the creak of the floorboards as she walked across the room.

'Goodnight, Bay.'

'Goodnight, Sisi.'

In the Dark Room

'WHY, CHARLOTTE, LADY D TOLD ME YOU were a paragon of every conceivable virtue, but she didn't let me know that you had such an eye. I am quite jealous. Such a luscious composition, all these girls tumbled together in one great, wanton heap. It looks so artless and yet every detail is perfect.' Caspar Hewes was holding up Charlotte's print of the Melton maids. They were in the studio of Lady Dunwoody's house in Holland Park, a large room with a great north-facing window, which was rattling in the wind. There was no fire in the studio; Lady Dunwoody believed strongly in living with beauty but was indifferent to comfort.

As he talked, Charlotte could see Caspar's breath condensing in the chilly air, like a dragon or a steam engine.

'When Lady D comes back, I shall tell her that this just *has* to be included in the exhibition. Everything we have is so stiff. This will add the essential note of decadence – loose and languorous, with just a touch of the harem.' Caspar turned to Charlotte and smiled a dazzling, very un-English smile that revealed a gleaming row of sharp white teeth; the puff that followed was definitely dragon-like, thought Charlotte – a Chinese dragon. Today he was wearing a green velvet jacket over a yellow brocade waistcoat and nankeen trousers. The splendour of his outfit was in contrast to the stained linen apron that he wore on top, but somehow he managed to make his costume look exotic rather than absurd. As Lady Dunwoody had predicted, he had barely drawn breath since his arrival at the house that morning. His voice was so different to an Englishman's: when Fred and his friends spoke in their club drawl they sounded as if they really did not have the energy to finish pronouncing their sentences, but Caspar gave every word its own privileged existence, rolling its around in his mouth before releasing it into the world. Charlotte thought that she had never met anyone who enjoyed talking as much as this American. The only word that was not in his extensive vocabulary was silence.

'You are very kind, Mr Hewes, but I doubt if the Queen will be interested in a group of servant girls. All the other portraits are of distinguished personages: Lord Beaconsfield, the Poet Laureate, Miss Nightingale, and members of the court. I am not sure that house-maids, however decadent, would be allowed to hang beside them.'

'Everyone needs youth and beauty, however distinguished they are,' Caspar said, and then, spinning round so that his face was so close to Charlotte's that she could smell the limes in his cologne, 'but why won't you call me Caspar? Mr Hewes makes me sound like a minister of the lord and I have to tell you, Charlotte, dear Charlotte, that I have Doubts, so when you call me Mr Hewes I feel like an imposter. Now I don't believe that a young lady as charming and as personable as yourself would want a poor foreigner like me to feel like a fraudulent man of God, by the constant use of his last name, now would you?'

Charlotte laughed and put up her hands in surrender. 'Enough, enough. I will call you Caspar, but only if you promise to stop talking, just for a minute.'

'But why? What is the point of being in a room with a lovely and talented young woman if you don't make every effort to talk to her? To be silent would be a terrible waste of a golden opportunity. Unless, of course, you want me to be silent while I cover your face with burning kisses?'

'Burning kisses? Well, it is rather cold in here, so only if you could guarantee they would be burning . . .' said Charlotte.

'You are teasing me now, an orphan all alone and friendless in a strange country.'

'Friendless! I am quite sure that you have more friends in London than I do. I suspect that there can't be many people you want to know who aren't already your intimate friends,' said Charlotte.

'Mere acquaintances. They are not soulmates. If you only knew, dear Charlotte, how I long for a confidante. I don't feel that I have had a genuine conversation since I left America.'

As he was talking Caspar took out the other prints from Charlotte's portfolio and arrayed them on the table in front of him. Charlotte noticed that, for all his height and lankiness, Caspar's movements were deft and precise. His hand hovered over the picture of Bay and his horse and he pointed at it with one long finger.

'Why, Carlotta! I think I like Carlotta more than Charlotte, it suits you better. You are not the prim little English miss that you appear; I know by your pictures that you have a dangerous soul. Already you are making me jealous. Do you know how fearsome I can be when my passions are aroused?' He held out out his hand with a thespian flourish.

'I know very little about you, as we only met yesterday,' said Charlotte.

She could feel a blush reaching her ear lobes. There had been nothing from Bay at breakfast, no letter, no telegram. But then he did not know where she had gone. She had a sudden image of Bay standing on the steps at Melton and laughing with Fred and

Chicken and she felt her mouth go dry. She would write to her aunt and ask her to tell Bay where she was. Adelaide Lisle might have some reservations about Bay, but the prospect of the house in town and the barouche with the matching greys that came with her role as Charlotte's chaperone might overcome her scruples.

Caspar saw the reddening of Charlotte's skin and continued, 'Already you are taunting me with this Adonis on horseback, with his tight breeches and his gleaming boots. But I will not despair, no, I will not lose heart – because as I look at this picture I see that this man is not in love with you. No, he only has eyes for his horse, who is a fine animal, undoubtedly, but compared to you, Carlotta . . . The man must have water in his veins.'

'Do you talk to every lady you meet like this?'

Caspar opened his eyes in theatrical outrage.

'Carlotta, how can you say such a cruel thing? Do I look like a man who makes love to every woman he meets? A rake, a reprobate, a Lothario?'

Charlotte shook her head, laughing. From another man, Caspar's declarations would be not just eccentric but alarming; however, there was something about the smooth fluency of his speech and the way that he was examining all her prints with painstaking care even as he declaimed undying love, that made her think that his extravagance of word and gesture was just as much an affectation as his style of dress.

'I don't know what you look like, an American, perhaps.'

'Oh, Carlotta, you make my nationality sound like an unfortunate disease. And yet I think you would like America. It is the land of the free, you know.' He began to sing 'Yankee Doodle Dandy' in a remarkably true baritone, while at the same time picking up Charlotte's box of undeveloped plates.

He stopped singing. 'You have two plates here that you haven't printed yet. Shall I develop them for you? It would be an honour. I long to see what else you have done. Please allow me to render you this one small service.'

Charlotte hesitated a moment. She felt a little uncomfortable about Caspar's offer – it was as if he was offering to wear her clothes – but she could think of no good reason to refuse.

'If you really want to. And now that you have looked at my portfolio, can I see yours?' she said.

'Oh, Carlotta, nothing would make me happier. I don't have much here. Perhaps one day I can lure you to Tite Street, but Lady D was kind enough to pull out a few things that she thought were worthy of being in the exhibition.'

He pulled a morocco folder down from one of the shelves.

'Here they are. Now I am altogether too bashful to stand by while you look at my work, so I am going to hide myself in the dark room with your plates, and then I won't have to squirm as you try to hide the contempt that it undoubtedly deserves.' Despite his words, Caspar did not look particularly apprehensive. He opened the portfolio with a flourish.

'There you are, Carlotta *mia*, the fruit of my labours. Be merciful, remember that I was not so fortunate as to have Lady Dunwoody as a teacher.'

He picked up her plate box and went into the wooden cubicle that Lady Dunwoody had built in the corner of the studio as a dark room. Charlotte could hear him moving around in there, still singing. She turned her attention to his portfolio, grateful for a brief respite from the torrent of chat. The first batch of photographs was of a desert dotted with huge cacti and strange, eroded rock formations. Charlotte had never seen a landscape like this before – no plants, no grass, nothing but sand and rock and sky. In one picture a young man was standing next to a cactus that topped him by at least two feet. The desert pictures were followed by a series of pictures of Chinese families – ten or more people, from the old men who wore pigtails and traditional costumes to their children who wore western clothes, right down to the babies swaddled in papooses. Some were studio portraits, some were posed outside the family's shop. Charlotte was surprised to see that all the signs were in Chinese characters. She wondered where Caspar had taken these pictures. It was an extraordinary thing to have these images from the other side of the world in front of her – the scenes they showed were so outlandish, and yet they were undoubtedly real.

Charlotte studied these pictures of strange people and savage landscapes and compared them to her carefully arranged pictures of maids and house parties, and she realised that she was jealous of Caspar's freedom and his palette. She felt a longing to go out and record an unknown world with her camera instead of always trying new ways to make the familiar strange. Charlotte had never been abroad – the most exotic place she had visited was the Isle of Wight. Fred and Augusta had offered to take her on their wedding trip to Italy, as a way of defraying the expense, she suspected. But even the prospect of the Colosseum by moonlight had not persuaded her to spend two months travelling with the newlyweds.

The last photos in the pile were a series of portrait heads, all of the same youth, the one who had been standing under the cactus in the desert. He had an angular face with high, flat cheekbones and a square jaw. Charlotte was surprised to see that his dark hair was very long and tied back behind his head. In some of the portraits, the boy, who couldn't have been much more than eighteen, looked straight into the camera, stern and unflinching, but there was one picture where he was looking back over his shoulder and smiling, and Charlotte had a sense of mutual affection on both sides of the camera. To catch a look like that, a moment rather than a pose, was very rare. She wondered who he was. In the last picture he was holding up a bunch of grapes, his head tipped back, revealing his long, supple throat. His eyes were tilted towards the camera and Charlotte saw something in his expression that she recognised. She had seen that look on Bay's face, once.

Caspar was now singing 'Silver Threads Among the Gold', attempting all the parts.

First he sang 'Darling, I am growing old', in a reedy baritone, 'Growing old' again in a sonorous bass, and then 'Silver threads among the gold' in a high-pitched falsetto. It was as if he was trying to recreate the sound of a barbershop quartet single-handed.

Charlotte put the print of the youth with the grapes down, and looked around the room. It was full of the props that Lady Dunwoody used for her photographs. On a chair there was a folded Union Jack and a cardboard helmet and shield which had been used for the famous and much reproduced portrait of Ellen Terry as Britannia. A collection of white pleated muslin tunics was hanging on a lacquered coat stand; on the shelf above was a pile of laurel wreaths. A crystal ball stood on a table next to a skull and a silver candelabra with three candles that had burnt down almost to the wick, with rivulets of wax hanging down like stalactites. On the wall next to the door a heavily embroidered Chinese mandarin's robe hung from a pole; above it on a small shelf that ran the length of the room was a collection of blue and white plates, lustre jugs and a marble cherub, one plump leg pointing towards the floor. Next to the bench where Charlotte was standing, was an easel displaying a photograph of a young girl dressed as Diana the huntress, her bow drawn back as she pointed her arrow at the sky. Charlotte recognised the model as one of Lady Dunwoody's maids. Even the most skilled retouching could not completely disguise the contrast between the girl's reddened hands and the classical whiteness of her neck and bare shoulder. But Lady D had caught something savage in her expression which gave the photograph an unexpected ferocity. This Diana looked as though she would hit her prey. Charlotte wondered what the model had been thinking of to produce that shaft of cruelty. Did she dream of taking up arms and bringing down her enemies, or was she perhaps thinking of Lady Dunwoody's collection of Japanese porcelain that had to be dusted with a single goose feather?

The singing stopped mid-phrase, there was a moment when Charlotte thought she heard a sigh, and then Caspar began to sing again, picking up the song exactly where he had left it.

The verse finished and Caspar emerged from the cubicle, his arms raised in benediction.

'I feel that we have consummated our artistic union, dearest Carlotta. I have brought your negatives into glorious life, and you have seen my humble offerings.'

Charlotte heard her cue.

'Oh, but you have *nothing* to be humble about. Your photographs are exceptional. I have never seen anything like them before. Oh, how I envy you your deserts and your endless light. We have nothing like that here, that's why we have to create little tableaux in studios,' – she gestured to the print on the easel – 'housemaids dressed up as goddesses. But you, you can just go out and find the perfect composition right in front of you.'

Caspar made a little bow of acknowledgement, but he was, for once, silent, and Charlotte realised that she had not said quite enough.

'But only a photographer of great skill and talent could do those astonishing landscapes justice. Don't worry, I know how good you are. Even if you hadn't had such raw material to work with, I would have known it just from this picture.' Charlotte picked up the print of the boy looking back over his shoulder and laughing. 'Only someone with an uncommon gift could have produced something like this. It is so rare to see real emotion in a photograph. But here it is quite naked.'

Charlotte did not know why that last word had come out of her mouth. She felt as if she had said something improper. Caspar looked at her directly for a moment and then he dropped his gaze and made her another sweeping bow.

'I am overwhelmed by your appreciation. To be praised by you is the pinnacle of all my life's achievements. I feel like stout Cortez on the Darien peak.'

Charlotte interrupted him, 'Who is the boy, the one holding the grapes? I can't imagine coaxing a look like that from any of my sitters.'

'But what about the gallant officer and his horse? You captured the love and affection between them perfectly.' Caspar raised an eyebrow.

'Such an unusual face. What is his name?' Charlotte asked.

'His name? Abraham Running Water. His father was a Sioux Indian and his mother was an Irish girl who came west in the gold rush. Abraham was the product of their brief union. I met him in the desert. He helped me carry my equipment, he showed me things. There was the skin of a rattlesnake, completely whole, lying on the sand. I would never have seen it if Abraham hadn't stopped me and made me look.' He paused for a second, and Charlotte asked the question to which she was afraid she already knew the answer.

'Where is he now?'

'Somewhere in the Mojave. I took a picture of the exact location. There were no trees, so I made a pile of stones. Not big ones, there are no boulders there, just pebbles really. He had consumption. I wanted to take him to the city, to see doctors, but he wouldn't leave the desert.'

'I am sorry. But these photographs are better than a gravestone,' said Charlotte.

'That is a delicate thought. I can appreciate it now, but I came very close to smashing the plates afterwards. But somehow, some of my best work . . . I just couldn't bring myself to do it.'

'To have a photograph of someone you cared for must be a consolation.'

'Perhaps, but they are also a permanent reminder of what you have lost. Memories fade, after all, but I will never have to struggle to remember Abraham's face. Is that really such a boon? Perhaps it is better to let things grow dim. Every time I look at one of these pictures I am reminded so vividly of how alive he was once.' He shook his head and waved his hands in front of him as if trying to banish unpleasantness.

Charlotte thought of the photograph of her mother in her coffin that her father had kept in his study. The one she had never wanted to look at.

Caspar clapped his hands.

'But enough of this, we have strayed down a very morbid byway, my Carlotta. We are not here to philosophise, but to work. What would Lady D say if she could see us now? She would condemn us as lilies of the field, gilded parasites, who indulge in idle conversation when we should be toiling.'

'I may have been idle, but you have been developing my plates. Are the prints dry?'

Caspar blinked. 'I suppose they must be. Let me check.' He disappeared into the dark-room cubicle.

Charlotte wondered if it would be too conspicuous to send Aunt Adelaide a telegram about Bay. She decided that it probably would. A telegram would be talked about, and after all, there was no urgency.

She could hear Caspar banging about in the dark room. He was singing Mozart now, '*Ma in Ispagna son già mille e tre . . .*'

The aria finished and Caspar emerged holding a print.

'Here she is, your tragic heroine.' He placed the photograph in front of Charlotte. It was the picture she had taken of the Empress on the morning of Major Postlethwaite's accident. She was in profile.

The focus of the picture was the Empress's narrow waist between the abundance of her hair above and the spread of her skirts below. Her face was tilted away from the camera but it was possible to see the delicate angle of her jaw and the long cord of her neck.

'What makes you say tragic?' said Charlotte.

'She has a melancholy shape. Something about the cast of her head. And she is clearly someone who is at the centre of things – look how everyone around is looking at her. I must say, I am curious. Is she an acquaintance of yours?'

'Hardly. She is the Empress of Austria. She came to a hunt at the house I was staying at.'

'An empress? Yes, I can see that.'

'Do you think she is beautiful?'

Caspar narrowed his eyes at the picture. 'If you had asked me that question before telling me who she was, I would have wavered. But now that I know, well, I have to say I do think she is beautiful, I simply can't separate the form from the function. A beautiful empress is so much more romantic than a moderately attractive one. Even though I am a proud republican, I can't deny that there is something irresistible about a crown.'

He glanced at Charlotte and then said, 'But I suspect from the brittle set of her head that she might be rather . . . taxing. Not like you, dearest Charlotte, you are so easy to be with.'

'That's because I am not an empress.'

'Oh, I know that you would be delightful anywhere.' He made her a little bow and then he took out his hunter from his waistcoat pocket.

'Is that really the time? I promised Lady D that we would meet her at the gallery at noon. We shall have to leave at once. Lady D does not like to be kept waiting.'

Charlotte helped him to pack up all the prints in a portfolio, carefully interleaving each one with tissue paper. Caspar insisted on including her picture of the maids, and the picture of Bay with Tipsy. She countered by putting in his portrait of Abraham Running Water. Just as she was placing the tissue paper over the last print, Caspar picked up the picture of the Empress.

'You can't leave out royalty.'

Charlotte remembered that she had taken more than one picture of the Empress. 'What about the other plate? I wasn't sure if I had the picture or not, because the Empress took out a fan to hide her face.'

'How tiresome.' Caspar put the leaves of the portfolio together and tied the strings. He put his hand on Charlotte's elbow, shepherding her to the door.

Charlotte hesitated. 'But did the other picture come out? I would like to see if I caught her before the fan.' Caspar's grip on her elbow tightened, but she broke away and entered the little dark room. In the darkness she could see one print hanging from string by a single peg. She took it down and brought it out into the light.

The photograph had come out perfectly. But the focus of the picture was not the Empress, who was bringing the enormous fan up to her face, but the rider just behind her. For a moment Charlotte didn't recognise Bay. The expression on his face, which was turned towards the Empress, was one she had not seen before. His pale eyes were completely intent; he was gazing at the woman in front of him as if she were some precious object that would fall and break if he looked away. His mouth was open slightly. It might have been the beginning of a smile, or a grimace of pain, Charlotte couldn't tell. He had never looked at her that way.

She felt a touch on her elbow and the photograph was taken out of her hand.

'Photographs can be so deceptive, don't you think?' Caspar said as he pushed her out of the dark room. 'That fellow there, your captain, looks as though he has seen a ghost. It's the way the light catches his eyes. A sunny day and a short exposure and you can be seeing all sorts of things. I remember once I took a picture of a butcher at work in Chinatown, he was holding up his cleaver in such a way that it looked that he was about to murder his assistant. Just a trick of the light, of course, but so alarming – he could have been Sweeney Todd himself.'

Charlotte allowed herself to be borne along by the torrent of Caspar's chatter out of the house and into a hansom. It wasn't until the cab had reached the Albertopolis in the park that she spoke.

'It wasn't a trick of the light, was it?'

Caspar was looking out of the window at the shiny new statue of Prince Albert sitting under his canopy.

'I can't help feeling that he looks rather morose sitting there. I think if I was a prince, I would want to be remembered as dashing and brave, rather than brooding.' Still looking out of the window, he continued, 'Trick of the light, really I couldn't say. You know the gallant captain, I have only seen the picture. And I have always said that photographs can be very misleading.' He turned to her and smiled.

'Promise me that when I die, you will commission a statue that makes me look like a hero. I really couldn't bear to be a lowering presence like that.'

But Charlotte was not to be diverted.

'If you had to describe the look on Captain Middleton's face; if you thought that expression was a real one, and not a photographic mirage, what would you say?'

Caspar sighed.

'I would say, my dear Carlotta, that the good Captain was enchanted.'

The Widow of Windsor

SISI LOOKED OUT OF THE TRAIN WINDOW AT THE snowy fields rushing by, stained pink by the rising sun. But she did not notice the keen sherbet colour of the snow; if she noticed the landscape at all, it was the fences and hedges that caught her eye. This was not good hunting country. It was typical of Queen Victoria to live in an unsporting landscape. Such a dowdy little woman, with no style at all. The summer before last when she had visited the Isle of Wight, she had been forced to call on the Queen at Osborne. She had been given a grindingly thorough tour of the sculpture gallery and the Swiss cottage where the royal children had their gardens. It had been one of the most tedious afternoons of her life.

But today would be quite different. She looked across at Bay, who was sitting opposite her. His eyes were closed and she wondered whether he had fallen asleep. He must have felt her gaze, even in his dreams, because he opened his eyes and smiled at her. His eyes were such a pale blue, like the stained glass in the Peterhof.

The train went over a junction and Sisi saw Bay grimace as the movement jolted his shoulder, which was still strapped up.

'Is it very painful, Captain Middleton?'

'Only now and then,' said Bay and winked.

'I have a tincture that is very good. From Vienna. The doctors there do not believe in suffering.' She turned to Countess Festetics, who was sitting at the other end of the carriage reading a novel in Hungarian.

'Do you have my solution, Festy? I think the Captain needs it.'

The Countess opened the crocodile skin dressing case at her side. She took out a phial with a silver top and handed it to Sisi.

'Open your mouth, and I will put the drops on your tongue,' said Sisi.

'It is really not so bad,' said Bay. 'Nothing that a little brandy wouldn't cure.'

'Open your mouth, Captain Middleton!'

Bay did as he was told and Sisi put six drops on his tongue. The train shuddered as she was administering the seventh and the drop fell onto Bay's moustache, where it glistened.

'Missed,' said Bay and licked it off with his tongue. He winked again. Sisi smiled and then glanced at the Countess, who was apparently too absorbed in her book to notice them, although she had barely turned a page since the journey began. Her presence in the carriage was necessary to avoid a scandal; the Empress of Austria could not be seen travelling in a carriage alone with her pilot. It did not matter how many hours they had spent alone on the hunting field, a train was different. Sisi had long ago learnt that it paid to observe the outward conventions. Nopsca had winced when she had announced that Captain Middleton would be coming with them to Windsor, but so long as Festetics sat there with her Hungarian novel, he could pretend that all was well.

The train was slowing down now, they must be almost there. The journey had been commendably swift, just under three hours. They had not had the indignity of changing trains; Nopsca had arranged it all very cleverly, procuring a private train which was routed round the outskirts of London. Sisi looked at her pocket watch, it was a few minutes before eleven. It was all quite an effort for a call that would last no more than half an hour, but monarchs could not always follow their inclinations. She put her hands to her hair automatically, to check that her crown of plaits had not slipped.

There was a red carpet at the station, of course, but not a band. This was a private visit by the Countess Hohenembs to Queen Victoria, not a state visit by the Empress of Austria to the Queen of England. Sisi pulled her veil right down; in England there were photographers everywhere.

She turned to Bay. 'There is quite a party to meet us. Are you ready, Captain Middleton?'

Bay stood up and made a little bow. 'Quite ready, Your Majesty.'

There was a knot of men on the platform. The Ambassador, Count Karolyi, stepped forward to kiss the Empress's hand. As he lifted his head his eyes flickered over to Bay, who was standing behind the Empress.

'Welcome, Majesty,' he said in German and then, turning to the man beside him, in English, 'May I present Sir Henry Ponsonby, Her Majesty's chamberlain.'

Sisi nodded and waited as Karolyi introduced the rest of the party who merited introduction, 'Countess Festetics, Her Majesty's lady-in-waiting, Baron Nopsca, her household comptroller, and,' with an almost imperceptible pause, 'Captain Middleton, her pilot.'

There were three carriages waiting outside. Sisi beckoned to Bay to join her in the first carriage with Karolyi and Ponsonby.

The Ambassador gave Middleton his best courtier's smile as they waited for the Empress and then Ponsonby to climb into the carriage.

'Is this your first time at Windsor, Captain Middleton?' he said. 'It is.'

'An exciting day for you, then, to visit your sovereign.' Karolyi lingered over the word sovereign. 'You are moving in exalted circles, Captain Middleton.'

Bay looked Karolyi in the eye. 'It is an honour to be of service to the Empress, Count.' He gestured to Karolyi that he should follow the Empress into the carriage. The older man put one foot on the step and turned to Bay.

'I have spent my life in the service of the Hapsburgs, Captain Middleton. It has been,' he paused for a moment as if searching for the right word, and then said with emphasis, 'the business of my life.'

Bay was about to reply, but the Empress called from the carriage, 'Count Karolyi, did you know that my son is to visit England?' The Count turned his head and the moment of tension between the two men passed.

When they were all seated in the carriage, Ponsonby began to point out the sights on the way. The streets were empty but for a few couples in their Sunday best, hurrying to church. No one stopped to look at the procession of carriages making its way towards the Castle.

As the turrets of Windsor Castle came into view, Ponsonby said, 'Windsor is Her Majesty's oldest residence. The Queen always comes here at this time of year, to remember the Prince Consort. He died here on the fourteenth of December, 1861.'

'So sad.' Sisi sighed. 'Such an enlightened man. I remember we had a long talk once about plumbing. He had a passion for hygiene. And then, poor man, he dies of typhus. I suppose the drains at Windsor are very old.'

Ponsonby nodded. 'Everything at Windsor is old. But with the greatest respect, Ma'am, I would hesitate to say that in the presence of the Queen.'

The carriages drove up the avenue of trees that lined the drive to the Castle. When they arrived at the Great West Door, the Austrian party was shown into an empty drawing room, clearly one of the Queen's private apartments as it was full of silver-framed photographs. There were group portraits of Victoria and her children and grandchildren, on lawns, steps and yachts. Franz Joseph was for ever imploring Sisi to sit for one of these dynastic pictures, so that he too could send out a family photograph that would gather dust in the royal drawing rooms of Europe. But Sisi stood firm; she had stopped sitting for photographs when she was thirty. She hated the idea of her image being pored over by strangers, royal or otherwise, examining her appearance for signs of ageing. '

Sisi looked over at Bay; he caught her glance and smiled. She examined another photograph – this one was of the Queen mounted on a Shetland pony which was being held by a tall, rather handsome man in Highland dress. It was the only picture in the room that showed the Queen with anyone other than a member of her family.

'Who is this?' she asked Sir Henry, pointing at the photograph. The Chamberlain, who had just taken out his watch for the second time since their arrival, said with some nervousness, 'That is John Brown, Ma'am. He is the Queen's personal servant.'

'Her servant?' Sisi could hardly keep the surprise out of her voice. Franz Joseph might have had his picture taken with his groom, but he would never put it in a silver frame and exhibit it for public view.

A series of clocks began to strike the hour, making Sisi aware that she was being kept waiting. She looked at Karolyi and said in German, 'But where is the Queen? Does she know I am here?'

The Ambassador pulled at his whiskers.

'I believe, Majesty, that the Queen did not expect you so promptly. I understand that she is still in church.'

He spoke in German but Ponsonby behind him caught the word *Kirche* and murmured in English, 'The Queen always likes to have a few words with the Chaplain after the service. It's a custom that began when the Prince Consort was alive, and the Queen does so like to carry things on.'

Sisi felt a shiver of impatience. She had come all this way and now she was being kept waiting. Her tone was querulous as she said in English, 'And how long do you think that these "few words" will take?'

Ponsonby exchanged the briefest of glances with Karolyi before replying, 'I believe just a few minutes more now, Your Majesty.' His tone was diplomatic and neutral, avoiding any semblance of retort to her raised voice, but Sisi had caught the look he had shared with the Ambassador, a look which conveyed their common helplessness in the hands of unreasonable women.

Sir Henry kept inviting her to sit down on one of the overstuffed sofas, but Sisi had been sitting down all morning. She began to pace up and down, her button boots making no sound on the thick carpet. It was difficult, though, to pace satisfactorily as the room, though large, was crowded with small tables covered with china models of the Queen's dogs, glass paperweights of Alpine scenes, watercolour albums, and of course the photographs. Sisi found herself threading through the clutter, hoping that her skirts would not knock anything down. Every inch of wall was covered in paintings – some of them by painters Sisi recognised. She thought that the group portrait of the royal family must be by Winterhalter – he really was the most flattering painter; the young princes and princesses looked like angels and while Victoria looked, as ever, like a goose, she was at least in Winterhalter's hands a handsome one. The floor was covered in a violently coloured carpet – Sisi could see patches of burgundy, mustard yellow and carmine red. She thought that it was fortunate that there was so much furniture in the room, as the carpet undiluted would give anyone a headache.

She walked over to Bay, who was standing by a wall. 'I thought we might look at some hunters this afternoon. Some English ones. You will help me choose them?'

'With pleasure.'

'We will go as soon as we are finished here.' Sisi lowered her voice, 'I do not intend to stay long.'

Just then there was a cough from Ponsonby, and Sisi turned to see two liveried footmen throwing open the door for the Queen. She was small, round and dressed entirely in black apart from her white widow's cap. Immediately behind her walked John Brown, who was almost a foot taller than his mistress. Behind him was a selection of ladies, including a young girl whose close-set blue eyes and long nose made her unmistakably one of Victoria's daughters.

There was a rustle as the men bowed and the women curtsied. Only Sisi did not move. She waited until Victoria was halfway across the room before she moved to kiss her on both cheeks.

'Your Majesty.'

'My dear Empress,' the Queen said in her high, childish voice, 'how delightful to see you. And on a Sunday too, such an unusual day for a visit.' There was a glint of steel in her bulbous blue eyes. Behind her Ponsonby cleared his throat nervously.

'This is my youngest daughter Beatrice.'

Beatrice curtsied and Sisi kissed her too on both cheeks. Then she smiled and said in her gayest voice, 'But how lovely you are, Beatrice. One day you must come and stay with me in Vienna. The archdukes will be fighting over you, I guarantee.'

Beatrice blushed and mumbled something about Mama needing her here. The Queen settled herself on one of the vast plaid buttoned-back sofas, and gestured to Sisi to join her.

'Oh, but Beatrice would be miserable away from me. She is such a little home bird.'

Sisi saw that Beatrice was clenching her fists; she wondered how miserable exactly the girl would be to be separated from her mother.

'Oh, but it is so important to travel at that age. I so regret not seeing the world before I married.'

Queen Victoria raised her head and her many chins wobbled. 'How fortunate then that you are able to travel so much now. When did we last meet? I believe it was two years ago at Osborne. You had your little girl with you. Such a dear little thing. Is she travelling with you now?'

'Valerie? No, I left her in Vienna with her father. He dotes upon her, and I couldn't bear to deprive him of her.'

'How is the dear Emperor? Such a *shame* that he is not with you.' Queen Victoria spoke with very definite emphases as if she was underlining the words as she spoke.

'My husband asked me to give you his warmest regards. He is very sorry not to be able to be here in person.'

'I am surprised that you can bear to leave him behind. I know that I was always quite *miserable* when I was parted from Prince Albert, even if only for the night.' The Queen gave a sigh that made her lace tippets flutter and placed one white hand to her breast. After a little pause while she collected herself, she asked, 'Tell me, how long do you intend to stay in England?'

'Till the end of the hunting season, I hope. To ride to hounds here is such a pleasure. We have nothing like it at home.'

The Queen sighed again, 'My dear husband always used to say that there was *nothing* to surpass a day out in the hunting field. If only he had been spared so that he could have enjoyed *more* of them. But he had so many duties here. There was no time for his own pleasure. He always put duty first.' The Queen turned her head to gaze at the portrait of Albert at his desk that hung over the fireplace.

Sisi caught the implied reproach. She replied in the same, slightly pious tone, 'The Emperor is the same, diligent beyond all measure. It was very hard for me to leave him, but he insisted. Dear Franzl, he swears that the only thing that gives him real joy is to know that I am happy and healthy. The winters in Vienna always make me ill, so he was so delighted when I decided to come here.'

There was a little pause as the Queen absorbed this speech. Sisi looked at the boulle clock on the mantelpiece. It was only fifteen minutes past the hour; she would have to stay for at least another twenty minutes. She sat up a little straighter, conscious of the Queen's shapeless black bulk. Only Victoria's head and the bulbous blue eyes had anything regal about them.

'But the Emperor must worry about you so. Hunting is *so* dangerous. The Prince of Wales had such a nasty fall only the other day. Dear Alix was quite beside herself. You must promise me, dear Empress, that you will not do anything *reckless*. After all, we are *grandmothers* now.' Queen Victoria nodded at Sisi, waving a plump white hand to indicate their similarity. Sisi smiled thinly. She did not altogether care to be called a grandmother. It made her sound so old and staid, when she was a mere thirty-eight. The Queen, on the other hand, fully deserved the grandmother label. She was only twelve or so years older than Sisi, but she looked like a contemporary of Sisi's mother. Sisi could not understand how anyone could allow themselves to spread quite so much. And those dreadful clothes. Of course she was in mourning, but even mourning clothes did not have to be so dowdy. Sisi reflexively smoothed the green worsted skirt of her travelling dress.

Victoria continued, 'I have never allowed my daughters to hunt, although Louise *begged* me to let her. But I told her to take up archery, *so graceful*. Really you should consider archery, Empress, such a fetching costume Louise had made, all in green with a peaked hat with a feather. Really quite charming. I believe I shall write to the Emperor and suggest archery. I am sure that he would be very happy to know of a sport that is *perfectly* safe.'

Victoria paused for breath and Sisi broke in, 'Oh, but I am quite safe. I have my pilot, Captain Middleton, to protect me from harm.' She gestured at Bay with her hand. 'Earl Spencer was kind enough to recommend him.' Bay, who had been looking at the floor during this exchange, straightened up and bowed low before the Queen.

Victoria turned to look at Bay, making no attempt to hide her scrutiny. She clearly liked what she saw, saying with almost a regal twinkle, 'We hope you will be *very* careful, young man. If anything were to happen to the Empress on English soil, it would be an *unspeakable* tragedy.'

Bay bowed again. 'You have my word, Ma'am, that no harm will come to the Empress in my care.'

'We are pleased to hear it. You must be *vigilant* at all times. But you seem to have injured yourself? I hope it is nothing serious.' Queen Victoria was all tender concern. There was nothing she liked more than a medical drama.

'Oh it's nothing, Ma'am. I fell from my horse and dislocated my shoulder.'

'Dislocated your shoulder? How dreadful. Was it *very* painful?' Victoria leant forward.

'It wasn't pleasant at the time, Ma'am, but luckily the Empress was able to set it for me right away. It's when the arm is hanging loose that it hurts.'

Victoria looked at Sisi and back at Bay. 'I had no idea, Elizabeth, that you had *medical* training. How very *fortunate* that you knew what to do.'

Sisi laughed. 'I didn't, but Captain Middleton is an excellent teacher.'

Queen Victoria considered this for a moment and then she turned to John Brown. 'I wonder if I would be as useful if anything like that were to happen to you, John?'

'I have nae intention of dislocating anything, Ma'am,' Brown said. 'And I if I did have a mishap then I would not be asking Your Majesty for assistance. My job is to look after you.' He did not look at Bay, but his air of superiority was impregnable.

Queen Victoria flushed with pleasure at this manly declaration. 'Oh, I am sure that Captain Middleton didn't *intend* to hurt himself. A fall like that could happen at *any* time. And besides, John, there have been times when you have been a little *unsteady* on your feet.'

'I've nae broken any limbs, Ma'am,' said Brown.

The Queen tapped him on one kilted thigh. 'You have been lucky then.' She turned back to Bay. 'And which regiment are you with, Captain Middleton?'

'The Eleventh Hussars, Ma'am.'

'Then the Prince of Wales is your Colonel in Chief. I believe he is *very* fond of the uniform. But it doesn't fit him so well these days. Too many dinners and parties. So unlike his poor dear father, who was always so *careful* about what he ate.' Victoria turned to John Brown, who was standing behind her, for corroboration.

Brown nodded. 'The late Prince was always verra dainty with his food.'

Sisi thought that it was a pity that the Queen did not show some of her late husband's restraint. She must be quite as broad as she was tall.

The Queen beckoned to her ladies. 'Can we offer you any

refreshment, Empress? You will stay to lunch, of course. And afterwards we can drive round the park. Fresh air is *so* important at this time of year.'

Sisi looked at her ambassador with reproach. She had made it quite clear that this visit was to be a call and nothing more.

'Oh, that would have been lovely, on another occasion I should like nothing better, but we have to go back. There is some urgent business I must attend to.'

Queen Victoria blinked. There was a muffled gasp from the courtiers behind her. The Queen's invitations were never refused. But Sisi did not flinch. She had kept her promise by paying this visit, but she would not ruin a whole day by staying for lunch. She continued, 'I hope you will meet Rudolph, my son, when he comes. He is such an admirer of all things English. He wants to know everything about your engineering – bridges and tunnels are all he talks about. Not Viennese at all.' She laughed and Karolyi, behind her, did his best to muster a smile. The English courtiers stood frozen, waiting to see how their mistress would react.

Victoria gave a little nod. Her voice was high, clear and unmistakably cross.

'We shall be delighted to see the Crown Prince. Let us hope *he* will not be so *pressed* for time.'

The royal lips were set in a straight line, but Sisi only laughed. 'I shall tell him that he must work very hard to make up for his mother's shortcomings.'

Queen Victoria did not smile back. Henry Ponsonby pulled at his whiskers.

Sisi, seeing Karolyi's pained expression, realised that she must repair the damage. She looked around her in desperation.

'But this is such an *interesting* room. We have nothing like this in Vienna. I know Franz Joseph would admire your decorations

exceedingly. So *gemütlich*. He ordered all the furniture for his apartments in the Hofburg from Maples of London.' Sisi pointed at the
polychrome carpet. 'What a pity he isn't here to see this. I know
he would admire it very much.'

Mollified, Victoria leant forward. 'That is the royal tartan. Dear
Albert designed it. He loved Scotland so much, he wanted to be
reminded of it *at all times*. We were always *so* happy there.' The Queen
looked fondly at John Brown as she said this.

'You really must visit Scotland, dear Kaiserin. So *picturesque*. I am
never so carefree as when I am in Scotland. Such happy memories
of my beloved Albert.'

Sisi thought that, despite her frequent references to her late
husband, the Queen looked remarkably content in the company of
John Brown.

'Perhaps one day you will visit Bad Ischl in the Tyrol. People say
it is very like Scotland.'

The Queen shook her head sadly. 'I am afraid it is too late for
me to visit Austria. Dear Albert was never there and I would not
like to go anywhere that he had not seen. I would feel disloyal.'

Sisi could think of nothing to say in answer to this. To her relief,
the boulle clock started to strike noon, its precise melodious chimes
echoed by the deeper notes of the chapel bells outside. There was
a brief hiatus as the party waited for the noise to subside.

This, Sisi decided, was her cue. She leant over to the Queen
and said, 'I must trespass on your hospitality no longer, Victoria.
I shall write to the Emperor today to say that I find you in good
health and to convey any other messages you would like to charge
me with.'

Sisi wanted to stand up, she was almost rigid with boredom, but
protocol meant that she could not rise before the Queen.

Victoria shook her head.

'What a pity you cannot stay longer,' she said again, although she did not look particularly sorry. 'I had hoped we might have more of a chance to talk together. It is not often that I am able to converse woman to woman with another,' a little pause, 'empress.' She made a little pecking motion of her head as she said this, and there was a gleam in her eyes. Ponsonby made a noise somewhere between a cough and a warning.

The Queen ignored him and carried on.

'You may tell your husband that I am to be Empress of India, as well as Queen of England. So you see, we are both empresses now, Elizabeth. Although, of course, there is a difference as I am a *sovereign* and you are a consort.' She beamed, the smile of a child who has been given an enormous box of chocolates.

Sisi saw that she would have to acknowledge this triumph adequately or be condemned to sit in this hideous cold room for ever. Clearly Victoria did not think it was enough to be the Queen of the world's most powerful nation; it had irked her that there was a still grander title that she did not yet possess. Sisi, who had been an empress since she was sixteen, could not share her excitement. To be a queen or an empress, what did it matter? Both titles were gilded cages. Any crown grew heavy. But Victoria would not understand any of this. The little queen was so like Franz Joseph. They both believed that God had chosen them to be monarchs, never doubting their position for a moment. The two monarchs might occasionally tremble at the burden of the duties imposed upon them, but they would not relinquish the tiniest fragment of their powers. Sisi wondered what it would be like to have that certainty, to wake up every morning knowing that you were God's anointed put on this earth to rule over your subjects.

She picked up one of Victoria's hands and pressed it.

'Although mere words can hardly express my feelings, I am so happy to be able to congratulate you in person.'

'Empresses and grandmothers. We stand *alone* on the World Stage, dear Elizabeth.' Victoria was at her most gracious.

'But you are superior to me in this way as in every other. I only have one grandchild,' said Sisi.

This speech seemed to strike the right note with Victoria, and she squeezed Sisi's hand in return and with much rustling rose to her feet.

'You will send my very best wishes to the Emperor. I often think of his poor dear brother. He was such a favourite with us here.'

Sisi lowered her eyes. Maximilian, her brother-in-law, had been crowned Emperor of Mexico eleven years ago, but his brief reign had ended three years later in front of a revolutionary firing squad.

'Poor Max. It was a terrible thing.'

'What a *dreadful* country. You can be sure that we expressed our indignation in the *strongest* terms through the British consul. An anointed sovereign put to death like a common criminal. The Mexicans are little better than *savages*.'

'Yes, we are fortunate to be in Europe,' said Sisi. 'But Max so wanted a kingdom of his own. He wanted to be an emperor like Franzl.'

'Such a mistake to think that a *monarchy* can be manufactured. It is a *sacred* trust.' For affirmation Victoria looked at John Brown, who nodded solemnly.

Sisi did not point out to the new Empress of India that her title was equally artificial, although she would have been liked to see the look on her face.

'Goodbye, Victoria, it was such a pleasure to see you.' She kissed the Queen and Beatrice. Sisi did not think she would say goodbye to John Brown, who after all was only a servant.

The Queen walked with the party to the entrance to the Tower.

'You *must* be *careful*, Elizabeth, I beg you. Please don't take any unnecessary risks.'

She turned to Bay. 'I am relying on you, Captain Middleton, to make sure that no harm comes to the Empress on British soil.'

Bay bowed and said, 'I will watch over the Empress night and day, Ma'am.'

Bay saw a flash in the blue eyes and wondered if he had gone too far, but the Queen smiled and said, 'I feel sure that you will.'

They were halfway down the corridor when the Queen stopped and said, 'Beatrice, you have forgotten the book! Run and fetch it at once.'

The party waited as Beatrice set off down the corridor without evident haste. She returned with a parcel which she pressed into Sisi's hands, 'From mama.'

Ponsonby came back to the station with them in the carriage. This time they were in a landau where the seats were directly behind each other rather than facing. Sisi invited Bay to sit next to her, while the Ambassador and the Chamberlain sat in the seat behind.

'You promised the Queen that you would look after me night and day,' said Sisi, looking straight ahead. 'You will be very busy, Captain Middleton.'

'*Very* busy. But I can hardly disobey my sovereign,' said Bay.

But as they walked up the red carpet to the waiting train, Bay remembered the kilted mass of John Brown standing behind Queen Victoria's chair. He had seen the cartoons in *Punch* of the Queen and her Highland Servant and had laughed in the club at the jokes that circulated about 'Mrs Brown'. There was no similarity, of course, between John Brown's situation and his own, but there had been something about the way that the Queen had looked at him that had made him uncomfortable. It did not surprise him that she had looked. What disturbed him was not Victoria's scrutiny, the slow flick of her blue eyes across his body, but the little turn of her head as she looked over to Brown and back. She had been *comparing* them.

Bay glanced over at Sisi, who was flicking through the book that the Queen had given her. 'Leaves from our Sketchbook of our *life in the Highlands,*' she read, imitating Victoria's emphatically accented delivery. 'What charming pictures. But how dull their life is – just ponies and picnics and those dowdy shawls always. And all the men showing their legs. How do you call the skirt that the Scots men wear? Not a flattering garment, I think.'

'It's called a kilt,' said Bay.

'I am so glad you don't wear a kilt, Captain Middleton, like that great mountain of a man standing behind the Queen. What a brute, and yet she clearly dotes on him. But he is a very odd choice. She needs someone, perhaps, but even at her age she might do better.' Sisi looked over at Bay and smiled. Bay knew that it was a smile of triumph. By choosing him, Sisi had shown her superiority over the dowdy English Queen. He smiled back automatically, the easy smile of a ladies' man. But if Sisi had been observing him closely she would have seen that his pale blue eyes were distant.

But by the time they arrived at Waddesdon to look at the Rothschild stud, the Empress was so reliant on her pilot to tell her which of the many magnificent animals would be best suited to carry her in the field, that Bay's mood lightened. There really was nothing so pleasant as spending someone else's money. And later still when Sisi visited him in his room and together they mocked the hideous carpet, the downtrodden princess and the general dowdiness of Windsor, Bay felt altogether himself again.

The Royal Mail

*I*N HOLLAND PARK CHARLOTTE WAITED FOR A REPLY from her aunt Adelaide. Her letter had been as nonchalantly phrased as she could manage – after the usual enquiries about her aunt's health, Lady Crewe's health and the trousseau preparations of Augusta, Charlotte had said as if in passing, 'Although I find the work here enormously interesting, I do miss our little party at Melton. Do write with some news of Captain Hartopp and Captain Middleton – I suppose they will have left to take up their shooting box.' Then she went on to describe to her aunt the gallery where the exhibition was being held and the heated disputes that were taking place over the hanging. She went into rather more detail about this than her aunt's interest would warrant, but it was necessary to disguise the real purpose of her letter.

Three days after writing to Aunt Adelaide, Charlotte came down to breakfast to find an envelope in Lady Lisle's handwriting. She must have made some sound as Lady Dunwoody looked up from her letters and said, 'I wish I still got letters that made me gasp with delight.'

Charlotte shook her head. 'It is from Aunt Adelaide.'

'Ah.' Lady Dunwoody looked sceptical. 'Well, your aunt must have improved as a correspondent.'

Charlotte waited till her godmother had left the room before opening her letter. She scanned it quickly, looking for Bay's name, but Lady Lisle had never got out of the old habit of crossing the pages so it took her quite ten minutes to decipher her aunt's pinched hand. At last, after detailed, and in Charlotte's view, interminable instructions about the monogrammed tortoiseshell dressing case that her aunt wanted Charlotte to order from Asprey's as a wedding present for Augusta, she finally reached the paragraph she was looking for.

> *The atmosphere here at Melton is not nearly as gay as when you were here, dear Charlotte. Captain Hartopp has gone to hunt on the other side of the county and poor Captain Middleton has not been here since his accident.*

Charlotte felt her stomach lurch. There had been only one accident in her life, and that was the one on the bright winter morning that had left her motherless. She gripped the edge of the breakfast table and for a moment she thought that she might actually be sick, but then her wits returned. It could not be a fatal accident; Aunt Adelaide had said that Bay had not been there, which meant that he must be still alive. She tried to read on, but her hand was shaking so much that she had to put the letter down before she could decipher it.

> *The Empress has quite taken charge of him. Some servants came over to fetch his belongings and his horses. Such livery! We were quite dazzled by the gold braid. But he sent a very charming note to Lady Crewe, saying that his visit had been quite memorable. I think we both know what he means by that! Lady Crewe read the note aloud after dinner and Augusta said that Bay had become*

quite the courtier and that quite soon he would be too grand to consort with his old friends. Lady Crewe wrote back at once to tell him that she would be very honoured to entertain the Empress if she were to suggest a visit. We have not yet received a reply but Lady C has ordered all the footmen to have their wigs repowdered, just in case.

As Charlotte read on and she realised that Bay could not be seriously hurt, she felt the tide of terror that had swept through her body subside and the tightness at the back of her throat ease. She put the letter down and drank some tea, uncomfortably aware that her chemise was clammy with sweat. She would have to go and change. It was unthinkable that she could stand next to the fragrant Caspar like this. It was only when she had got to her bedroom and was trying to unlace her corset (she had felt too embarrassed to ring for her maid), her hand behind her back struggling to undo the corset laces which had been tied into a particularly intractable knot, that she realised that although Bay was not in all likelihood badly injured, he was now staying at Easton Neston with the Empress.

There was a knock at the bedroom door and without waiting for a reply Lady Dunwoody walked in. She looked at Charlotte's state of undress in surprise.

'Do you want me to ring for the maid?'

'If you could just undo this knot for me, I think I can manage.'

Lady Dunwoody gave a sharp tug and the laces came free. Charlotte opened the chest of drawers, looking for another chemise. She felt awkward undressing in front of her godmother, so she turned away from her as she took off the old garment and put on the new one, but Lady Dunwoody carried on talking regardless.

'I came to give you some good news. The hanging committee

has looked at your work and they have decided to show four of your prints. Before you think that there might have been some influence on my part, I must tell you that I submitted the pictures quite anonymously. It is true that I voted for their inclusion, but on a committee of twelve I felt that was quite fair. And to be truthful the votes were unanimous. *Such* an honour for you, Charlotte. I am so very proud of you.'

Charlotte turned round and saw that her godmother's craggy face was quite soft with pride. She put her arms around the older woman's neck and embraced her.

'Not having children myself I have never known what it is to feel a mother's pride, but now that I have seen you succeed, Charlotte, I feel I know something of that emotion.'

Charlotte kissed the leathery cheek. 'If I have succeeded, it is because I had the best teacher.'

Lady Dunwoody straightened up, her briskness returning. 'Well, at least I have managed to put something in your head other than waltzing and cavalry officers. Men are all very well, and a good husband can be enormously useful, but women like us need something to *do*.'

'But you have a good husband, Aunt Celia, you can't blame me for wanting one too,' said Charlotte.

'Of course! But a man will only make you happy for a while, while a skill, an occupation – learning something – will always satisfy you. If only your poor mother could have realised that. She was such a clever, charming creature, but her whole life was about *sensation*. She never understood the value of accomplishment.'

'I believe she rode very well,' said Charlotte, who did not like to hear her mother dismissed so lightly, 'my father always said she had the best hands in the kingdom.'

'She may well have done. But to ride well to hounds is simply a diversion. It leaves no *record*. But already, my dear Charlotte, you have created something, a legacy. When you have children, you will be able to say to them, this is the picture that was picked by the greatest experts in the field, to hang before the Queen. That is something, is it not?'

Charlotte nodded. She did not point out that the inheritance her mother had left her had affected every aspect of her life. Everything she did lay in the shadow of the Lennox fortune. It was true that her godmother had shown her how to take photographs, but it was her inheritance that paid for her cameras, the dark rooms and her freedom to indulge her hobby. If she had been forced to earn her living as a governess she would not have had the time or space to create a legacy.

'Anyway, to show you that I haven't entirely forgotten what it is to be young and foolish, I suggest that if there is anyone you would like to invite to the opening next week, you should do so. I am sure that Fred will want to come with the Crewe girl and Adelaide Lisle, if you must, but I am sure there are *other* friends you would like to ask. I believe that one of the selected pictures is of a very special friend.' Lady Dunwoody raised an eyebrow with an archness Charlotte had not known her to possess. 'Of course you will make Caspar terribly jealous when he sees how handsome your cavalry officer is, but he will survive. The point is that all your admirers should cluster in front of your pictures and acknowledge your talent. That would be a fine thing.'

Charlotte found herself blushing. She had not had enough compliments in her life to know how to acknowledge them. Compliments inspired by her own self, that is, rather than by the Lennox fortune: that kind of flattery she knew exactly how to deal with.

'You are right, Aunt Celia. It is a very great honour and I shall certainly invite people to come. Of course it is very short notice, so I fear that—'

'Nonsense,' interrupted her godmother, 'this is an *event.*' She opened the door and delivered her parting shot, 'Anybody who truly cares for you will be there.'

The door closed and Charlotte picked up her green velvet bodice. Realising that she could not do up the line of hooks down the back unaided, she rang the bell.

While she waited for her maid, she sat down at the bureau and took out some writing paper.

'Dear Bay', she wrote, and then, deciding that was too intimate, she took a fresh piece and wrote, 'Dear Captain Middleton'. She would have liked very much to start with 'My dearest', but she thought of the print that Caspar had been so reluctant to show her, and she knew that this letter must be carefully phrased.

My aunt writes to tell me that you have had an accident. She did not vouchsafe the extent of your injuries, simply that it was serious enough to warrant you staying at Easton Neston. So I am writing to you there to wish you a speedy recovery. I was so sorry not to see you before I left Melton. It was rather a sudden departure; my godmother Lady Dunwoody is organising an exhibition of photographs to be presented to the Queen and she needed my help. I thought I would be perhaps more useful to her than to Augusta and her trousseau preparations. Once I had announced my decision I decided to go to London at once – Augusta's reaction made it uncomfortable for me to prolong my stay. I left you a note but I believe that it may have been given to Captain Hartopp by mistake. I hope that he passed it on.

The maid came in without knocking and Charlotte quickly covered the letter with her blotter. She didn't know if the maid could even read, but she had spent enough time listening to servants' gossip to know that if she could, everything about her letter would be public knowledge below stairs. As the maid did up her bodice with impatient fingers, sighing because she had been called away from her breakfast, Charlotte looked at her reflection with distaste. Her hair looked dingy and her complexion sallow. It was all very well for Lady Dunwoody to talk about achievements, but what use was public approval when what she wanted was Bay's admiration? She thought of Grace, the maid who had arranged her hair so prettily at Melton. She had always resisted having her own maid – it was one of the trappings of heiressdom that she despised – but now Charlotte thought she would like to have someone who could make her look charming. When she had finished her letter to Bay, she would write to Lady Crewe.

When the maid had finished Charlotte picked up her letter again.

The exhibition opens next Thursday, the 18th, at the Royal Photographic Society. The Queen is coming to open the show. There are around four hundred prints on display, and it may surprise you to hear some of my work has been selected. My godmother tells me that this is a great honour and has suggested that I should invite my friends to the opening.

I realise that you must be very busy with your duties as the Empress's pilot, but as you are in one of the pictures to be exhibited, I thought it might be interesting for the spectators to see whether my lens has done justice to the original.

Charlotte wondered whether that last sentence was too obvious an appeal, so she added,

It is a pity that I cannot extend the invitation to Tipsy, who I am sure will be much in demand as a photographic model. I am writing to the Melton party and to Captain Hartopp, and I hope that some of them will find the time to make the journey. I wonder if the prospect of a Royal encounter might tempt Augusta away from her trousseau preparations?

I hope that you are making a good recovery from your injury and that it won't interfere with your plans for the Grand National. You see I remember our conversation . . .

Charlotte paused, wondering if this sounded too significant. She wanted Bay to know that her feelings had not changed, without writing anything that would sound like a reproach. Casting her mind back over their brief courtship, she tried to think of something that would remind him of their past intimacy. She thought of the last time she had seen Bay, standing on the steps of Melton laughing with Fred and Captain Hartopp. Picking up her pen again she wrote,

*. . . and your promise to tell me the story of how Captain Hartopp came to be called Chicken. I will be **most** disappointed if you do not enlighten me. Even if it is an indelicate story I promise not to get the vapours. We women are stronger than you think.*

Hoping very much to see you at the exhibition, and certainly at Fred and Augusta's wedding,

I remain your friend and photographer,

Charlotte Baird

Having read the letter through twice, once silently and once aloud, alert to any suggestion of missishness, she sealed it and addressed it to Captain Middleton, Easton Neston, Northamptonshire. She then quickly wrote to Lady Crewe to beg for the loan of Grace, and to Lady Lisle, Augusta and Chicken Hartopp to invite them to the exhibition.

As she placed the letters in the Japanese bowl in the hallway that Lady Dunwoody used as a post tray, the doorbell rang and Caspar walked in, shaking the snow from his ulster like a wet dog. He began talking the moment he walked through the door.

'Carlotta *mia,* have you heard the news? Your pictures. Unanimous decision. Everyone agog. You are the youngest contributor by far.' He seized her hands and whirled her around for a moment. Charlotte laughed. His delight was clearly genuine and she was touched.

'Aunt Celia told me. I am delighted, of course, but I can't help feeling like an imposter. My photography is just a hobby, I feel embarrassed to be compared to professionals like you.'

Caspar gripped her by the forearms and pretended to shake her.

'Shame on you, Miss Baird, for the crime of false modesty. If you have a talent, why not revel in it instead of protesting against it? Are you are afraid of being unladylike?'

'Not at all,' said Charlotte, pushing him away. 'If I had been afraid of that, I would be painting watercolours of highland scenes and making pictures out of shells.'

'Then you should be proud of your accomplishments. I am delighted that my pictures will be hanging next to yours.'

The faint note of reproach made Charlotte realise that she had forgotten to ask Caspar about his pictures. Quickly, she added, 'Your portfolio is outstanding, I expect the committee wanted to select everything.'

Caspar smiled, mollified. 'They have taken ten pictures. Not bad for an American interloper.'

'Now who is being falsely modest? You know that you are the

equal of anyone here. The society's members must be beside themselves with jealousy.'

'I believe there have been mutterings. Some members tried to exclude me because I was not British, but Lady D would have none of it. She told them that photography was an international medium and that they should celebrate excellence wherever it came from.' As Caspar said this he stuck out his chest to suggest Lady Dunwoody in full flow.

'I hope they chose the picture of your friend. The one with the grapes,' said Charlotte.

To her surprise, Caspar's shoulders dropped, his buoyancy gone.

'Abraham will hang before the Queen of England, a woman he had never heard of,' he said quietly, brushing a snowflake from the sleeve of his coat.

Charlotte saw the pain in his face. She remembered the photograph he had taken of a pile of stones in the desert that was Abraham's gravestone. For all his ebullience, Caspar was, she realised, still in mourning. Even though there was no black band on his sleeve, he obviously felt Abraham's loss as keenly as if it had been a close relative. She tried to soothe him.

'But as your friend, he would have been so happy to have done you this service.'

'No doubt. He was a generous boy. He would have been delighted to make me famous.' Caspar took a yellow silk handkerchief from his pocket and wiped the snow off his moustache. 'No, *I* am the one who minds that he is to be hung before strangers who know nothing more of him than the image I have presented. All they can see is what I have put before them – a savage with a bunch of grapes.'

'But that's not true! Anyone could see that he has a great soul. *I* did. You aren't so great a photographer that you can give your subject a character they don't have,' Charlotte protested.

'Perhaps.' He folded up the yellow silk square carefully and put it back in his pocket. 'But even if they don't see what a remarkable person he was, he will still hang there as an example of my photographic skill.'

Smiling ruefully he continued. 'I do *have* scruples, just not enough of them. Abraham will become a plate in the *Illustrated London News* and I will sigh a little as I cash the cheque.'

To end this exchange Caspar began to look through the letters in the Japanese bowl. Charlotte would have protested but she was relieved that his sudden fit of melancholy seemed to have passed. It struck her that Caspar's high spirits, the torrent of chatter and jokes, was something he turned on to mask his true feelings. It made her like him more, as she knew how hard it was sometimes to disguise the most painful thoughts.

As she watched him flick through the heavy white envelopes, she could see him trying to work himself back to his normal playful pitch. When he spoke, his voice was light again.

'I see you have been busy – these are in your hand, are they not?' He took one out and sniffed it. 'No perfume, Carlotta? Not even for your billet-doux to the handsome captain?'

'Do I look like the sort of girl who sends letters smelling of violets? Lady Dunwoody suggested that I invite some people to the opening, and I have, of course, obeyed her instructions.'

Caspar made a mock bow. 'Lady Dunwoody must be obeyed, certainly, but I wonder if perhaps in this case you might want to consider—'

He broke off as Lady Dunwoody herself burst through the green baize door that led to the servants' hall. She was dressed to go out and fizzing with impatience. She barked at Charlotte, 'Have you forgotten that the carriage is ordered for eleven? The hanging committee meets at twelve. You have exactly two minutes to get ready, Charlotte. I have no intention of being late.'

In the rush and confusion as Charlotte tried to adjust her hat to the least unbecoming angle, find her gloves and button up her boots, she forgot to ask Caspar what he had been about to say before her godmother had interrupted them. Rushing through the hall and down the steps, she didn't even glance at the letters in the blue and white Japanese bowl.

At eleven-thirty the butler collected the letters as he did three times a day and took them to his pantry. There he selected seven penny stamps from his postage book and stuck them to the letters, using a specially moistened pad. The butler did not think it was his place to use his own saliva. After recording the number of stamps used and the destinations of the letters – despite her bohemian leanings, Lady Dunwoody was never vague about household accounts – the butler put the household correspondence in a red velvet bag embroidered with a D. Then he called the footman whose job it was to take the letters to the new red pillar box on the Kensington Road. Despite the snow, the footman was not only the only person converging on the letter box in order to catch the midday collection. There was another footman from Holland House, a maid from Leighton House and a boot boy belonging to the Burne Jones household. The post box had only been there since the new year, so there was still some novelty about watching the letters disappear into its shiny red maw. Sometimes the footman would read out the addresses on the letters in an imitation of an aristocratic accent for the delectation of the Leighton House parlourmaid, who was the reason that he never shirked this particular chore, but today the snow was falling too thickly. Lady Dunwoody's footman watched as the parlourmaid deposited the Leighton House correspondence and then did the same, taking care that the snow did not fall on the envelopes and make the ink run.

Charlotte had not sealed her letter with wax. She had used one of the new envelopes that used dried xanthan gum to stick the flaps together. This made it much easier for the Foreign Office agent whose job it was to intercept all mail to the imperial household at Easton Neston. As it contained no reference to foreign policy that he could detect, he noted its contents in the ledger put aside for this purpose, resealed it and sent it on so that it was loaded onto the 4.10 to Northampton.

The letter was delivered to Easton Neston at seven a.m. the next morning where it was steamed open again, this time by Baron Nopsca, who had made it his business to know everything about the Empress's new favourite. He found its contents marginally more interesting than the Foreign Office man. Although his English was far from fluent, he knew enough to understand that this was a letter from a woman, who if not a mistress was certainly more than a friend. This did not surprise him as he had already assessed Captain Middleton as *ein galant* and a *herzensbrecher*, his only concern was for the happiness of his mistress. For a moment he thought of destroying the letter; the Empress would not be happy about the Captain going to London to visit another woman. In Austria he would not have hesitated to burn the letter, but then in Vienna no woman would be foolish enough to write publicly to the Empress's favourite while he was in residence. After a moment of reflection Nospca decided that there was no need to interfere; the attachment between his mistress and the Captain was too new and too mutually exciting. It would have to be an exceptional woman to summon the Englishman away from the Austrian Empress. He scanned the letter again and decided that there was nothing to fear.

As he got to the mention of Chicken Hartopp, the Baron sighed. Only an Englishman, he thought, would be named after a fowl.

The Monkey's Paw

COUNTESS FESTETICS HAD GIVEN BAY A FLASK OF schnapps as they rode out that morning. 'I think you must have need of this,' she said.

The flask was now empty and for the first time in his hunting career Bay was longing for the chase to end. Every bump, every stumble made his shoulder throb. He needed his good hand to hold the reins so he couldn't use his whip, which made it hard to keep up with the Empress. She was leading the field on one of the new hunters that she had bought at Waddesdon from the Rothschilds. She had bought five horses in all and Bay had made a tidy commission. The blue roan called Liniment, was everything a great hunter should be and showed no sign of flagging after a long day on soft ground, but now Bay was regretting his gift for spotting a good horse.

After clearing one particularly high fence Bay heard her say to Count Esterhazy in English so that he could understand, 'Aren't you jealous of my English Pegasus, Count? You have to admit that the Captain was right about English hunters.'

'The Captain is certainly good at picking winners,' said Esterhazy, also in English.

The Empress did not hear Esterhazy's reply as she had already gone ahead to the next fence, but Bay did. Despite the throbbing in his shoulder he made himself smile at the Count and said, 'If you change your mind about English horses, I would be happy to find some for you.'

'Thank you for your kind offer, Captain Middleton, but I don't think that I need your assistance to choose my horses.'

Bay's smile did not falter. 'I'm always happy to help if you change your mind.'

Count Esterhazy gave him the very smallest inclination of the head, somewhere between a nod and a gesture of distaste.

'Too kind. But unlike the Empress, I never change my mind.' He turned his head to look at the Empress wheeling round the edge of the field on the blue roan. 'I believe I am keeping you from your duties, Captain Middleton.'

Bay gave Tipsy a nudge with his spurs. When he drew alongside Sisi, she turned her head and frowned.

'There you are,' she said.

At the end of the day, the Empress had a carriage to take her home. Normally Bay would have hacked home on Tipsy but he knew he was at the end of his strength. Reluctantly he climbed into the closed carriage, with the Empress, Liechtenstein and Esterhazy. Esterhazy was sitting next to the Empress so he had to take the seat next to Liechtenstein, who shrank into the corner as Bay sat down. The Austrians chatted away in German, the two men doing their best to ignore Bay. The Empress smiled at him from time to time, but she did not insist on speaking English. Bay closed his eyes and instantly fell asleep.

A searing jolt of pain woke him up with a start. Lichtenstein must have poked him in his bad shoulder. To his surprise he saw that the three others were laughing at him.

Sisi said, 'Don't be angry with Felix, Captain Middleton. You were snoring a little loudly, and I asked him to wake you up. I had forgotten about your bad shoulder. Forgive me.'

Bay smiled as broadly as he could. 'I am the one who should be asking forgiveness. To disturb you with my snoring, that is a heinous crime. I deserve the most severe punishment.'

'It is a good thing we are not in Austria, Captain Middleton, as then your punishment really would be severe,' said Count Esterhazy. 'There no courtier would dream of falling asleep in the presence of royalty.'

'How fortunate, then, that we are in England,' said Bay evenly.

'Yes, it is so nice to be here and not in Vienna where everybody takes etiquette so seriously,' said Sisi. 'Everyone must be allowed their frailties. I would have left you to sleep but you were making such a noise that we could hardly hear ourselves talk.' She laughed and Bay could see that she was enjoying teasing him in front of the others, so he forced himself to laugh too.

'And why are you so weary, I wonder, Captain? What are you doing at night that means that you fall asleep in the day?' Sisi said. Bay saw the merest glimpse of her tongue as she licked her lips.

'It can be difficult sometimes to fall asleep in a strange house, Ma'am. Even one as welcoming as Easton Neston.'

'Perhaps you should consider staying somewhere else,' said the Count.

Bay met his gaze without flinching. It was a direct challenge; both men waited to see how the Empress would react. Her cheeks were flushed and her eyes glinted. Picking up her fan, she tapped Esterhazy on the arm, harder than was strictly necessary.

'Do I need to remind you that the Captain is my guest? I have asked him to stay and I will be the one to ask him to leave. We may be in England, but you are an Austrian, and as you were so quick to remind Captain Middleton, a courtier knows the penalty for being rude to royalty. By insulting him you have insulted me. Please apologise at once.'

'I apologise to you, Kaiserin, unreservedly,' said the Count. 'Perhaps I did not understand your feelings completely. But you cannot expect me to apologise to this, this . . .' he was spitting out his words now, 'this groom.'

Bay recoiled from the force of his anger, but he had had years of experience dealing with people who thought themselves superior to him; he knew that the most effective response was deflation. So he smiled affably, the smile of a cavalry officer dealing with a drunken soldier.

'No need to apologise, old man. No need at all. No offence meant, I am sure, and none taken. I don't think either of us would want to embarrass Her Majesty with a petty squabble. That may be the way you do things in Austria, but an English gentleman does not give way to his feelings in the presence of a lady, let alone a queen.'

Sisi clapped her hands.

'Bravo, Bay Middleton. We are not in Vienna now, Count.'

Esterhazy saw that he had been outmanoeuvred. Subsiding into his corner, he was silent for the rest of the journey.

Nopsca was on the steps to greet them, with a footman holding tumblers of negus on a salver. Bay took his and drained it in one gulp. The quarrel with Esterhazy had unsettled him. He did not enjoy being the focus of so much hostility.

Nopsca was distributing the day's letters to Esterhazy and Liechtenstein. The Empress's correspondence was set out in a red morocco casket. Nopsca murmured something about the Crown Prince and the Empress started to go upstairs. Bay, who did not want to be left alone with the Austrians, made to follow her when the Baron called him back.

'One moment, Captain Middleton. There is a letter for you too.'

Surprised, Bay took the letter. Not recognising the handwriting, he put it in the pocket of his coat and had just put his foot on the first marble tread when the whole hall was pierced by a shriek that made the crystals of the great chandelier rattle. A quick grey shape jumped from the top of the balustrade at the top of the staircase onto the stairs and started to bounce from step to step, chattering as it did so. As the creature came nearer to him Bay saw that it was a monkey about the size of a terrier, wearing a red waistcoat with gold braid and a golden collar round its neck.

As it passed the Empress, she cried out, 'My little Florian, you have escaped. Nopsca, we must put him back in his prison or the English housekeeper will hand in her notice.' Behind him, Bay heard Nopsca sigh. Catching the monkey was not going to be easy.

Bay found a sugar lump in his pocket that he kept there to reward his horses, and he bent down and offered it to the monkey. The little animal skittered around him for a moment, coming towards the outstretched treat and then retreating. Bay kept up a a stream of soothing chatter, the sort of small talk he made to his horses.

'Don't be scared, Florian, I'm not going to hurt you, look at this lovely lump of sugar, you know you're hungry.' The monkey's movements began to slow down and at last he came very close to Bay's outstretched hand and one paw darted out to take the treat. Bay let him take the sugar lump and then started to stroke the animal's head and back. Then slowly and carefully he scooped up the little creature with his good arm and held it close to his body.

The monkey, who was blissfully eating the sugar, did not protest, and Bay was about to hand him over to Nopsca's outstretched arms when Liechtenstein said in a stage whisper to the Count, 'Why, even little Florian finds the Captain irresistible.'

Esterhazy gave a sharp bark of laughter which echoed through the vast marble hall and frightened the monkey, which leapt out of Bay's arms and began to dance around him. Cursing under his breath, he dug around in his pocket for another sugar lump, and in doing so he dislodged the letter which fell to the ground. The monkey, who had seen exactly where the supply of treats was coming from, saw the envelope as manna from heaven. He picked it up with both paws and began to scamper up the stairs. Bay went after him, but with only one arm, it was too easy for Florian to jump out of his grasp. He made a grab for the monkey, which had jumped on the handrail, and losing his balance, fell painfully onto the marble steps, narrowly avoiding a headlong tumble down the staircase.

'Florian, you are a wicked creature,' said the Empress, who had been laughing so much there were tears on her cheeks. 'Come here at once and receive your punishment.' The monkey looked at her for a moment, nibbled the envelope he was holding, and then jumped into the Empress's arms.

'Good boy! And now you must apologise to the Captain.' Bay had to pull himself up by the marble banister. At that moment he would have happily throttled Florian. He could see that Nopsca was having similar thoughts. Standing up shakily, he shook the tiny paw that was being held out to him by the Empress.

'Look how sorry he is. But I suppose he is like any caged

creature, desperate to enjoy his freedom.' Bay did not trust himself to reply.

'And here is your letter, only slightly damaged. I hope it isn't too important?' Her tone was pointed.

Bay took the envelope. In a moment of sudden clarity he realised that the letter must be from Charlotte and that the Empress had sensed that it was from a woman.

'I doubt it, Ma'am,' he said, as nonchalantly as he could. He turned the letter over in his hand. 'It's probably from Lady Crewe, wanting to know when I am coming back.'

As Bay had hoped, this distracted the Empress. 'There is no question of you going back. You must write and tell her that I insist that you remain here.'

'Yes, Your Majesty,' said Bay with a mock flourish. Sisi either ignored this gesture or accepted it as her due, Bay could not be quite sure.

Then the Empress swept past him to give Florian to his gaoler, and Bay took his chance to escape.

As he read the letter, he could hear Charlotte's small, clear voice and see the wry tilt of her head. With a pang, he realised that there had been no caprice about her departure from Melton. Hartopp had seen an opportunity to queer things between Bay and Charlotte and had taken it.

He heard the appeal in Charlotte's letter, understanding that she had hedged it around with banter, as if unsure of how he would receive it: he must, he decided, go to the exhibition. It would make Charlotte happy. Whatever happened here at Easton Neston, he liked the idea of making Charlotte happy.

With some relish he thought that he would tell Charlotte exactly how Hartopp had come to be called Chicken – in normal circumstances he would never dream of betraying a fellow officer, but given Hartopp's treachery he felt no compunction. But as he sat down at the walnut writing bureau and tried to pick up a pen he realised that his injured arm was not capable of doing even that, let alone writing a letter. Bay rocked back on his chair. He tried to write something with his left hand, but as he was right-handed his efforts were hardly legible.

In another house, Bay might have asked someone to take dictation for him, but that was not possible at Easton Neston. There was no one in the household whose discretion he could trust. There was the telegraph, of course, but even that would involve getting one of the servants on side.

He was wondering how to solve this problem when the footman who had been assigned to valet him appeared, holding a bowl of hot water.

Bay had cut himself shaving that morning, and it was difficult to hold the razor steady with the wrong hand, so he asked the footman to do the job for him. The footman, who was a tall teenager with a freckled countenance that suggested he had red hair under his wig, was unexpectedly deft.

'Thank you. What's your name?'

'Albert, sir.'

'You could be a barber, Albert.'

'Thank you, sir. Grew up on a farm, so I've been shearing sheep since I was a lad. Got to have a steady hand for shearing.'

'How did you come into service? Doesn't your father need you on the farm?'

'I am the youngest of eight brothers, sir. Would have been ten but two of them died of fever.'

'I see. Do you like it here?'

Albert hesitated.

Bay, sensing this, said, 'Don't worry, I never betray a confidence.'

'Well, sir, I was happy enough here working for Lord Hesketh, but I can't say as I enjoy the current situation. I haven't worked for foreigners before. They've got some funny notions. The housekeeper and the cook are beside themselves. Last week in the middle of the night, the bell rings – Her Majesty's bell. I was still up, so I had to go up there. The Countess, the older lady, tells me to go and fetch some raw veal, quick as I can. So I have to wake up Cook and get the key to the meat safe and fetch the meat up there on a silver salver. Next morning the maid that was doing the room brought it down again. They hadn't touched it.'

Bay thought he had found his man.

'Albert, would you like to earn a sovereign?'

'Yes, sir.'

'Can you write?'

Albert looked puzzled. 'Not copperplate, sir, but I know my letters.'

'If I give you a message, could you write it down and take it to the telegraph office for me?'

'I think so, sir.'

'The important thing is that no one in the household should know anything about it. Not the message, nor the fact that I want to send a telegram.'

Albert looked worried.

'But suppose someone sees me go into the telegraph office, sir. What will I say?'

'If it is one of the English servants you can tell them I sent you, something about a horse. If it is one of the Austrians, just pretend that you don't understand what they are saying.'

The footman smiled. 'That'll be easy enough, sir.'

'Excellent. When you've done it, there will be another sovereign for you.'

'Thank you, sir.'

After Albert had left, Bay picked up Charlotte's letter and tucked it into the inside pocket of his riding coat. Then after a moment he took it out, read it through again and threw into the fire, where it blazed for a moment before crumbling into the ash.

Bay did not go down to dinner that evening. His shoulder was aching and he did not relish the prospect of another encounter with Liechtenstein and Esterhazy. He knew that Sisi would not be pleased by this dereliction of duty, and he wondered whether she would come to his room that night.

By eleven o'clock he decided that she wasn't coming. He rang the bell and asked the footman to bring him some brandy. He had subsided into a pleasant, alcohol-tinged haze, so when he heard the tap on the door just before midnight, he felt a moment of irritation at being disturbed.

Her hair was down, hanging over one shoulder, and she was holding the length of it up with her arm like a train. She was wearing a floor-length velvet gown with a high neck and frogged fastenings all the way down. Bay, as always, found himself moved by the sight of her hair unbound.

She smiled at him. 'I would have come sooner, but I had to write some letters.'

He walked over to her and took the rope of hair and shook it out. The weight of it pulled her head back a little and he kissed her as her mouth tilted up to his.

He slipped his hand under her gown and felt bare skin. He stroked her ribs and the underside of her breast, tiny feathery touches until he could hear her breathing change. He tugged at the fastening of the robe with his good hand but the little knots of silk wouldn't budge.

'Are you trying to keep me out?' he said.

'Aren't I worth a little perseverance?' said Sisi.

She liked to hedge their encounters with these small tests of his patience. After the days spent behaving as Empress and Pilot, it took them both a moment to assume their night-time roles. She always came to him, but she did not instantly surrender. As Bay struggled with the slippery silk fastenings, he knew that in her eyes he was proving himself worthy of the prize.

At last, his fingers aching, he unfastened the last knot at the hem. Kneeling before her, he tugged the robe from her shoulders so that it pooled on the floor.

She looked down at him. 'I don't think that even John Brown would work so hard to possess his queen.'

'But my reward is so much greater,' said Bay.

Later, as they lay side by side on his bed, Bay said, 'I so long to put *both* my arms around you, Sisi.'

'I think you manage quite well.' She laughed.

'I need to see the doctor in London who attended to my shoulder before. I don't think the man here has strapped it up properly.'

'Oh, but you don't have to go all the way to London. What's his name? I will ask Nopsca to send for him,' said Sisi, stroking his injured arm.

'You are very kind, but I think it might be easier if I went to see him myself. I will only be gone for a day and a night.'

'But I will miss you,' said Sisi, pouting.

Bay kissed her. 'You have Liechtenstein and Esterhazy to entertain you. I am sure they won't miss me.'

'No. They are horribly jealous of you. Not because of me, you understand, not in that way – they are more interested in each other. But they are scared that now I have you, I will send them home.'

'And will you?'

'Oh no, they would run back and gossip about me. No, they are better here. They will get used to you.'

'I wish I could agree with you.'

She laughed. 'I thought Max was going to call you out this afternoon.'

'May I remind Your Majesty that duelling is illegal in this country.'

'Oh, it is in Austria too, but it doesn't stop them.'

'Well, I value my life too highly to lose it because someone calls me a groom. And besides, I would rather be called a groom than a courtier.'

'So what do you want to be called, Bay?'

'Your pilot and your friend.' He stroked the length of her side.

'Special friend,' said Sisi, putting her head on his chest.

Bay tried not to flinch as her weight fell on his bad arm. Sisi quite often forgot his dislocated shoulder. He hoped that she would not fall asleep.

The stable clock struck two-thirty and Sisi roused herself. As she stood fastening the blue velvet gown she said, 'Who was your letter from? The one that poor Florian nearly ate.'

Bay was glad he had burnt the letter.

'Oh, it was from Lady Crewe. She wanted to know if I could persuade you to call on her at Melton.'

'But why would I want to do that?'

'The house is an architectural curiosity. It is one of the most famous examples of the Gothic style.'

'Does it have tartan carpets?'

'Oh no. Lord Crewe is a very cultured man. '

'And what is she like?'

'Ambitious.'

'Then I see no reason to call on her. Unless, of course, you have a reason for going there?'

'None at all,' Bay said truthfully.

Sisi seemed satisfied. Fastening the collar, she said, 'I had a letter today too. From my son.'

Bay looked up, surprised. Sisi hardly ever mentioned her children. He had assumed it was from some delicacy about their situation.

'I don't know if he will come here. Rudolph doesn't care for hunting.' She frowned. 'I think perhaps that he is afraid. But I cannot ask him.'

'No,' Bay agreed.

'He has come to look at factories and shipyards. Or so he says.' Sisi paused. 'I think there may be other reasons, but he would not tell his mother those.' She shrugged. 'They took him away from me when he was very young. I had been ill, and my husband's mother did not trust me to bring up the heir to the throne. But I would have managed him better. He is more Wittelsbach than Hapsburg, but they do not listen to me.' She pulled her hair across her shoulder and flicked the ends against her other hand like a switch.

'But if he does come here, we must be discreet.'

'Yes, Your Majesty,' said Bay.

The Crown Prince

THE AMBASSADOR LOOKED AT HIS POCKET WATCH. it was twenty-three minutes past eleven. He had told the Crown Prince that he would come for him at eleven and he had now been waiting in the lobby of Claridge's for twenty-three minutes. He decided that he must chivvy the Prince along. It would not do to arrive at the exhibition after the Queen, who, being an English queen, was always punctual.

The door to the suite was opened by the Prince's valet.

'Where is His Highness? I think perhaps he has forgotten that I was to call for him at eleven.'

'The Crown Prince is still dressing, Your Excellency,' said the valet wearily.

'Perhaps I can be of assistance,' said Karolyi, and followed the valet into the bedroom.

Rudolph was standing in front of a cheval glass, trying to fasten the gold buttons of his uniform. One look at the young man's ashen face told the Ambassador why he had been kept waiting. The Prince had been kept to a strict schedule of improving activities approved by the Emperor – the evening before he had been to a lecture at the Mechanics Institute, but afterwards he had made his own amusement. He was a slight young man, only a little taller than his mother, and this morning he looked weighed down by the gold braid on his uniform. The whites of his black eyes were bloodshot and the Ambassador could see what looked like a bite mark on his throat.

'Good morning, Your Highness.'

'Karolyi.' Rudolph gave him the barest acknowledgement.

The Ambassador sighed inwardly. Although he did not wish to delay their departure any more, he would have to tell the Prince that wearing the uniform of a colonel of the Imperial Guard, while perfectly normal in Vienna, was not appropriate at the opening of a photographic exhibition in London. The Prince, he knew, would not welcome his advice. Like all the Hapsburgs, he loved to dress up, but the Ambassador dreaded the inevitable sniggering about tinpot princes that would follow in the English press if Rudolph was allowed to appear in all his military finery.

'If I might suggest a morning coat, sir . . .'

Rudoph looked at him with distaste, but the Ambassador pressed on.

'The English do not wear uniforms to this kind of event. As you are here on an unofficial visit, I think morning dress is more appropriate.' Rudolph was scowling now and the Ambassador looked around him with desperation. He saw the morocco boxes containing the Prince's impressive assortment of medals and other honours. 'But you could certainly wear one of your Orders. The Golden Fleece, perhaps?'

Like a small child who has been distracted from the edge of a precipice by a glittering bauble, Rudolph picked up the order which signified that he was a chevalier of the Golden Fleece and twirled it around so that the gold- and diamond-encrusted surface of the fleece caught the light.

'Very well,' he said, the scowl subsiding. 'When in Rome.'

Karolyi gestured to the valet, who had been listening to this exchange, and went outside to wait. At eleven forty-five, the Prince emerged wearing morning dress, with the Order of the Golden Fleece prominent on his lapel. He still looked pale and Karolyi could smell last night's alcohol beneath the imperial cologne, but he was presentable.

To the Ambassador's surprise Rudolph smiled at him.

'I am sorry to have kept you waiting.'

Karolyi bowed. 'My time is of no account, but as Queen Victoria is opening the exhibition . . .'

'We must not be late.' The Prince finished the sentence.

'Exactly, sir.' Karolyi said, relieved at the Prince's sudden change of mood.

As the carriage made its way down Regent Street to the Royal Society of Arts just off the Strand, Rudolph stared out of the window at the passers-by.

'The girls are better in Vienna, don't you think?'

Karolyi murmured something non-committal, and tried not to look at the bruise on Rudolph's neck that was only just concealed by his high collar. Then, to change the subject, he said, 'Are you intending to visit your mother while you are here, sir? Easton Neston is very beautiful. One of the finest houses in the country.'

'If my mother asks me I suppose I must go, but I have come here to learn, not to fraternise with my mother's *friends.*'

Karolyi, who had not anticipated this reaction, decided to probe a little further. 'The hunting there is very fine, though. The Empress is very pleased with the sport.'

'No doubt. But I can't stand those popinjays, Esterhazy and

Liechtenstein. I don't know why Mama takes them everywhere. And now Aunt Maria tells me she has taken up with some English groom.'

The Ambassador coughed. 'If you mean Captain Middleton, sir, with respect he is hardly a groom. He is a cavalry officer on Earl Spencer's staff. The Earl asked him to be your mother's pilot. It is true that he does not have a title, but in England this is quite usual.'

'Aunt Maria says that he is insolent and a man of bad reputation. She says that he has been flirting with my mother.'

'I believe that your aunt tried to engage Captain Middleton's services herself before he became the Empress's pilot. As to the flirting, well, your mother is still a great beauty, I am sure Captain Middleton is not the only man to engage her attention in that way.'

'But she is the Empress of Austria. He should have more respect.'

'Having seen them together, sir, I think that the Kaiserin rather enjoys the attentions of Captain Middleton.'

The Crown Prince relapsed into moody silence, drumming his fingers on the window frame. Karolyi thought how much he looked like his mother.

Charlotte had been at the exhibition since ten o'clock that morning. Lady Dunwoody had been ready to leave from half-past eight, and although her husband and Charlotte pointed out that it would not take more than an hour to reach the Strand from Holland Park, she refused to listen. 'Suppose the carriage's axle breaks? Or one of the horses goes lame? These things do happen.'

Sir Alured, who was not a photographer and had only agreed to attend the exhibition because his wife had insisted, said that he would leave when he had finished his kipper and not before. Charlotte was grateful to him. She had got up at six so that the maid, Grace, who had arrived the day before from Melton, would have time to do her hair, and even at eight-thirty she was not entirely happy with her appearance.

Bay's telegram had arrived a couple of days ago. It had been delivered when Lady Dunwoody was in the dark room so Charlotte had been able to open it alone. TIPSY LOOKING FORWARD TO MEETING THE QUEEN HAS GOT NEW FROCK STOP SHOULDER CROCKED SO CAN'T WRITE BAY. Charlotte had smiled with relief.

She spent the extra minutes afforded by the deboning of Sir Alured's kipper getting Grace to coax a few more curls at the nape of her neck with tongs. She was wearing a new dress in a mauve and white striped silk. It was far more elaborate than her usual day dresses, but Lady Dunwoody had been clear that none of her existing wardrobe was suitable for meeting royalty. The dress had a bustle with a small train, which took some getting used to. She had already knocked over a jardinière in her room by turning round suddenly; she wondered how she would be able to manoeuvre through the crowds at the exhibition.

Charlotte studied herself in the pier glass. She pushed her pancake hat down a little on one side as she had seen Augusta do. She knew from taking pictures that a good image needed just a little asymmetry. She was aiming for jaunty but she pushed it too far, making her look simply dishevelled. She righted it again and stared at herself critically. If she was going to put herself in one of her animal photomontages, she thought, she would be a field mouse – eyes a little too large for her face, nose rather pointed. Her mouth – just the right shape for nibbling. All she needed were some whiskers. In winter, at least, she wasn't covered in freckles. It was not a face to launch a thousand ships. The only thing that she liked about it, the feature that gave her distinction, was her chin. It was firm but with just the suggestion of a dimple.

'Are you sure you don't want to try a false fringe, miss? Lady Augusta wears one, and the Princess of Wales. It softens the hairline.'

Grace held up the curly patch in front of Charlotte's forehead. But Charlotte looked at herself in the mirror, grimaced and pushed it away.

Seeing the maid's disappointed face, she said, 'I am sorry, but I can't wear the fringe. I would feel like a French poodle. I'm afraid I will never live up to your idea of a fashionable lady.'

The toilette was interrupted by a bell being rung violently in the hall. Sir Alured had clearly finished his kipper. Charlotte gave her hat a last-minute adjustment in the mirror and ran down the stairs.

Lady Dunwoody was resplendent in a red and gold figured silk which reminded Charlotte irresistibly of the dragons on the Japanese screen in the studio. There was something quite regal about her – it was the combination of her height and her assumption that she was being listened to with full attention. Charlotte thought that the real Queen could hardly be more intimidating.

Just as they had seated themselves in the carriage, there was a knock at the window and Caspar peered in.

'Good morning, ladies, Sir Alured. I know that I said yesterday that I would meet you at the exhibition, but when I woke up this morning I felt my heart beating like it was fit to burst and the only way to calm my nerves is to be in your company. Will you take pity on me? If there is no room, I will happily walk alongside. I feel that unless I do a great deal of talking now I will splutter like a firework in front of the Queen.'

Ignoring her husband's sigh, Lady Dunwoody opened the carriage door.

'You may ride with us, Mr Hewes, but you must not crush Miss Baird's dress. Or talk too much.'

'I promise to make myself as thin as a pencil and as quiet as a mouse. Miss Baird will emerge unruffled, her ears unsullied by my noisome chatter. But before I embark upon my vow of silence I must just observe the splendour of the feminine apparel in this carriage.'

Caspar climbed in and sat beside Charlotte, making a great play of twisting his lanky limbs into the smallest possible knot.

'That lilac stripe is so à la mode, Charlotte. You look like the most delicious ice, a confection of Parma violets and cream. I don't suppose that anyone will bother to look at the photographs when they have such loveliness before them.'

Sir Alured banged on the carriage roof to give the coachman the signal to drive off and opened his copy of *The Times* with an ostentatious rustle.

'And as for you, Lady D, such splendour. There are not many women who can wear that particular shade of red and emerge the victor, but you have vanquished the colour quite decisively. I bask in your reflected glory.'

Caspar let his ulster fall open a little to reveal that he was wearing a waistcoat of a rose figured silk that did indeed look like a dilution of Lady D's vigorous crimson.

'I think you may be assured of your share of attention in that waistcoat,' said Lady Dunwoody.

'Do you think perhaps that is a little too much for the morning?

I did toy with something a little more discreet, but then I decided that as all the photographs are monochrome it was my duty to add a splash of colour.'

'But Caspar, you don't need a waistcoat to add colour,' said Charlotte, 'your pictures are so magnificent they will attract all the attention you could possibly want.' Caspar smiled. Like all flatterers he longed to be praised in return.

'Now Caspar, if you have the good fortune to be presented to the Queen,' said Lady Dunwoody, 'you bow very low and call her Your Majesty, and if she engages you in conversation you may call her Ma'am. But remember that, hard as it will be for you of all people, you may only speak if you are spoken to. You cannot chat away to the Queen as you would to us.'

'Don't worry, Lady D, even a Republican like me is awed by the presence of royalty. The only unsolicited noise I will make is a sigh as I contemplate Her Majesty in all her pomp.'

There was an audible snort from behind *The Times*.

Lady Dunwoody turned to Charlotte. 'And you must talk to that goose of an aunt of yours, and warn her that the Queen must be allowed to look at the pictures in peace. Caspar is positively taciturn in comparison with Adelaide Lisle.'

'I will do my best,' said Charlotte.

Caspar turned to Charlotte. 'What about the gallant Captain? Is he coming? I am *consumed* with jealousy already. I may have to challenge him to a duel. I am surprisingly good with a pistol.'

'I believe that Captain Middleton is coming, but I shall turn him away at the door if you don't promise to behave,' said Charlotte sternly.

Caspar put up his hands in surrender. 'I will be a model of discretion. I shall fade into the background.'

'Not in that waistcoat, you won't,' said Charlotte.

As the carriage entered the Park, Lady Dunwoody leant forward and said, 'I believe that the Queen will not be the only royal presence at the exhibition. There is a possibility that Crown Prince Rudolph, the son of the Austrian emperor, will be there too. Alured arranged it with the Austrian ambassador. The Crown Prince is very interested in photography, isn't that right, Alured?'

Her husband grunted behind his paper, but after a nudge he put the paper down for a moment and said, 'Apparently so. Although from what I hear about the Crown Prince, his interest in photography may be in its less salubrious forms. I hear that he is quite a volatile young man. Not like a Hapsburg at all. They are stolid to the point of dreariness, but Prince Rudolph clearly takes after his mother.'

'Is the Empress volatile?' asked Charlotte.

Sir Alured folded his hands. 'If our own queen was to behave as the Empress does, I feel confident that we would be a republic before very long. Of course, she is only a consort and there is no doubt that Franz Joseph is the most diligent of sovereigns, but he has indulged his wife in a way that could not be tolerated here. Karolyi says that she can be extraordinarily wilful. In Vienna she hired a circus troupe to teach her to do tricks on horseback. She is most reluctant to go to court functions, but she is quite happy to appear in public jumping through a ring of fire.'

'How splendid,' said Caspar, 'now that would make a great picture.'

Sir Alured looked at him over his half-moon glasses. 'Making a great subject for one of your,' he paused, 'photographs is not the role of an empress.'

'Well, as a Republican, Sir Alured, I would happily trade in one of our presidents for an empress who can do circus tricks,' said Caspar.

'You may joke about these matters, Mr Hewes, but I suspect that as a Republican you do not understand that the mystique of royalty is a precious thing. Majesty cannot be taken lightly. It is inconceivable that our queen would jump through hoops of fire.'

Caspar whispered to Charlotte, 'It would have to be a very big hoop.'

Lady Dunwoody said hastily, 'Have you seen the Queen before, Charlotte?'

'I once saw her riding out in her carriage. But she was a long way in the distance, so the impression I had was of a small black shape. Her lady-in-waiting was about twice her size.'

'But haven't you been presented? Surely Adelaide has arranged it?'

'Not yet. Augusta wants to be my sponsor this season.'

'They are always long afternoons. I remember when I was presented, one of the girls ahead of me fainted from the fatigue. She fell down in a dead swoon and all her feathers were crushed, poor thing. She couldn't be presented after that, of course, and the Queen was asked if the girl could be counted even though she hadn't actually made it to the throne. But the Queen said no, and the poor girl had to do it all over again. We all thought it rather unkind at the time, but I suppose it's very important to stick to the rules.'

Sir Alured nodded. 'How can you doubt it, my dear? That is the difference between our queen and the Austrian one. Our queen knows that she has a divine duty to perform, while the Empress Elizabeth seems to have no sense of the responsibilities that come with her position.'

'I suppose you are right, Alured.'

The carriage was now travelling down Pall Mall and Charlotte had her face pressed to the window in case she spotted Bay coming out of one of the clubs. But a light drizzle had started to fall and the faces of the passers-by were concealed by their umbrellas. She could feel her heart beating so loudly in her chest that she thought everyone else in the carriage must surely hear it. It had been two weeks since she had seen Bay. She tried to picture him in her head but the only image she could summon was the photograph she had taken of him when he had been staring at the Empress. Caspar had tried to persuade her that the photograph should be entered into the competition, but she had resisted. It was a powerful image; the framing and the depth of field was perfect. But Charlotte had felt that it was not a photograph to put on public view. Whatever that expression on Bay's face had been, it was a private matter.

In Harley Street Bay was putting his shirt on. He was in some pain. Dr Murchison had manipulated his shoulder, and while he now had much more range of movement, the deft twist that the doctor had given his scapula had been so agonising that Bay had cried out.

'There, Captain. It's all done. You should be able to use it normally now. But you can't keep doing this. Once a shoulder joint gets loose like this, it could pop out any moment. It's probably useless my saying so, but you should really avoid situations where you are likely to fall and dislocate it again.'

'Perfectly useless, I'm afraid, doctor,' said Bay. 'I don't intend to fall off my horse but sometimes it happens. I can't stop riding.'

'You could stop riding so fast,' said Dr Murchison. 'It is the velocity with which you hit the ground that makes these injuries so dangerous. The next time you fall and put the joint out, I may not be able to fix it.'

'That's a chance I will have to take,' said Bay. 'Meanwhile I am grateful to you, doctor, for giving me the ability to button my shirt.

It's a damned nuisance to be dependent on other people just to get dressed.'

'Well, if you don't take care of that shoulder, you will have your arm in a sling for the rest of your life. And who will button your shirts then?' said Dr Murchison.

'Once again, doctor, I suppose that is another chance I will just have to take.'

It was a quarter to twelve when Bay left the doctor's. He had intended to walk to the Strand but the drizzle was developing into solid rain. He hailed a hansom and then immediately regretted it. The traffic in London was infernally slow in bad weather. He looked out of the window at the women sheltering in shop doorways, trying to protect their expensive new hats.

The hansom had stopped moving entirely. Bay put his head out of the window and saw that a dustcart had lost an axle and was blocking the down traffic along Regent Street. The dustman was trying ineffectively to prop up the cart so that it could be moved out of the way, but the vehicle was too heavy for him to make much headway on his own. The rain was turning the road to mud and the drover kept slipping as he tried to prop up the broken axle. The carriages coming the other way had all slowed down to look at the spectacle. Bay thought that he would have to walk and cursed himself for not bringing an umbrella. Then he saw a group of navvies and other workmen emerging from a public house – he rapped on the carriage roof and said to his driver, 'Tell those men I will give them a sovereign if they will get the cart out of the way.' The coachman climbed down from his box and went to negotiate with the workmen.

As the navvies set to work – clearly too drunk to mind much about the mud – Bay noticed another carriage had drawn up alongside him. It was a private carriage with a coat of arms on the side. The crest was splashed with mud, but Bay recognised the double-headed eagle crest of the Hapsburgs. He could hardly fail to recognise it; the crest was on everything that the Empress's household used at Easton Neston, from the butter pats to the soap dishes. Curious, Bay peered into the carriage. The Empress was hunting with the Cottesmore today after much grumbling about having to ride out 'quite alone' with only Liechtenstein, Esterhazy, and three grooms for company. He glimpsed a profile in the carriage, and until its owner turned and Bay saw the luxurious moustache, he thought for an uncomfortable moment that the Empress had abandoned the Cottesmore to follow him to London. Then the owner of the moustache lit a small cigar and Bay saw that it was a young man not much more than a boy. The high cheekbones and those deep-set eyes were so similar to Sisi's that the man in the carriage could only be Rudolph, her son. Then the other passenger leant forward and Bay recognised Karolyi, the Austrian ambassador. The Ambassador was clearly trying to persuade the Prince of something; he was leaning forward and almost but not quite putting his hand on the Prince's arm. But the Prince was evidently in no mood to be persuaded. Ignoring the other man, he turned his head and stared out of the window, looking directly at Bay. Bay wondered if he should smile or even touch his hat in acknowledgement, settling for a civil nod. But there was no response from the Prince, it was as if Bay did not exist.

There was a shout of triumph from the navvies as the dustcart was pushed to the side of the road. The hansom driver picked up his reins and set off at a brisk clip. Bay threw a sovereign to the mud-splattered men as he passed. As they positively cantered to

Piccadilly, Bay looked back out of the window and saw that the men were brawling in the road, fighting no doubt over Bay's sovereign. The Hapsburg carriage was trapped behind the scrapping navvies. The chill that had come over Bay when he saw the blank, arrogant face of the Crown Prince was replaced by an ignoble flush of triumph.

The rain had stopped by the time the hansom had negotiated its way across Trafalgar Square to the Strand. The queue of carriages stretching down the Strand was stationary, so Bay decided to walk the rest of the way. He skirted the front of the Charing Cross Hotel and turned right onto John Adam Street. The pavements were thick with people. As Bay tried to make his way through to the Royal Society building he could hear a hum from the spectators, 'the Queen, the Queen'. There was a distant noise that sounded like a cheer coming from the Strand. Bay pushed his way to the pillared portico at the entrance of the Royal Society; he knew that he had to get into the building before the Queen arrived or he would be stuck outside for ages. The cheers for the Queen were getting louder. At last Bay squeezed his way through a gap in the crowd and made his way up the white marble steps.

The liveried footman at the door looked at him with suspicion – visitors to the exhibition did not generally arrive on foot and Bay looked a bit dishevelled after his struggle through the crowd. But Bay sprang up the steps with such confidence that the footman did not dare to challenge him.

'What name shall I give, sir?'

'Captain Middleton.'

On the other side of the room, Charlotte heard the words she had been waiting for all morning.

Pictures at the Exhibition

HE TURNOUT FOR THE EXHIBITION WAS VIGOROUS
for a wet morning in March. The lure of royalty was enough
to draw the politicians from the chamber, the artists from their
studios, the writers from their desks and the ladies from their
morning calls. The large salon on the first floor had an Adam ceiling
and a fine Grinling Gibbons chimney piece, but its eighteenth-
century splendours had been eclipsed by the wonders of the modern
world. Every inch of wall space was covered with photographs:
studio portraits of the great and the good, staged tableaux of scenes
from the Bible or the novels of Sir Walter Scott, studies of little
girls in white dresses and grizzled old men in kilts. There were
photographs of trees struck by lightning and crowds in Piccadilly,
the Pyramids in Egypt and the Pavilion at Brighton. The majority
of the pictures were monochrome and hung sombrely against the
venetian red of the walls, but every so often a spot of colour was
introduced by the brush or pen of a photographer who had needed
the punctuation of a red lip or a blue sky. Most of the works
displayed were no bigger than a family bible, and as there were
nearly four hundred pictures crammed together on the walls, the
initial effect was almost overwhelming.

Many of the spectators had never seen so many photographs

gathered together before, and as they entered they paused, uncertain where to begin. This was not like the Royal Academy where everybody knew who this year's lions were, and which pictures were to be the talk of the season. Here there were no familiar names to cluster around and no movements to discuss. Most visitors went straight to the portraits of the famous – where at least there was some possibility of judging the photograph against the original. The likeness of Lord Beaconsfield was considered most flattering, making him look so youthful that there was speculation that some artifice had been involved. Several women of a certain age, who had always resisted the pitiless lens of the *carte de visite*, made a note of the photographer's name in their catalogues and resolved to enquire about having their portrait done after the same manner.

A few brave souls who had got all the way to the far wall found pictures that astonished them – women floating in thin air, a girl looking into a mirror and seeing the reflection of an old crone, a man with three legs. A Canon of St Paul's whispered to his wife that he wondered if these pictures were quite suitable, 'had there perhaps been occult practices?' he murmured. His wife, who was ten years younger than him and a keen photographer, told him not to be such a fuddy-duddy. The pictures were 'artistic'. Photographs could be manipulated just as much as paintings, and to achieve the effects in front of them had required an inordinate amount of skill.

Augusta and Fred were looking at a picture of a Highland scene. Or rather, Fred was looking and Augusta was surveying the room. She was not entirely at ease. This was not a milieu that she was comfortable with: royalty notwithstanding, so far she had not seen anyone she considered 'smart'. There were several cabinet ministers in the room, a Poet Laureate and a number of fashionable painters, but none of them met Augusta's exacting standards for smartness. A home secretary was no substitute for a duchess. Augusta was surprised that the Queen should patronise such a ramshackle gathering; it was the sort of occasion that she associated with Charlotte, who had no idea of what constituted 'good form'. Augusta once again felt the unfairness of Charlotte being the heiress to a fortune, while she was marrying a Borders squire who didn't even have a house in town. Augusta knew just what to do with that money – she knew that with sixty thousand a year, she could be one of the foremost hostesses in the land. If only Charlotte wasn't so awkward. She had always wanted a younger sister, but not one like Charlotte. Augusta sighed.

Fred said, 'I say, Augusta. Have a look at this one – ain't those the housemaids from Melton?'

Augusta peered at the photograph through her eyeglass. 'Why, yes. Although you would hardly recognise them; they look quite feverish. This must be one of your sister's photographs. Number forty-seven. What does it say in the catalogue? A group study by Miss Baird. I do think that she might have mentioned Melton. I mean, after Mama went to all the trouble of giving her the old nursery for her photography, she might have had the courtesy to mention that she was at our house.'

'Perhaps she has mentioned it somewhere else, Gus.' Fred sighed; he wished that Augusta wasn't so obsessed with her own position as a daughter of Melton. Although he was happy to be marrying an earl's daughter, it would be more seemly if she remembered that his family had status too.

'I am going to look for all of Charlotte's photographs. I wouldn't be at all surprised to find that she has included the picture she took of us and forgotten to mention our names!' said Augusta.

Fred looked around for a diversion and saw Chicken Hartopp standing behind a bishop. He was stooping to examine a photograph that was hung at waist level.

'Hello, Chicken. Thought you were with the Cottesmore today?'

'Changed my mind. Have you seen this?'

The two men looked at the photograph of Bay and Tipsy in the Melton stables.

'Don't understand how they select the photographs,' said Chicken.

'No. You would think that they would look for interesting subjects.'

'I mean, how is a picture of Middleton and his horse right for a Royal Exhibition? Middleton's a nobody and the horse hasn't won anything.'

'Middleton thinks he'll win the National with that mare.'

'I wouldn't put money on it. Horse is only fifteen hands. You need a big beast for the National. Anyway, Middleton's too busy being a royal horse dealer these days. Someone told me at the club that the Empress bought a whole string of hunters on Middleton's say-so. He certainly hasn't lost any time.'

'Yes,' said Fred, 'Bay has been very busy.'

Lady Lisle was saying to Charlotte, 'And where are your photographs, dear?'

'They are scattered about, Aunt. Only the most distinguished photographers are hung together. I don't even know where all my pictures are, because all the hanging was changed last night. I believe that Mrs Cameron felt that not enough of her photographs were on the line.'

'On the line?' asked Lady Lisle.

'At eye level. That's where they hang all the most important photographs. You won't find any of mine there.'

'But eye level depends on how tall you are,' said Lady Lisle. 'I believe the Queen is quite a small person.'

Charlotte smiled. 'I hadn't thought of that.'

Lady Lisle started to examine the wall behind her. She found the mass of images rather dizzying; watercolours were so much more peaceful. But then she found a picture that punctured her happy blur. This must be one of Charlotte's photographs. That was Captain Middleton, she was almost sure, but who was the lady on horseback that he was staring at so intently? Lady Lisle turned to ask Charlotte, but her niece had disappeared into the crowd.

Charlotte was looking for Bay. After hearing his name announced she had been trying to work her way across to the door, but the room was now packed and the train on her dress made it difficult for her to move through it unimpeded. She saw the back of a head with reddish brown hair and set off in that direction, only for the man to turn around and reveal himself to be wearing a dog collar. Charlotte stopped by a table in the middle of the room that held a stereoscope and stood on her tiptoes to see if she could catch a glimpse of Bay.

'Goodness me, Charlotte, why are you standing here all alone?' Augusta tapped her on the shoulder with her programme. 'Shouldn't you be enjoying your triumph?'

Charlotte was looking at a knot of people clustered around an easel at the front of the room. Was that Bay standing next to a woman in red velvet?

'I am glad you think it is a triumph. I feel rather nervous.'

'I can't think why. It's not as if you are one of the principals. I very much doubt that the Queen will single you out.'

'How kind of you to point that out. I shall stop worrying immediately.'

'I was disappointed to see that you failed to mention that the maids in your photograph belong to Melton. I thought it customary for an artist to thank their patron.'

Charlotte turned round to look at Augusta.

'The photograph is of three young women with their lives ahead of them. It's a study in character and composition. I don't believe there is anything to be gained from knowing that they are house-maids. I wanted viewers to see their characters, not their situation in life.' As she spoke, the chatter in the room dimmed and was replaced by an expectant murmur.

'You will have to excuse me, I believe that the Queen is arriving and Lady Dunwoody has asked me to be in the receiving line.'

Charlotte found her way to the door. At the bottom of the steps she could see a very small woman in black making her way up the red carpeted steps. The crowd in the room drew back to make room for the royal party. Charlotte saw Bay on the other side of the room. She waved to him but he was looking in the other direction. She dug her nails into her palms. To cross that empty floor to greet him now would be tantamount to announcing their engagement in _The Times_. If only he would look her way. She stared at him as hard as she could, willing him to turn his head.

'There you are, Charlotte,' said Lady Dunwoody. 'You must come and stand next to me. I am relying on you to make sure that Caspar behaves himself.'

Charlotte followed her and took her place in the line of people waiting to be presented to the Queen, Caspar on one side, Lady Dunwoody on the other. Caspar whispered in her ear, 'Is that your beau standing over there? Shall we make him jealous? If you smile at me now while I whisper in your ear, he will think that we are having a flirtation.'

'But I don't *want* to make him jealous,' said Charlotte.

'Carlotta *mia*, every romance needs a little tension. If the gallant captain turns his head and sees you gazing at him as you are now, he will know precisely what is in your heart, but if he turns to see you confiding in me, well, he will be confused, and that would not be such a bad thing. Everybody desires a thing more when it is not straightforward.'

'Perhaps that is the way that it works in America, Mr Hewes, but I don't care to play games.'

'What I am suggesting is simply self-defence,' murmured Caspar in a more serious tone than he had used previously.

Charlotte did turn to look at him then, but at that moment the Queen reached the top of the steps and the sounds in the room were muffled by the approach of royalty.

The Queen was even smaller than Charlotte had expected. She barely reached the chest of her Highland servant. But her lack of height was balanced by her considerable girth, the stoutness accentuated by the old-fashioned width of her skirts. The crowd instinctively shrank back another foot as if they hadn't quite anticipated her wideness.

Behind the Queen and John Brown, came a couple of ladies. One of them, who was a little taller but almost as stout as the Queen, must be her youngest daughter, Princess Beatrice. She had the same bulbous blue eyes as her mother. At the rear of the party were two men. Without quite knowing why, Charlotte assumed they must be foreigners – there was something about the younger man's goatee and the cut of his frock coat that made him look quite different to the Englishmen in the room.

Caspar said under his breath, 'Who is the fellow with the gold pin who looks so uncommonly put out?'

'I think that must be Prince Rudolph, the Austrian Crown Prince.'

The Queen was talking now in her high, clear voice with its exaggerated emphasis, and slight German accent.

'What an extraordinary display, Sir Peter,' she said to the President of the Society, who had greeted her at the top of the stairs. 'To see so *many* photographs in one place. How pleased Prince Albert would have been to see this. He was so *interested* in photography. He made us sit for them many times. I remember he would say to me that he always preferred a photograph to an indifferent painting. The camera does not lie, he would say.'

Sir Peter bowed. 'The Society will be for ever grateful to the Prince for his patronage. Such a remarkable man.'

The Queen nodded, satisfied with this tribute. 'Today you have another royal visitor. We are very pleased to see the Crown Prince Rudolph here. The Ambassador was good enough to suggest that the exhibition might form part of the Crown Prince's itinerary.'

The Queen turned to Rudolph. 'What a pity your mother could not join you here today. She came to visit us at Windsor and she looked *very* well. I hope she is still enjoying her visit.'

'I believe so, Ma'am, but you have the advantage of me as I have not seen the Empress since I arrived in England.'

Queen Victoria blinked. 'I trust that she is not overexerting herself. She told me that she rides out every day, but at her age she really should be careful. A gentle ride every day is good for the constitution, but hunting is quite another matter.'

'The Emperor is of the same opinion, Ma'am.'

The Queen was about to reply when Princess Beatrice, who could see the receiving line that was waiting for the royal party, said,

'Perhaps you should move inside, Mama. It is very draughty here, and you might catch a chill.'

The Queen shivered and the royal party moved into the room and began to make their way down the line. Thirty of the photographers in the exhibition were to be presented.

Charlotte was about halfway down. The progress of the royal party was uncommonly slow and she rocked on her heels with impatience. The crowd was still blocking her view of Bay.

'Really, Charlotte. Stop moving about. The Queen won't get here any faster if you fidget.' Lady Dunwoody spoke out of the corner of her mouth, all the while looking straight ahead with a fixed smile on her lips.

Charlotte muttered an apology and tried to stand still, but she could not help craning her head to see if Bay was looking at her. But he had disappeared from where she had seen him last. If only the Queen would move a little faster. At that moment Charlotte would have happily given up her chance of curtseying before royalty if it meant that she could go and find Bay, but she knew that Lady Dunwoody would never forgive her if she left her place in the receiving line, so she balled her hands into fists and tried to count in her head, as if she was playing hide and seek.

Fifty-eight, fifty-nine, sixty, at last the Queen had reached Lady Dunwoody.

'I remember the picture you had at the last exhibition, Lady Dunwoody. It was the Lady of Shalott, I believe. I am so fond of Tennyson.'

'You are too kind, Ma'am. I hope I may be allowed to present you with a print of the picture.'

The Queen nodded, satisfied that her hint had been taken. 'We would be delighted.'

'May I present my goddaughter Charlotte Baird, who has a

number of photographs on display, and my assistant Mr Caspar Hewes, who has given us some splendid views of his native America.'

Charlotte made her curtsey and was gratified to observe that she had been quite right about the Queen's resemblance to a codfish. It was the heavy jowls on either side of the tiny, pursed mouth that quite resembled gills, and the glassy, bulging eyes that glistened moistly as if only recently placed on the fishmonger's slab. Princess Beatrice, who hovered next to her mother, was also fish-like, although not so august a fish as a cod, a haddock, perhaps.

'You are very young, Miss Baird, to be in the exhibition.'

'I have been fortunate to have Lady Dunwoody as a teacher, Ma'am.'

'Your modesty does you credit, Miss Baird. Young women today can be quite *brazen*.' She turned her head slightly to John Brown, who murmured in reply, 'Indeed, Ma'am. Brazen is the wurrrd for it.'

Charlotte bowed her head in what she thought was a reasonable facsimile of demureness. She hoped that Augusta was watching this exchange. Royal favour was not something that Charlotte had ever considered, let alone sought for its own sake, but there was a certain satisfaction in receiving something that would so thoroughly enrage Augusta.

Now Caspar was bowing before the Queen. It was a very low bow, one that would have been more suitable to the court of the Sun King at Versailles than a modern queen, but Victoria nodded with approval, finding nothing extravagant in his gesture.

'Your Majesty,' said Caspar, in a voice that would have filled the Albert Hall.

'Which part of America do you come from, Mr Hewes?'

'I come from California, Ma'am.'

'Such a *romantic* sounding name.'

'It is a spectacular country, Ma'am. I am afraid that my

photographs do not do it justice. There are trees there the height of your cathedral spires and the earth is so fertile and the weather so clement that the settlers call it the land of milk and honey.'

'I am surprised that you could bring yourself to leave such a paradise, Mr Hewes.' The corners of the Queen's mouth were pointing down. Charlotte heard Lady Dunwoody gasp. Sir Peter, who was standing behind the Queen, stood very still, his mouth slightly open as if preserved in aspic. John Brown gave a long rolling sniff.

But Caspar was not deterred. 'Natural beauty is all very well, but there is no culture there. We Americans are forced to travel a long way to find the patina of civilisation that your subjects take for granted, Ma'am.'

He bowed again as if to emphasise the subjugation of the New World to the Old, and this time the Queen's lips flickered upwards.

Sir Peter jerked out of his temporary paralysis and moved to shepherd the Queen further down the line of photographers.

There was a short pause, and then Caspar said, 'Who was the guy in the skirt?'

A Groom

THE QUEEN HAD REACHED THE END OF THE FORMAL presentations and was now making her way around the gallery in the company of Sir Peter. Prince Rudolph and the Austrian ambassador were circulating around the exhibition in the opposite direction. The rest of the crowd were following the royal parties at a respectful distance.

Caspar had been led away by Lady Dunwoody for a scolding. Charlotte scanned the room – she could see Chicken Hartopp's burly frame standing by the door, and Fred and Augusta with Lady Lisle following the Queen, but there was no sign of Bay. Her mouth was dry with impatience.

She felt a touch at her elbow, and a voice murmured in her ear, 'Do I have the honour of addressing the celebrated Charlotte Baird, the promising photographer?'

'Bay! I have been looking for you everywhere.' Charlotte had to stop herself from clutching at the lapels of his coat.

'But I have been here all the time,' he said, smiling down at her.

'I wasn't sure if you would come.'

'Didn't you get Tipsy's telegram?'

'I did, but—' Charlotte broke off. 'Oh, but I haven't asked you about your accident, how thoughtless of me. What happened? Do you feel better? Was it terribly painful?'

Bay held up a hand, laughing at her torrent of questions. 'It was no more than a passing inconvenience, as you can see. My shoulder was sore for a few days and my right arm unusable, which meant that I couldn't write to you. But now I am practically recovered and instead of an illegible letter you have my imperfect self.'

'Oh, I am so glad to see you,' said Charlotte, overwhelmed by how good it felt to stand next to Bay.

'Are you? I would have come to speak to you sooner but you seemed very thick with the fellow in the splendid waistcoat. I didn't like to interrupt.'

'Mr Hewes is a photographer. He also has some pictures in the exhibition.'

'A photographer. How foolish of me to think that he was an admirer.'

'Mr Hewes is my godmother's assistant. We have been working on the exhibition together.'

'And naturally you have become close.'

'We have become friendly, yes. Isn't that often the case when you share an interest with someone? I daresay that you have made many friends on the hunting field.'

'Not with Mr Hewes's taste in waistcoats.'

Charlotte laughed. 'Mr Hewes is an American.'

'That explains a great deal. Now, you must show me where I can find Tipsy's portrait. She is so disappointed not to be here. She has always wanted to meet the Queen.'

'Even though she is riding out every day with an empress?'

Bay looked at Charlotte. He said quickly in a low voice, 'I didn't know what to think when you left Melton. I thought perhaps I had offended you and that our understanding was at an end. There was nothing for me there after you left.'

Charlotte put her hand on his arm. 'But how could you think that, Bay? Why would I change my mind?'

But before he could reply, Lady Dunwoody's voice interrupted them. 'There you are, Charlotte. The Queen is looking at your pictures.' She stopped and surveyed Bay. He bowed and kissed the hand that was held out to him. 'You must be Captain Middleton. I recognise you from Charlotte's photographs.'

'Oh, I am so sorry. Aunt Celia, may I present Captain Middleton. Captain Middleton, Lady Dunwoody, my godmother and mentor.'

'I am sorry to interrupt your tête-à-tête. But, Charlotte, you will want to hear the Queen's verdict on your work.'

'I think we would all like to hear that, Lady Dunwoody,' Bay said.

The Queen's party had stopped in front of a group of pictures that included Charlotte's portrait of Bay and Tipsy. Sir Peter was pointing out compositions by the celebrated Mrs Cameron and Charles Fox Talbot, the son of the man who had invented photography. Victoria had the slightly glazed look of a woman who was being forced to listen when she much preferred being listened to. As Sir Peter talked about the rule of thirds and shutter speeds, Victoria's head snapped forward like a tortoise and peered at a photograph in front of her.

'I have seen this young man before.' She turned to John Brown. 'He was with the Empress. What was his name?'

'Middleton, Ma'am,' said Brown.

'Oh yes. He had had some accident, his poor arm was in a sling.'

Sir Peter coughed. 'This is one of Miss Baird's photographs, Ma'am.' He beckoned to Charlotte, who stepped forward.

'I met the young man in the photograph with Prince Rudolph's mother, the Empress. What a coincidence.'

'Yes,' said Charlotte, 'it is.' Collecting herself, she continued, 'In fact, Ma'am, Captain Middleton is here today.' She stepped aside so that the Queen could see Bay.

The Queen looked at him with interest. Bay made his bow.

'Captain Middleton, did you leave the Empress well?'

'Yes, Ma'am. She is hunting with the Cottesmore today.'

'And you have left your post?' An eyebrow hovered over one bulging blue eye. 'I don't think you have ever left my side, have you, John?'

'Nivverrr, Ma'am,' said John Brown.

Bay said quickly, 'If you remember, Ma'am, I had the misfortune to dislocate my shoulder when I saw you at Windsor. I came to town to consult a doctor.'

'And to admire Miss Baird's photograph of you,' said the Queen, the eyebrow still hovering.

'That too, Ma'am. Although I would say that the true subject of the photograph is my horse Tipsy.'

'What would you say, Miss Baird?' said the Queen, her eyes gleaming with interest. 'You must have had something in mind when you took the photograph?'

'I would say that a good photograph can find favour with spectators for different reasons. I was taking a picture of a man and a horse.' Charlotte spoke as calmly as she could. She was keenly aware that this side of the room had fallen silent to hear her interrogation by the Queen.

'Well, if young ladies are more interested in horses than they are in young men, then the world has changed a great deal since my youth,' said the Queen, smiling at her own joke. 'I only wish my maids of honour were as interested in four-legged animals.'

There was a general murmur of amusement from the people gathered near the Queen. Charlotte felt herself reddening. She could not see Bay, as he was standing directly behind her. She longed to turn her head, but she did not want to give the crowd any more reason to gossip. It was unbearable to be branded publicly as a lovesick girl by the one person against whom there was no defence. In her peripheral vision she could see Augusta whispering to Fred. Charlotte fixed her eyes on the parquet floor, hoping that the Queen would approve of this display of maidenly modesty and move on. But help came from another quarter.

'Your Majesty.' Thirty heads swivelled to see Caspar Hewes on the other side of the room. 'May I show you one of my photographs? I have only one aim when I take a picture and that is to capture a moment.'

The faces of the crowd turned like sunflowers following the sun. Everyone, including the Queen, was now looking at the American who had dared to interrupt a royal conversation. Charlotte allowed herself to look up and caught Caspar's eye; he was smiling broadly.

'I thought you might like to see my picture of the Grand Canyon, Ma'am. It is one of the wonders of the West, almost three miles deep. I don't believe there is anything like it anywhere in the world.'

The company held its breath. Sir Peter put up his hand as if to shield his monarch from the uncouth American. John Brown's ruddy face turned a few shades more towards magenta; Lady Dunwoody wore her most fixed smile; her husband had the smugly moist expression of someone whose worst predictions had been fulfilled. But the Queen, with the capriciousness that can only come from a lifetime of being indulged, surveyed Caspar's improbably lanky form, the pink waistcoat and the unabashed candour in his wide blue eyes, and decided that she liked what she saw.

'The Grand Canyon. What picturesque names Americans give to their landmarks.' She took five steps across the floor, followed by Brown and Princess Beatrice, to where Caspar was standing. He pointed to his photograph, which had been hung above the line, far too high for the Queen to see it.

'John, I can't see this gentleman's photograph.'

'Ma'am.'

For a moment it looked as though the kilted giant was going to pick up his mistress, as you would pick up a child, so that she could put her face quite next to the picture, but then he reached up one enormous arm, took the photograph off its hook and put it in the Queen's hands.

The photograph was taken from a mountain top; it showed the forested slopes of the Canyon's banks bisected by the black snake of the ravine.

The Queen peered at the print.

'Such a *wild* landscape. It reminds me of the Highlands.' She turned her head a fraction and John Brown picked up his cue.

'Sairtainly, Ma'am, verrry like the hills beyond the Dee.'

Caspar leant forward. 'The most extraordinary thing about the Canyon is that it can be snowing on the slopes here, while at the bottom of the gorge the rocks are so hot that you can fry an egg on them.'

'How very convenient for picnics,' said the Queen.

The crowd murmured in amusement and the tension slackened. The Queen demanded to see all Caspar's pictures of America, much to the indignation of the British exhibitors, and as John Brown handed them down to her (all Caspar's pictures had been hung high above the eyeline) she examined them minutely.

Looking at one of the studies of Abraham she said, 'What a handsome boy. Such an exotic face. He looks very like one of my Indian subjects.'

She tilted her head and John Brown followed with, 'He could verra' well be a Hindoo, Ma'am.'

'Abraham's mother was Irish and his father was from the Hopi tribe,' said Caspar, frowning slightly, 'Ma'am.'

'I wish you had brought him with you, Mr Hewes. We would be so interested to meet an *American* Indian.'

'And Abraham, if he were still alive, would have been delighted to meet the Queen of England, not that he had any knowledge of queens or indeed England.'

Queen Victoria stared at the American. A world without royalty was incomprehensible to her. Rather than admit this terrifying prospect, she chose not to believe it.

'I am sure that the American Indians have their own kings and queens. It is the natural order of things.'

'Yes, Ma'am, it is. That is why the Founding Fathers made sure that our presidents have to be re-elected every four years so that none of them could assume the trappings of royalty.' The Queen's eyes protruded from her head like marbles, but Caspar carried on, 'Because, of course, real kings and queens must be born to the purple. A grocer's wife can become First Lady but she can *never* become a sovereign Queen,' and he made another very low bow. The Queen's eyes subsided into their sockets and she blinked, mollified. John Brown, who had begun to swell at the sound of Republican heresy, shrank back to his normal bulk.

Sir Peter, who felt that it would now be safe to intervene, came up on the Queen's other side. 'Perhaps you would like to see some other pictures of picturesque landscapes, Ma'am. Mr Trelawney has made a most remarkable series of photographs of the Holy Land which have been much admired.'

The Queen allowed herself to be shepherded towards a study of the Holy Sepulchre, and the crowd began to disperse a little. Trelawney's sepia-toned photographs of the sea of Galilee were unlikely to provoke an amusing reaction.

'Your American friend has some nerve,' said Bay to Charlotte. 'Sailing very close to the wind there. Thought the Widow might erupt, but he got away with it.'

'Caspar isn't someone you can be angry with,' said Charlotte. 'And I am grateful to him for taking the attention away from me.'

Bay had raised an eyebrow at her use of the American's Christian name.

'You seem to know him very well, for such a short acquaintance.'

'And you are quite the favourite with the Queen. You didn't tell me that you and she were friends already,' Charlotte retorted. 'I thought John Brown looked rather put out.'

Bay smiled. 'I am so very glad to see you, Charlotte.' He leant towards her and she felt his moustache brush her cheek as he whispered in her ear, 'Are you sure you don't want to elope with me? We could take a train to Scotland tonight, and be married by morning.'

'Or we could wait a few short months and get married properly without a scandal,' said Charlotte.

'But how can I be sure that you won't succumb to the transatlantic charms of Mr Hewes?' said Bay lightly.

'And how can I be sure that you won't be swept away by the Empress?' said Charlotte with equal lightness. 'Augusta thinks that I should be jealous.'

'Do you think that we could go somewhere to talk privately?' Bay said. 'I can see Chicken heading this way. And I must spend a moment with you alone.'

Charlotte considered. 'There's a room on the floor above where they frame the photographs. If you go up there now, I will follow as soon as I can.'

Bay started to move across the room, but his progress was impeded by the crowd which had coalesced to the left of the door. The two royal parties had both completed their separate orbits of the exhibition and were now standing together. The Queen was talking earnestly to the Crown Prince, who looked tired and kept fingering the Golden Fleece hanging from his lapel.

'You must be sure to visit the Crystal Palace while you are here. It was my dear Albert's great achievement. I think the opening of the Great Exhibition was one of the happiest days of my life.'

'Indeed,' said Rudolph without animation, 'your late husband was an example to us all.'

'He would have been *so* pleased to see you here. Albert thought it was one of the sacred duties of royalty to promote greater under-standing between nations. When my first grandchild, Wilhelm, was born, Albert called me the Grandmama of Europe.'

Rudolph bowed slightly. 'A noble title, indeed. Although it is not one that would please my mother, I think.'

'Well, the Empress was not blessed with nine children,' said the Queen with satisfaction. 'Now tell me, what do you think of the exhibition?'

'It is most impressive. I think we should institute something similar in Vienna. The Imperial Photographic Society sounds very well. I might even design a uniform.'

Victoria's eyes began to protrude. 'A uniform. That is an unusual idea. It might deter the lady members, don't you think?'

Rudolph looked at her blankly.

'Some of the most talented photographers in this country are women. Are there no lady photographers in Vienna?'

'I have no idea.'

'Your mother is not interested in photography then? I suppose she prefers more active pursuits?' said the Queen, looking at the photographs on the wall in front of her.

'My mother has developed an aversion to photography. I think the last one was taken ten years ago. My father the Emperor would like very much to have our photograph taken as a family but Mama refuses.'

'How curious. I always find it such a comfort to know that my children can always have my likeness with them.' She made the little jerk of the head that was John Brown's cue.

'A verra great comfort, Ma'am.'

Rudolph could make no answer to this. He knew that his mother's dislike of photography was because she did not want to be reminded that she was getting older and that her beauty was fading. This was not, clearly, a matter of concern to Queen Victoria.

The Queen was staring closely at a photograph directly in front of her.

'Now this is a curious thing,' she said. 'You say the Empress refuses to be photographed, and yet here is a picture of her and Captain Middleton.'

Rudolph, who had been admiring the ladies in the crowd, turned around sharply.

'A picture of my mother, but that's impossible. You must be mistaken, Ma'am.'

Queen Victoria looked up at him, the jowls on either side of her mouth pendulous, her mouth pursed.

'We are not in the habit of making mistakes.' She pointed one diamond be-ringed finger at the photograph.

'That is most definitely the Empress.'

She tilted her head slightly and John Brown echoed her, 'Most definitely.'

Rudolph's pallor was interrupted by two red patches on his cheekbones. He stood quite still as the Queen pointed at the portrait. When, at last, he moved, it looked at first as if he was going to turn away and walk out of the room. But the Ambassador, who was standing next to him, angled his body so that it would be impossible for the Crown Prince to move in that direction without pushing him aside. Checked, the Prince sighed and walked slowly towards the photograph at which the Queen was still pointing.

'Here is your mother. She is bringing a fan up to her face, but with all that hair, she is quite unmistakeable.'

Rudolph bent down to look at the photograph.

'My apologies, Ma'am. This *is* a picture of the Empress. But it can only have been taken without her knowledge or consent.'

'How unfortunate.' The Queen looked at the picture again. 'Of course, Captain Middleton, the gentleman behind the Empress in the photograph, is here. He will know what happened.' She turned from the photograph to the crowd, looking for Bay.

Bay was at the door on his way to the rendezvous with Charlotte, but stopped when he heard his name spoken by the Queen in that high, clear voice. Stepping forward into the room, he saw that the royal party were clustered around a photograph. As he approached them, he saw Rudolph turn to look at him. It was only a brief glance, but Bay felt the Prince's scorn like a slap. He stopped, wondering if he should go any further, but the Queen had seen him now and was looking at him expectantly.

'Captain Middleton, I hope you can enlighten us about this photograph.' The Queen's voice was not unfriendly. She had been shocked by Rudolph's outburst. A young prince in a foreign country should know better than to make a scene, and certainly should know better than to contradict that country's sovereign.

'If I might look at it, Ma'am?' said Bay. Victoria moved aside so that he could see the picture. Rudolph turned away so that he would not even have to look at Bay.

Bay saw the elegant curve of the Empress's silhouette, the narrow waist, the coronet of hair, the leather fan she was bringing up to conceal her face. He saw the bulky figure of Earl Spencer leaning down towards her, the Roman nose, the thick neck, the massive thigh. But most of all Bay saw his own face – his eyes wide, his mouth slightly open, staring at Sisi. He saw himself as he must look to others and he felt a chill of shame sweeping through him.

The Queen said, 'I am sure you can explain to the Crown Prince how this photograph came to be taken when the Empress is so *very* set against it.'

Bay took a deep breath and bowed to Rudolph. 'Your Highness, I believe there has been an unfortunate—'

But before he could finish his sentence, the Crown Prince put up his hand and without even looking at Bay, said to the Queen, 'I have no interest in "explanations". I do not talk to grooms.'

The room went quiet. The Ambassador laid a hand on the Prince's arm as if to check him but Rudolph shook it away.

'In that case,' said Bay, 'I will not trouble you with my presence any longer.' He bowed to the Queen and backed out of the room.

Queen Victoria looked at Rudolph with distaste. 'This time it is *you* who are mistaken, Prince Rudolph. Captain Middleton is not a groom. How could he be? He is an officer in *our* Army.'

The contrast between Rudolph's scarlet cheeks and his ashen complexion heightened.

'Please forgive me for casting a slur on the British Army, your Majesty. *That* was not my intention.'

'Indeed,' said the Queen, her pale blue eyes as glassy as marbles.

Count Karolyi murmured, 'Your Majesty must excuse the Crown Prince for any infelicity of expression. He is, of course, a most devoted son, and like any son is anxious above all to protect the dignity and honour of his mother.'

Rudolph said, 'On my mother's behalf, I demand to know who took the picture and how it came to be exhibited in public.'

Queen Victoria turned to Sir Peter. 'Who did take the picture, Sir Peter?'

Sir Peter, his face slack with horror at this unforeseen contretemps, made a show of consulting his catalogue.

'This wall was rehung late last night. I wasn't aware that this picture had been selected, there must have been a mistake. What's the number . . .' He fumbled with the card, inserting his monocle so that he could read the label.

'I took the picture, Ma'am,' said Charlotte from the other side of the room. The crowd shrank away from her as she approached the royal party.

'Miss Baird.' The Queen looked at her and smiled. 'You could not resist taking another picture of Captain Middleton, perhaps?'

Charlotte shook her head. 'I wanted to take a picture of the Empress. She is a magnificent subject. I didn't know at the time of her objection to photography. I can only apologise for the intrusion. I never meant for this picture to be displayed; it must have been included in my portfolio by mistake. Let me take it away.' She walked towards the photograph and took it down from the wall.

Queen Victoria gestured towards the Prince. 'Well, there is your explanation, Prince Rudolph. I am quite sure the Empress would forgive Miss Baird for her mistake. Particularly since it is such a *flattering* photograph.'

Rudolph clicked his heels and bowed. 'If you say so, Ma'am.'

'As an empress myself, I *do* say so.'

Having given the final word, the Queen nodded to her entourage, allowed Sir Peter to kiss her hand, and swept towards the door, John Brown following in her wake. Count Karolyi took his charge's arm and propelled him in the same direction.

The room was silent for a moment after the royal exit, and then, as if at a prearranged signal, the hubbub began.

Broken Glass

CHARLOTTE HELD THE PHOTOGRAPH IN HER HANDS so tightly that later that day she found red weals in her hands where the frame had cut into her skin.

Lady Dunwoody put a hand on her shoulder. 'My dear girl, what a drama! But how splendid that the Queen defended you. No one can blame you now that she has so publicly declared herself in your favour.' Lady Dunwoody's smile was wide but she spoke a little too loudly to be completely convincing.

Charlotte said nothing, but Lady Dunwoody did not wait for a reply.

'And how strange that the photograph was hung without your knowledge. We put it in because it was such a striking image; those three heads made such a pleasing composition. I had no idea that it was the Empress.'

'If you'll excuse me, Aunt Celia, I think I should like to get some air.'

'Of course, shall I ask Caspar to accompany you?'

'No. I would rather be alone.'

Charlotte hurried away from her godmother, keeping her eyes on the parquet floor. She had almost reached the door when she heard Augusta's voice.

'I can't tell you how grateful I am to you for asking me here today. Most entertaining. Poor Captain Middleton, though. To be snubbed like that in public.'

Charlotte kept moving, but Augusta was blocking her way.

'Is that the famous photograph? Oh, do let me have a look.' Augusta reached for the photograph, but Charlotte held onto it firmly. Augusta tried to pull it out of her hands but Charlotte would not let go.

'Please show me, Charlotte. I am beside myself with curiosity.' She turned to her fiancé, who was standing a little apart. 'Fred, do persuade your sister to let us have a look.'

Fred shuffled his feet. 'Actually, Augusta, I have seen the photograph and I don't need to see it again. If my sister chooses to keep it to herself that is her decision.'

Augusta almost spat with fury. 'Oh Fred, don't be so tiresome. It's not fair if I'm the only one who hasn't seen it.'

But Fred did not waver and Charlotte walked past Augusta, through the double doors and onto the landing, the photograph still clutched to her chest.

The marble staircase with its red and gold carpet stretched in two directions: down to the street or up to the framing room, where she had arranged to meet Bay.

She hesitated for a moment. Would Bay be waiting for her? Did she want to see him?

'Carlotta, there you are! Lady D said that you wanted to be alone, so of course I came at once. So much excitement. There has been quite a run on the sal volatile among the RPS matrons. The Bishop's wife is having palpitations.' Caspar came round to stand in front of Charlotte, blocking her way to the staircase.

'I don't understand how *this*,' Charlotte held up the photograph, 'came to be in the exhibition at all. *I* didn't submit it.'

Caspar shrugged. 'No. *I* did.'

'But why? I would never have submitted it.'

'I know. But it was too good to be left out.'

'It would have been bearable if you had put in the picture of the Empress by herself. I think there are worse crimes than taking photographs of royalty without their knowledge. But *not* this one.' She tapped on the glass cover of the plate with her nails.

'But why not, Carlotta? It has a much better composition.'

'Damn the composition!' said Charlotte.

Caspar held up his hands in mock horror.

'Why, Miss Baird, that is not an expression I expect to hear from a lady.'

'No. But I don't feel like a lady at this moment. Not only have I been humiliated in front of everyone I know, but Captain Middleton has as well. There would have been no reason for Prince Rudolph to snub him like that, if it hadn't been for this!' Charlotte was trying to keep her voice down, but it rose at the end into something like a sob. She realised to her mortification that tears were pouring down her cheeks.

Caspar pulled out a large silk handkerchief from his pocket and deftly wiped the tears away.

'Now, now, we can't have tears. You don't want that ghastly sister-in-law of yours to see you crying. After all, what have you got to cry about? It's not your fault that Prince Rudolph is jealous of Captain Middleton.'

'Jealous? But why would he be jealous of Bay?'

Caspar sighed. 'For the same reason that you are clutching that photograph to your chest. Because he thinks that Captain Middleton is more than a pilot to his mother.'

'I don't understand you. Bay and I are going to get married. He asked me to elope with him, just now, before all this happened.'

'And what did you say?'

'That I wanted to wait until we could get married properly.'

'Did he know you were going to say that?' Caspar asked.

'Perhaps. I have told him before that I see no reason to run away. Why create a scandal when there is no need?'

'How sensible you are, Charlotte. But I am afraid that Captain Middleton is not as prudent as you. Look at that photograph you are holding. You know what it reveals. He may well want to marry you, why wouldn't he? You are clever, lovely and extremely rich, but you are not the only woman in his life. So I suppose the question is, do you want to marry him?

'That's none of your business.'

'Of course it's my business. I think you have great talents. I don't want you to waste all your promise and potential on a man who isn't worthy of you. If I thought I could make you happy I would propose to you myself, but I know my limitations. However as your friend and admirer, I can't stand by and see you throw your life away. I know he is handsome and I am sure he is charming, but he isn't good enough for you.'

'I suppose you think he is a fortune hunter.'

'Perhaps. Who wouldn't be interested in your money, dearest Charlotte? I am sure he likes you too, but he has been dazzled by that woman. The camera doesn't lie.'

Charlotte looked at the photograph again. She remembered when she had taken it. It was the day the hunt had come to Melton. She had taken the photograph in the morning and in the afternoon Bay had proposed to her and kissed her for the second time. She felt a little pop of anger explode in her head.

Walking to the balustrade, she hurled the photograph down onto the marble floor below. The sound of the glass shattering brought the porter out of his cubbyhole. He looked at the mess of glass and wood in amazement and then looked up and saw Charlotte's face.

'How clumsy of me,' she said, 'I am so sorry.'

'Don't worry, miss, it's only a bit of glass.' He stooped down. 'Here's a lucky thing, the photograph's undamaged.'

Charlotte began to laugh.

Caspar stepped forward. 'I think I am going to take you home now.'

'But he is waiting for me upstairs,' said Charlotte breathlessly.

'Let him wait.'

Caspar took Charlotte's arm and marched her down the stairs. At the bottom, the porter came towards Charlotte holding the photograph.

'Here you are, miss.'

Charlotte took the picture. 'Do you see this man here?' She pointed to Bay's face in the photo. 'His name is Captain Middleton. At some point he will come down the stairs. When he does, I would like you to give it to him with Miss Baird's compliments.'

At Bay

THE FRAMING ROOM SMELT OF VARNISH AND ammonium salts. The windows had the blinds drawn in case the more delicate prints were damaged by the sunlight, so the room was dark, apart from a few stripes on the floor where the wintry light came in through the gaps in the blinds.

Bay pulled out his hunter from his waistcoat pocket. It was twenty-five minutes past the hour. He had been waiting now for thirty minutes. He went to the window and looked down into the street. The crowds had gone now the Queen had left. There were a few people standing on the pavement waiting for their carriages. Bay saw a clergyman hand a younger woman into a carriage and drive off. The woman had been wearing striped silk and for a moment Bay thought that it might be Charlotte, until the clergyman had put an unmistakeably uxorious hand on her waist. There were now two men and a woman standing on the pavement. From his bird's eye view Bay could tell that the woman was not young. The hair falling out from under her hat looked grey. The woman turned her head for a moment and he could see now that it was Charlotte's aunt, Lady Lisle.

He continued to look out of the window as Lady Lisle was handed into her carriage, wondering if at the last moment Charlotte would run down the steps to join her. When the carriage drove off, he looked at his pocket watch again. He would wait another five minutes, in case Charlotte had been waiting for her aunt to leave before coming to find him.

The hunter gave its tiny peal on the hour and Bay finally conceded that she wasn't coming. He opened the door and walked down the stairs to the first floor. The building was silent. Bay put his head around the door of the exhibition hall; it was empty.

He wanted to have another look at the photograph of him and the Empress. It wasn't that he had forgotten the image. It was in the hope that his recollection of the picture was somehow faulty. The glimpse he had got had been terrifying. He had barely recognised himself. The man in the picture was not someone he wanted to be: transfixed by the Empress, eyes wide with desire and – he could barely admit it – greed.

He tried to remember where the picture had hung. He wheeled around the empty salon, trying to identify the scene of his humiliation. But there were so many photographs. He found the portrait that Charlotte had taken of him and Tipsy. She had understood how much the horse meant to him.

At last, accepting that the photograph was no longer there, he realised that there was no point in staying. The hall was clearly empty; only the smell of wet wool remained of the crowd that had been there earlier.

Bay walked slowly down the stairs, towards the door, which was open. Outside, two men were rolling up the red carpet that had been laid out for the Queen's visit.

'Excuse me, sir, but are you Captain Middleton?'

Bay turned to see the porter.

'Yes.'

'Then I have something for you.' The porter went behind his desk and pulled out a package wrapped in brown paper.

'This was left for you, sir. By Miss Baird. With her compliments. I wrapped it up, though, didn't want the print to get dirty.'

'Miss Baird. When did she leave?'

'About an hour or so ago. She left with a gentleman.'

Bay undid the brown paper and string and was confronted with his own face.

'Did she say anything else, leave any other message for me?'

'No, sir. Just her compliments.'

Bay gave the man a half-crown.

'Thank you, sir, thank you very much indeed. Do you want some more paper to cover up the print? Shame that the glass and the frame got smashed.'

'Smashed?'

'Yes, Miss Baird dropped it from the landing. It made quite a mess, but the print's all right. That's the main thing.'

Bay turned out of John Adam Street into the Strand. He stood there for a moment as the crowds milled around him, wondering which direction to take. He could go west to Lady Dunwoody's house in Holland Park and try to speak to Charlotte. He could go north to Marylebone station and take the train back to Easton Neston where the Empress would be expecting him. He could go to his set in Albany but he had shut it up for the winter and had let his valet go. None of these options appealed.

He could not pursue Charlotte. She had decided not to see him and he could not blame her. The photograph had changed everything. Bay could not bear the glimpse of his soul that it had revealed, and he felt ashamed that Charlotte had seen it too. To go there now would be to declare himself a man completely without honour, the fortune hunter everyone took him to be.

Nor could he bear to go to Easton Neston. He did not want to be the man he had seen in the photograph. Besides, the repercussions of his encounter with Rudolph would be profound. He wondered what the Empress would do when she heard about the incident.

In the end, almost without realising it, he found himself walking along Pall Mall to St James's Street and his club. His shoulder was aching and he needed a drink. In the smoking room he ordered a brandy and, not seeing anyone he knew, he sat down and started to leaf through an old copy of *Punch*. But soon the heat from the generous fire and the fumes from the cigars overwhelmed him, and he fell asleep in one of the club chairs.

'Well, if it isn't Bay Middleton, the man of the hour.'

Bay came to with a start. Chicken Hartopp was standing over him, his face ruddy with drink.

'Hello, Chicken.' Bay took out his pocket watch. It was six o'clock. 'Good heavens. I have been asleep all afternoon.' He gestured to Chicken to sit down and called to the club servant to bring them both a drink.

'But what are you doing in town? I thought you would be out with the Cottesmore,' said Bay.

'Same as you, old man – came up to see the photographic exhibition. Charlotte Baird sent me a card.'

Bay understood now why Hartopp looked so exultant.

'So you saw my encounter with the Crown Prince?'

'Infernal insolence. I am surprised you didn't challenge him. I would have been happy to act as your second.'

'In front of the Queen?' Bay said.

'*I* wouldn't have stood for it. I would have called him out there and then.'

'Then you are a braver man than I am,' said Bay

Hartopp finished his drink and signalled for another. He shook his head and said, 'Damn peculiar that the Prince should have taken against you like that.'

'Indeed,' said Bay.

'Maybe he's heard the rumours about you and the Empress,' said Hartopp, slapping Bay on the shoulder, the bad one. Bay tried not to wince.

'As I don't know what rumours you are referring to, it's hard to say,' said Bay as evenly as he could.

'It's all right, old fellow. No need to get on your high horse. You know how these stories go around. One minute you are leading her in the field, next thing we hear you've been to Windsor Castle with her. Royal visits aren't the usual duties of a pilot, maybe old Rudolph thought you were getting above your station and he didn't like it.' Hartopp peered at Bay from behind his thicket of whiskers, clearly hoping for a response.

'The Empress asked me to accompany her. I was not in a position to refuse.'

Bay stood up.

'I have to be going now, Chicken. I have a dinner engagement.'

'Well, don't let me stop you old man. It wouldn't do to keep royalty waiting.' Chicken was guffawing at his own wit as Bay left.

Bay walked across Piccadilly to Brown's Hotel and took a room. He sent a wire to Easton Neston saying that he would not return that night. In the morning he would write to Sisi and explain that, under the circumstances, he could not act as her pilot any longer.

It would spoil the rest of the hunting season but there were still point-to-points and, of course, the National later that month. Tipsy was definitely ready. As he thought of his horse, he felt a little better. But then he remembered the photograph that Charlotte had taken of him and Tipsy in the stables at Melton and felt much worse.

After dinner, he wandered over to Covent Garden, to the Opera House. He thought that music might soothe his miserable state of mind. An opera by Meyerbeer was playing. Bay took a seat in the stalls, hoping that he would not see anyone he knew.

But at the Crush bar in the interval, he realised his mistake. All the ladies who had been at the exhibition in the morning had spent the afternoon paying calls, making sure that their closest friends were aware of exactly how close they had been to the Queen when Prince Rudolph had called Captain Middleton 'a groom'. The news could not have travelled faster if it had been published in a newspaper. As Bay walked through the mirror-lined room he saw the fans go up as the women whispered about him. He decided to leave, making a point of sauntering through the crimson velvet corridor as if he didn't have a care in the world. As he walked down the stairs to the foyer he saw Blanche Hozier, blonde and immaculate, accompanied by her cousin George Spencer. They were coming up the stairs on the other side, so he could not escape them. Bay bowed and waited to see if Blanche would acknowledge him. He was surprised to see that she stopped and smiled at him. Lord George nodded.

'Captain Middleton!' said Blanche. 'I am surprised to see you in town in the middle of the hunting season. Whatever can have torn you away from the Quorn?'

Middleton saw from her expression that Blanche knew precisely why he was in London and had heard every particular of the morning's incident. George Spencer looked embarrassed.

'Oh, I have always been very fond of music.'

'And yet you appear to be leaving. How strange.' Blanche opened her blue eyes wide and Bay was struck both by how beautiful she was and how little desire he felt for her now.

'I find that I have had my fill of sensation for the day. Goodnight, Lady Hozier, Lord George.' And he had to stop himself from running out into the cold night air.

Mother and Son

ESTY, I AM COMPLETELY CHILLED. I NEED A BATH, a really hot one.' Sisi was pulling off her gloves and unpinning her hat, which she dropped on the floor. She stood still for a moment as the Countess unbuttoned the skirt of her riding habit, revealing the suede breeches beneath.

'It is waiting for you, Ma'am. How was your day?'

'Very tiresome. I can't stand it when no one will keep up with me at the front. It is not the same without Captain Middleton. Everyone else is so slow. Even Max and Felix.'

'Some beef tea, perhaps, with a little schnapps?' The Countess thought that her mistress looked thin and pale.

'My bones are aching, Festy. I need the medicine.'

The Countess went over to the dressing table and opened the wooden case where all the Empress's medicines were kept. The cocaine solution had been made up for the Empress in Vienna, where she used it all the time. Festy had brought a full bottle of the mixture from Austria. In the Hofburg, the Empress would get through one of these vials in a fortnight. They had been in England for weeks now and the bottle was almost unused. The Countess took out the syringe from its velvet-lined compartment, put the needle into the liquid and drew up the plunger.

The Empress took off her bodice and held out one white arm. She looked away as the Countess pushed the needle into one of the thin blue veins.

'Thank you, Festy.' And the Empress smiled for the first time that day.

Countess Festetics waited until the Empress had had her bath and the effects of the cocaine were well advanced before showing her the telegrams. She knew their contents, because Baron Nopsca had already steamed them open. There were two telegrams – one from Bay saying that he was detained in London and that he would not be coming back for dinner. Sisi read it then scrumpled it up and threw it on the floor.

'Captain Middleton is not coming back tonight. It is too bad of him, I have had such a miserable day. I will tell him that he must come back at once. I can't hunt without him.' Festetics did not point out that there was no return address on the telegram.

But the second telegram made the Empress smile.

'Rudolph is coming for dinner, Festy. You must tell Nopsca to have a room made ready.' Festetics nodded, knowing that the Baron had made the arrangements hours ago.

'What a son I have. He doesn't write to me for weeks and now he is coming just like that.' Sisi snapped her fingers. 'Tell the cook to make something with chocolate. Rudolph adores chocolate.'

The Countess nodded again; that too had already been taken care of.

Sisi decided to wear her hair down in a loose plait. She remembered how Rudolph had liked to hide behind her hair when he had been a little boy; that was before he was taken away from her to be 'trained'. They had tried very hard to turn him into the perfect prince, but Rudolph was too like her and not enough like his father to make a good pupil. He would never get up at five every morning, ready to be the 'father of his people'. Rudolph had no sense of duty. He lived simply to be amused. The only thing he had in common with Franz Joseph was their love of uniforms.

Sisi felt her thoughts fizzing through her head. As well as relieving the pain in her joints, the cocaine made her restless. She must send a wire to Bay tonight. If he did not come back tomorrow she did not think she could bear to stay here without him. But why had he not come back? Surely if he had gone to see his doctor he would not be detained for a night. Sisi realised that Bay's life outside Easton Neston was completely unknown to her. He never spoke about his family or his friends and she had never thought to ask him.

At least Rudolph's arrival would relieve the tedium of the day.

There had been another pilot earlier, but he had hung back at every fence as if she had been a china figure. Riding with Bay was like continuing a conversation; she would turn her head and he would be there at her flank. He knew before she did which way she was going. She never hesitated when she was following him. They hardly spoke to each other when they were alone in the field, or later in bed. They did not need to. But now that unspoken thread had been broken. How could Bay bear to miss a day's hunting with her?

'I will wear the green velvet, I think, with the emeralds.'

It was fifty paces from one end of the drawing room to the other. Sisi had taken a thousand steps before Rudolph's carriage finally drew up at Easton Neston.

She noticed at once that he was not wearing a uniform. Just the Golden Fleece decoration. And Karolyi had come with him, which surprised Sisi. She had assumed that Rudoph had come down here to escape from the Ambassador.

'Dearest Rudolph, I am so pleased to see you.'

Rudi kissed her hand, but Sisi pulled him towards her and kissed him twice on both cheeks, in the Hungarian way. Rudolph held himself stiffly and he smelt faintly of alcohol.

'You look taller, or am I imagining it? And even more handsome, surely I am not imagining that. But a little pale. How long is it since we saw each other? Two months?'

'Five months, Mama.'

'Then we must toast to our reunion here in England. Nopsca, please bring some champagne.'

Sisi turned to Karolyi. 'Count, I must thank you for looking after my son and for bringing him here to me. I know that you must have been behind it.'

'Actually, Mama, it was my decision to come. I need to speak to you.'

Sisi saw the red patches on her son's cheeks and heard the urgency in his voice.

'Count Karolyi, I expect you would like to see your room before dinner. Countess Festetics will show you the way.' She turned to Nopsca, Liechtenstein and Esterhazy who were standing in a group round the fire.

'You may leave us.'

When they were alone in the vast room, Sisi sat down on one of the sofas and gestured to Rudi to sit next to her.

But he stood in front of her, legs apart, one hand nervously pulling at his decoration.

Sisi waited. Finally Rudolph burst out, 'I saw your "friend" Captain Middleton today. Did you know that there is a photograph of you and him hanging in an exhibition in London? A picture where he is gazing at you like a lovesick puppy? I was so ashamed. The Empress of Austria and a groom! He even had the impudence to speak to me!'

The Order of the Fleece finally snapped under Rudolph's constant fidgeting and he looked at it in his palm. He was close to tears.

'You saw Captain Middleton? In London?'

'Yes, this morning, at the exhibition. Karolyi made me go because the Queen would be there.'

'Victoria was there?'

'It doesn't matter who was there, Mama! What matters is that you have made yourself ridiculous. Everyone in London is talking about you and this Middleton. You must get rid of him at once.'

Sisi stood up and put her hand on her son's arm. 'Oh Rudi, you have broken the Fleece. Do you remember when you were given that, in the cathedral in Buda? How old were you then? Thirteen or fourteen? I was so proud of you. My little knight.'

'Mama, I am not thirteen now! You cannot pretend that nothing has happened. You must get rid of this man and go home. You are never in Vienna.'

'You want me to go back to Vienna where I am quite miserable? How can you be so cruel to your mother, Rudi? You know what it is like to stand there in those endless receptions, knowing that everyone is whispering about you. Don't you want me to have some happiness in my life? I have been the Empress since I was sixteen, younger than you are now. For twenty-two years I have been watched and measured and criticised every minute of the day. I am so tired of it. You know how hard it is, you feel it too.' She stroked his cheek. 'You are my son.' Rudolph stood for a moment under her touch, but then he broke away.

'But the picture, Mama!'

'Are you so very shocked that someone should admire me?' said Sisi.

'You are my mother.'

'Wait till you are married, Rudi. You will find that not everything is as simple as it seems to you now.'

'I just don't understand how you can be so careless of your position. Aunt Maria says that you and this Captain Middleton are inseparable.'

'Did she also tell you that she wanted Captain Middleton to work for her and that he refused her? Please don't base your judgement of me on what Maria tells you. She is bitter because she thinks that I have all the things that she has lost – a crown, a son like you. You must understand that. She is deliberately trying to make trouble between us.'

'So there is nothing between you and this Captain Middleton?'

'You have no right to ask me that!'

Sisi walked away from him, angry now. This frightened Rudolph, who followed her.

'I'm sorry, Mama. I have no right to ask you anything.'

Sisi stopped pacing and turned to embrace her son. She could feel his breath coming fast and shallow.

After a moment she released him and said, 'Do you like it in England, Rudolph?'

'I don't know. I haven't really had time to take it in. Karolyi keeps me so busy touring factories and visiting printing presses. We have hardly stopped. This will be the first evening where I am not attending a dinner with speeches.'

'I am sure Nopsca can arrange a speech if you like,' said Sisi, smiling.

'Oh, it will be a relief just to speak German and not to have to be polite to Englishmen who talk about their machines.'

'I have asked Festy to arrange for a chocolate cake.'

'Oh Mama, how did you know I have been dreaming of chocolate cake?'

After dinner, Rudi came into his mother's room while the maid was brushing out her hair. The girl had to bend over to take the brush all the way to the bottom. He watched as if hypnotised as the silver-backed brush was drawn through the long chestnut hair, leaving a trail of static crackling in its wake. He addressed his mother's face in the mirror.

'I was thinking that I might stay here for a few days. I have had enough of factories and machine looms. And I thought it would be nice to spend some time with you here, away from Vienna.'

'Of course, my darling. Will you want to hunt? I am sure that Captain Middleton could find you a horse.'

'I don't need anything from Captain Middleton.'

'Oh don't be silly, Rudolph. I thought we had settled this.'

'I don't think the Captain will want to be here with me.'

'But why not?'

'I called him a groom at the exhibition this morning and he was not pleased.'

'Of course he wasn't. How could you be so boorish? He is a cavalry officer, not a servant. Well, you will just have to apologise to him. I am sure he will forgive you.'

'That is beside the point, as I have no intention of apologising. Indeed, Mama, if Captain Middleton returns here then I cannot remain.'

'Oh Rudolph, why do you have to make things awkward? I have come here to hunt. Captain Middleton is my pilot. I cannot hunt without him. So he must come back.'

'But why does he have to stay here?'

'He stays here because I have asked him to.'

'Then you will just have to tell him to go somewhere else,' said Rudolph, standing up.

Sisi heard the petulance in his voice. There could be no reasoning with him in this state. He had drunk heavily at dinner, and he was not a happy drunk. She could not face a scene and besides, there was enough of the little boy he had once been to make her want to protect him.

Sisi signalled to the maid to leave them and she got up, her hair swirling around her, and put her arms around her son.

'My poor boy,' she said.

When she woke up the next morning, Sisi asked Festetics if there had been any word from Bay. When the Countess said there had been nothing since the telegram of the night before, Sisi asked her to fetch Nopsca and the Ambassador to her sitting room. The Crown Prince was still asleep.

As they came in Sisi could see that both wore the all too familiar courtiers' expression of wary neutrality. Neither of them wanted to offend so they would pretend to have no opinions until she did.

'Perhaps you can tell me what happened yesterday, Count Karolyi.'

'Well, Majesty, it was a most unhappy series of events. I took the

Crown Prince to the exhibition in order that he might have an opportunity to meet the Queen. He was not perhaps himself, a late night had left him nervous. I believe that he was very shocked to find a photograph of Your Majesty and perhaps he expressed himself more forcibly than he might otherwise have done. Captain Middleton, prudently in my opinion, decided to leave. But it is fair to say that the Queen, who of course met the Captain on your visit to Windsor, was surprised by the Crown's Prince's rudeness towards him.'

'I see. And can you tell me how my picture came to be included in this exhibition?'

'I believe it was taken by a young lady, a Miss Baird, who appears to be a friend of Captain Middleton. She had taken some other pictures of him which were also at the exhibition.'

'I see. I trust that the picture is no longer on display.'

'No, Majesty, the young lady was very quick to remove it. She appeared to be most distressed by the incident.'

Baron Nopsca remembered the note that he had steamed open the week before and cracked his knuckles with satisfaction, now that the situation was clear to him.

Sisi turned to him.

'Baron, I want you to find Captain Middleton. Tell him that I want him to return as soon as my son has gone. I do not think it would be wise for them to meet again.'

The men nodded in agreement.

'Ambassador, I am relying on you to take my son back to London tomorrow at the latest. You must persuade him, I want no part of it. But he must go back. Can I rely on you?'

'Of course, but the Prince can be headstrong and not always open to persuasion.'

'My son is easily bored. I don't think he will find it amusing here for very long. I am sure you can tempt him to return to London.'

Karolyi bowed. He had thought it was his job to keep Rudolph away from those kinds of temptation, but he understood the Empress's predicament. The longer that the Prince stayed at Easton Neston and Bay was banished, the greater the scandal.

'I will do my best, Majesty.'

Sisi nodded to the men. 'You may leave us.'

When the men had gone, she turned to Festetics.

'Did you know anything about this Miss Baird, Festy?'

Festy smiled. 'A man like Captain Middleton will always have female friends, Majesty. He is a *herzensbrecher*.'

'He didn't tell me that he was going to the exhibition.'

'Maybe he was embarrassed to admit that he was going to look at pictures of himself.'

'Perhaps.' Sisi shook herself. 'I am so cross with Rudolph.'

'But Majesty, he is young and jealous. You know how much he loves you.'

Sisi shrugged. 'If he loves me he should want me to be happy.'

The Countess knew it was useless to say any more.

Baron Nopsca's Mission

BAY WOKE UP WITH A SORE HEAD. AFTER THE OPERA he had taken a bottle of brandy to bed with him and now he was feeling the results. He wondered what time it was. He stumbled out of bed and looked at the clock on the mantelpiece. It was past noon. He rang the bell and asked the valet to bring him some shaving things and a pot of coffee.

When he was dressed and shaved he felt a little better. But then he saw the brown paper parcel containing the photograph lying on the writing desk.

Last night, halfway through the bottle of brandy, he had decided that he must go to Holland Park and talk to Charlotte. But sober, he knew that this would be impossible. She didn't want to see him; the message she had left with the photograph had been quite clear. He could write to her, but he did not know where to begin. He could not explain his behaviour to her. Away from Easton Neston, away from the Empress, Bay could hardly explain it to himself.

There was a knock at the door. Thinking it was the valet come to collect the shaving things, Bay said, 'Come in.' But to his surprise Baron Nopsca walked into the room.

'Baron, what are you doing here? I am sorry, that sounded rude, but how on earth did you find me?'

The Baron waved his hands.

'Oh, there are ways, but that is not important.' He coughed. 'The Empress asked me to come. The Crown Prince came down to Easton Neston last night.'

Bay gestured to the Baron to sit down in the hotel room's only armchair. He sat on the ottoman at the foot of the bed.

'So the Empress knows what happened yesterday?' Bay asked.

Nopsca nodded unhappily. 'Her Majesty is aware of the incident. She regrets the Prince's behaviour towards you very much. She would like you to return to Easton Neston, but unfortunately that will not be possible while the Prince remains at the house.'

Bay was wondering how he could explain to the Baron the impossibility of his returning to Easton Neston at all, when the waiter returned with a tray bearing a coffee pot. He set it up on the table and poured out two cups. Bay fumbled for a coin in his dress trousers to tip the man.

The Baron added three teaspoons of sugar to his coffee. He stirred it vigorously, took a sip and grimaced.

'We would not call this coffee in Wien.'

Bay took a sip. 'I am afraid I can't defend it either. So the Empress wants me to cool my heels here until the Prince leaves?'

The Baron plucked at his lapel. 'I would not put it quite like that; she is not happy about the situation but she thinks that under the circumstances it would be better if you were not under the same roof as His Highness.'

'But when he leaves, she would like me to come back and be her pilot just as before?'

The Baron nodded.

Bay stood up. 'Surely the Empress must see that it is impossible.'

The Baron leant forward. 'But nothing has changed, my dear

Captain. The Empress is very happy with your services. She has come to depend on you. You have made this visit very,' he smiled, 'agreeable for her.'

Bay found the Baron's smile infuriating. 'But her son insulted me. He made it quite clear that he did not think that I was a suitable companion for his mother.'

The Baron heard the anger in Bay's voice. He stood up and put his hand on Middleton's shoulder. 'You must understand that the Crown Prince can be . . . volatile. He has not yet learnt to think before he speaks. I feel sure that he will realise his mistake.'

'But I am not to come to Easton Neston while he is there.'

The Baron shrugged. 'The Crown Prince will probably leave tomorrow.'

'I am sorry, Baron, but I want no part of this. You can tell the Empress that I shall stay in town.'

The Baron looked dismayed. 'I cannot possibly deliver such a message.'

Bay felt almost sorry for him. 'Tell her that you did your best to persuade me, but I am a stubborn Englishman. She can't blame you for that.'

'You misunderstand me. It is not for myself that I am concerned but for the Empress. I have been in her service for many years, and I know her moods. She has formed a very strong attachment to you, Captain Middleton. I can see that you have made her happy. She has not had so much happiness in her life.'

The Baron was wringing his hands in real distress. Bay could see that this was more than a courtier's reluctance to be the bearer of bad news.

'Do you really think that I make her happy?'

The Baron nodded. 'You did not see her before. Since she has met you she is eating and laughing. The Countess and I, we both know that you are responsible. And Captain Middleton, I think that she makes you happy too.'

Bay walked over to the window. In the street below a hurdy-gurdy grinder was playing. A small crowd had gathered who were dropping coins into a bag carried around by a monkey.

'Yes, she does,' he said slowly, 'but the situation is impossible. It is not just the Prince, what about Liechtenstein and Esterhazy? They loathe me.'

'Perhaps, but they do not signify. Please, Captain Middleton, do not let your pride make the Empress unhappy.'

The monkey was standing on the peddler's shoulder now, waving his miniature fez in the air.

Bay thought of the Empress that night in the stables with the stars in her hair. He had wanted her so much. The moment when he felt her respond had been so triumphant.

'But I can't lurk about here waiting for the Crown Prince to leave.'

The Baron was silent.

A policeman came along the street and told the hurdy-gurdy man to move along. The monkey tried to pick off one of the shiny buttons on his tunic and put it into his bag.

Bay made a decision.

He turned to the Baron. 'Have you heard of the Grand National?'

The other man shrugged. 'It is a horse race, I believe.'

'It is the best steeplechase in the country, the world, probably. Every hunt jockey dreams of winning the National. I was going to run in it five years ago, but I lost the horse. Since I bought Tipsy I have been thinking of running her, and now I have made up my mind. The race is on the twenty-fourth. The hunting season is almost over and I don't want her to break a leg before the race. If you tell the Empress that I am going to Aintree to train for the National, she will understand.'

The Baron looked dubious. 'Perhaps the Captain would like to write her a letter to explain. I know that Her Majesty will ask me many questions.'

Bay sat down at the desk and began to write, conscious that the Baron was reading over his shoulder.

Your Majesty,

I have decided to enter Tipsy in the Grand National. It is the most magnificent race in the world and to win it has long been my dearest wish. Nopsca has asked me to come back to Easton Neston, but I know you will forgive me if I don't return as I must spend the next days preparing for the race. I can be sure you will forgive me because I know that if you were in my position you would not only enter the Grand National but you would undoubt-edly win, as you are the greatest rider I have ever known.

I remain, dear Madam, your most obedient servant,

Bay Middleton

He blotted the letter and gave it to Nopsca, unsealed. He wanted Sisi to know that he had written the letter for public consumption.

'Don't look so worried, Nopsca, the Empress will understand.'

'I hope so, Captain.'

When the Baron had gone, Bay went for a walk in the park. The trees were still bare but the weather was beginning to turn, and every now and then the sun appeared from behind the clouds. The afternoon carriage drives had begun and Bay watched as the ladies went past in their barouches and phaetons. It was not a huge turnout, it was too early in the season for that, but there were a few faces that Bay recognised. It felt strange to be walking in the park instead of riding but on foot there was no danger of running into anyone he knew. The only other pedestrians were nursemaids pushing perambulators.

His mood lifted in the fresh air. The thought of the National made him feel buoyant, and as he walked along the Serpentine he felt as if he was floating above the tangle of his life. Riding in the steeple-chase, for all its dangers, felt ridiculously simple. He had the right horse; if only his shoulder would hold out, then surely he stood a chance of winning.

A woman cantered past on a chestnut mare and for a moment Bay fancied it was the Empress, but then he saw the rider bounce a little in the saddle, looking for a moment as if she would lose her balance. Bay realised that in the weeks he had been riding out with the Empress, he had never once seen her falter.

Mayfair

'LOOK UP, LADY AUGUSTA. SUCH A LONG NECK SHOULD be given every opportunity to be swan-like. And turn your head a little towards me, that's the ticket. Now think of drifting down the Grand Canal on a gondola.'

'But I have never been to Venice,' objected Augusta.

Caspar smiled. 'You don't need to have been there to imagine it, dear Lady Augusta. You are a bride on the eve of her wedding thinking of the pleasures to come. Ah, you are blushing, that is just what I want. Now just keep thinking of the gondola while I take the picture.' He disappeared beneath the velvet cloth and pressed the shutter button.

'Perfect! Now I am going to play with your veil a little, like this. Your eyes have such depths to them, I want the lace to act as a frame. Yes, hold it up a little like that. That is enchanting. I believe you are a natural model, Lady Augusta. In America we would be putting your image on advertising hoardings.'

'How perfectly dreadful,' said Augusta, looking pleased.

She was standing on a small dais in one corner of the Crewe drawing room in Portman Square. Behind her was a painted backdrop of a classical temple, a pair of cherubs blowing their trumpets in the left corner. Charlotte thought that the backdrop was vulgar, but Caspar had overruled her – 'Women like your sister-in-law-to-be, dear Carlotta, cannot be flattered enough. She will find it quite appropriate to be put in a goddess-like setting, believe me.' He had been right. Augusta was delighted.

Charlotte could only admire the ease with which Caspar handled Augusta. Despite being an American with no fortune or connections, he had coaxed and flattered Augusta into regarding him not just as an equal but as quite indispensable.

It had started after the exhibition. Augusta had come to Lady Dunwoody's house to see Charlotte, ostensibly to persuade her to return to Melton, but her real object had been to goad her about Bay's relationship with the Empress. 'The Crown Prince was terribly rude to Captain Middleton, of course. But he must have been provoked. What a difficult position for you, Charlotte. But if you had stayed in Melton, as I urged you, none of this would have happened.'

To Charlotte's intense relief, Caspar had interrupted Augusta's torrent of malice, and had effortlessly turned her into his creature, by remarking as she turned her head, 'But what a profile! It is quite Grecian in its purity. I must photograph you, Lady Augusta. To leave such perfection unrecorded would be a crime.'

Charlotte had expected Augusta to bristle at the impudence, but instead she had succumbed to his charm and been swept off to the studio, where Caspar had photographed her looking into a hand mirror. He had sent the print to Melton the very next day and Augusta had been so delighted with the result that when Caspar had begged to be allowed to photograph her in her wedding dress, she had not only agreed but had asked him to take photographs of the wedding party, and had even sent him his own invitation.

Now Augusta was standing in her wedding dress and tiara, her Honiton lace veil arranged by Caspar to hide the jutting Crewe jaw, looking at the American with a great deal more affection than she ever showed to her fiancé.

'Mr Hewes is so good at putting his subjects at ease,' she had said to Charlotte. 'I had no idea that sitting for a photograph could be such a pleasant experience.' Charlotte had understood the implied rebuke.

'One more, I think, and then I must leave you both to prepare for tomorrow.' Caspar turned to Charlotte. 'Why don't you stand behind the bride and hold up her veil?' Charlotte glared at him, but did as she was told.

'Now that is charming. The bride and her attendant. What would make it perfect is if, Charlotte, you could look a little wistful. As if you were wondering when your turn will come.'

'One day you *will* be the one in the veil and tiara, Charlotte. It takes time to make the right match. I always think it is a terrible mistake to marry the first person who comes along,' said Augusta.

'Evidently,' said Charlotte, 'Fred was lucky that you were prepared to wait.'

Augusta glanced at her, but Charlotte was busy arranging the veil.

'Now that's charming,' said Caspar, 'what a delightful composition. Now I want you both to think about tomorrow. Perfect, I could call this one, Almost Sisters.'

Charlotte dropped the veil as if it had been poisoned.

'I think that's enough, Caspar, you mustn't tire Augusta out.' Charlotte walked over to the table covered in Caspar's photographic paraphernalia and started to put things away.

'Very well,' sighed Caspar. 'You are right, of course, Charlotte, but it is hard to tear myself away when Augusta is looking so exquisite.'

Charlotte looked over at Augusta, wondering if she could really believe Caspar's flattery, but the bride-to-be looked as if she could have listened to the American for ever.

The carriage was waiting outside to take Charlotte back to the house in Charles Street. She had moved back there from Holland Park a week ago when Lady Lisle had come back from Melton. She would have preferred to stay on in Holland Park, but she felt a little sorry for her aunt. When Fred and Augusta returned from their honeymoon, Charlotte would live with them and poor Lady Lisle would soon have to go back to the little house in the cathedral close.

But it was a sacrifice for Charlotte. In Charles Street there was nothing to distract her. Lady Lisle had only two topics of conversation: the forthcoming wedding or the drama of the photographic exhibition. Charlotte could not muster much enthusiasm for the former, and wanted very much to forget the latter.

Fred, who saw no reason to let his impending nuptials ruin his hunting, had only arrived that morning.

Caspar, of course, did not have a carriage waiting. He sighed as he stood on the pavement with his photographic equipment, contemplating the long journey back to Chelsea. He would have to take a hackney cab or even an omnibus. Charlotte knew that Caspar did not enjoy taking public transport. He would happily walk for miles but found the packed buses, or worse, the underground railway, to be altogether claustrophobic. 'In the West you can go for days without meeting another soul. To find someone's nose pushing between your waistcoat buttons on an omnibus is very hard to get used to.'

Despite Caspar's treachery in forcing her to pose with Augusta,

Charlotte decided to ask him to Charles Street for dinner. Since the exhibition, when he had taken her back to Holland Park, Caspar had become an indispensable part of her life. While she had been staying at Lady Dunwoody's he had been there every day – helping at the Thursday salons, printing up Lady Dunwoody's plates, entertaining the ladies during afternoon calls. But Caspar's charm was not confined to Holland Park; since the photographic exhibition he had become the toast of Mayfair too. Augusta had been his first conquest, then he had charmed Lady Crewe with his passionate advocacy of Sabbath Day Observance and had seduced Lord Crewe by taking a picture of him dressed as Merlin. Caspar had been down to Melton for a Saturday to Monday, without Charlotte, and had laid siege to Fred – imploring him to sit as Lancelot to Augusta's Guinevere. Charlotte had blinked in disbelief when she saw the picture being developed in Lady Dunwoody's dark room. Fred had put on the knightly costume that had been hired from Maskelyne's and had gone down on one knee in front of a be-kirtled Augusta with her hair loose. They looked delighted with themselves.

A light rain started to fall and Caspar began to do up the buttons on his plaid ulster. As he reached the penultimate button, Charlotte said, 'Caspar, you can't go home in this weather. Come back to Charles Street and stay to dinner. I am sure my aunt will be delighted to see you. You can leave the camera there and then it will so much easier to pick it up for the wedding.'

Caspar stopped buttoning and made a low bow.

'Thoughtful as ever, my Carlotta. Now you have suggested it, it is clearly the best of all possible arrangements. But I am wary of imposing myself on your brother's last night as a free man.'

'Fred will be delighted, I know.'

As the carriage made its way from the Crewe house in Portland Square across Oxford Street and into Mayfair, Caspar sat opposite Charlotte with his back to the horses, keeping up a steady flow of chatter. But as they turned into Grosvesnor Square, he leant forward and said, 'I will only stop talking if you tell me what the matter is. No, let me guess. You see, I can read your mind as easily as I can make the fearsome Augusta invite me to her wedding. You are fretting because you suspect that Captain Middleton will be there tomorrow and you do not wish to see him.' Caspar put his finger to his temple.

'No, that is not right.' He gestured as if he were practising Mesmerism. 'You *do* want to see him, but at the same time you don't. He attracts and repels you equally. And now you are cross with me for reading your mind. But you make it so easy, Charlotte. I don't think I have ever seen someone whose face expresses so exactly what they are thinking.'

Charlotte shifted on the leather buttoned seat. 'Nobody else finds me easy to read.'

'Because they are not as interested as I am. If you would let me photograph you I could show you what I see in your face. But you won't let me because you are afraid of what I will find.'

'I don't know what you are talking about.' Charlotte looked out of the window.

'You see, I am the only one who knows what a remarkable person you are.'

Charlotte put her hands up in front of her face.

'I don't feel very remarkable at the moment,' she muttered.

'That is because you thought that you and the Captain had an understanding. Or rather, he was the man that understood you. And I am sure he did, or rather does. But you are not the only woman that he cares for. And that makes you doubt everything he has ever said to you.'

Charlotte took her hands away from her face. Caspar's analysis of her state of mind had put into words feelings that she had tried not to define. She wished more than anything that she had never taken that photograph, but now it was there it was impossible to ignore. Bay was not, as Fred and Chicken had hinted, using the Empress for his own ends; it was far worse, he was in thrall to her.

Charlotte looked at Caspar. His big, freckled, farm-boy face belied his intelligence. She wondered if a photograph would reveal the shrewdness beneath his flamboyance. In a collage he should be a peacock but she couldn't quite reconcile that small head with Caspar's intelligence. His flamboyance was not an end in itself like a peacock's display. Charlotte thought that it was perhaps a diversion, or even a shield. She could not help remembering the strain in his face when he talked about the short life of Abraham Running Water.

But Charlotte did not want to listen to Caspar talking about Bay. Even though she knew that he was right, at that moment she could not bear to hear it. She leant forward and touched his arm.

'Tell me about America, Caspar. I should very much like to think about something other than my own situation.'

Caspar cleared his throat and held out his hands as if preaching from a pulpit.

'The first thing to realise is that it is a country that is still being imagined. Here every patch of earth has a story, all your places have nuances; if you say Cornwall to an English person, they think of smugglers, and King Arthur and fish. But there are great parts of my country about which Americans know nothing beyond an idea of unimaginable vastness. Of course the Indians that live there know the spirits of these places, but that is not the point. You can't imagine how blue the sky is in the West, Charlotte. So much space. It's really wild, not like your Lake District with its little stone walls. In the West the landscape is unmarked by man.

'That's why I like to photograph it; those landscapes are so strange that they defy the viewer. If I had painted the Grand Canyon, you would not believe me – but with my photograph I have shown you the truth and you will have to find a way to imagine it. Even the cities like San Francisco are making themselves up. They change their character completely in two years – I expect that I shall hardly recognise the place when I go back. Here we are in Mayfair going to Charles Street. An address that has been respectable, respected even, for centuries. Perhaps the buildings may change but to live in Charles Street is something. But we don't have a Charles Street in the West, not yet, anyway. In San Francisco there are fancy streets, of course, but they weren't there five years ago. There aren't any layers yet, the paint is still wet. We don't really have time for the past out West; we are too busy imagining the present.'

With impeccable timing, Caspar brought his speech to a close just as the carriage drew up outside the house in Charles Street.

'There!' he said. 'Did I distract you with my vision of the land of the free? You should come to America, Charlotte, with your camera.'

'Oh, I would love to, but how could I, Caspar? I can't just get on a boat and go.'

'Why not? When Fred and Augusta have gone on their wedding tour, there will be nothing between you and America but your aunt, and I think she is quite manageable.'

'But I can't go to America alone, Caspar. I don't know anybody there.'

'You can take your maid, the one who does your hair so nicely. Oh and of course,' he smiled, '*I* would come with you.'

From any other man that was tantamount to a proposal, but not with Caspar. He was offering her something even more than marriage; he was giving her the chance to escape.

But before she could reply the footman opened the carriage door and there was Lady Lisle standing on the steps.

'What do you know about America, Grace?' Charlotte asked later that evening, as she was changing for dinner. The Melton maid was trying to coax Charlotte's hair around a pad to give it some volume.

'Not much, miss. The blacksmith's son went over there from the village. He is doing very well. Sent his mother a photograph of himself wearing a suit. Mrs Street hardly recognised him.'

'I am thinking of going to America myself. To take photographs. Do you think you would like to come with me?'

'To America? I can't really say, miss. It's too much for me to imagine it. Coming to London was an adventure, but at least everyone speaks English.'

'Oh, I think they speak English in America.'

'Maybe they do, but I wonder how easy it is to understand them. When Mr Hewes starts talking fast I can't barely make out a word he says.'

'I don't think many people in the world speak as fast as Mr Hewes,' said Charlotte, smiling.

'If you go, I think I should like to go with you. But not for ever, Miss Baird, I would miss my mother too much.'

'No, not for ever. I just want to go for a . . . visit.'

'But, excuse me for asking, miss. What about Captain Middleton?'

'What about him?'

'I thought that you and the Captain had an understanding.'

'Sometimes understandings turn into misunderstandings. I doubt that Captain Middleton will care whether I stay or go.'

'Oh, Miss Charlotte, I think you are being too hard on him. He has a good heart. Always popular in the servants' hall. Pleasant with everyone and very generous, even though he isn't a rich man. He didn't keep a valet, but nobody minded polishing his boots or starching his hunting collars, and that can't be said of all the young gentlemen at Melton. I don't know what is passing off between you and the Captain, miss, but he isn't a bad man. He never forgets to be kind to people like me.'

Charlotte wondered if Bay had simply been kind to her in the way that he was instinctively generous with servants like Grace, animals and children. She could not really believe that he had only wanted the money. Avarice she recognised, but kindness was so unfamiliar to her that it was possible she might have mistaken it for love. But as soon as the thought came into her mind, she batted it away. She could not bear to think about him. Caspar had been right, she had thought that Bay had understood her, but it turned out that she had misunderstood him.

Firmly, she made herself think of other things. The idea of going to America was beginning to take shape in her mind. If she had not seen the pictures she would have dismissed Caspar's talk about the West as just another of his gaudy exaggerations. But the pictures were undeniable.

On the other side of Piccadilly, Bay was walking down St James towards his club. He had taken the train down from Cheshire, where he had stabled Tipsy in preparation for the National. In his pocket he had a card for Lady Augusta's Crewe's wedding to

Frederick Baird Esq. He had not expected to get an invitation, but he had reckoned without the social ambition of Augusta, who, despite Fred's protests, saw no reason to banish the most talked about man in London, to spare Charlotte's feelings. 'If we don't invite him, people will say it is because he has jilted Charlotte, but as they were never officially engaged, the best way to put the rumours to rest is to have him at the wedding.' Fred had reluctantly agreed to the sense of this and Augusta had taken great pleasure in telling Charlotte what she had done. 'If he comes, you must just treat him like anybody else. When people see that you are perfectly civil to him, they will stop gossiping about the whole affair.'

At the club Bay found a card game and played until midnight, losing mostly and having to put up with the joshing of the others. 'Unlucky at cards, eh Middleton?' Two of the drunker members had started to whirl each other around the room in an improvised Viennese waltz. Bay had borne it all with an easy smile. He knew how to handle the envious teasing of his contemporaries.

Crombie, a tall major from the Blues who had ridden against Bay at a few point-to-points the year before, accosted him on the stairs.

''Spect you will be too busy with your royal duties for the National, Middleton.'

'Nothing would keep me away this year. In fact I've just been up to Aintree to feel the course.'

'Are you riding that mare of yours? The one you bought in Ireland?'

'God willing. I think we have a chance at getting round.'

'Indeed. I don't think there's a book yet. Maybe I'll take a punt on you. Mind you, it's a bloody course. Might be too much for a mare.'

'Tipsy is a finisher. She will make it past the post even if I don't.'

Crombie nodded. 'Nothing like an Irish horse. Well, I shall look forward to seeing you at Aintree.'

'So long, Crombie.'

Bay was on his way out when he saw Hartopp weaving up the steps. He missed one and would have landed rather heavily if Bay hadn't caught him before his face hit the granite.

'They keep moving the damn steps. Goin' to take it up with the Club Secretary. Damn cheek,' grumbled Hartopp. 'Oh, hello, Bay. What you doin' here? Thought you were too busy bowin' and scrapin'.'

'Came up for Fred's wedding.'

Chicken was brushing the dust from the steps from his evening clothes without much success.

'Well, do me a favour, old man, and keep away from Charlotte Baird. I have a chance there now you are out of the picture. I've had my eye on her for years. Would have got her too if you hadn't come along and turned her head. So stay away from her tomorrow, or you will have me to answer to.'

The threat present in Chicken's words was undermined by his inability to focus properly. He addressed this speech somewhere behind Bay's right ear.

'Can't promise that, Chicken. But I will tell you one thing, if Charlotte won't have you, it has nothing to do with me.'

'Is that so? At least I didn't lead her on and then abandon her when a more attractive offer came along.'

Bay's punch sent Chicken sprawling down the steps. He scrabbled to his feet and tried to have a swing at Bay, but Bay evaded him easily. Chicken's nose was bleeding heavily, staining his shirt front. Bay was already regretting his flash of temper. He went inside and called out the club porter.

'Captain Hartopp seems to have fallen down the steps. Can you see to him?' He pressed a half-sovereign into the man's hand.

The porter touched his cap. 'Certainly, sir. We are quite used to Captain Hartopp.'

Chicken pointed a huge hand at Bay as the other man set off into the night.

'You won't get away with it, you know.'

St George's, Hanover Square

NO CHURCH PEWS WERE COMFORTABLE, BUT THE ones in St George's Hanover Square had been made by a nonconformist carpenter who saw no reason why worshippers, especially rich and fashionable ones, should sit at their ease in the Lord's House. So he had made the bench seats intentionally half an inch narrower than was customary, which made it impossible for the sitter to do anything other than perch. Visiting preachers were always gratified by the attentiveness of the congregation to their sermons; no one ever closed their eyes in St George's, as a momentary loss of attention inevitably resulted in an embarrassing and noisy tumble.

So the congregation awaiting the arrival of the bride did not view her tardiness with indulgence. It was early in the year for a society wedding and quite a number of the guests had come up to town for the day, in order to avoid the expense of opening up their town houses so far ahead of the season proper. The guests who lived near Melton wondered why Crewe had decided to hold the wedding in town when he had that chapel at home that he was so proud of. The women who had come out the same year as Augusta knew exactly why she had chosen St George's; it was a way of showing the world that she was no longer on the shelf but a matron to be reckoned with. It was not a fabulous match for the daughter of an earl to be marrying a Borders squire, but by having the wedding in town, Augusta was making it plain that she did not intend to be written off.

The restless guests had little to do but survey each other as the organ launched into yet another Bach cantata. Captain Hartopp's black eye was a cause of much speculation. There was a rumour that he had been knocked down by Bay Middleton, yet they were today both standing at the groom's side. A drunken tumble seemed a more likely explanation, as Chicken was not a graceful drunk. Those guests who had heard about the now famous incident at the photographic exhibition were most curious to see Captain Middleton. Could the rumours about him and the Empress of Austria possibly be true? Middleton was known to be a ladies' man, but for an officer on half pay to become a royal paramour, well, it was the stuff of novels.

Earl Spencer was particularly uncomfortable. The narrow slat barely supported his massive thighs. It was a beautiful spring day, a perfect day to be out with the Quorn on one of the last days of the hunting season. But Spencer knew his duty. Baird had been one of his adjutants in Ireland, but he might have ignored that tie if it hadn't been for Bay. As far as he was capable of remorse, Spencer felt some responsibility for Bay's current predicament. For that reason he had put on his morning suit and was now perching awkwardly on his pew. There could be no question of people cutting Bay if Spencer was at his side.

Bay stood between Fred and Chicken at the altar steps. He had shaken hands that morning with Chicken, and while neither had forgiven the other, they were now standing side by side as fellow officers, resplendent in their dress uniforms. Hartopp was sporting an eyepatch but the swelling underneath was so bad that it hardly covered the affected area. Because of Chicken's shiner, Fred had asked Bay to hold the ring. 'If Augusta sees Chicken looking like that she might faint.'

So Bay stood next to the groom rolling the ring around in his pocket, listening to Hartopp's stertorous breathing, every exhalation sounding like a complaint.

At long last, the organist pulled out the trumpet stop and the congregation stood up as Augusta came down the aisle on her father's arm. Bay looked over his shoulder at the approaching confection of lace, orange blossom and diamonds, and out of compassion he whispered to Fred, who was shaking with nerves, 'You're a lucky man, Baird.' Fred looked surprised and grateful.

The service took place without incident, although it was noted that, unusually, the bride's vows were considerably louder than the groom's. When it was time for Bay to hand Fred the ring he tried to look at Charlotte, who was standing beside Augusta holding her bouquet. But either by accident or design, Charlotte's face was hidden behind the voluminous folds of the bride's veil. Despite this, Bay had thought it was a good sign that he had been invited to the wedding. He hoped that it was at Charlotte's instigation. As the wedding party formed to make their way down the aisle, Bay thought for a moment that he would be able to take Charlotte's arm, but somehow he ended up with Lady Crewe. Charlotte was behind him with Chicken.

As they came out of the church, the bride and groom made their way through the raised swords of Fred's guardsmen. There was a shout of huzzah for the happy couple, and the congregation were enthusiastic in throwing rice at them as they drove away in the carriage drawn by wedding greys.

Bay tried to find a moment to talk to Charlotte outside the church, but he could not get near her. She stuck close to Chicken Hartopp until she disappeared into the carriage that was to take the bridesmaids to the wedding breakfast in Portman Square.

Bay stood in the throng on the steps, listening to the excited chatter all around him, and wished that he was riding on Tipsy with the hounds in front of him and the wind at his back. For a moment he hesitated, wondering whether he should go on to the wedding breakfast, but before he could decide he felt Spencer's heavy hand between his shoulder blades.

'You managed to hand over the ring then.'

'It was the least I could do,' said Bay, trying to smile.

'Come with me to the breakfast. My wife has gone with Edith Crewe.'

Spencer did not wait for an answer but swept Bay along in front of him, until they were seated in the carriage.

'I saw the Empress last night at the Ambassador's. The Crown Prince was there, which is why, I imagine, you weren't.'

'I wasn't invited.'

'But you might as well have been there, as the Empress talked about you all night.'

'The Crown Prince must have enjoyed that.'

'He glowered like a sulky child. But the Empress wouldn't let him be; she teased him all night until he finally relented and smiled. Funny fellow. The way he looks at her is damned peculiar. Never seen the Prince of Wales look at his mother like that!' Spencer, as always, laughed at his own joke. Bay did not join in.

'The Empress was complaining that you have deserted her for the National.'

'The timing is unfortunate.'

'The Empress means to be at Aintree, so you had better perform.'

Spencer shifted in his seat and tugged at his waistcoat. 'I meant to ask you, how are you getting on with the Baird girl now?'

'She will have nothing to do with me,' Bay said.

'Pity, she's a nice girl, and rich too. But you can't have both, I suppose. Girls can be a bit snappish about these things. Way I see it, you dance to the Empress's tune until she gets tired of you, which she will one day. And then you go back to Charlotte Baird and ask her if she will still have you. My guess is that once she has got over her missishness, she will come round all right. Women like a man who is in demand. Don't think the Countess would have accepted me if she hadn't thought that her sister was keen on me. You mark my words, when the day comes and the Empress decides she doesn't need you any more, you can still have a crack at the Lennox fortune. I think the royal connection will only increase your charms. And if not her, there are plenty of others out there looking for a man like you.'

'Charlotte Baird is the only girl I have ever thought of marrying,' said Bay.

'Understandably. You don't find an heiress like that very often.'

'My reasons for wanting to marry her are not mercenary.'

'Of course not. You like her because she is a sweet young thing who worships the ground you walk on, but would she be so quite so sweet if she didn't have sixty thousand a year? Hard to tell. Man like you is bound to fall for the rich ones. How else are you going to keep a decent string?'

Bay knocked on the roof of the carriage to signal the coachman to stop.

'What on earth are you doing, Middleton?' said Spencer in surprise.

'I am going to walk the rest of the way.'

'But why?'

'Because I don't want to hit you,' said Bay, opening the carriage door.

Baron Nopsca, who had been following the Earl's carriage since Bay had got into it, sat back in his seat so that he wouldn't be seen. But when he saw Bay's face he realised that the Captain was not in a state to notice anything or anybody. He stood on the pavement in his dress uniform, the hilt of his sword gleaming in the spring sunshine, looking as if he might take out the sabre and run through a few pedestrians. The Baron told his driver to wait in a side street. He looked at his pocket watch and observed the hands pass for two minutes, before Bay shook himself and began to walk north towards Portman Square. The Baron waited until he saw Bay disappear into Crewe House, then told the carriage to go back to Claridge's Hotel.

The Wedding Breakfast

'NOW I WOULD LIKE THE NEWLYWEDS IN THE centre here. Perhaps the groom could smile just a little? I know that marriage is a serious business but surely not that serious. You have only been in wedlock for an hour.' Caspar had arranged the wedding party on the orchestra dais of the Crewe House ballroom. The bride and groom were standing slightly in front.

'Miss Chambers and Lady Violet, if you could move a little to your left, I think we want to see those beautiful dresses and their lovely owners. Very nice. Now, Charlotte, if you could move a little closer to your brother. No, there is something wrong with the drape of your skirt, if you will allow me?'

Caspar was fiddling with the volumes of fabric, when the door was opened by a footman and Bay walked in.

'Am I too late?'

'Not at all, Captain Middleton,' said Caspar smoothly. 'I am still arranging my subjects. Why don't you come and stand over here between Lady Violet and Miss Chambers?'

'As the best man, I believe I should stand next to the maid of honour.' Bay found a spot next to Charlotte, who did not turn her head.

Caspar gave a tight smile. 'Oh, the English, such sticklers for etiquette. Please don't worry about the composition of the photograph,

Captain Middleton. What's a little asymmetry if the laws of precedence are being observed?'

Tapping her fan on her head rather menacingly, Lady Crewe said, 'We must get on, Mr Hewes, tempus fugit.'

'Indeed, Lady Crewe, I am practically ready; all I require now is for you all to look at me and imagine that you are ankle-deep in melted chocolate.'

The bizarre image he conjured up broke the stiffness in their faces, and Caspar took the picture.

'Well, I think I have it,' said Caspar.

'Wait,' said Charlotte, stepping forward. 'May I be allowed to take one picture? Caspar, why don't you stand in there, I am sure Augusta would like a picture of you as well.'

Ignoring Lady Crewe's sigh and Caspar's look of horror, Charlotte took a plate from the case and inserted it into the camera.

'Now if everyone could look at me, that's it. Now *I* want you to imagine me going on a tour of North America to take photographs. Remember, quite still, everybody.'

She disappeared under the cloth, squeezed the bulb and took the picture.

When she emerged the bridal party broke up, Lady Crewe hurrying to the drawing room to take charge of the wedding breakfast, followed by Augusta.

But Fred broke away from his wife to say to Charlotte, 'The going to America thing was a trick to shock us like the chocolate, wasn't it?'

'Not exactly.'

'But you can't be serious! You must know that I would never allow it,' said Fred.

'Don't worry, Fred, I understand your objections,' said Charlotte, taking the plate out of the camera and putting it in its case, 'but I am still thinking about it.'

'It's a preposterous idea. You can't go gallivanting round the world on your own just because you've had a disappointment.'

'It's got nothing to do with disappointment. *If* I go it's because I want to take pictures of something more interesting than our friends, their servants, their houses and their animals.' She looked at Fred and smiled. 'And I have no intention of going alone. I am sure Mr Hewes will come with me if I ask him.'

Fred laughed. 'You shouldn't tease me like that, Mitten. For a moment there I thought you were serious.'

But before Charlotte could reply, he was summoned by a shrill cry from his wife, 'Fred, I am waiting.'

As the rest of the wedding party left the room, Charlotte was engaged in conversation by Lady Violet Anson, her fellow brides-maid. Lady Violet had never paid much attention to Charlotte on the few occasions that they had met, but now she seemed eager to make friends.

'Charlotte, my dear girl, I had no idea you were so *skilful*, you must give me some instruction. I long to take photographs. Such a sociable thing to do. You have everybody quite at your command.'

'I wouldn't say that. You can't guarantee that the sitters will like the results,' Charlotte said, wondering how much Violet knew about what had happened at the Royal Photographic Exhibition. But as she saw the other girl's eye flicker towards Bay, who was talking to Lord Crewe, it was obvious that her fellow bridesmaid knew every detail of the story.

'That must be *very* trying. But if you were to take a photograph of me I am sure I would be delighted.'

'If you want a portrait you should sit for Mr Hewes. Everybody likes his pictures. Augusta was thrilled with hers. Come let me introduce you.'

Charlotte shepherded Lady Violet towards Caspar, who was shutting up his camera. 'Caspar, I want to present you to Lady Violet Anson. She wants to have her photograph taken and I told her that you would do a much better job than me.'

'Well, I dispute that entirely, you are easily the more talented, but as I can never resist photographing a beautiful woman, I would be delighted to photograph you, Lady Violet.' He stood to one side considering her.

'With your colouring I think I would pose you as Ophelia.'

Lady Violet, who was so pale that she looked quite spectral in her bridesmaid's dress, looked delighted.

Charlotte left them together and joined the group that was heading towards the wedding breakfast. As she stood in the hall waiting for the clump of guests on the staircase to disperse, she felt a touch on her elbow.

'You can't ignore me for ever,' said Bay.

'But I have nothing to say to you.'

'You aren't really going to America.'

'That's funny, Fred said exactly the same thing. But I suppose he has a reason to ask as he is my brother. You, on the other hand, do not.' She turned to go but Bay stepped in front of her.

'Charlotte, please don't be haughty. Whatever you think of me, it cannot be worse than the opinion I have of myself. You are the person I care for and yet I have wronged you. Won't you let me explain?'

Charlotte tried to push past him. 'There is nothing to explain. I have seen the photograph: it speaks for itself.'

Bay blocked her way, his hand on the hilt of his sword.

'That wretched photograph. It is just a moment – an instant where, perhaps, I was dazzled by the Empress. But it is not a picture of my heart.'

'I am not sure I believe you,' said Charlotte.

'But why not? I am only here because of you. Take a photograph of me now and judge what you see in my face.'

'I just did. But whatever it shows, I am afraid it's too late.'

Bay leant towards her and she could see tears in his pale blue eyes. 'Really, Charlotte? Are you sure?'

She shook her head. 'No, I am not sure about anything. But that's the point. I have to be sure about the man I am going to marry.'

She pushed past Bay and started going up one arm of the double staircase.

Bay followed her. 'Couldn't I just come and talk to you? I miss you.'

'Talk to me?' said Charlotte.

'Tell you stories. Try and make you laugh. I used to be good at that. I could even tell you how Hartopp came to be called Chicken.'

Charlotte tried not to react. She carried on climbing the stairs, her hand gripping the balustrade as if she were afraid she might fall.

'Do you think that I am really so easy to win over?'

'Admit it. You are consumed with curiosity.'

'You don't mind betraying your friend?'

'I don't think he would call me his friend at the moment.'

Charlotte turned her head. 'You gave him the black eye?'

'I am afraid so.'

'But why?'

'Because he told me to leave you alone so that he could "have a crack" at you, as he put it. I told him that it wouldn't make any difference as you would never accept him.'

'Then you have done me a service. Does he really imagine that I would change my mind about him so quickly?'

'You changed your mind about me,' said Bay.

They were at the top of the stairs, behind a throng of guests waiting to go down the receiving line. Some people coming up the other arm of the double staircase looked at Bay and Charlotte with interest. Charlotte noticed this and tried to separate herself from Bay and become part of the group ahead of her. But Bay stayed close.

'People are looking at us,' said Charlotte.

'Let them look,' said Bay.

'It's easy for you to say that, but I don't want to be gossiped about any more than I already am, thanks to you. Please go away.'

'Only if you promise to let me see you.'

'Absolutely not.'

'Then I will tell Chicken that you have confessed to me your overwhelming desire to be Mrs Hartopp and that he should propose to you at once.'

Charlotte could not help smiling, but she put her hand up in front of her like a shield.

'You are not going to win me over, Bay.'

Bay was about to answer, but Caspar and Lady Violet had walked up the other side of the staircase and had drawn level with them.

'Captain Middleton, it is such a pleasure to meet you finally, having seen you on a photographic plate. It is fascinating to observe the original.' Caspar bowed.

'I am afraid I am bound to be a disappointment,' said Bay.

'Not in that uniform. In my country we rarely see anything so splendid. Not man-made, anyway.'

'It's a bit awkward to walk around town in, although it's quite reassuring having a sword.' Bay put his hand on the hilt of his sabre.

Caspar laughed. 'In the West everybody carries a gun. I feel quite naked without mine.'

'But nobody needs a gun in London!' said Lady Violet. 'We are not savages here.'

'We are not savages in San Francisco either,' said Caspar, looking at Bay, 'but we like to be prepared.'

There was a general bustle from inside the drawing room which suggested that the speeches were about to begin. Charlotte hurried inside. One of her duties as chief bridesmaid was to give flower favours from the bride's bouquet to all the female guests. Augusta thought that this was a charming custom, and had told Charlotte it would give her a chance to meet more people. 'You can never have too many female acquaintances. With your fortune you will never lack for male admirers, but it's the women who make the rules.'

She took the bouquet from the table that displayed the couple's wedding presents. Charlotte's gift to the bride of a pearl and topaz necklace was displayed in its red velvet case; but her real gift to the bride had been the loan of the Lennox diamonds. Charlotte had taken a certain pleasure in not conferring this boon until the day before the wedding. It had been enjoyable watching her sister-in-law's delight in snubbing Charlotte, fighting her desire to be resplendent on her wedding day in the Lennox tiara.

Bay's present to the couple was a pair of Meissen figurines of a shepherd and shepherdess. They were exquisite things, standing out from the heavy silver candelabra, pearl-handled fish knives and tortoiseshell dressing cases that made up the majority of the couple's tributes. Meissen porcelain was not something that Charlotte would have expected Bay to choose, but then, she reflected, there was a great deal about Bay that she didn't know.

She picked up the bouquet and circulated, giving out white narcissi and waxy stephanotis to the ladies. As she made her way through the tables and chairs Lord Crewe made a speech on the joys of matrimony, drawing his examples entirely from the Arthurian legends, which perhaps was not the most fertile ground, as Arthur and Guinevere, Lancelot and Elaine and Sir Bedivere had not been known for the felicity of their marriages. Then Fred stood up and made the shortest possible speech, with a great deal of throat clearing and spluttering before and after, but as he looked so genuinely pleased to be married, his awkwardness was forgiven, although Augusta watched him beadily throughout.

Then Bay stood up. Hartopp had been vetoed by Augusta, on account of the black eye.

Bay started off by congratulating Fred for his good fortune in being accepted by a bride as exceptional as Augusta. Charlotte tried not to smile at Bay's use of the adjective. Then he went into flattering detail about Fred's army career, his prowess in the saddle, and his skill at the game of quoits they used to play in the officers' mess with napkin rings and candlesticks. He was a natural speaker and his audience relaxed, satisfied that he would not embarrass them or himself. He told an anecdote about Fred's time in Ireland when as a young adjutant he had been expected to dance with all the young ladies at the vice-regal balls and had to have a consignment of dancing slippers sent over from London because he was getting through the shoe leather so quickly.

Bay took a sip of champagne and continued, 'We are here to celebrate a marriage. There is nothing more noble than the words of the marriage service which pledge to have and to hold from this day forward. I wish Fred and Augusta every blessing in their married life,' and here he looked directly at Charlotte, 'I can only pray that I will be granted the same chance to devote myself to another person's happiness.'

A gust of interest blew through the room at this obvious statement of intent. Charlotte, who had been trying to find an undamaged flower to give to the Dowager Countess of Trent, blushed despite herself. As everyone stood up to drink the health of the bride and groom, she slipped outside to give herself a moment to recover.

As she stood on the stone landing holding onto the balustrade with one hand, the dismembered bouquet with the other, Charlotte looked down into the hall and saw the footman open the door. A man in splendid livery stood outside and there was a muffled conversation between them. At last the footman admitted the man, who gave him a card which the footman carried upstairs on a silver tray. Charlotte watched as the card was handed to Lady Crewe and saw that lady start with surprise and nod violently. She leant over to whisper something in Augusta's ear which made the bride look more animated than she had all day. The footman was sent downstairs again.

This time the liveried servant opened the double doors to Crewe House.

From her vantage point, Charlotte saw the hair first – the medusa-like crown of auburn plaits cascading out beneath the tiny top hat trimmed with peacock feathers.

She tried to retreat into the drawing room but Lord and Lady Crewe were coming through the door to greet the Empress, so Charlotte retreated back onto the landing, trying to tuck herself away behind the double door.

The Empress climbed the white marble steps surprisingly quickly, the Countess Festetics hurrying to keep up with her.

'Lady Crewe,' said Sisi. 'You must forgive me for intruding. But when Captain Middleton told me that he was attending the wedding of your daughter I suddenly thought how nice it would be to see an English wedding. In my country it is the custom for members of the royal house to bless the brides of good families, so I thought you would excuse my visit. I should so much like to offer your daughter my congratulations.'

Lady Crewe had a little difficulty extricating herself from her extremely deep curtsey.

'We are honoured, Your Majesty. Augusta and Fred will feel doubly blessed. Please come in and let me introduce them to you.'

Charlotte thought that the Empress was rather less alluring close to, than she had been as a silhouette upon a horse. From a distance she was an exciting idea; three feet away Charlotte could see the lines around her eyes, the grooves between the nose and the mouth and the red knuckles on her hands. She was graceful, the carriage of her head was impeccable and she moved as if she was on castors instead of feet. But the Empress was a woman whose claim to beauty was now an effort of will rather than a self-evident truth.

The Empress processed into the room and there was much bowing and curtseying. Augusta, pink with excitement, offered the Empress her chair as the place of honour. But Sisi demurred and put her hands to Augusta's face.

'No, my dear child, I wouldn't dream of usurping your place on this your special day. We have brought a wedding gift. Festy!'

The Countess opened her reticule and brought out a small leather box which the Empress presented to Augusta. Inside was an enamelled brooch containing a miniature of Sisi surrounded by diamond brilliants. Taking it out of the box, the Empress pinned it onto Augusta's white satin bosom. 'There, now you will have something to remember my visit by.' Augusta, for once, had nothing to say.

Charlotte, who had crept into the drawing room in the Empress's wake, noticed that everyone in the room looked excited by the new arrival, apart from Bay. He looked, thought Charlotte, as if someone had slapped him in the face. He clearly had not been expecting this. She caught his eye and he shook his head.

She heard Caspar's voice in her ear, 'Do you know, I almost feel sorry for Captain Middleton. I don't think he was expecting a royal visit.'

The Empress was processing throughout the room, with her hosts on either side. When they got to where Bay was standing, Sisi stopped and held out her hand for Bay to kiss.

'Captain Middleton, you did not tell me how charming your friends were or I would have insisted on meeting them before.' Sisi turned to Lady Crewe. 'Easton Neston is close to your house, no?' She smiled without showing her teeth.

Lady Crewe simpered, 'The Melton park runs next to Easton Neston. Such a remarkable house. I hope Your Majesty is comfortable there.'

'Oh, but I didn't come to England to be comfortable, Lady Crewe. I came to hunt your foxes. I would happily sleep in a tent if it meant I could ride to hounds in Leicestershire.'

Lady Crewe looked aghast. 'Oh, I hope there will be no need for that.'

'Ah, here is my great friend, Milord Spencer, and the Countess. How delightful this is. Of course in Vienna we could never be so informal, but what I love about England is that you do not stand on ceremony for its own sake.'

Earl Spencer said with clumsy gallantry, 'Where you are concerned, Ma'am, the normal rules do not apply.'

'You are too chivalrous, but there are some rules that even I cannot break, like hunting on a Sunday.'

'You have to respect the religious affiliations of the foxes, Ma'am.' Sisi laughed.

A suitable chair was produced for the Empress so that she could preside in state over the rest of the reception. As she sat down, she said to Spencer, 'Tell me, where is the young woman who took the picture that made Rudi so angry? I take it that she is here.'

The Earl looked embarrassed. 'I am not sure I know who you mean, Ma'am. I know there was some incident but I was not there.'

'Ah, then I will ask Bay. He will know, of course.'

Remembering the odd scene with Bay in the carriage, Spencer decided it would be better if the Empress did not ask Bay about Charlotte. So taking a chair, he sat down next to the Empress. 'I think you must mean Charlotte Baird, she is the bridegroom's sister.'

'Can you point her out to me?'

The Earl turned his great head to survey the room. He saw Charlotte standing against the wall holding the remains of the bride's bouquet; she was talking to a tall young man who was wearing trousers of a most peculiar cut. He could also see that Bay, who was the only person in the room who was not looking at the Empress, was staring at Charlotte so intently that it was as if he was trying to memorise her face.

'I take it that Miss Baird is the girl holding the bouquet.'

'Yes, Ma'am, I believe it is.'

'I should like to meet her. Would you ask her to come here?'

'It would be my pleasure.'

The Earl walked slowly to the spot where Charlotte was talking to Caspar.

'Miss Baird, the Empress has asked to meet you. May I introduce you to her?'

Charlotte looked up at him. 'Can I refuse, Earl Spencer?'

The Earl said nothing, but Caspar clapped his hands. 'Charlotte, you goose, every girl in the room is dying to meet the Empress. Come along.'

The Earl looked at the American with surprise. Charlotte said, 'Earl Spencer, may I present Caspar Hewes. He is a photographer from America.'

The Earl bowed his head a fraction, in acknowledgement of the introduction.

'Will you follow Mr Hewes's advice and allow me to present you to the Empress?'

'If Mr Hewes may accompany me.'

The Earl nodded. 'But I warn you that the Empress is not fond of photography, Mr Hewes.'

'So I understand, but let's hope that she has nothing against photographers.'

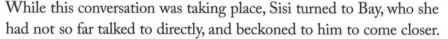

While this conversation was taking place, Sisi turned to Bay, who she had not so far talked to directly, and beckoned to him to come closer.

'This is such a picturesque event. I am so glad to see an ordinary English wedding party.'

'I am not sure that the bride would call this an ordinary wedding, Ma'am, but I am glad you are amused by it.'

'I remember you telling me that the Crewes were very dull, and yet they seem quite pleasant to me. I am sorry not to have met them earlier.'

'You have been busy, Ma'am.'

'Indeed.' Sisi looked across the room, and saw that Spencer was approaching with Charlotte. As they came into earshot she said to Bay, 'Oh Bay, I think I have one of my headaches coming on and I have left my drops in the carriage.'

Bay hesitated for a second and then said, 'Let me fetch them for you, Ma'am.'

'Your Majesty, may I present Miss Baird.' Charlotte made a perfunctory curtsey and Caspar stepped forward so that Spencer had no choice but to say, 'And Mr Hewes, an American gentleman.' Caspar's bow was so low that his forehead almost brushed the Empress's skirt.

The Empress signalled for them to sit, and Caspar pulled up two gilt and velvet chairs.

The older woman's gaze swept over Charlotte.

'I have heard about you, Miss Baird.'

Charlotte lowered her eyes.

'You are the young lady who took the photograph that upset my son.'

'Yes.' Charlotte paused for a moment, 'Your Majesty.'

The Empress laughed. 'Oh don't worry, I haven't come here to scold you. In fact I must apologise if Rudi insulted you. He can be so headstrong.'

Charlotte did not smile back. 'It was Captain Middleton your son insulted. I don't think he noticed me.'

Earl Spencer, who was listening to this exchange, studied the floor with great attention.

Sisi continued, 'Poor Rudi. He is so protective of me, he knows that I cannot bear to be photographed.'

'But how can that possibly be, Your Majesty?' Caspar broke in. 'Someone as lovely as you should be photographed all the time. As a photographer I feel it is a crime to hide your beauty from the public gaze.'

Sisi looked amazed at this interruption, but Caspar's smile did not waver.

'But I do not wish to be gazed on by the public in a photograph. I don't care to be gaped at in magazines, or displayed in shop windows. I am a queen, not a mannequin.'

Countess Festetics broke in, 'Majesty, you sound a little hoarse. May I fetch you some water?'

'No, no, I am fine.' Sisi waved her away.

Charlotte was about to reply, but Caspar forestalled her.

'Well, that is a great pity. The history of art would be much poorer without the great royal portraits – Velazquez, Van Dyck; I believe Your Majesty has been painted by Winterhalter. We photographers only want for the same privilege. How can we ever be respected as artists if we are denied access to the great subjects?'

'A painting is quite different. It is a product of hours of thought and labour. A great portrait shows the soul of the sitter; that is something a photograph can never do.'

Charlotte spoke up now. 'I disagree, Ma'am. A royal portrait is bound by its very nature to flatter its subject, but a photograph cannot lie.'

'You are young, Miss Baird, and if you will forgive me, obscure. You cannot know what it is like to be photographed constantly without your consent. Photographs taken in those circumstances cannot be the truth, as you put it. They are founded on deceit.'

Charlotte considered this. 'I sincerely regret taking your photograph without your knowledge, but the photograph itself was not a lie.'

There was a pause, and then Sisi smiled.

'Ah, but you are young and we all have great opinions when we are young. I think when you are a little older you will see things differently. Here is Captain Middleton. You know Miss Baird, I think?'

'Yes, Ma'am.'

'We have been having a delightful discussion about her hobby.' She turned to Charlotte. 'Tell me, my dear, do you still have the photograph, the one that so upset my son?'

'No. I destroyed the negative. You need have no fears on that score.'

'How very thorough. I feel almost sorry that you had to destroy your handiwork.'

'I had good reasons, Ma'am,' Charlotte said, looking briefly at Bay.

The Empress caught the look and signalled to Countess Festetics that she should gather her things. Having seen the Baird girl, she was no longer worried about her effect on Bay. The girl was insignificant.

'I am afraid I can no longer fight my headache. We shall have to go. Such a delightful occasion, but I am afraid it has quite tired me out.'

The Empress rose, and as the room noticed, they too got to their feet.

'Such a pleasant occasion, Lady Crewe, and such a lovely bride. Thank you so much.' The Empress glided towards the door, followed by Countess Festetics and Lord Crewe. At the door she stopped and said in a clear voice, 'Captain Middleton, I am sure you want to say goodbye to your friends.'

Bay, who had not followed her to the door, stood in the middle of the room – the focus of all eyes. He turned to Charlotte and said, 'You will remember your promise.'

Charlotte said, as evenly as she could, 'If you have time to call before I go to America, then I shall be delighted to see you.'

'You are actually going?'

'I wasn't sure before, but now I am. But you don't have time to stand here talking to me. Your mistress is waiting.'

Bay looked at her, his face contorted with regret. But before he could say anything in reply, Augusta walked to where they were standing and placed herself between them, her cheeks red.

'Captain Middleton,' she hissed, 'the Empress is waiting.'

'Goodbye, Bay,' Charlotte said.

The room fell silent as Bay walked towards the door where Sisi stood, her body turned in motion like Diana fleeing Actaeon. When he was about five paces away, the Empress, seeing that he was coming, turned and went through the door and down the stairs, leaving Bay to follow.

He paused at the door and looked back at Charlotte, before disappearing.

Caspar, who was standing next to Charlotte, said, 'Poor fellow, it can't be easy being an imperial lackey.'

'No, and he doesn't have your talent for flattery either, so it must be harder still.' Charlotte turned her face away from him.

As Bay came down the stairs, Countess Festetics appeared as if from nowhere and took him by the arm.

'Captain Middleton, I am so glad to be seeing you.'

Bay smiled at her.

'How are you, Festy?'

'I am worried, dear Captain. It was not kind of you to disappear like this. It has been most sad without you. The Empress has not smiled, I am thinking, since you left. It is necessary that you should come back.'

'But the Empress asked me to stay away.'

'For one day, maybe two when the Crown Prince was there. She does not want any unpleasantnessess with her son. But since then she has been waiting every day for you to come back. That is why we came here today, not to see some wedding, but to see you.'

Bay looked at the floor. But the Countess dug her fingers into his arm and forced him to look at her.

'I know that you do not love my mistress as I do, Captain, but I think you care for her. You made her happy, now you are making her unhappy.'

Bay said slowly, 'I wish she hadn't come here today.'

'I also. I have tried to stop her, but she is not listening. Now, dear Captain, you must go, she is waiting for you.' The little countess almost pushed him out of the door.

The coachman was waiting to open the carriage door. As Bay climbed in, he saw that Sisi was sitting in the corner opposite him, her face hidden by her fan. The carriage blinds were drawn.

When the coachman closed the door Bay said, 'Sisi?', but still she did not lower the fan. He waited for a moment and then, sitting directly opposite her, he gently pulled the hand holding the fan away from her face.

The Empress was crying.

Bay saw that her even her tears were elegant: they left her eyes shining, but had not made her nose red.

He found a handkerchief in his pocket and started to wipe the tears away from her cheeks.

She caught his hand in hers.

'Oh, I am sorry, Bay. I should not have come today. But I have missed you so.' She looked up at him through wet lashes.

Bay could not resist the appeal in her eyes. Even though he knew it was a mistake, he could not stop himself. He took her other hand in his and began to kiss away the tears until he found her mouth.

The carriage began to move.

'I am not worth crying over, dearest Sisi.'

'I was so happy here in England with you. But then Rudolph has to spoil everything. He doesn't understand. Please tell me that you have forgiven him.'

'There is nothing to forgive,' said Bay.

This time Sisi, her tears dried, kissed him.

'Oh, I am so glad. But I will make sure that your paths do not cross again. Then we can be happy as we were before. We will hunt every day and forget about my crazy son.'

The scent of her hair, that heady mixture of brandy and eau de cologne, made feel Bay feel quite dizzy. He thought that he would like to open the window.

'But I can't come back to Easton Neston now. The National is on Saturday.'

'The National? I know it is a race but is it really so important?'

'The Grand National is the greatest steeplechase in the country.' Seeing that she did not understand, he continued, 'Imagine the fastest ride to hounds you have ever had with a different jump every minute. Four miles, and sixteen fences against the best riders in the country.'

'But *you* are the best rider in the country.'

'Gentleman rider, perhaps, but there are professional jockeys riding too. Irish boys who ride like banshees. I have seen them at Aintree, they have no fear.'

Sisi put her fingers to his lips. 'You will have no fear – because I will be there. I shall come and watch you win your race.'

She was smiling now, her mood light again.

'I will tell Nopsca to make the arrangements.'

The carriage had slowed down, and Bay lifted the blind. He recognised the gates of Devonshire House. A shaft of light fell across the interior of the carriage. He noticed that there were tiny lines forming around Sisi's lips as she smiled.

'Oh Bay, I am so glad that we have no more misunderstandings,' and she held his hand to her breast so that he could feel her heart beating.

As he sat in the carriage, his hand against the Empress's heart, her eyes fixed on his face, Bay heard a paperboy shouting the evening's headlines and it occurred to him what the world would think of Captain Middleton riding around London in the Empress of Austria's carriage with the blinds drawn. Most people would think it was scandalous; some more worldly spectators would think it was perhaps a little ostentatious. All of them would assume that he, Captain Middleton, was the Empress's acknowledged lover. The Empress was smiling at him, her eyes shining, her face radiant under the hat with the peacock feathers. Bay wondered if she was aware of any of this. Had she in fact drawn the blinds to the carriage before starting to cry? But if it had been a trap, Bay thought, then he had walked into it quite willingly.

The carriage came to a halt. Bay looked through the blinds and saw that they were outside Claridge's Hotel.

The Empress said, 'Will you come in?'

'I must go back to Aintree. I don't trust the grooms to feed Tipsy properly.'

'Till Saturday then.' Sisi leant over and kissed him.

'Till Saturday,' said Bay.

The Adelphi

Liverpool

Dear Fred,

I hope that your wedding trip has been everything you hoped for and that Augusta has found Italy to her taste. I must apologise for not being there to welcome you on your return, but by the time you read this letter I will be somewhere in North America. Depending on the length of your wedding trip, I might be in New York, or possibly at the bottom of the Grand Canyon. At any rate I will not be in Charles Street.

I suspect that you will be very much vexed by my departure. I know that you will be worried about my safety and Augusta will be disappointed not to be able to guide me through the season. But I promise you that I will be exceedingly careful. It may temper Augusta's disappointment to know that I enclose the key to my jewel case. I have left the diamonds in the vault at Drummonds, except for the tiara, which I had to pawn in order to pay for my passage. I would be grateful if you could redeem it on your return. I imagine that Augusta might like to wear it. Please do not worry about me, Fred, I shall only be gone for a few months. But if you want me to return you will have to wire me money to New York as I *don't think the tiara will take me across the Atlantic and back. Grace, the Melton maid, is with me – so you don't need to worry about me being unchaperoned, and Mr Hewes will be travelling on the same boat, the SS Britannic. He promises to translate American into English for me.*

This is not an elopement, dear Fred, I did not elope with Captain Middleton at a time when I would have been very happy to become his wife, to spare your feelings. I am not eloping now.

I suspect that you may be angry when you read this, but not, I hope, for long. I am sure Augusta will look very splendid in the Lennox diamonds.

I remain, despite my temporary absence, always your affectionate sister,

Charlotte

Charlotte sealed the letter and rang the bell. A page appeared wearing the Adelphi Hotel's red and gold livery. The boy was about twelve but he was small for his age and the uniform swamped him.

She held out the letter and showed him a half-crown. 'I want you to post this for me, and when you've done that I want you to come back here and I will give you this.'

'Yes, miss.' The page took the letter and scampered off.

Charlotte went back to her desk in the hotel library. The room smelt strongly of varnish and morocco leather. The hotel was brand new. Caspar told her that it had sprung up in the year since he had arrived in Liverpool from America. Through the sumptuous red and gold brocade curtains she could see the storm clouds hanging over the horizon and could hear the rain lashing the windows in an endless round of applause.

The library was empty, which was a relief. The train from London had been crowded with parties coming up for the Grand National

Steeplechase, as well as passengers bound for America. Even in the first-class carriage (Caspar had insisted on the most expensive tickets: 'If I have to go back to America I want my last memory of England to be a fragrant one') the atmosphere had been verging on the rowdy. The racegoers had availed themselves of their hip flasks and the America-bound passengers had been voluble about their anxieties concerning the primitive conditions they expected to find there. Caspar had attempted to reassure one particularly nervous lady that most Americans had stopped wearing feathers in their hair, and no longer cooked on an open fire, but both his vocabulary and his waistcoat were so florid that the woman's fears were exacerbated rather than soothed.

Charlotte had no such worries. Her decision to leave had been sudden, but she had not regretted it for one minute. Anything was better than sitting in the drawing room of Charles Street, waiting for something to happen. Or worse still, having to listen to Chicken Hartopp talking about Bay and the Empress.

She picked up her pen and wondered if she could actually bring herself to write to Bay. But as had happened so often before, Charlotte found that she could not find the words. She wanted to write a letter that would both scald him for ever and at the same time bring him to her side. It was easier to pack her trunk, pawn her diamonds and go halfway across the world than it was to know what she wanted to say to him. He had sent a letter to her after the wedding – a note that looked as if it had been written in the dark.

My dearest Charlotte,

I will still call you that in my head even if I can never say those words to you myself. My dearest Charlotte, my offer to explain the truth of how Captain Hartopp earned the name of Chicken still stands. I have nothing else to offer you except my heart and Tipsy's services as a photographic model. The letter broke off here as if Bay had thought better of this jauntiness, and then started again, the handwriting here much less regular. *I wish I could kiss you again: I remember it so clearly – your lips a little dry – the freckles on your eyelids. I would like to kiss every one of those freckles. You see I am quite reckless now; now that it is too late. But you should know how much I want to hold you and how I will always adore you even if we never meet again. You have my photograph but nothing could be clearer than the picture of you that is in my head. A photograph can be destroyed but the image I have of your dear face is* **indelible**. [This last word was underlined several times.]

I will always remain, now and for ever,
your own Bay Middleton

It was her first and only love letter. It was the letter that she had longed for after the fracas at the exhibition. But it was, after all, only a letter. If Bay had said these words to her face, Charlotte thought that she would never have been able to resist him, but he hadn't. She had read it so many times that she knew its words by heart, had murmured them to herself as she packed her trunk full of the things she would need for a world three thousand miles away from Bay.

The library door opened and Grace came in. The vivid magenta dye used in the silk trim of her bonnet had run in the rain, so that her face was daubed with amethyst streaks.

'It's terrible out there, miss. I went to buy some hat pins, British ones, you know, but I wish I had stayed here now. I was lucky that there was a gentleman with an umbrella to escort me back to the hotel. He is staying here too on account of the racing.'

Grace caught sight of herself in the mirror over the mantelpiece and gave a little scream. She started to rub at her face with her handkerchief and it came away purple.

'Heavens above! Excuse me, miss, while I go and make myself presentable. And the racing gentleman never said a word. He must have been laughing his head off inside, while all the time he was pretending to be pleasant and talking about the Grand National. He said I should put my money on Dancing Bear at fifty to one. It's a sure thing, he said.'

'You shouldn't trust racing tips from strangers,' said Charlotte.

'Don't worry, miss, I wasn't born yesterday! I told him it was too late for me to bet, even if it was guaranteed, because we were off to America tomorrow. He said if I gave him my address he would keep the money for me. He must have thought I was not right in the head – on account of this,' she scrubbed at her face with her handkerchief.

Charlotte went over to where the newspapers were hanging on the wall on their wooden posts. In the *Manchester Guardian* she found what she was looking for. Halfway down the list of jockeys was Middleton, J.M., riding Tipsy (grey). She felt the jolt of seeing his name in print and realised that she had no idea what his initials stood for. She had only ever known him as Bay.

'Please, miss . . .' It was the page; his scarlet livery was soaked, and the rain had washed his cheeks clean. Charlotte gave him the half-crown and added another shilling.

'I am sorry you got so wet on my account. You should have taken an umbrella.'

'I did, miss, but it got blown inside out, the wind's that strong.'

As the servant went off to get into dry clothes, Charlotte went back to the newspaper. There was an article about the race which she found almost incomprehensible. What she could glean was that there were forty horses in the race. Five of the horses were Irish, two French and only ten of them were mares. She could not see Bay or Tipsy's name in among the list of likely favourites. The shortest odds were being offered on a horse called the Governess, ridden by Ned Beasley.

Charlotte found that she was pleased that Bay had, after all, entered the race. She remembered him telling her about his desire to win that first night at Melton. It meant that he was more than the Empress's creature. It was strange to think that for tonight at least, they would be only a few miles apart. Aintree, the course where the Grand National was held, was, she had gleaned from the racegoers on the train, only a carriage drive away from Liverpool. But tomorrow when Bay was lining up at the start of the race, she would be halfway across the Irish Sea.

She rang the bell to order some tea. Caspar would be back soon. One more night and they would be at sea. It was a terrifying thought but also a great relief to know that for a few months at least she would not be the Lennox heiress or even the girl who was jilted by Bay Middleton; she would simply be Charlotte Baird, the photographer. If things went well she might never come back. She thought that Fred would probably support her till she came of age if it meant that Augusta was able to sparkle through the season in the Lennox diamonds.

Of course, if she did come back there would be talk about her decision to travel with Caspar Hewes. People who did not know Caspar would assume they had eloped. This, Charlotte thought, would be more damaging to his reputation than hers. The worst that would happen to Charlotte was that she would no longer be invited to the smartest parties. There would be duchesses who would no longer think her a suitable match for their younger sons. Augusta would never get over the humiliation of being related by marriage to a social outcast – but these were all consequences that Charlotte felt that she could tolerate. But Caspar's burgeoning success as a society photographer was based on his unique ability to flatter and charm all his sitters into believing that he alone saw their true beauty. If his society sitters thought that his affections were spoken for, especially by someone as insignificant and dingy as Charlotte, he might not be able to cast the spell that made even the plainest of his subjects blossom into the goddess-like being of Caspar's rhetoric.

The night before, as they were eating in the cavernous dining room of the Adelphi, Charlotte had said, 'It feels quite scandalous to be eating alone with you in a restaurant. If Augusta could see us she would die of mortification.'

'But what on earth could be scandalous about a man and a woman having dinner in public? It would be much more shocking if we were having dinner upstairs in your room,' said Caspar.

'Unmarried girls are not meant to be out in public unchaperoned, especially with unmarried men.'

'But you seem remarkably unconcerned, Carlotta, to be consorting with me. Aren't you worried that I might make demands on your virtue?'

It had been a light-hearted question, but Charlotte knew that it had a serious undertone.

'No, I am not worried. Should I be?'

Caspar smiled and Charlotte thought she saw a flicker of relief in his face. He raised his glass to her.

'You are the only woman in the world I could ever imagine proposing to, but even in the unlikely event that you would have me I think I know that I am not the marrying kind.'

'Not even for the Lennox fortune?' said Charlotte, laughing.

'Now I am sorely tempted, but no, not even for that.'

And at that moment Charlotte thought that Caspar was the closest thing she had ever had to a friend.

A waiter brought in the tea.

'Shall I set the table for two, miss?'

'Yes, thank you.'

Caspar should be back from the shipping office by now. Charlotte had bought their passages in London, but Caspar had insisted on going down to the Liverpool office to make sure that they were given decent cabins. This had not seemed to Charlotte like a good enough reason to go out in a thunderstorm, but Caspar had been adamant. 'You have no idea how much these things matter. Trust me, Carlotta, you may be defying convention by running away to America, but you don't want to end up in a cabin next to the engine.'

She was eating her third slice of anchovy toast when Caspar burst into the library, his ulster dripping with rain water. He gave his wet things to the waiter who was hovering in the background and collapsed into a chair.

'Forgive me for leaving you alone for so long. I have bad news, I'm afraid. A timber ship lost its load during the storm and the port is rammed with floating logs. None of the ships can move until the logs have been plucked out of the Mersey. The quayside was full of men with chains shouting their heads off and accomplishing very little, so I suspect that the task may take some time. So we will have to amuse ourselves in Liverpool for another day at least.'

Charlotte handed him a cup of tea.

He looked at her. 'I thought you would be disappointed. And yet you look quite cheerful. Have you changed your mind about going?'

'No, not that. But if we are going to be here for another day, I have an idea as to what we might do tomorrow.'

'And what would that be?'

'I think we should go to the Grand National. The racecourse at Aintree is only a carriage ride away.'

Caspar narrowed his eyes at her. 'I had no idea, Carlotta, that you followed the sport of kings.'

Charlotte blushed. She did not want to admit to Caspar, or even to herself, the real reason for her interest in the Grand National.

'Oh, but this race is famous. It will be a splendid place to take photographs,' she said. 'We could probably make all our passage money by taking pictures of the horses with their owners. There are forty starters.'

'You are remarkably well informed, Carlotta.' Caspar raised an eyebrow.

'Oh, Grace told me all about it,' Charlotte said, as easily as she could. 'It sounds rather interesting. The course is four miles long, and there are sixteen fences.'

'Sixteen fences?' said Caspar. 'Fancy that.'

'Yes, and only about half the horses finish the race. It's tremendously difficult.'

Caspar shook his head. 'It sounds like a supremely English occasion. Incomprehensible and pointless to the uninitiated. But it can't be any worse than a cricket match, so we might as well go.' He looked Charlotte straight in the eye. 'Who knows who we might run into?'

Charlotte could not return his gaze.

The Grand National

HE DAY OF THE NATIONAL WAS FINE. THE STORM had passed over entirely, leaving the sky a watery blue. There was even a weak sun fighting the chilly breeze from the Atlantic. The change in weather was a great relief to the many female racegoers who had bought new trimmings for their bonnets in honour of the great day; it was heralded as a good omen by the seasoned racegoers from London, who knew from experience that the stands at Aintree were not adequately covered; the Prince of Wales was happy because he would be able to wear his new Homburg hat and his view would not be obstructed by umbrellas, which he thought deeply vulgar inventions. The Empress of Austria, who was travelling with him in the royal train, thought that the good weather was entirely in keeping with her present disposition, which was cheerful – she was always irritated when the weather was at variance with her mood. Countess Festetics was happy because her mistress was smiling. For her the only weather that mattered were the clouds that gathered in her mistress's eyes.

Only Bay, who was walking the course that morning, was indifferent to the sunshine. For him the damage had already been done. The ground after two days of rain was soft, and as he led Tipsy round the jumps to show her the treacherous dips and shallows that lay in wait for them later that day, Bay, despite the spring weather, felt a cold ripple of fear. It had been a frosty winter, and the going all season had been hard, but now the ground was muddy and waterlogged. After the first lap of the course it would be a quagmire. Bay hated soft ground: it unsettled the horses and the spray from the puddles made it impossible to see. Horses stumbled on sodden turf; even if they took the fence at the correct angle there was no guarantee that they would land safely.

Bay felt a twinge in his bad shoulder as he walked around Becher's Brook, named after the man who had fallen there in 1856. His doctor had been very stern about the dangers of another fall. He knew that he should have his shoulder strapped up properly before the race, but that would put his whip hand out of action. Was it really worth endangering his whole future for the sake of winning this one race? There was only one possible answer to that. For Bay at that moment, victory at the National was the only thing that mattered. It was the one thing in his life that seemed to be under his control.

A rabbit darted across the ground and Tipsy neighed in alarm. As Bay calmed his horse, he thought that the mare was the only female in his life with whom he was in perfect accord. He was still good with horses, even if he had lost his touch with women. Tipsy nuzzled his ear and Bay tried not to think about Charlotte. He had almost won her over at the wedding before the Empress had arrived and declared her interest. He no longer felt the desire for Sisi that had flooded his senses at the beginning, but that urgency had been replaced by something more insidious; to be so publicly needed by the most beautiful woman in Europe was quite something. But even stronger than the appeal to his vanity was the call on his compassion; he knew he had the power to make her happy.

'Morning, Middleton!' Bay recognised Major Crombie from his club. 'How do you like the course?'

'Too soft for my taste. Could have done without the storm,' said Bay.

'Favours the Irish, they like it boggy.'

'What odds are they giving for Tipsy?'

'Twenty-five to one. Mares are very sticky and a grey has never won the National.'

Bay said nothing.

Crombie laughed. 'Personally I am delighted at the length of your odds. I saw you and Tipsy ride at the Cottesleigh point-to-point last year. Never seen a braver ride. So my money's on you. Some of the Irish horses will give you a run, but none of the jockeys are in your class. I put a monkey on you last week, so don't let me down.'

'I'll do my best,' said Bay.

'The royal box will be full, at any rate. The Prince and Princess of Wales *and* the Empress of Austria. I expect half the crowd will be too busy watching them to pay any attention to the race. But so long as the jockeys don't get distracted, eh Middleton?'

Crombie waved Bay farewell as he turned back towards the stands, which were already beginning to fill up six or so hours before the race was due to begin.

When he got back to the stables, the lads were sitting down to a race day breakfast – porridge, bacon, eggs, ham, devilled kidneys. Bay had ordered it from the local inn the night before but now he found he could not face even a mouthful.

He sat down on a mounting block and pulled out his cigarette case. Perhaps a gasper would help calm his nerves; what he really wanted was a shot of brandy, but even the Irish jockeys never drank before a race. As he fumbled with the match, he heard a familiar voice.

'Feeling a bit shaky, Bay?' It was Hartopp.

'Chicken! This is a surprise.' Bay looked at the other man warily.

'Don't worry, old boy. I haven't come to get my revenge. Anyway, that bird has flown. Paid a call at Charles Street yesterday only to find that Miss Baird has gone to America. To take photographs, if you please. Lady Lisle was in quite a state about it. First thing she knew about it was the note that Charlotte left her on the breakfast table.'

'America?' Bay finally lit his cigarette.

'Desperate measures, I know! That photographer chap she was hanging about with has gone with her.'

Bay took a long draw. 'They've eloped?'

'Lady L says not. But then she would, wouldn't she?'

'Perhaps.' Bay stood up. 'Sorry, Chicken, but I have a few things I must do before the race.' Before Hartopp could say anything more, Bay went round to other side of the stables and was violently sick into a bale of straw.

As the special trains laid on from London and the north-east disgorged their passengers into Liverpool Lime Street, it seemed as if the whole city was migrating north-west. Every wheeled conveyance had been pressed into service and the road was jammed with carriages, omnibuses, governess carts, even a dustcart. Caspar had managed to get seats on one of the special race day omnibuses. Charlotte and Grace were sitting inside; Caspar was clinging to the top deck. It took the best part of the morning to travel the six miles or so to the racecourse as the road was unpaved and the horses and the carriages kept getting stuck in the ruts.

Mud, it seemed, was the great leveller. Even the carriage carrying the royal party found itself defeated by the treacherous conditions and nearly capsized into a hidden ditch. Fortunately for all concerned, the Prince of Wales was sitting on the opposite side of the carriage, and by using his considerable bulk as a counterweight he was able to keep the vehicle from toppling over. When the royal carriage was righted and on its way again, there was a rousing cheer from the spectators, 'God bless the Prince of Wales', as well as more raucous shouts of 'Good old Tum Tum'.

After the second hour of sitting wedged between Grace and a lady who smelt strongly of eau de cologne and who was wearing a hat with orange feathers, Charlotte was ready to get out and walk the rest of the way. But at last the gates of the course came into view and the mass exodus began.

Charlotte felt almost physically assaulted as she walked through the gates. She had never been to a race meeting before and the tumult around her was extreme. The crush was impassable because people moved not as individuals but in packs. There were families, three generations of them in their Sunday best, who had decided that there was safety in numbers and so moved everywhere in a solid clump. Then there were the Irish, who had come over on the boat train and were packed around the show ring waiting for a sight of Glasnevin, the Irish favourite. Charlotte was struck by the gaudiness of the crowd after the monochrome colours of the London streets. Her neighbour on the bus with the orange feathered hat was not the only racegoer who had chosen to wear colours as bright as the jockeys' silks; the milliners of the north-west had clearly been busy. Charlotte saw one woman with a hat consisting of a pheasant in its nest with chicks poking out over the brim. Anyone who could afford it had clearly ordered a new frock for the race, and the array of the latest mauve and lime-green silks was dazzling. Even the men were splashed with colour, sporting spotted silk handkerchiefs, scarlet waistcoats, and suits in mustard check. Charlotte, wearing a fawn travelling dress whose greatest recommendation was that it hardly showed the dirt, felt like a wren in a peacock enclosure.

Caspar, on the other hand, fitted in perfectly. His green and orange check ulster, which in London turned heads, here in Aintree looked exactly right. He had taken out his camera and was setting it up by the owners' enclosure. As he worked, the crowd concentrated around him, and when Sholto Douglas, the celebrated Scottish owner, asked him to take a picture of his horse, the Governess, an excited murmur ran through the racegoers.

The Governess was nervy before the race, and both Douglas and the jockey had to stand on either side to keep the horse still. But Caspar's way with society women seemed also to work on thoroughbreds: he stroked the racehorse on the muzzle and kept up a stream of soothing chatter which had the animal almost hypnotised as he disappeared under the cloth and squeezed the bulb.

Douglas offered to pay for the print, but Caspar said, 'It was a privilege to take a picture of such a magnificent animal. I wouldn't dream of asking for money, but if you could find a suitable place for my companion Miss Baird to watch the race, I would be enormously grateful.'

Douglas looked over at Charlotte, who was looking at the horses being walked round the ring by their lads, and shook his head. 'I'll give you both a pass to the owners' stand. This part of the course is not really suitable for a lady.'

Caspar bowed. 'Thank you, sir. As an American there are so many things I don't understand, and I don't suppose Miss Baird has been to a racecourse before, either.'

'Well, everybody should see the Grand National at least once. It's the finest race in the world. And make sure you place a bet. You can't really enter into the spirit of the thing, unless you have some money down. You can still get decent odds on the Governess and she is definitely going to win.'

Douglas called over one of the race day stewards and asked him to take Caspar and his party up to his box in the stands. Charlotte was relieved to be away from the hubbub. Her one aim, a desire she could barely admit to herself, was to catch a glimpse of Bay, but she was too small to see over the bowler-hatted crowd. But as they were shepherded from the melee of the public grounds to the relative calm of the stands, Charlotte felt a moment of unease. Here the orange feathers had been replaced by mink and sable – the loud checked tweeds by subtle heather mixtures, which meant that it was entirely possible that she would see someone she knew.

As if to prove her point, a tweedy back in front of her turned to wave at a friend and she caught sight of Chicken Hartopp's unmistakeable profile with its dundreary whiskers. She stopped, clutching Caspar's arm to pull him away, but it was too late; Chicken had seen her, and he greeted her with a roar. Even from where she was standing Charlotte could smell the brandy on his breath.

'Charlotte, I mean Miss Baird! What on earth are you doing here? I mean, what a surprise . . . To see you, I mean,' he faltered, checked by the expression on Charlotte's face.

'Good morning, Captain Hartopp, I believe you have met Mr Hewes.'

Chicken looked Caspar up and down in a way that was only a shade away from insolence. 'Indeed.'

Charlotte could see that Hartopp was about to boil over with curiosity. To forestall him she said, 'It is quite an accident that we are here. We were meant to be sailing to America today but there has been a delay. And since we were in Liverpool on the day of the National it seemed that we must come to Aintree.'

Caspar rushed in, 'Such a promising place for photography,

Captain Hartopp. I should like very much to photograph the winner. I have always wanted to capture a moment of total joy.'

Hartopp looked at Caspar in bewilderment. He could not understand how the man could walk around with Charlotte Baird without a trace of embarrassment. Surely if they were eloping, they would not appear in such a public place.

Caspar said, 'Lord Sholto has offered to introduce me to Major Topham, who owns the course. Charlotte, would you mind very much if I left you with Captain Hartopp for a moment? I want to make sure of my place at the winning post.'

Charlotte did mind, but she could see that Caspar was determined to get his picture. She turned to Chicken.

'Captain Hartopp, I would be so grateful if you would go through the race card with me. I am so confused by all the different terms, and I think I should really like to place a bet.' She smiled at Chicken with a charm that made his skin redden under the whiskers. 'Grace, my maid, tells me that I should be backing a horse called Dancing Bear.'

'Your maid is here?'

'Of course my maid is here. Do you think I would come here without a female companion?' Charlotte said in mock outrage.

Chicken looked at the floor.

'Forgive me, Miss Baird. But I don't know what to think. I called on your aunt in London and she said you were going to America with that fellow. She was in a terrible to-do. Everyone in London is talking about it. The word is that you have eloped. But dash it all, you can't marry a creature like that. I don't believe it.'

Charlotte pulled off the kid glove she was wearing on her left hand. She held it up for Chicken to inspect.

'No ring, Captain Hartopp, no ring. Mr Hewes is my travelling companion and colleague, nothing more. I am going to America to take photographs, and he has kindly agreed to act as my guide. So you can tell "everyone" in London that there is no scandal, beyond that of a young woman making a decision about her own life. I don't suppose that will satisfy anyone, but it is the truth. My maid is with me, and while Mr Hewes may not qualify in your mind as a gentleman, he has shown me nothing but kindness.'

Chicken Hartopp could not meet her gaze; he tugged at his whiskers so hard that Charlotte feared that he would pull the hairs out by the roots.

'But dash it, if you are going to America, why are you here? Don't you know that Bay is a runner?'

Charlotte tried to look composed. 'Yes. But coming here was never part of my plan. I should have been on the Irish Sea by now, but when the crossing was delayed and I heard about the race, and I discovered that Captain Middleton had entered, well, I decided to come.'

'But, damn it, I don't understand. The man has treated you monstrously. Humiliating you in public. Carrying on with the Empress like that. I am surprised you can even look at him.'

Charlotte put her glove back on, deliberately smoothing and stretching the leather over her shaking fingers.

'Perhaps you are right to be surprised, Captain Hartopp. But I don't consider myself humiliated, whatever the world may think. Now are you going to be kind enough to explain this race card to me, or will I have to find another guide?'

But Chicken, now that he had begun to speak his mind, could not be diverted so easily.

'But Charlotte, I mean Miss Baird, did you know that the Empress is here too? In the royal box with the Prince of Wales. If you come to the front here you can see her quite clearly.'

He pushed to the front of the stand and pointed to the royal box, which was about twenty feet away. Charlotte hesitated. In her impulsive decision to come to Aintree it had never occurred to her that the Empress might have made the same choice. At first she thought that she could not bear to look, but then a scalding wave of curiosity and jealousy swept her reluctance away. She followed the direction of Hartopp's finger and saw the portly figure of the Prince of Wales in a homburg, a cigar clamped between his teeth. He was flanked by two women. The nearest one Charlotte recognised as the Princess of Wales; the Empress was on the other side. She was wearing a dark blue costume, almost as plain in cut as her riding habit. But the severity of her costume was offset by the sable stole she wore round her shoulders, which even at this distance Charlotte could see was a miracle of softness. The Empress was leaning forward slightly, holding a pair of binoculars which she had trained on the parade ring. The Prince of Wales leant over to her and said something, and the Empress smiled but she kept on looking through her glasses at the horses and riders below.

Hartopp turned to Charlotte with a smile almost of triumph.

Willing herself to sound as light as possible, she said, 'The Empress has a splendid pair of field glasses. I think that they are exactly what I need. Do you know where I might get some, Captain Hartopp?'

'Field glasses?' Chicken seemed not to understand.

'Yes, isn't that what they are called? Like opera glasses, only rather more powerful, I imagine. Fred has some.'

Chicken shook his head from side to side and pulled on his whiskers again, only this time meditatively rather than urgently. Charlotte said nothing while he ruminated. Finally he said, 'Does Fred know you are here?'

'Of course not. He and Augusta are on a boat heading to the Bay of Naples, so he won't come in here if that's what you are worried about. Now, are you able to help me find some field glasses? I can see that something is happening down there, and I really would like to see the race properly.' Charlotte tapped her foot.

'Bay doesn't stand a chance, you know. He's a decent enough rider, but Tipsy doesn't have the stamina for the National. A mare hasn't won at Aintree since the Fifties.'

'All the more reason to find some glasses, so that I can have a chance of seeing him lose,' Charlotte said with some tartness.

Captain Hartopp looked as if he was about to make another protest, but a glance from Charlotte stopped him and he mumbled something about borrowing some glasses from a fellow he knew, and stumbled off.

The stand was filling up by the minute and Charlotte beckoned to Grace to stand by her to protect her vantage point. She wondered if Caspar would photograph Bay in the ring. She hoped he didn't disapprove too vehemently of her desire to come here. After all, it was the purest coincidence that they should be in Liverpool on the day of the National. There was no surrender in coming to watch Bay run in the race of his life. He wouldn't even know that she was there. But even as she rehearsed these arguments, Charlotte struggled to ignore the deep current that had brought her there that day. At a level that she could barely give words to, Charlotte felt that it was fate that had tipped those logs into the Mersey, fate that had led Grace into conversation with the racing stranger. She was meant to be here, that was all.

In the jockeys' changing rooms, Bay stepped onto the scale to weigh in. To his great relief, he was given the lightest possible handicap. He glanced at his pocket watch, the race was due to start in just under an hour. It was time to get changed into his jockey's outfit. When racing, he always wore the scarlet and gold colours of his regiment.

As he took the now rather faded silks out of his Gladstone bag in the changing room, he heard a familiar cough behind him. He turned to see Nopsca holding a flat cardboard box out to him. He took the box and put it down on the boot bench. Nopsca reached into his inside pocket and brought out a letter. Bay did not need to see the crest on on the back to know that it was from Sisi.

'The Kaiserin asked me to give you this before the race.'

'Thank you, Baron.' Bay kept his voice down, as the other jockeys in the room were looking at them curiously. Nopsca, who was wearing a frock coat and spats and was fragrant with attar of roses, was an incongruous figure in the gentleman riders' vestibule, which was strewn with discarded racing stocks and smelt of leather, rubbing alcohol and sweat.

Bay opened the letter first:

My dear Bay,
Please wear these for me when you win,
Your own Sisi

Undoing the string that fastened the box, he saw a set of racing colours in black and gold. As he held them up, he saw that not only were they precisely the right size but the Hapsburg crest had been embroidered on the back.

His horror must have been evident on his face because the Baron shrugged apologetically. 'In Wien, it is the custom for the riders always to wear the arms of their owners.'

Bay turned his head away, and the Baron said quickly, 'I think perhaps I have the word incorrectly. I mean to say patron.'

Bay put the Empress's colours back in their box. He took a deep breath to let out his emotion but still he sounded angrier than he would have liked. 'Tell her that I mean no disrespect, but I can't possibly wear these. Tipsy is my horse and I am not some medieval knight who wears his lady's colours.'

Nopsca held out his hands, about to plead with Bay, but when he saw the other man's face he stopped short, his mouth open, the placating smile frozen. He dropped his arms, picked up the colours and packed them away in their box.

'I understand that you have no use for these. I think, perhaps, that it was impossible to find you here among the crowds.'

He made Bay a stiff bow, clicking his heels together in the Austrian way.

'For my part, Captain Middleton, I wish you good luck.'

A Royal Wager

LUNCHEON WAS BEING SERVED IN THE ROYAL BOX. There had been a generous breakfast on the train, but the Prince of Wales felt that was no drawback to the consumption of a sumptuous lunch of the kind he had when out shooting. There were four different kinds of raised pies, salmagundi, chicken in aspic and truffled riz de veau, as well as pheasants stuffed with foie gras, and a terrine of hare and salsify. To drink there was champagne, hock, burgundy and a warm claret cup to which the Princess of Wales was extremely partial.

Sisi, as usual, only toyed with the food on her plate. She knew that if she looked up Festy would be gazing at her, willing her to eat something, but although from time to time she would cut off a morsel and take it to her mouth, it would always return to the plate untouched. This part of the day was taking far too long, she wanted the race to begin.

The Prince of Wales sat on one side of her at the table which had been set up at the back of the royal box, and Earl Spencer on the other. The Princess of Wales sat at the other end of the table, her lovely face unruffled by the conversation that flowed around her as she was almost completely deaf. The Prince was in a benign mood – his lunch had been plentiful and punctual, and he was delighted to have the Empress as his guest. He knew all about Elizabeth's visit to Windsor and he could not help but admire a woman who had defied his mother. '*Not nearly as pretty as dear Alix, and after coming all that way she refused to stay for luncheon.*'

But he thought she was beautiful, and it was a rare treat for the Prince of Wales to find beauty in a woman of his own rank. And she was not Prussian, which was a relief. He knew that the Empress shared his loathing of Bismarck. They had a most enjoyable gossip about the dreariness of the Prussian court and the awfulness of the food at Potsdam. There was an enjoyable frisson when the Empress, in order to emphasise a point about the dowdiness of the Hohenzollern ladies, briefly touched his hand. His eyes flickered to see if Alix had noticed, but she was smiling dreamily at the equerry sitting next to her; she had long ago learnt not to observe her husband too closely.

At a quarter to three, Major Topham, the owner of Aintree Racecourse, came in to let the royal party know that the riders were about to parade around the ring.

The Prince of Wales clapped his hands and said to the table, 'Does anybody want to place a bet before the race begins? This will be your last chance.'

The Empress looked at him sideways. 'I think perhaps that I shall make a bet.'

'Splendid, splendid. Topham will arrange it.'

Topham's bow was a touch reluctant; he had many things to do, and acting as a royal bookie was not one of them.

Sisi beckoned to Festy, who was standing in a corner. 'I need some money.'

Festy nodded. 'How much, Majesty?'

'Let me see, I think five hundred guineas.'

The Prince of Wales exhaled. 'I say, that's brave, which horse?'

'The horse is called Tipsy. But I am not being brave, my dear Prince, Tipsy is being ridden by Captain Middleton.' She smiled at him. The Prince, who, of course, had heard all the rumours about the Empress and her pilot, smiled back.

'In that case, Empress, I shall match your bet.'

Edward waved to his equerry and instructed him to give a note to Topham. The racecourse owner looked surprised.

'I think Tipsy was being quoted at twenty to one, sir.'

'Capital, better get down there before the odds shorten.'

As the Prince's party took their place in the front of the box, a cheer went up from the crowd. The Prince of Wales touched his homburg and the Princess waved one kid-gloved hand. Sisi bowed automatically as she always did when she heard cheering in public, and like her royal companions she stretched her mouth into what she thought of as her public smile. She hoped that there were no photographers in the crowd.

The horses began to come out into the ring. Sisi picked up her field glasses so that she could take a closer look. Earl Spencer, who was standing behind her, was checking the numbers off against his race guide.

'Twenty-three, that's Glasnevin, Leinster's horse, odds-on favourite with Sir William. Listen to the crowd, sounds like half of Dublin has come over to see him run.'

Sisi picked up her own race card, looking for Bay's number. She wished that she could stand down by the ring and speak to him before the race, but it would be impossible for her to go without the Waleses, and the Prince showed no inclination to leave the comfort of his box. But it was of no matter, she would be able to see him after the race. Rudolph had, at last, gone home, so there was no reason why Bay shouldn't return to Easton Neston, although the hunting season was almost over. It might be time to go to Gödöllő. The estate in Hungary was always so pretty in the spring, when the cherry orchards were in bloom. It would be the ideal place to breed horses. How smart it would be to have her own stud farm.

Bay was number thirty-eight. This gave her a little thrill, as it was the age that she was now. It must be a good omen. It would be something to see him wearing her colours. Peering through her field glasses she tried to catch a glimpse of number thirty-eight. But the field was forty strong and although the ring was full of horses, there was no sign of Bay.

Spencer was looking for him too. 'No sign of Middleton yet. Wonder where he's got to. Probably getting some Dutch courage. Fences seem to get higher every year. Last year there were six horses down and two jockeys with broken arms. In 'sixty-nine a fellow died when his horse fell on top of him. Still, makes it more interestin', you never know who is going to finish.'

Countess Festetics did not fully understand what the English Lord was saying, but could see from her mistress's face that it was upsetting her. She said quickly, 'Earl Spencer, please to tell me why that man down there is standing on a box and waving his hands like a *puppe*, sorry, I don't know the English word.'

Sisi said, 'Puppet.'

'So who is the man, actually there are many of them, who are the puppets?'

Spencer laughed. 'Oh, you mean the bookies.'

'Bookies?' said Sisi. 'I do not know this word.'

'They take the bets, and set the odds. They wave their hands around to tell each other how people are betting. Once Topham has gone down there and put your bets on Tipsy, they will be waving at each other like crazy, just wait and see.'

But Sisi was no longer listening to him. Through her glasses, she had seen the magic number, thirty-eight. She sighed with relief as Bay rode in on Tipsy, the only grey in the ring. But he looked wrong, not somehow as she expected. It took her a minute to work out the problem: he was not wearing the black and gold colours of the Hapsburgs.

On the other side of the cast-iron and wood partition that divided the royal box from the rest of the stand, Charlotte was also watching number thirty-eight. After her outburst, a chastened Hartopp had found her some field glasses, so now she could see every detail of the riders and their horses as they paraded around the show ring. She spotted Tipsy at once. As she peered at Bay's familiar profile through the magnifying lens, it felt odd to be looking at him when he could have no idea that she was there. He would know about the Empress, of course, and Charlotte watched attentively to see if Bay looked up at the royal box. But to her great satisfaction, so far he had not.

'Big field today,' said Chicken. 'Forty riders. Got to get ahead quickly at the start, otherwise there will be a terrible crush at those fences. I was here in 'seventy-three when six horses went down at Becher's. Only five horses finished that year. Good year for the bookies, that one.'

Charlotte interrupted him. 'How long before the race starts, Captain Hartopp?'

Chicken looked at his pocket watch. 'Oh, not long now. They will go down to the starting line any minute.'

Charlotte wondered what had happened to Caspar; she did not relish the thought of spending the whole race with Captain Hartopp. She thought she might go and look for him, but the stand was now filled with bellowing tweed – suited men and some loud women – and she did not want to lose her vantage point at the rail. Watching the race up here, even with Hartopp, was better than getting lost in the crowd below.

The course steward, who had shown them into the stand, came up to her and handed her a note.

'Miss Baird? The American gentleman asked me to give you this.'

It was a folded betting slip, a receipt for a fifty-pound bet on Tipsy to win at odds of twenty to one against.

Charlotte folded the paper up carefully and put it in her pocket. She understood that the betting slip was a message. Caspar was making it clear that he knew exactly why they were there and where her loyalties lay.

A band started playing 'God save the Queen', and the crowd began to sing the national anthem. Charlotte turned her field glasses on the royal box and saw that while the Prince and Princess of Wales were singing, or at least mouthing the words, the Empress was staring at the riders, her face rapt. Even at this distance, Charlotte could see that the Empress's face at that moment would make a wonderful photograph, there was so much feeling in it. She was looking at Bay, of course, and Charlotte recognised the look. She had never thought, or perhaps she had never allowed herself to think, that the Empress might actually care for Bay. It was easier to think of her as the Snow Queen of fairy stories, a woman with ice in her heart. But the Empress in the sables was not heartless. She was in love with Bay.

This was not a welcome discovery. Charlotte wanted to have the monopoly on feeling. The idea that the Empress might care for Bay as strongly as she did was uncomfortable. The thought that had consoled her as she made her preparations to leave for America was that Bay would be miserable with the Empress. But if the Empress loved him then his misery was not guaranteed. The unfairness of this stung Charlotte, and for a moment she thought she was going to cry.

The strains of 'God Save the Queen' finished and the singing was replaced by a rumble of expectation from the crowd. The horses were making their way to the starting line. They jostled for position, the riders trying to hold back the excited horses who were desperate to get going.

Bay had found a place at the outside edge. It was not a favoured position, but it was a long race and he had been bunched in before when steeplechasing, so he had decided that the only way to win the National was to be as far outside the field as possible. Next to him was one of the Beasley brothers, Ned, riding the Governess. He nodded at Bay. Ned's two younger brothers Jack and Tom were also riding in the race. Bay felt reassured that Ned, the most experienced jockey, had also taken an outside edge position.

Now that he could see the course in front of him, Bay wished that he had taken a nip from his flask. The race caller was announcing the names of all the horses and riders. As their names were called, the jockeys put their whips in the air. There was a great cheer when they got to Glasnevin, the Irish horse, and by now the odds-on favourite. By the time the caller had worked his way down to his end of the field, Bay's hands were shaking as he lifted his crop into the air.

He knew that Sisi would be looking at him from the royal box, waiting for him to acknowledge her, but he kept his eyes straight ahead.

The starter pistol cracked and the line of horses surged forward, Glasnevin leading from the middle of the field. Bay felt his nerves fall away as his horse got into her stride. This was where he was meant to be: riding Tipsy in the Grand National.

Tipsy cleared the first fence effortlessly, but out of the corner of his eye Bay saw a horse stumble and his rider fall. Glasnevin was still at the front of the field. Bay could feel Tipsy straining to get ahead, as she always liked to be at the front, but he restrained her; he did not want to make his bid for the race until the second lap. At Becher's

Brook two horses refused the fence, and several came down at the sharp left-hand turn that took the course back towards the stands. There was a groan from the crowd that lined the course, standing on old railway carriages, when the jockey riding Glasnevin the favourite fell to the ground as the horse made the right-angled turn towards the main stand.

Bay glanced to his right to check on Beasley and the Governess. The big black horse had an easy stride and both horse and rider looked ominously relaxed.

A huge cheer came from the crowd as the horses came into sight of the main stands. The field was about two thirds of its original size. On the second lap the going was much worse; the horses' hooves had churned the soft ground into slippery mud. As Tipsy cleared the second fence Bay felt her stumble on landing, and for a second he thought he was about to fly over the mare's head. All he could do was hope that he would his break his neck instantly and that would be that – but Tipsy found some purchase with her back legs and she managed to get back into her rhythm, Bay clinging not just to her reins but to her mane as well.

'Thank you, my darling Tipsy,' he shouted into his mount's ear, sobbing with relief that his National was not over.

Becher's again, and this time six horses came down as they tried to make the jump and ninety-degree turn. Bay looked up for a moment and saw that while there were about twelve horses left in the race, only eight of them still had their riders on their backs. Glasnevin, the riderless favourite, was still galloping away at the front. But while the stallion was establishing his dominance over the other horses in the field, the racegoers who had backed him to win were crumpling their betting slips, as horses without jockeys were disqualified.

In the royal box, Sisi gasped as the horses came round for the second lap. Where was Bay? She held up her glasses but her hands were shaking so much that she could not hold them steady. She heard the Prince of Wales say, 'Now where is our horse, eh Empress? Hope it hasn't fallen on the first lap. What was the number again?'

'Thirty-eight,' said Sisi.

'Oh, I can't see it. Pity.'

Sisi tried to keep her face still but she was seeing Bay spreadeagled on the ground, his head twisted to the side, his neck broken. She felt a touch on her shoulder and knew that it was Festy trying to give her comfort in her distress.

Then there was a great bellow from Earl Spencer. 'There's Middleton, I can see him, but his horse is so muddy you can hardly tell it's a grey. Time to move up now, Bay. Come on.'

Sisi picked up her binoculars again and fiddled with them until at last she found number thirty-eight. Spencer was correct, horse and rider were so splashed with mud as to be almost unrecognisable. She followed Bay through the glasses until he went round the bend. Tipsy, she could see, was still running well and Bay was as buoyant in the saddle as ever.

'Our horse is still in the running, Empress,' said the Prince of Wales. 'My goodness, the field has taken a battering. Only about ten horses in it now. Your man is good, no doubt about it.'

'Not good. He is the best,' said the Empress softly.

Charlotte missed seeing Bay come into view for the second lap as she had her hands over her eyes. She had picked up the glasses earlier and had focussed on a horse and rider, only to see the horse stumble and fall and the rider being thrown to the side and curling himself into a tight ball as the other horses galloped over him. She knew that it was not Bay that had fallen but the violence of the fall horrified her. The image of her mother's body being carried over the fields on a five-bar gate came into her head and refused to shift.

Chicken nudged her. 'There they are, coming round now. By Jove, Bay is still in there. Glasnevin's lost his jockey, but the Governess is still in it.'

Opening her fingers a fraction, Charlotte saw the horses rush by. Her heart was beating so fast she could hear the blood drumming in her ears. She thought that she could not bear it any more. She turned, thinking that she would push her way out so that she could be somewhere – anywhere – else, but there were so many people pressing down to the rail now that the horses were coming round into the final stretch, that she found she could not move.

Chicken said, 'Middleton is coming up the field now. Now that's a good bit of riding,' he said grudgingly.

Charlotte was making all kinds of bargains with the God she did not much think about, promising anything if only Bay would be delivered safely.

Bay and Tipsy were hurtling towards the last fence. There were three horses ahead of them including the Governess. Now was the time to let Tipsy go. Bay raised his whip to urge his horse on to the final effort and found that he could not move his arm. A bolt of excruciating pain ran down from his shoulder and he saw black spots in front of his eyes, but, gripping Tipsy with his knees, he took the whip in his other hand and gave her a whack.

They sailed over the fence, another horse down. Now there were only two horses in front on the home stretch. Bay, biting his lip so hard that he tasted blood in his mouth, dug his heels into Tipsy's sides. Leaning down, he urged her on. She responded at once and passed the chestnut, so now there was only the Governess between him and the finishing line. He raised his good arm again and felt Tipsy straining forward, desperate to get to the front. But as both horse and rider strained every sinew, they could not edge past the black stallion. The roar from the crowd was coming nearer and nearer as they came closer to the finishing line. Bay saw the four-hundred-yard marker flash and he realised that victory was so close and yet he was about to lose. He saw the gap between the Governess's flanks and Tipsy's head begin to widen; the stallion simply had a longer stride. Bay knew that this was justice. The just punishment for his sins was that the thing he so desired would be held out to him and then snatched away.

His head down, Bay did not see the other horse coming up between him and the Governess but he felt Tipsy accelerate forward in alarm. The riderless Glasnevin was coming to take its favourite position at the head of the pack, and as the bay horse surged forward it veered to the side and crushed against the Governess. The last sound Bay remembered hearing was Ned Beasley's scream as his leg was crushed by the runaway horse, but from then on, as Tipsy galloped ahead to go first past the finishing post, he saw and heard nothing but a blur of faces and sound.

The Prize

THE PRINCE OF WALES SEIZED SISI'S HAND AND
kissed it.

'We won, Empress! We won. We must have champagne.'

'But, I think it was Captain Middleton who won,' said Sisi.

'Of course, but *we* have both won ten thousand pounds. Not quite a king's ransom, but good enough for the Prince of Wales.' The Prince was beaming. His win meant some new horses for his stud and several diamond bracelets for his mistresses.

He held up his glass in a toast. 'To the Empress, who has made me a very lucky man today. A lady who is as wise about horses as she is beautiful.'

Sisi smiled back. 'And to Captain Middleton, the best rider in England.'

More champagne was drunk, and then Major Topham appeared.

'Topham! Twenty to one, eh? All thanks to the Empress here. Is it time for the presentation?'

'Yes, sir.'

'Well, in the circumstances, I think we might prevail upon the Empress to hand over the prize to the winning jockey. You don't mind, do you, Alix?' he said, turning to his wife, who nodded vaguely, and then back to Sisi. 'Would you do Major Topham the honour of presenting the cup and what-have-you to the winner, Empress?'

'Nothing would give me greater pleasure!'

The Prince offered Sisi his arm, and the royal party began to make their way down through the cheering crowds to the winner's enclosure. This time the band played 'God Bless the Prince of Wales'.

Charlotte's fingers were stiff from clamping them over her face, and her thumbs from stopping her ears. She had watched Bay and Tipsy come into the home straight but as the noise around her grew louder and the horses got nearer, she realised that she could not bear to see any more. Whether Bay won or lost, it made no difference. He was safe, at least. When she judged from the muffled roar that the race must be over, she put her shield down and looked at Chicken. His expression told her everything. He was loose and shiny from the frequent nips he had been taking from his flask.

'He did it, he damn well did it! Deuced lucky, of course, Glasnevin coming up like that and cutting off the other feller, but then Bay always was a lucky devil.' He shook his head. 'Wish to blazes I had put money on him now. Knew he could ride, of course, but didn't think the mare was up to it. Should have known better, Bay always gets what he wants.'

He looked at Charlotte, his eyes full of drunken meaning.

But Charlotte said nothing. She was watching the crowd retreating like the tide as the royal party came down from the royal box towards the winner's enclosure. There was the Prince of Wales's homburg and at his side the Empress wreathed in sable. There was a dais covered in bunting in the winner's enclosure, with chairs and a stand bearing the silver trophy. The royal party arranged themselves on the dais, the Prince of Wales and the Empress in the middle.

There was a huge cheer as Bay and Tipsy came into the ring. People surged forward to touch the horse and rider, a few holding up their betting slips and kissing them.

Charlotte watched as Bay and Tipsy approached the dais. She watched as the Prince of Wales handed the trophy to the Empress. She watched as Bay was helped to dismount and carried on the shoulders of the crowd towards the Empress. And then she felt she could watch no more. She turned her back on the scene and touched her maid's arm.

'I want to go.'

Grace turned round reluctantly. As the two women began to fight their way out of the stand, Hartopp touched Charlotte on the shoulder.

'You are leaving without saying goodbye?'

Charlotte, still moving, said, 'Goodbye, Captain Hartopp. Thank you for the glasses.' She thrust them at him.

'But hang on! You might need me. It's a bit busy down there.'

Charlotte did not stop, but she looked back over her shoulder.

'I am going back to my hotel. If you would be kind enough to escort us to somewhere we can find a carriage that would be helpful.' She was grateful for Hartopp's bulk as he cleared a path for her through the teeming crowd of racegoers.

'What about your American friend? Would you like me to find him for you?' Hartopp asked Charlotte as they reached the gates.

Charlotte shook her head. She did not want to be there for another second. There was a line of carriages waiting for hire on the road that led back to Liverpool. She signalled to the driver at the front of the queue and he drove up to where they stood.

As Hartopp closed the carriage door, she remembered the betting slip in her pocket. 'I would be very grateful, Captain Hartopp, if you could find Mr Hewes and give him this.' She held out the slip.

Hartopp looked at it. 'By Jove, he will be glad. A monkey at twenty to one, that's a thousand smackers.'

Charlotte tried to smile. 'Then be sure you give it to him.'

Hartopp saw the effort on her face. 'You have my word. And what about Middleton? Do you have a message for him?'

Charlotte put her chin up. 'You may give him my congratulations if you like, Captain Hartopp. My sincere congratulations.' Then she put her hands up over her face to stop him seeing her cry, and Chicken, tactful for once in his blundering life, closed the carriage door and told the man to drive on.

The thing that surprised Bay as he slowly became aware of his victory, was that he felt no elation. All he could think of were the last few minutes of the race when he had known for certain that he was going to lose, and what's more that he deserved to. The pain in his shoulder was intense, but worse was the knowledge that even this, the greatest victory of his life, could not make him happy. As he rode into the winner's enclosure, he saw Sisi standing on the dais, her face lit up with joy. But he could not find the answering emotion in himself.

Hands were picking him up now and carrying him across to where Sisi was standing holding out the trophy to him.

'A splendid victory, Captain Middleton,' boomed the Prince of Wales.

Bay collected himself. 'I was lucky, sir.'

'Nonsense, nonsense, you rode a brilliant race. Now the Empress is going to present you with the trophy.'

Sisi held out the heavy silver cup with both hands. 'It is with the greatest pleasure that I give you this, Captain Middleton.' Her smile was so genuine that she showed all her teeth.

Instinctively Bay put out his hands to take his prize and then realised that he could not move his right arm. He took the cup awkwardly with his left and the weight of it, taking him by surprise, made him stagger slightly. Sisi saw him wince and cried out, 'Bay!' as she put her arm out to stop him falling over.

To the spectators of the scene on the dais and in the crowd it was proof – if any was needed – that the relationship between the Empress and her pilot, the man who had just won the Grand National, was a close one. Even the Princess of Wales, who generally remained aloof from the cross currents of life around her, opened her large blue eyes a little wider and murmured to herself, 'Careful.'

Bay got his balance back and found himself looking directly into Sisi's dark eyes.

'My Bay,' she said silently.

For a moment Bay thought he was going to be happy.

The Prince of Wales turned towards them, 'You kept us guessing right up until the finishing post, Middleton. The Empress and I didn't know where to look. Both of us had placed our shirts on you to win. But you did us proud in the end.'

The Empress smiled. 'I just wish that you had got my colours in time, Captain Middleton. I had them made up in London. It would have been so much easier to pick you out in the field.'

Bay shivered involuntarily. 'Perhaps, but I always race in these.'

The Prince looked at him with something like sympathy and said, 'Regimental colours of the Eleventh Hussars, aren't they? I am proud to wear them myself as your Colonel in Chief.'

'Yes, sir.'

The Prince turned to Sisi. 'An officer always rides under his regimental colours, unless of course, it's not his horse.'

Sisi laughed. 'You English and your rules. Well then, I shall buy your horse, Captain Middleton, and then the next time you win the Grand National, you will be wearing my colours.'

Bay said, 'I would never sell Tipsy.'

'Not even to me?' asked Sisi.

But before Bay could answer, Major Topham appeared at the dais.

'Captain Middleton, I wonder if you would consent to having your photograph taken with your horse. I am sorry to interrupt your celebrations, but I have been told that the light is failing and if we are to take a picture it must be done at once.'

The Empress looked at the Major with distaste. 'I believe that Captain Middleton is otherwise engaged.'

But Bay put his good hand up. 'Actually, if you will excuse me, Ma'am, I would like a photograph of the occasion. These things don't happen very often. But you will have to hold the cup, Major. My shoulder is a bit crook.'

Before Sisi could protest again, Bay followed the Major to where Tipsy was standing. He leant against his horse's flank and closed his eyes, trying to collect his thoughts. Just for a second he had felt Sisi's spell again and he would have surrendered if it hadn't been for the thought of the colours she had sent him. They had been a perfect fit, but he had been unable to put them on.

When Bay opened his eyes, Caspar was standing in front of him.

'May I add my congratulations to those of the entire racecourse, Captain Middleton. It was a thrilling victory. When you are ready, I would like very much to take your picture. I think perhaps you should be on your magnificent horse, do you agree?'

Bay looked at him in astonishment. 'What on earth are *you* doing here?'

'Taking photographs, Captain. That is, I like to think, my calling.'

'But how did you get here? And how can you even think of taking my picture?'

Caspar smiled. 'Because I have been asked by the good major to record your triumph.'

Major Topham came round to where they stood to help Bay up onto Tipsy. 'Are you acquainted with Captain Middleton, Mr Hewes? What a happy coincidence.'

Caspar picked up his camera and tripod and put them at a forty-five-degree angle to Bay and Tipsy. 'Captain Middleton and I have met before in London. I am very familiar with his image.' He fiddled with the camera. 'Now if you would turn your head towards me, Captain. You don't have to smile, unless you want to, of course.'

'I don't,' said Bay.

The Major laughed nervously. 'But perhaps you could look a little happier. After all, you have just won the National.'

Bay turned to look at Caspar, his eyes blazing.

'Splendid. You really are a great photographic subject, Captain Middleton. If you could hold it like that just for a moment.'

Caspar disappeared under his velvet cloth, came out and squeezed the bulb. 'Excellent. That, I can promise you, will be a splendid picture.'

Bay slid down from Tipsy, advanced towards Caspar and used his good hand to shove the other man. 'Where is Charlotte? What have you done with her?'

Caspar, who was a couple of inches taller than Bay, did not flinch. 'Charlotte is where she wants to be, Captain Middleton.'

Bay drew back his fist, but Caspar was too quick for him and caught his wrist. 'You have your prize, Captain Middleton. Remember that.'

Major Topham, who was watching this scene in alarm, came

bustling over. 'Captain Middleton, perhaps you would like to come with me. There is a reception laid on for you in the members' enclosure. After all your exertions I am sure you need a drink.'

Bay felt a profound weariness come over him and allowed the Major to lead him to a room full of cheerful strangers who clapped him on his sore shoulder and gave him glass after glass of champagne. As he had not eaten that day, Bay got swiftly and comprehensively drunk.

He was sitting between Major Crombie and Lord Sholto Douglas, one man celebrating his enormous win, the other drowning his sorrows, when Chicken Hartopp swam into view.

'Well done, Bay. Wish I had put money on you. Can't think why I didn't. You always were a lucky fellow.'

Bay squinted at him.

'Yes, that's me. I'm rich now too. Put a hundred guineas on myself to win. So I'm damn rich and damn lucky.'

But Bay looked so miserable that even Chicken felt curiosity rather than envy.

'What's up, old man? No reason for a long face. You should be on top of the world. What more could you possibly want?'

Bay looked at his boots.

Sholto Douglas nudged him. 'Cheer up, Middleton, you've won the bloody Grand National and the Empress of bloody Austria can't keep her bloody hands off you.'

Bay lunged towards him, fists outstretched, but Sholto ducked easily.

'Steady on, old man, I meant it as a compliment.'

Bay subsided. 'Sorry, Sholto, not quite the thing.'

Sholto got up. 'If you will excuse me, I must go and wring the neck of Glasnevin's jockey.'

Hartopp took his place next to Bay. 'Do you know who I watched you race with, Bay?'

'I don't know, Chicken. Queen Victoria?'

Chicken leant closer and said in his ear, 'Charlotte Baird.'

Bay pulled away from him. 'Of course you did.'

'No really, old man, I did. She told me to give you her congratulations. Her sincere congratulations.'

'She said that?'

'Yes, sincere congratulations, those were her words exactly. But it was damned odd. She came to watch you race but she had her hands over her eyes at the end. I don't think she saw a bloody thing.'

''Spect she was thinking of her mother,' said Bay.

'Her mother?'

'Broke her neck huntin'. That's why she doesn't ride.'

'Oh, is that the reason?'

'That's it precisely.'

There was a silence. Then Bay said, 'Is she still here?'

'No. She went pretty sharpish after the race. Back to Liverpool. Sailing tomorrow.'

'To America?'

'Yes.'

'With that American?'

'Well, he's going with her, but just as her travelling companion. She was pretty clear about that. Says she is going to take photographs and he's going to help her.'

'So they ain't eloping?'

'She says not. No ring, she showed me her hand. No ring.'

Bay went back to contemplating his boots. 'Why'd she tell you that, do you suppose?' he asked.

'Didn't want me to think that she was marrying him. Doesn't

make any difference, mind you. The girl is finished. Even the Lennox fortune won't be enough. No one will marry her now.'

'Is that what you think, Chicken?'

'Yes, that's what I think.'

'So you wouldn't marry her, even supposing she would have you?'

'No, not now. The girl's not respectable. Don't know what Fred and Augusta will say when they come back from their wedding trip. Terrible blow. Newlyweds trying to make a home with a scandal like that in the background. Better really if she *had* eloped with the fellow.' Hartopp started to tug at his whiskers. 'At least she would be married then. All this nonsense about taking photographs. Trouble with Charlotte is that she has been indulged.' He pulled on both whiskers at once so that he looked like a discontented haddock.

'Lady Dunwoody has a lot to answer for, putting ridiculous notions into her head. Photography isn't even a proper accomplishment. It doesn't require any skill, just a lot of equipment.'

Bay tried to consult his watch, and then he remembered that he was still wearing his racing silks and his watch was with his other clothes.

'So let's get this absolutely straight, Chicken, so there is no room for doubt. There is no circumstance in which you would marry Charlotte Baird?'

'None whatsoever, no chance at all.'

'Then, Chicken, you are an even bigger bloody fool than I thought.'

Bay got up and, clutching his bad shoulder to protect it from pats of congratulation from well-meaning racegoers, he stumbled towards the jockeys' enclosure. He needed to get back into his civilian clothes.

The royal party was winding up. The Prince was taking one last draw on his cigar as he looked out over the racecourse, secure in the knowledge that the royal train could not leave without him. His wife was pretending to listen to Major Topham's plans for bringing the railway to Aintree. Sisi was talking to Earl Spencer about her estate in Hungary, Gödöllő. 'You must come and stay with me in the summer, I don't want Bay to feel too lonely with nobody but Magyars for company.'

'I would be delighted, Ma'am. So Middleton is to set up your stable? What a splendid opportunity for him.'

'And then we can come back here in the winter to hunt. It is perfect, no? I must say, Earl Spencer, that I am most grateful to you for giving me my pilot. He has shown me so many things.'

The Earl avoided her gaze. The Empress's passion for Middleton was becoming rather unseemly.

'But where is Captain Middleton, actually? I have not seen him since a man took him away to take his photograph. Why hasn't he come back?'

'He can hardly come in here, Ma'am, without an invitation.'

'Then I shall invite him!'

Spencer coughed. 'I think you might want to consult the Prince. It is after all, his box.'

Sisi smiled. 'Of course, I must not forget that this is not my country.'

She turned to the Prince of Wales. 'I should like to see Captain Middleton before we leave. Would it be possible to bring him in here?'

The Prince blew out a perfect ring of cigar smoke. 'Certainly, Empress. To the victor, the spoils, eh Spencer?'

He waved his free hand at the hapless Major Topham. 'Can you ask Captain Middleton to come up here?'

As Topham set out on his errand, Countess Festetics followed him out onto the racecourse. 'If you please, I should like to come with you. Captain Middleton is my friend.'

The Major shrugged. The royal party was good for business, but he had had enough of being treated like a messenger boy.

They walked across the course, which was scattered with discarded betting slips, chestnut shells and spent cheroots. Now that the racing had finished, the prevailing current of the crowd was towards the gates and the road to Liverpool. Most people were quiet, intent only on getting home, but every so often a little eddy of clamour would erupt. Someone would burst into a snatch of song, or once, loud sobs. Nobody made a sound as two men in white aprons walked through the crowd and onto the course, one of them carrying a stretcher, the other a saw. A woman with drooping orange feathers in her hat, her face shiny with gin, screamed after them, 'Butchers!'

Topham walked fast and the Countess had almost to run to keep up. They went first to the members' enclosure but there was no sign of Bay there, and no one sober enough to know where he had gone. The jockeys' changing room was deserted, too. Major Topham made the Countess wait outside as he looked around, but he could see that Bay had taken his things.

He came out and shook his head. 'Don't know where the feller's got to.'

The Countess said, 'Do you think perhaps he might be with his horse?'

'Anything's possible.' Topham set off grimly towards the stables, but the Countess caught him by the arm.

'The stables are over there, no? You must have so many things to be doing, Major. I think you are too busy to be running every-where for my mistress, so let me help you. *I* will go to the stables and find the Captain.'

'*If* he's there.'

'Yes, but I think he will be.'

The Major looked irresolute for a moment and then said, 'If you are quite sure, then I will leave you. Thank you.'

The Countess set off towards the stables. Nopsca had told her what had happened when he had given Bay the Empress's colours, and she was worried.

She found him with his arms around Tipsy's neck. He had changed into tweeds. The Countess noticed that his waistcoat was buttoned wrongly, his eyes were bloodshot and his cheeks were pink.

He was singing something into the horse's ear and Tipsy was nuzzling his tweed shoulder. The Countess waited for him to notice her and when he did he looked at her warily.

'Hello, Festy. Have you come to fetch me?'

'In my country we would be giving you leaves to put on your head. When you are the victor.'

'Leaves? You mean a laurel wreath, I suppose. But I am afraid Tipsy would dispatch any leaves in short order. And so she should, she did all the work after all.'

The Countess could see that Bay was not sober, but she did not think he was quite drunk. He was in that dangerous state of intoxication where truth would erupt unimpeded by embarrassment or shame. The Countess could see that he was about to turn; she hoped that she had come in time.

She was considering how she could coax him to come with her, when Bay said, 'You really love her, don't you, Festy?'

The Countess nodded. 'She is everything to me.'

'I understand how you feel. She is . . . intoxicating. But I can't be like you, Festy, in her service. Did you know about the racing colours?'

Festy nodded.

'How could she think that I would wear them? I am not her creature!'

'She was trying to give you something, I think. In return for so much that you have given her. Some happiness. There is not so much for her otherwise.'

Bay sat down on a bale of straw, cradling his head in his good hand. Festy sat down next to him.

'Why did you come, Festy? Nopsca would have been so much easier.'

Festy stroked his head. 'But that is why I had to come. You must understand what you will be doing.'

Bay sat silent for a moment, feeling the Countess's fingers running over his hair, feeling her desire to smooth away his discontent.

'I can't be like you, for ever in her shadow, waiting for a smile. I want something else.'

'You will make her very sad, Captain Middleton.'

'Perhaps for a little while, until she finds another distraction. She still has her monkey.'

Festetics' hand stopped stroking his hair. 'You may leave her, if you must, but do not pretend that it will not matter to her.'

Bay found tears leaking from his eyes. 'I am sorry, Festy.'

Festy patted him on his head and stood up. 'You should be sorry for me, because now I shall have to tell the Kaiserin that you are going away. She will be angry with me, not you, because she will think that I did not say the right words to you. She will think that you can be coaxed to follow me like a horse with a sugar lump.'

Bay looked up at her and smiled. 'Your English is getting quite fluent, Festy.'

The Countess snapped her fingers. 'Any language is easy if you are Hungarian. I suppose now that you are finding the girl with the camera?'

'I am going to try. Though I don't suppose she wants to be found very much.'

'It is enough, I think, that you want to find her.'

'Perhaps.' Bay stood up. He bent to kiss the Countess on her cheek. 'Tell her, the Empress, that I will never forget our rides together, Festy. Please don't forget.'

The Countess touched his cheek. 'Do not worry, my Captain. I won't forget.' And walking back to the royal box, she murmured, 'And neither will she.'

Going West

CHARLOTTE WAS SITTING ON HER TRUNK. GRACE HAD told her that if she sat there for ten minutes, the contents would subside and she would be able to close it. There had been a message from the White Star Line when they had got back to the hotel. All trunks for the *Britannic* were to be sent down tonight, so that the ship could get away promptly on the morning tide.

She sat on the trunk waiting for the moment when the stuff inside would stop resisting and allow her to snap the lid shut. But her possessions remained stubbornly springy; they were not going to settle quietly. The easy thing would be to take some things out, but for some reason, Charlotte could not bear to do this.

Everything had happened so quickly. After Fred and Augusta's wedding it had just been so clear what she had to do. She kept thinking of Caspar's photographic plates of the desert. Those wide expanses of nothingness. Once she had imagined this new Charlotte, the rest had been easy. It was not so very difficult to be free if you had diamonds, and Caspar, of course. He had understood at once. He had even told Lady Dunwoody, which Charlotte could not bring herself to do. Her godmother should approve of her decision – she was the one, after all, who had encouraged her photography – but Charlotte also knew that for all her bohemian affect, Lady Dunwoody was completely conventional about what was suitable behaviour in unmarried girls. Lady Lisle was bribable, but Celia Dunwoody did not change her mind. Charlotte had been afraid that her resolve would wilt under her godmother's disapproval. But while she was quite happy for Fred and Augusta to receive the news by letter, she knew that Lady D would never forgive her if she had not been consulted. So she sent Caspar, who could talk his way in and out of any situation.

But today at the racecourse Charlotte had seen quite how much Caspar was giving up by coming with her. The effortless way that he had put himself at the heart of the event was impressive. Caspar was meant to be at the centre of things, and she was taking him back to the periphery of the world.

There was a tap at the door and Caspar walked in, still in his tweed ulster, brandishing a sheaf of notes in his hand.

'My winnings! One thousand pounds. Captain Middleton has been luckier for me than he has been for you.' He was turning to close the door when Charlotte stopped him.

'Don't shut the door, you shouldn't be in here alone with me if Grace isn't here.'

'Quite right too. I must protect my reputation at all costs. Why are you sitting on your trunk?'

'Because it won't close and it needs to be sent down to the quay tonight.'

'Would you like me to sit on it with you?'

Charlotte nodded. But even their combined weights could not make the lid close.

'Let's sit here for a moment, perhaps something will give way.'

'If you like.'

Charlotte looked at the notes that Caspar was still holding in his hands. 'A thousand pounds!'

'I placed the bet for you, of course.'

'I know.'

'In all it was a most successful day. I took some excellent pictures, including one of the winning jockey.'

Charlotte's sudden movement made the trunk lid sigh and with a click it subsided into line.

'You saw Bay? Did you tell him I was there?'

Caspar stood up. 'I think our work with the trunk is done.' He went over to the doorway. 'No, Carlotta, I did not tell Captain Middleton that you had come to watch him race. I did not want to give him the satisfaction. I thought that he had won quite enough victories for the day.'

Charlotte said nothing.

'Now you are cross with me. But I did it for your own good, and perhaps a little bit for my own satisfaction. He was so very cross. He even tried to strike me. Fortunately he had injured his arm, so I could not retaliate with honour. Which was a shame, as I would have enjoyed it.'

'His arm? What's wrong with his arm?' And then, 'But why would he want to fight *you*?'

'Because I wouldn't tell him where you were, and because I imagine he thinks that you and I have eloped.'

Charlotte turned her head away from him.

'Oh Charlotte, did you really want me to tell him that you had been there all day hoping for a glimpse of him? Far better that he thinks that you have eloped with me and care for him not a jot. It will be easier for both of you. You will have your glorious career in America and he will have his victory and the Empress. That is really the only happy ending.'

Charlotte bit her lip. Finally she said, 'But how do you know what a happy ending is for *me*? Or Bay?'

Caspar took her by the shoulders and shook her, gently but firmly. 'I know, because I understand what it's like to lose something you love. When Abraham died, I thought that I would never be happy again. That I would never take another picture. But I came here and found solace. That is why I agreed to come back to America with you, because you had the courage to start afresh. And you still do, whatever you think now.'

Charlotte looked down at the carpet where a cornucopia of fruits and flowers was erupting across the pile. She poked at a pomegranate with the toe of her boot.

'Now I suggest that you put on your bonnet and we can take a walk down to the quay and see our trunks being loaded onto the *Britannic*. There is nothing worse than discovering that your belongings have gone to Argentina by mistake. So run along and fetch Grace, and then we can observe all the proprieties.'

It was getting dark outside, so Caspar waved for a hackney carriage to take them down to the docks. As he helped Charlotte inside, he said, 'Thanks to the gallant captain, I can indulge myself.'

Charlotte and Grace sat on the seat opposite the driver with Caspar facing them. The streets were emptying now, but every so often they would pass a clump of people obviously back from the races, their best clothes rumpled – the feathers drooping and the neckties wilted – but clinging together with that sense of having shared a great moment. One or two held up their winning betting slips as talismans, proof that for one day only they were fortune's favoured ones. On the street corners, newsboys were still shouting 'Outsider wins National!' and 'Tipsy rides to Victory!', hoping to sell their last editions to the few people left in Liverpool who had not spent the day at Aintree. As they got closer to the docks, the public houses got closer together and every one was crammed with racegoers still enjoying their day out. By the Mersey itself, the Queen Adelaide was overflowing with Irish clans who were waiting for the Dun Laoghaire boat. They were bemoaning the loss of Glasnevin, and the singing had turned mournful.

When they got to the quayside, Caspar went down to the shipping office to find out when their luggage would be loaded onto the ship. 'I am going to tell them that I want to see each one of our trunks being carried up the gangplank. It is, I am afraid, the only way.' Charlotte noticed that Caspar was looking unusually cheerful, as if he had some splendid secret, but then, she thought, he had just won a thousand pounds.

The two women sat in the carriage for a few minutes until Charlotte could stand it no longer. She got out and stood on the cobbled quayside. The light was almost gone now, but the steamships at the dock were lit by lanterns and they loomed like Christmas trees in the twilight, the lights wobbling as the boats rocked on the wash of a passing tug. There were people everywhere; a large crowd had gathered further down the dock to wave goodbye to a boat bound for Canada. To the left of where she stood, a crew of Chinese workers in pigtails were unloading crates from a steamer into a warehouse, passing them from hand to hand in a human chain. The streets around the hotel had already taken on the subdued temper of the Sabbath, but here at the docks the activity was unceasing. It was an utterly exotic scene to Charlotte, and she thought how ironic it was that she was going all the way to America when she had seen more strange sights in the last two days in Liverpool than she had in the rest of her twenty years.

A black sailor was approaching carrying a parrot in a cage, and Charlotte thought what a wonderful picture he would make. How much more exciting to capture life in the raw than to recreate classical scenes in Lady Dunwoody's studio. In an instant the gloom that had enveloped her since her return from Aintree lifted, and she began to look forward to what she might do. To record the world in all its strangeness and beauty, that was a real ambition. It was something that she could actually accomplish. To make a record of the unexpected and the extraordinary, so that other girls like her, less fortunate than her, perhaps, could know that they could expect more than the confines of their drawing room or their kitchens. Standing here on the quayside, with the cold wind blowing off the water and the smell of rotting vegetables and brewing hops streaming past her, Charlotte felt suddenly and unexpectedly happy.

So she was smiling when she first heard the noise from the other end of the wharf. The crowds that had gathered to wave off the Canadian steamer were cheering now and throwing their hats in the air. They were surging around something, but it was too dark now to see clearly what it was. But then the crowd parted and Charlotte saw that it was a man riding a horse, and she realised that she could only see this because it was a white horse.

The crowd was following the white horse and they were singing. Charlotte could not make out the tune, she was staring too hard at the rider. Grace, hearing the singing, got out of the carriage and came to stand beside Charlotte.

'Oh look, miss,' she said, 'it's Captain Middleton.'

She stood there as Bay stopped in front of her, hundreds of hands ready to help the National winner to the ground and to hold the wonder horse's head.

He walked over to where she was standing and hesitated for a moment, then took her hand and kissed it. She remembered the first time he had kissed her hand, the night of the Spencer ball.

There was a roar of approval from the crowd behind them.

'You're smiling, Charlotte. Does that mean you are pleased to see me?' Bay looked so worried that she might have laughed.

'I am happy that you won the National, I know how much you wanted to.'

'You came to watch me?'

'I did.'

There was a silence. Charlotte saw that underneath his greatcoat, one of Bay's arms was in a sling.

'What happened to your arm?'

'My shoulder's gone. The joint is loose. I need to get it strapped up, but I've been busy.'

Charlotte looked him in the eye. 'I am catching a boat in the morning to New York, with Mr Hewes.' There was a cough behind her, and she said, 'And Grace.'

Grace smiled at Bay. 'Evening, sir, and congratulations on winning. I made some money on you, so I am very grateful to you, sir. What a finish! I didn't think you were going to do it, but suddenly that loose horse came out of nowhere and you were there.'

'I didn't think I was going to do it either, Grace, but sometimes things don't turn out in the way you expect. The Governess was a faster horse but I suppose I was lucky, and Tipsy never likes to come second.'

Charlotte could bear it no longer. 'Why did you come here, Bay?'

'To see you, of course. I knew you were here somewhere. Chicken told me.'

'Chicken?'

'Our mutual friend. He told me that you were going to America, but he also told me that you were not yet married to Mr Hewes, which was a relief, because I would like to marry you, dear Charlotte, if there is any chance at all that you will have me.'

There was a whisper through the crowd as the ones at the front, who could hear what Bay was saying, relayed it to the bystanders at the back. Some wag shouted, 'Put him out of his misery, Charlotte!'

Charlotte tried to turn away from him, but she found that she could not actually bring herself to move. 'But I am going to America tomorrow, to take photographs,' she said slowly, not meeting his eye.

'Can married women take photographs?' said Bay.

She looked at him now. 'I don't know.'

'Charlotte, I'm rich now. Well, not as rich as you, but I have enough money to support us both for years. You could give your fortune away to Fred if you wanted and we would still have enough.'

'But what about *her*?'

'I promise you that I will never see the Empress again. No, that sounds as if I am giving something up, when I am not at all. I never *want* to see her again.'

'Poor Empress,' said Charlotte, thinking of the lines around the other woman's mouth.

'I was under her spell, but I am not any more. Can you forgive me?'

There were shouts of 'Go on love, it's cold out here', from the crowd.

'But I am going to America tomorrow.'

'And I want to come with you. I could be the person that carries your camera.'

'Not with your arm in a sling, you couldn't.'

'But apart from that, am I a candidate for the job?'

Someone from the crowd started to sing 'Daisy, Daisy, give me your answer do', and noise swelled as everyone joined in the chorus.

Charlotte put one hand on Bay's good arm and, finding that no words came, she nodded.

'Really, Charlotte?'

She nodded again, and then she closed her eyes as Bay put his good arm around her waist and kissed her.

The cheers from the crowd were so loud that Charlotte did not hear Caspar calling her name, until he tapped her quite hard on the shoulder.

She looked up, her mouth already swollen from Bay's moustache.

Caspar put his head on one side and looked at Charlotte and then Bay, and then addressing Charlotte he said, 'So, I take it there has been a change of plan.'

Bay said, 'Charlotte has promised to marry me.'

'It's not her promise I am worried about, but yours, Captain Middleton. Are you going to keep your word this time?'

Bay tilted his chin at Caspar. 'I deserve that, I suppose. All I can say is that if she will have me, I will marry her tomorrow on the boat.'

Shouts of 'eager beaver' and 'steady on' came from the crowd.

Caspar turned his back on him and bent down to look at Charlotte. 'And you, can you really forgive him?'

'I think so. He is here, isn't he?'

'But do you really want to be a wife?'

'He says he will carry my camera.'

Caspar looked at her for a moment and then he laughed and raised his hands in a parody of benediction. 'Then I have no choice but to give you my blessing.'

It was late when they got back to the Adelphi. Caspar had insisted on riding Tipsy. 'I would rather ride a National winner than play the gooseberry.'

As they stood in the hotel lobby, slightly uncomfortable in their new arrangement, Bay said, 'I must engage a room for tonight. And arrange for stabling for Tipsy. Excuse me for a moment,' and he went to talk to the hotel manager.

Caspar sighed. 'I hope you know what you are doing, Carlotta.'

'He has chosen me, and I think we will be happy.'

'And it's not just because he likes you better than an empress?'

'I loved him first.'

'Then I surrender. And I wish you joy, I really do. I am sure you will take America by storm.'

'You're not coming?'

'No, Carlotta, you no longer have any need for my services, and I have duchesses to photograph. I shall be irresistible when I return to London as the man with all the details of the Lennox heiress's scandalous elopement. Don't worry, I shall do my best to console Augusta for your absence.'

Charlotte laughed and kissed him on the cheek. Then she remembered something. 'But what about your trunk? You must ask them to take it off the boat.'

Caspar winked at her. 'Really, Carlotta, what do you take me for? My trunk never left the hotel.'

❧

The sky was still pink as Charlotte and Bay stood on the deck of the *Britannic* waiting for the ship to sail.

They were standing on the promenade deck, looking back over the city.

Charlotte put her hand over Bay's. 'Now that we are about to be married, you have to tell me.'

'Tell you what?'

'How Chicken got his name.'

Bay laughed and kissed her. 'Darling Charlotte, I am afraid I will have to disappoint you. You see, if it wasn't for Chicken I would never have known that you weren't going to marry your American. I owe him my happiness, so I can hardly betray him by telling you his deepest, darkest secret.'

Charlotte squeezed his hand.

'Besides, if I tell you, what will you have to look forward to?'

Charlotte smiled.

'Oh, I'll think of something.'

Author's Note

My interest in Sisi began when, as a little girl, I was given a jigsaw puzzle of the famous Winterhalter picture of the Empress with diamond stars in her hair. When, many years later I was casting around for a subject on which to base a novel, I remembered Sisi and the more I learnt about her extraordinary bittersweet life, the more I wanted to write about her. This novel is based on fact: the cast of characters: Sisi, Bay, Charlotte, Earl Spencer even Chicken Hartopp are all real, even if their thoughts and feelings have been supplied by me. Sisi did come to England to hunt in 1875/6 and Bay Middleton was her pilot. Her hair did reach to the ground, and she did use raw veal as a face pack. But although the Fortune Hunter is grounded in fact, it is a novel and I have departed from the strict chronology of Sis's life when I felt my story demanded it.

Elizabeth of Austria was the Princess Diana of nineteenth-century Europe: famously beautiful but unfulfilled in her marriage to Franz Joseph, she spent most of her life trying to find the happiness that evaded her. Her early married life was dominated by her overbearing mother-in-law, who tried to mould Sisi (Elizabeth's nickname) into a perfect Hapsburg queen. But Sisi hated the stifling formality of the Austrian court, where every courtier had to come from four generations of aristocrats. She was politically liberal and supported the political aspirations of the Hungarians, who had rebelled against Hapsburg rule in 1848. For these reasons, Franz Joseph was not altogether sorry that Sisi spent so much time abroad travelling though Europe in her private train, or visiting her villa in Corfu on her private yacht. Sisi loved to hunt – partly for the adrenalin rush and partly, of course, because she looked so magnificent in her riding habit.

The second half of Sisi's life was marred by tragedy. Her only son Rudolph ended his life in a suicide/murder with his teenage mistress at his hunting lodge in Mayerling in 1889. Elizabeth wore black for the rest of her life, which came to an end in 1898 when she was stabbed to death by an Italian anarchist as she was boarding a steamer on Lake Geneva. The anarchist was hoping to assassinate a member of the Russian royal family. Franz Joseph lived on until 1916 – the assassination of his nephew and heir Archduke Ferdinand was the event that triggered the First World War.

Bay Middleton (a very distant relation of the future Queen of England) was famous for being the 'hardest rider in England'. He got his nickname from a Derby winner. He spent five years with Sisi 'piloting' her through the hunting seasons in England and Ireland. Their relationship has been the source of speculation ever since. It certainly aroused her son's Rudolph's jealousy. According to the Kenneth McMillan ballet 'Mayerling' it precipitated Rudolph's descent into madness and suicide.

Very little is known about Charlotte Baird apart from the fact that she and Bay did marry. I have given her an interest in photography, an art form which was popular with intelligent young women at that time.

Acknowledgements

I couldn't have written this book without the help and support of some people:

My two outstanding editors, Imogen Taylor and Hope Dellon, my agent Caroline Michel, who is as good as she is beautiful, Georgina Moore and her team at Headline, Dori Weintraub and her team at SMP, Emma Holtz and Silissa Kennedy for expert fielding, Rachel Street who is a brilliant copyeditor as well as being a superlative assistant, Penny Mortimer for the hunting edit, Janet Reibstein for her ability to spot the most important thing, Sam Lawrence who kept me going in a difficult year, Andrea Wong for her enthusiasm and kindness, my friends Shane Watson and Emma Fearnhamm for their patience, Jason Goodwin for the rewrite, my sisters Tabitha, Chloe and Sabine for their support, Richard Goodwin for his excitement on reading the first draft, my daughters Ottilie and Lydia for being my keenest supporters and fiercest critics and my husband Marcus for being the rock on which my flimsy edifice is built.